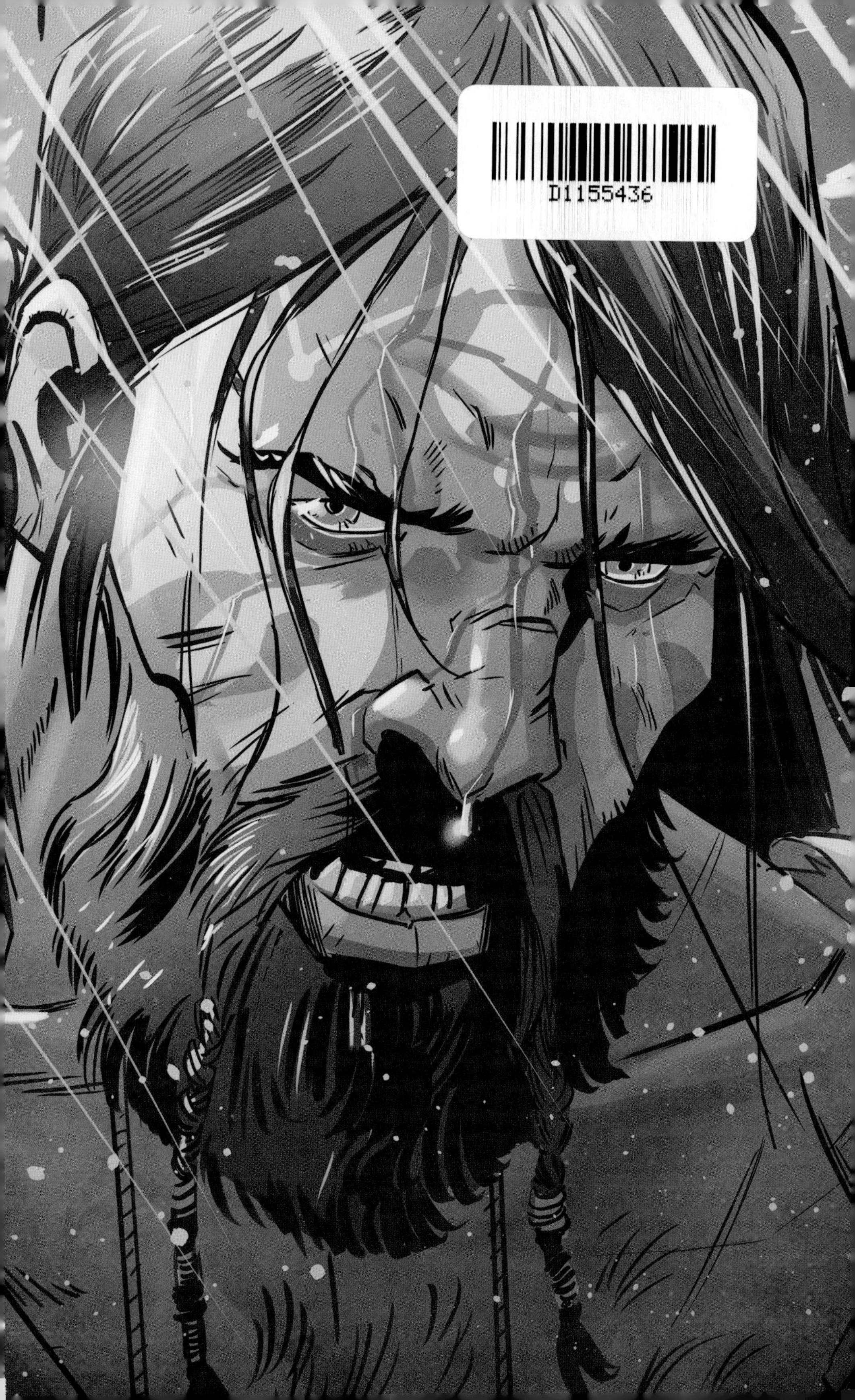

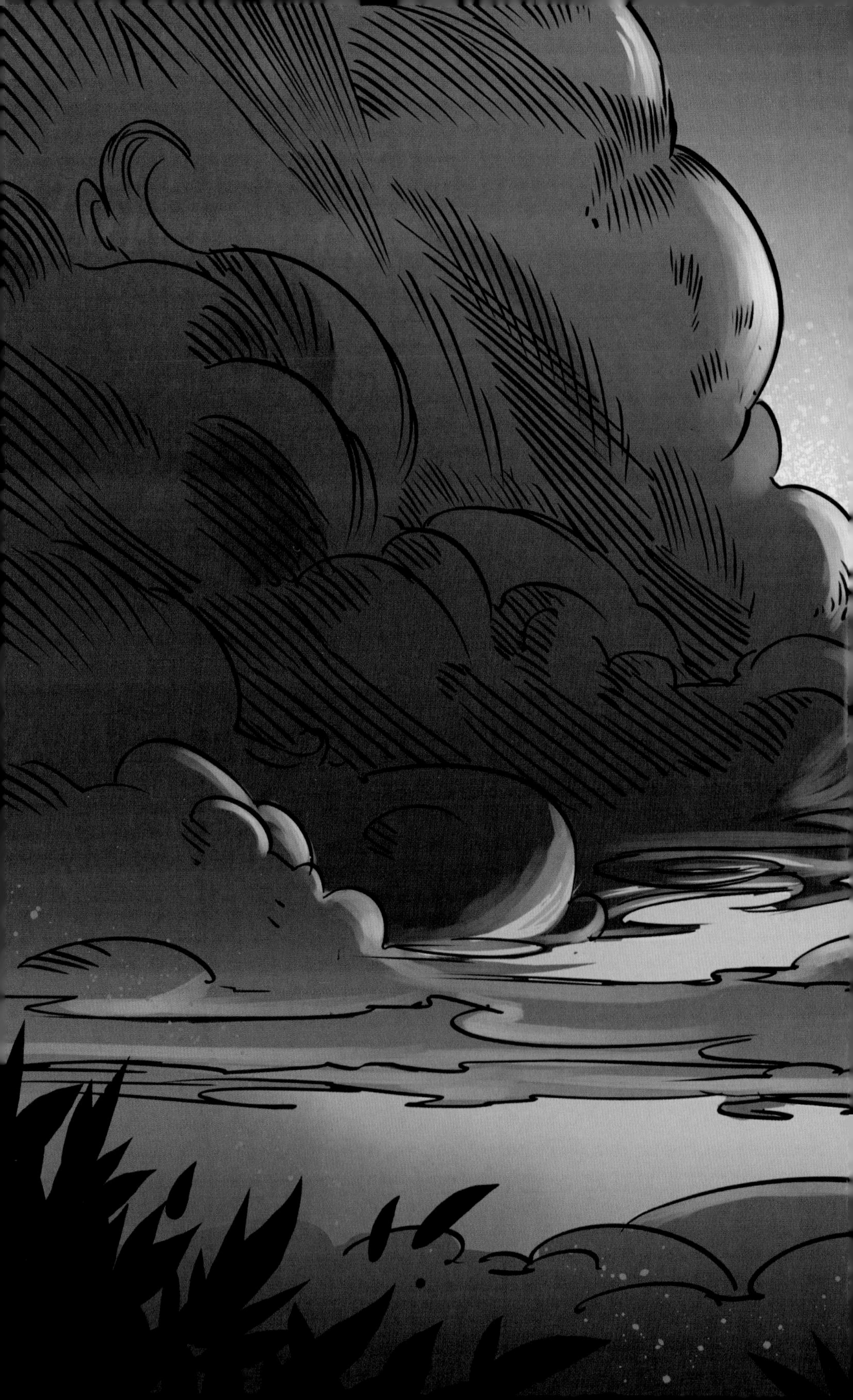

GOBLIN

Story By
ERIC GRISSOM

Art by
WILL PERKINS

DARK HORSE BOOKS

PRESIDENT & PUBLISHER
MIKE RICHARDSON

EDITOR
SHANTEL LAROCQUE

ASSOCIATE EDITOR
BRETT ISRAEL

DESIGNER
ERIC GRISSOM with BRENNAN THOME

DIGITAL ART TECHNICIAN
SAMANTHA HUMMER

Neil Hankerson, **Executive Vice President** • Tom Weddle, **Chief Financial Officer** • Randy Stradley, **Vice President of Publishing** • Nick Mcwhorter, **Chief Business Development Officer** • Dale Lafountain, **Chief Information Officer** • Matt Parkinson, **Vice President of Marketing** • Vanessa Todd-Holmes, **Vice President of Production and Scheduling** • Mark Bernardi, **Vice President of Book Trade and Digital Sales** • Ken Lizzi, **General Counsel** • Dave Marshall, **Editor in Chief** • Davey Estrada, **Editorial Director** • Chris Warner, **Senior Books Editor** • Cary Grazzini, **Director of Specialty Projects** • Lia Ribacchi, **Art Director** • Matt Dryer, **Director of Digital Art and Prepress** • Michael Gombos, **Senior Director of Licensed Publications** • Kari Yadro, **Director of Custom Programs** • Kari Torson, **Director of International Licensing** • Sean Brice, **Director of Trade Sales**

Published by Dark Horse Books
A division of Dark Horse Comics LLC.
10956 SE Main Street
Milwaukie, OR 97222

DarkHorse.com

To find a comics shop in your area, visit ComicShopLocator.com.

First edition: May 2021
Ebook ISBN 978-1-50672-473-7
Trade paperback ISBN 978-1-50672-472-0

10 9 8 7 6 5 4 3 2 1
Printed in China

Library of Congress Cataloging-in-Publication Data

Names: Grissom, Eric, author. | Perkins, Will, artist.
Title: Goblin / Eric Grissom, Will Perkins.
Description: First edition. | Milwaukie, OR : Dark Horse Books, 2021. |
   Audience: Ages 12+ | Summary: After a sinister human warrior raids the
   home of young goblin Rikt and leaves him orphaned, he vows to avenge the
   death of his parents and embarks on a perilous journey, learning of a
   secret power hidden in the heart of the First Tree.
Identifiers: LCCN 2020052341 | ISBN 9781506724720 (trade paperback) | ISBN
   9781506724737 (ebook)
Subjects: LCSH: Graphic novels. | CYAC: Graphic novels. | Fantasy. |
   Goblins--Fiction. | Revenge--Fiction. | Quests (Expeditions)--Fiction.
Classification: LCC PZ7.7.G776 Go 2021 | DDC 741.5/973--dc23
LC record available at https://lccn.loc.gov/2020052341

CHAPTER ONE
THE GOBLIN'S GIFTS

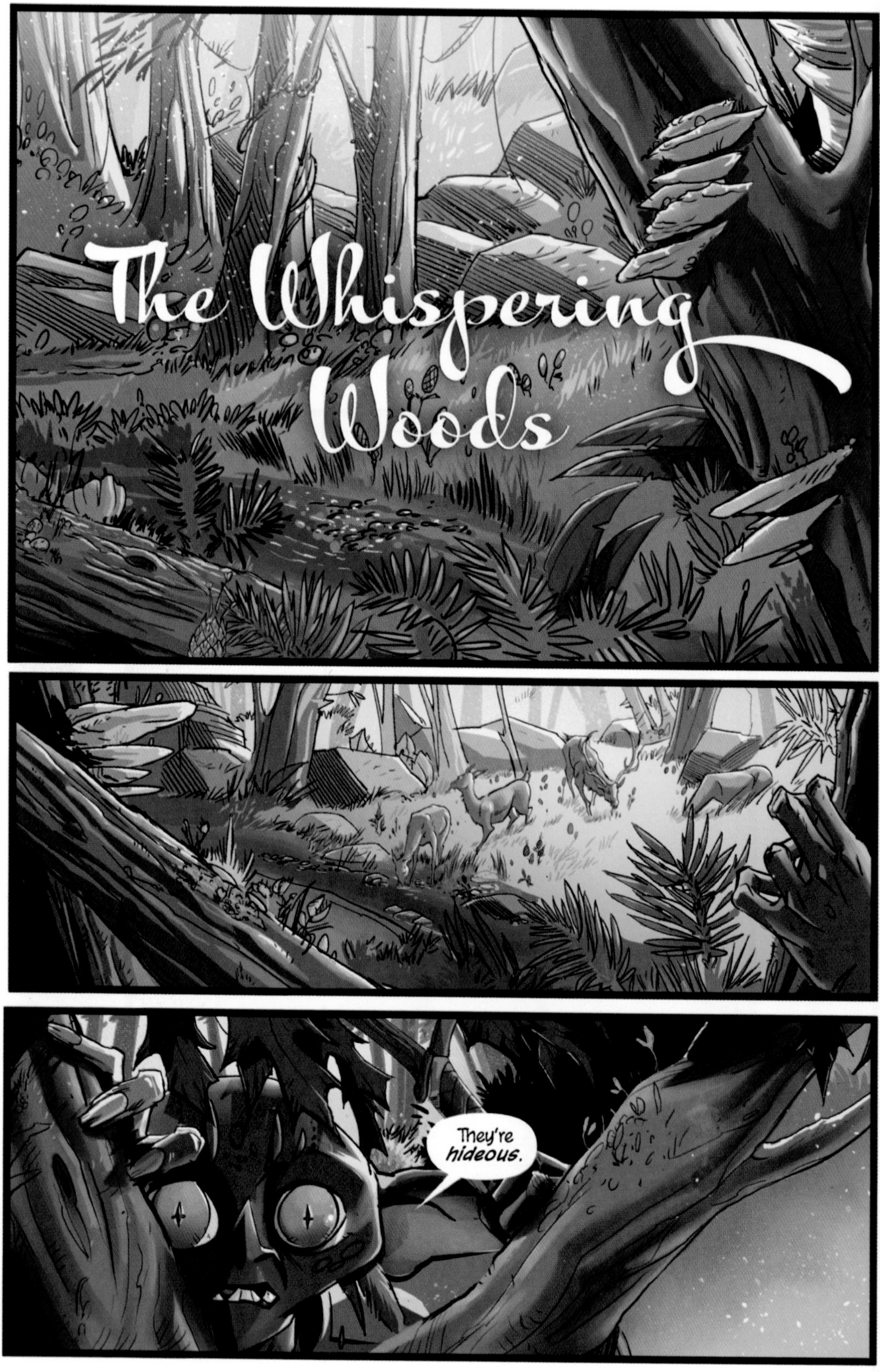
The Whispering Woods
They're hideous.

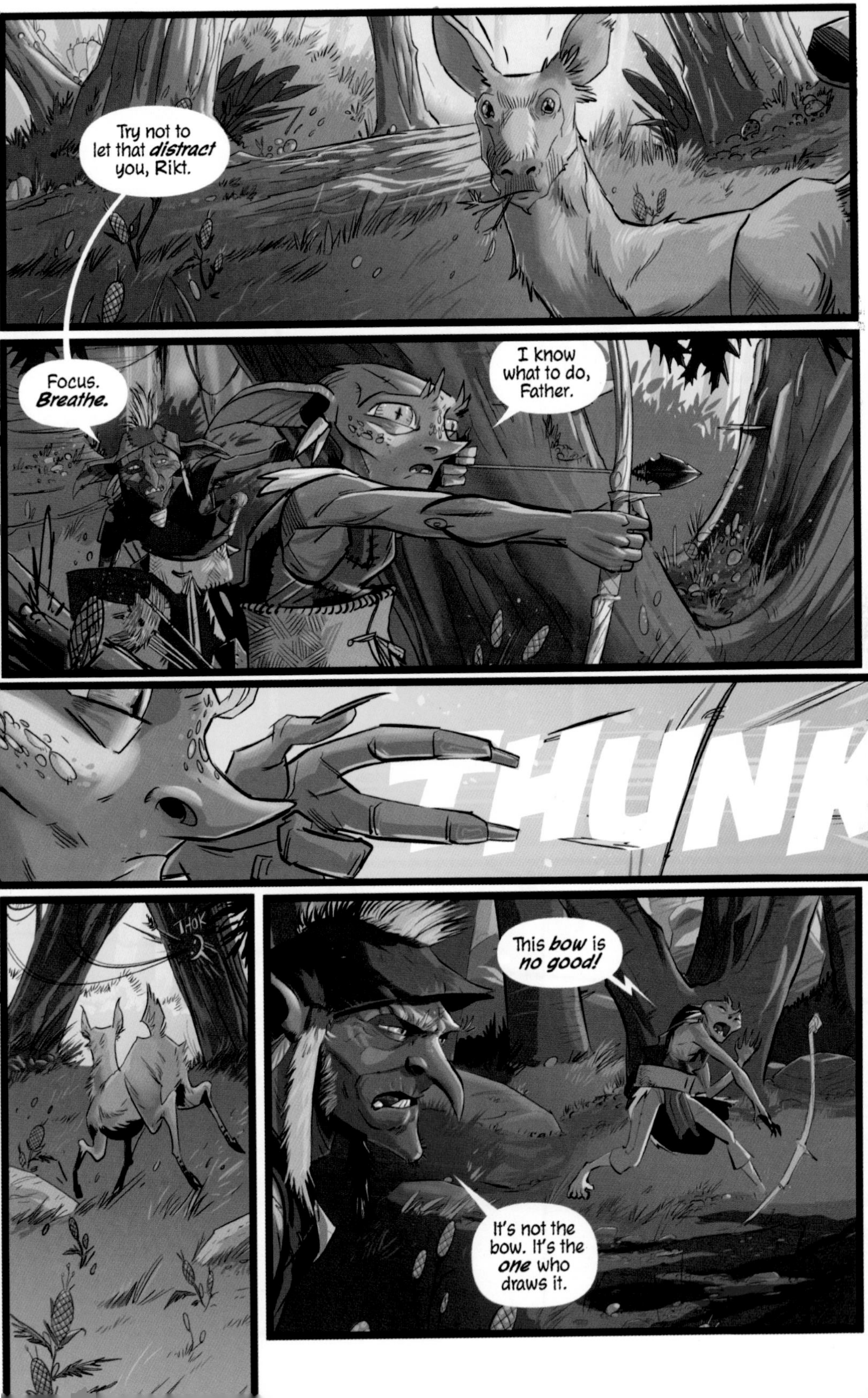
Try not to let that *distract* you, Rikt.
Focus. **Breathe.**
I know what to do, Father.
THUNK
THOK
This **bow** is **no good!**
It's not the bow. It's the **one** who draws it.

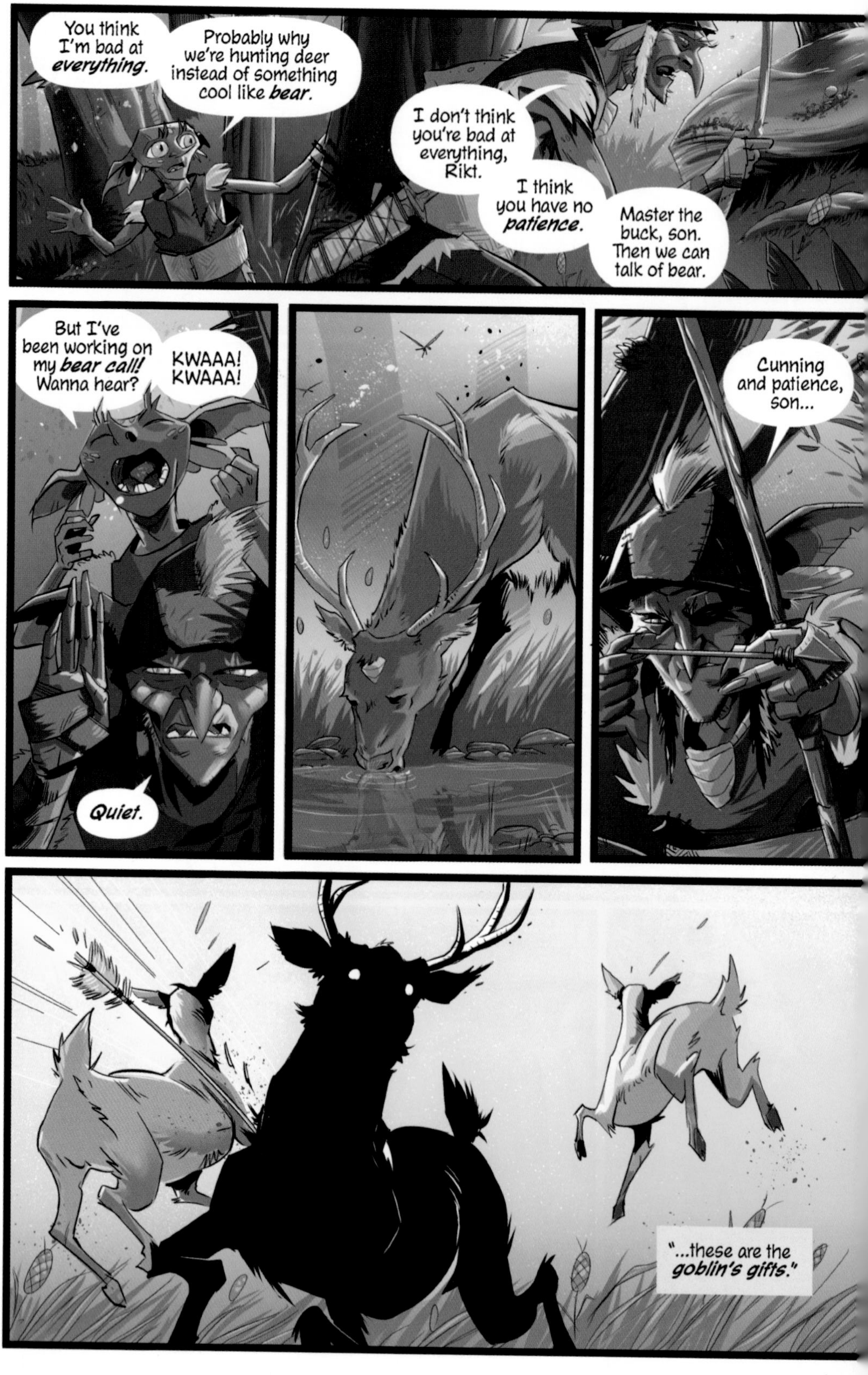
You think I'm bad at *everything*.
Probably why we're hunting deer instead of something cool like *bear*.
I don't think you're bad at everything, Rikt.
I think you have no *patience*.
Master the buck, son. Then we can talk of bear.
But I've been working on my *bear call!* Wanna hear?
KWAAA! KWAAA!
Quiet.
Cunning and patience, son...
"...these are the *goblin's gifts*."

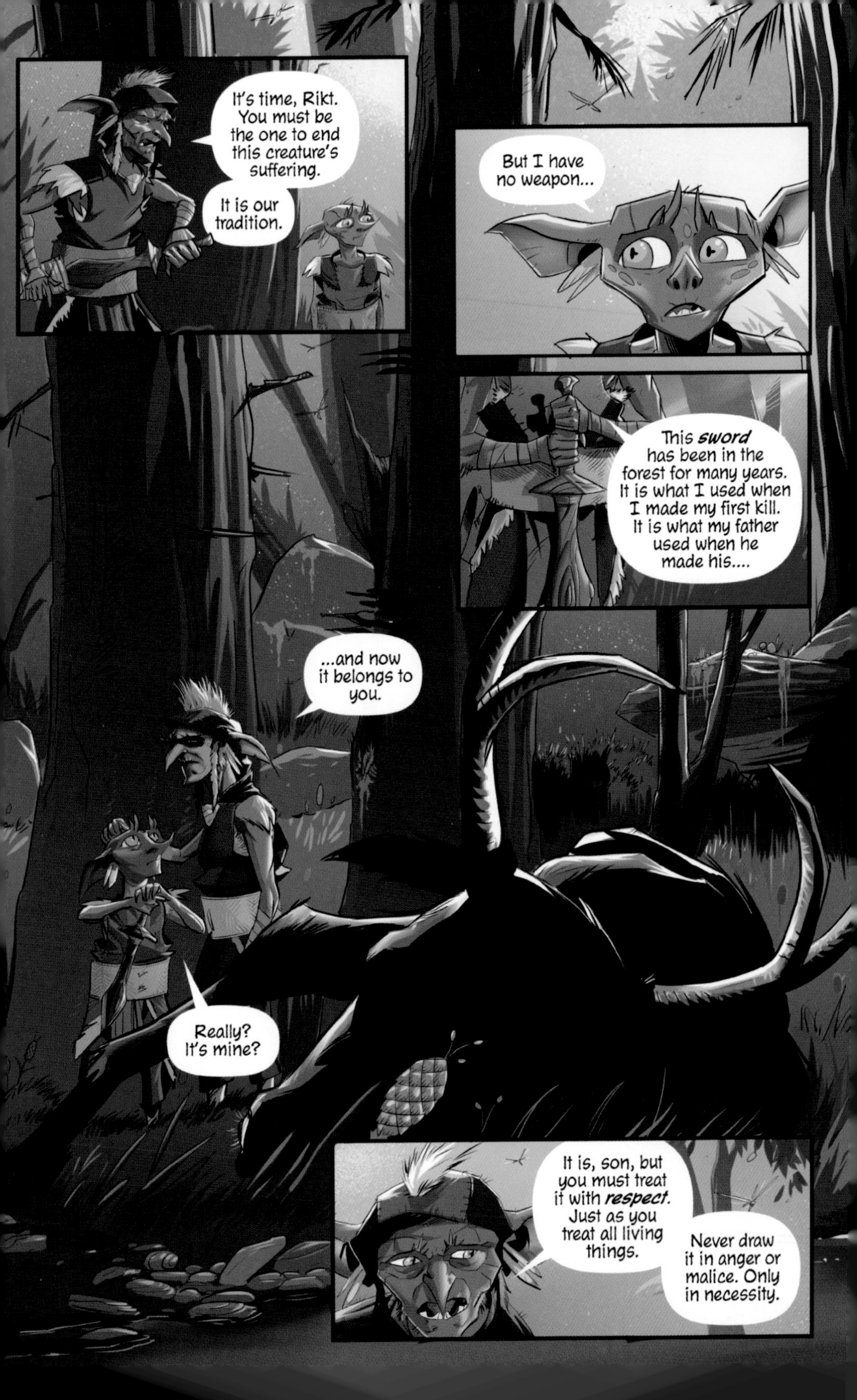
It's time, Rikt. You must be the one to end this creature's suffering.
It is our tradition.
But I have no weapon...
This *sword* has been in the forest for many years. It is what I used when I made my first kill. It is what my father used when he made his....
...and now it belongs to you.
Really? It's mine?
It is, son, but you must treat it with *respect*. Just as you treat all living things.
Never draw it in anger or malice. Only in necessity.

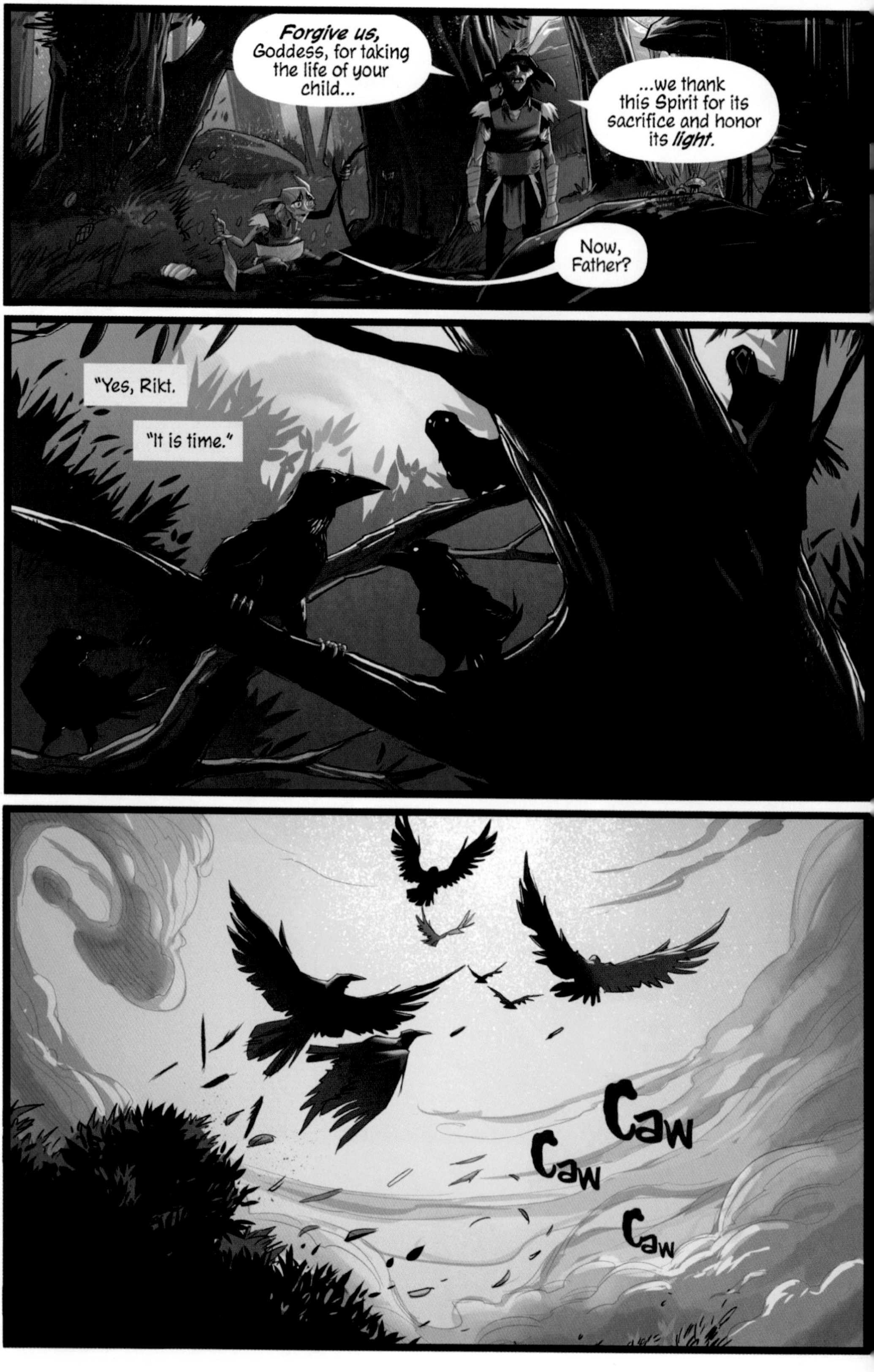
Forgive us, Goddess, for taking the life of your child...
...we thank this Spirit for its sacrifice and honor its light.
Now, Father?
"Yes, Rikt.
"It is time."
Caw
Caw
Caw

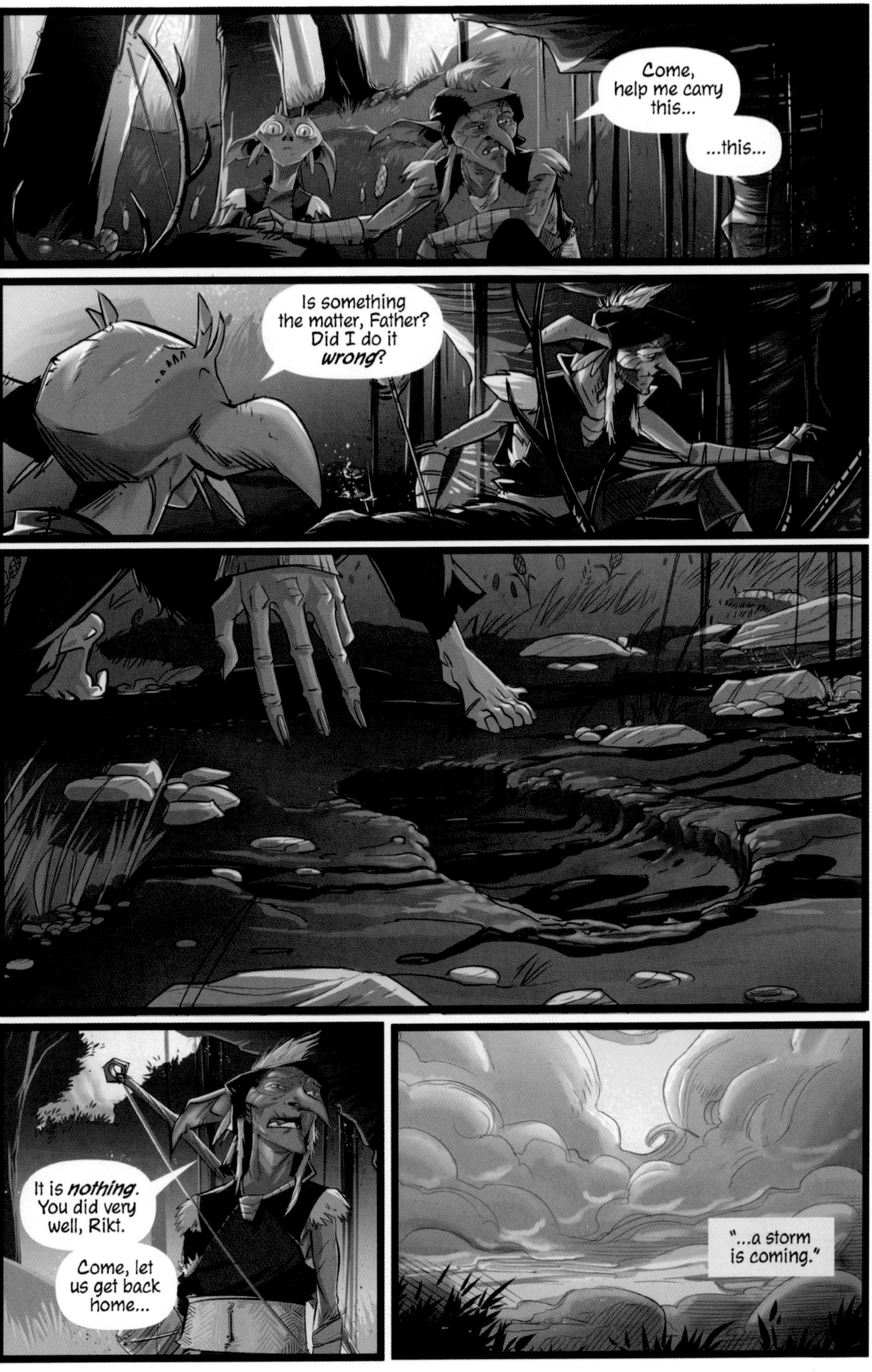
Come, help me carry this...
...this...
Is something the matter, Father? Did I do it *wrong*?
It is *nothing*. You did very well, Rikt.
Come, let us get back home...
"...a storm is coming."

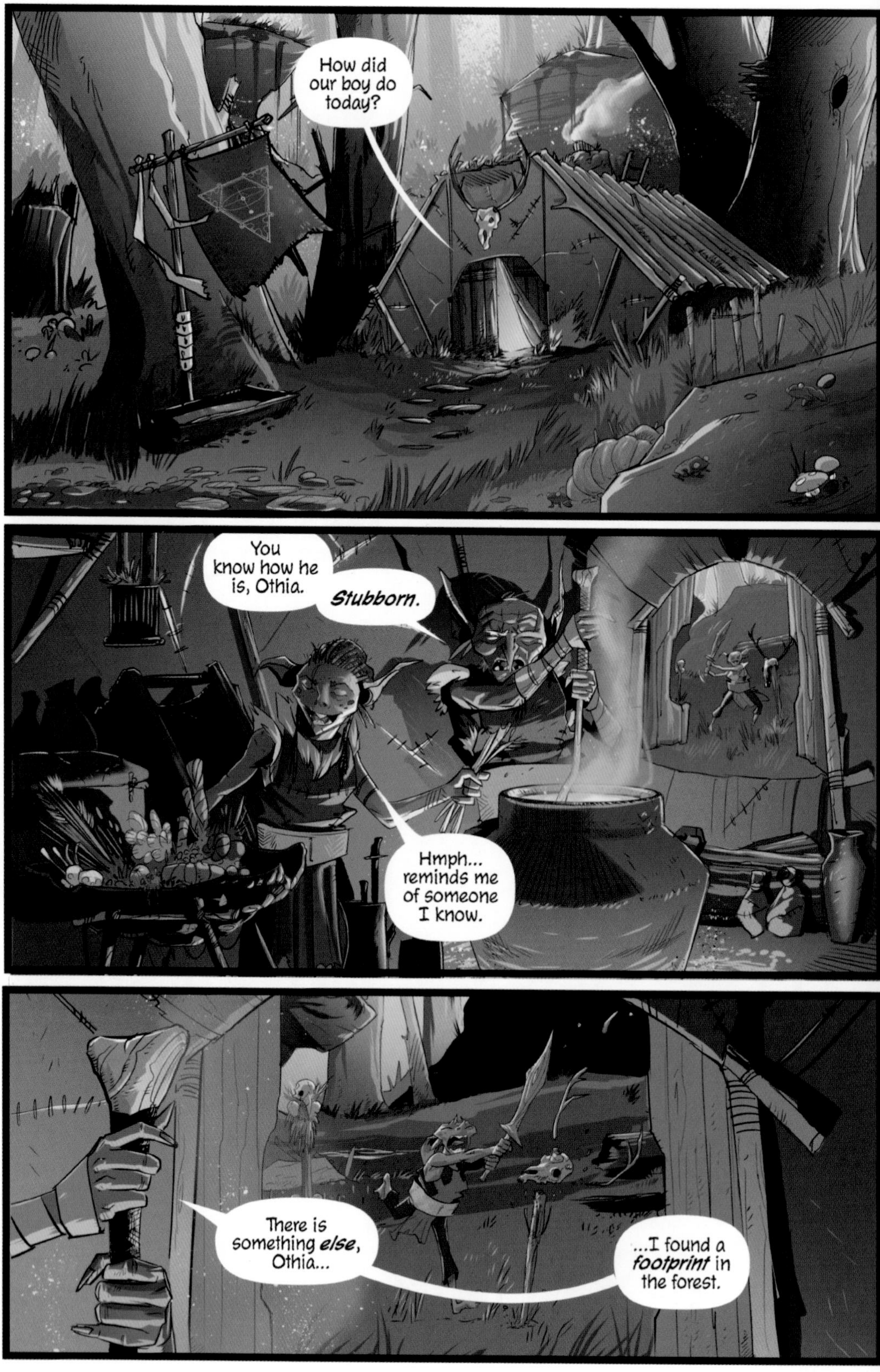
How did our boy do today?
You know how he is, Othia.
Stubborn.
Hmph... reminds me of someone I know.
There is something else, Othia...
...I found a footprint in the forest.

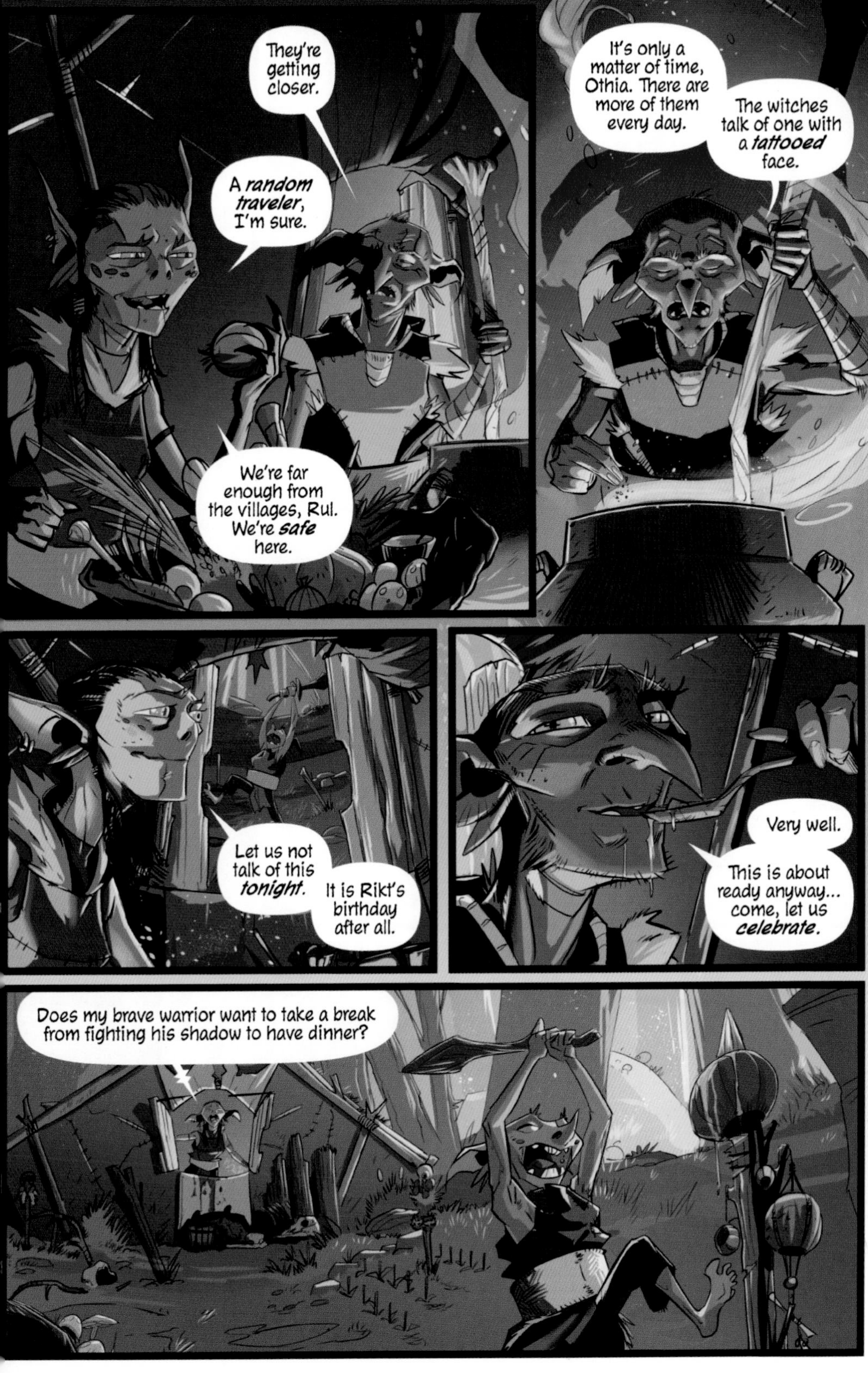
They're getting closer.
A random traveler, I'm sure.
We're far enough from the villages, Rul. We're safe here.
It's only a matter of time, Othia. There are more of them every day.
The witches talk of one with a tattooed face.
Let us not talk of this tonight.
It is Rikt's birthday after all.
Very well.
This is about ready anyway... come, let us celebrate.
Does my brave warrior want to take a break from fighting his shadow to have dinner?

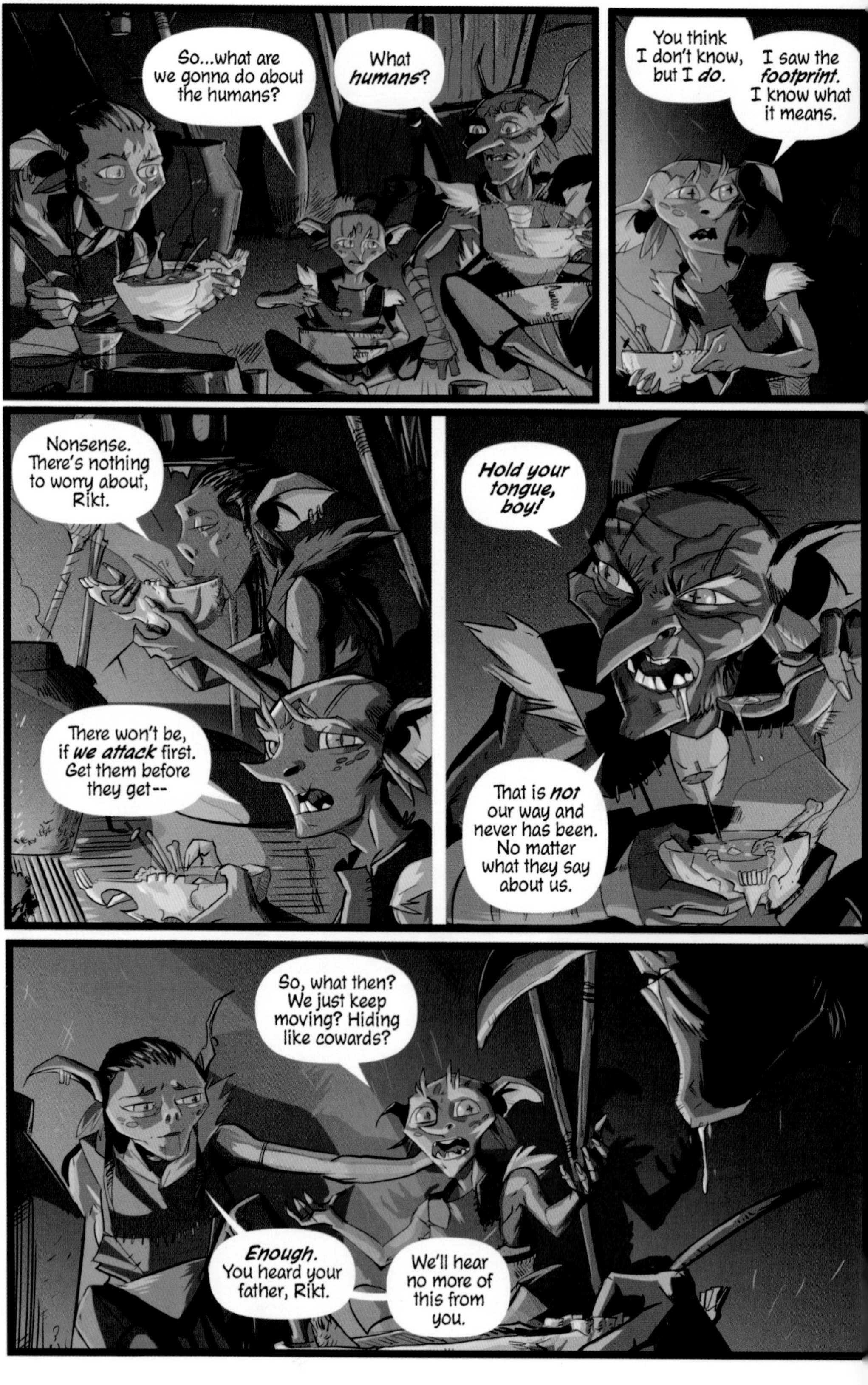
So...what are we gonna do about the humans?
What *humans*?
You think I don't know, but I *do*.
I saw the *footprint*. I know what it means.
Nonsense. There's nothing to worry about, Rikt.
There won't be, if *we attack* first. Get them before they get--
Hold your tongue, boy!
That is *not* our way and never has been. No matter what they say about us.
So, what then? We just keep moving? Hiding like cowards?
Enough. You heard your father, Rikt.
We'll hear no more of this from you.

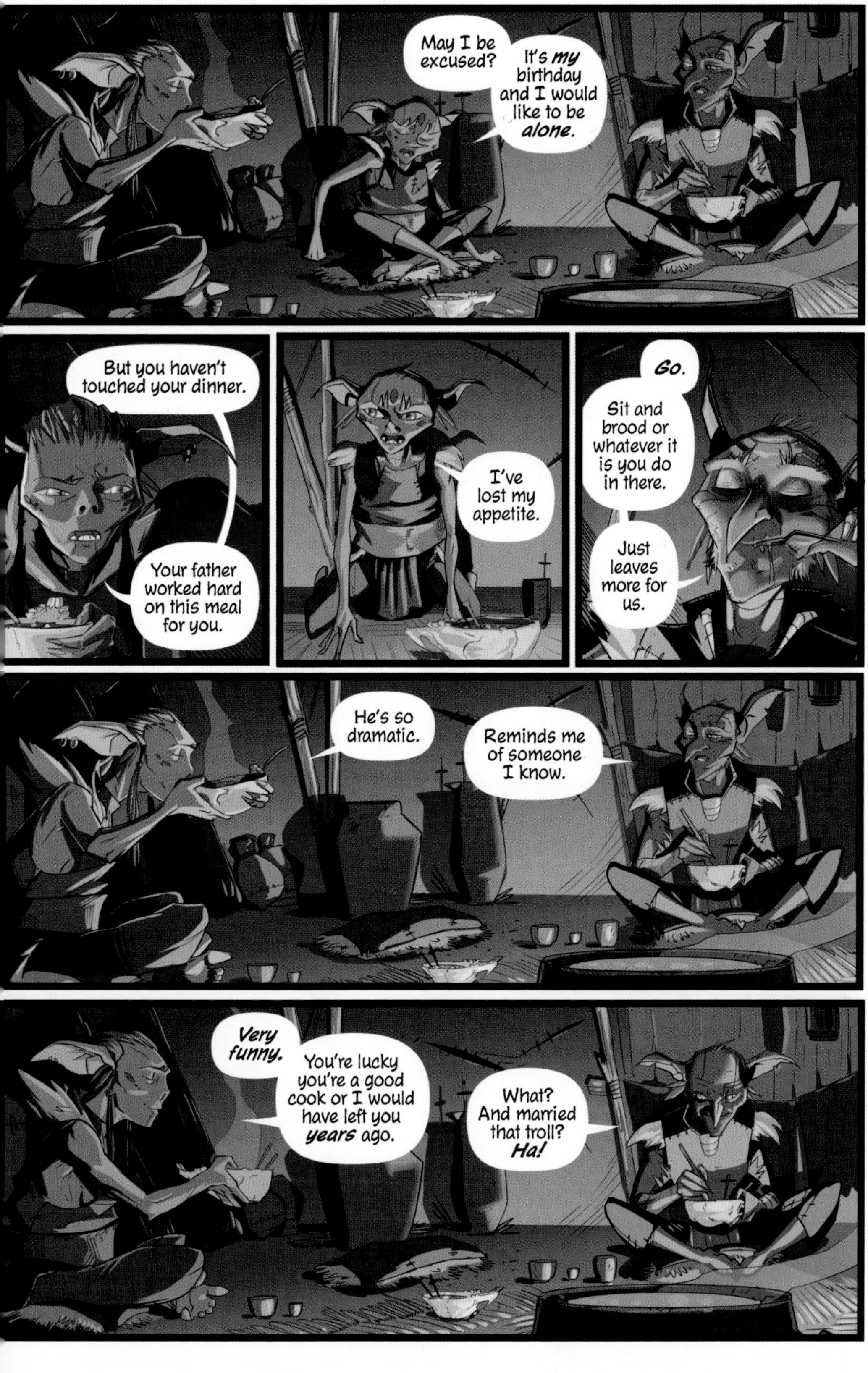
May I be excused?
It's *my* birthday and I would like to be *alone*.
But you haven't touched your dinner.
Your father worked hard on this meal for you.
I've lost my appetite.
Go.
Sit and brood or whatever it is you do in there.
Just leaves more for us.
He's so dramatic.
Reminds me of someone I know.
Very funny.
You're lucky you're a good cook or I would have left you *years* ago.
What? And married that troll? *Ha!*

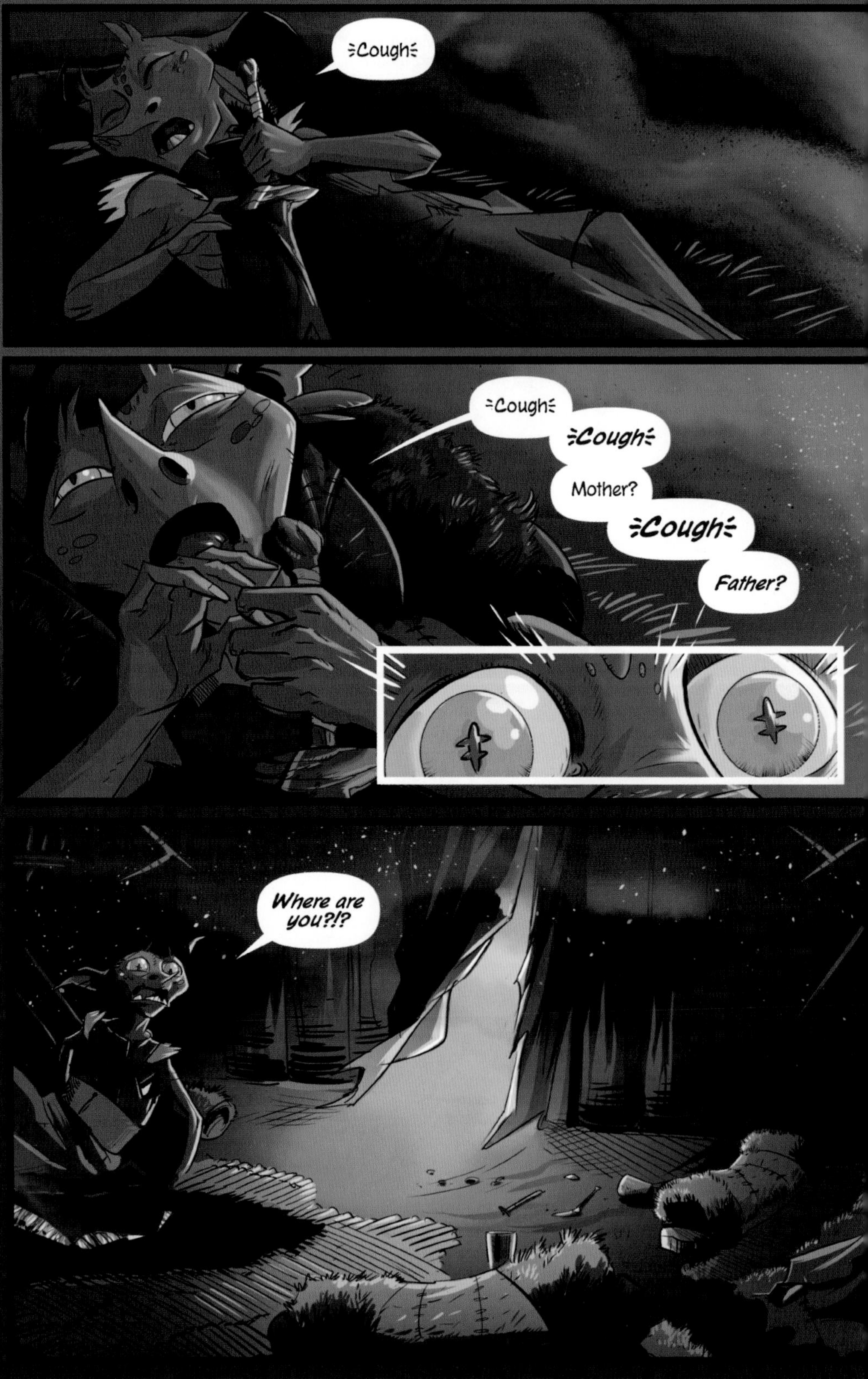
Cough
Cough
Cough
Mother?
Cough
Father?
Where are you?!?

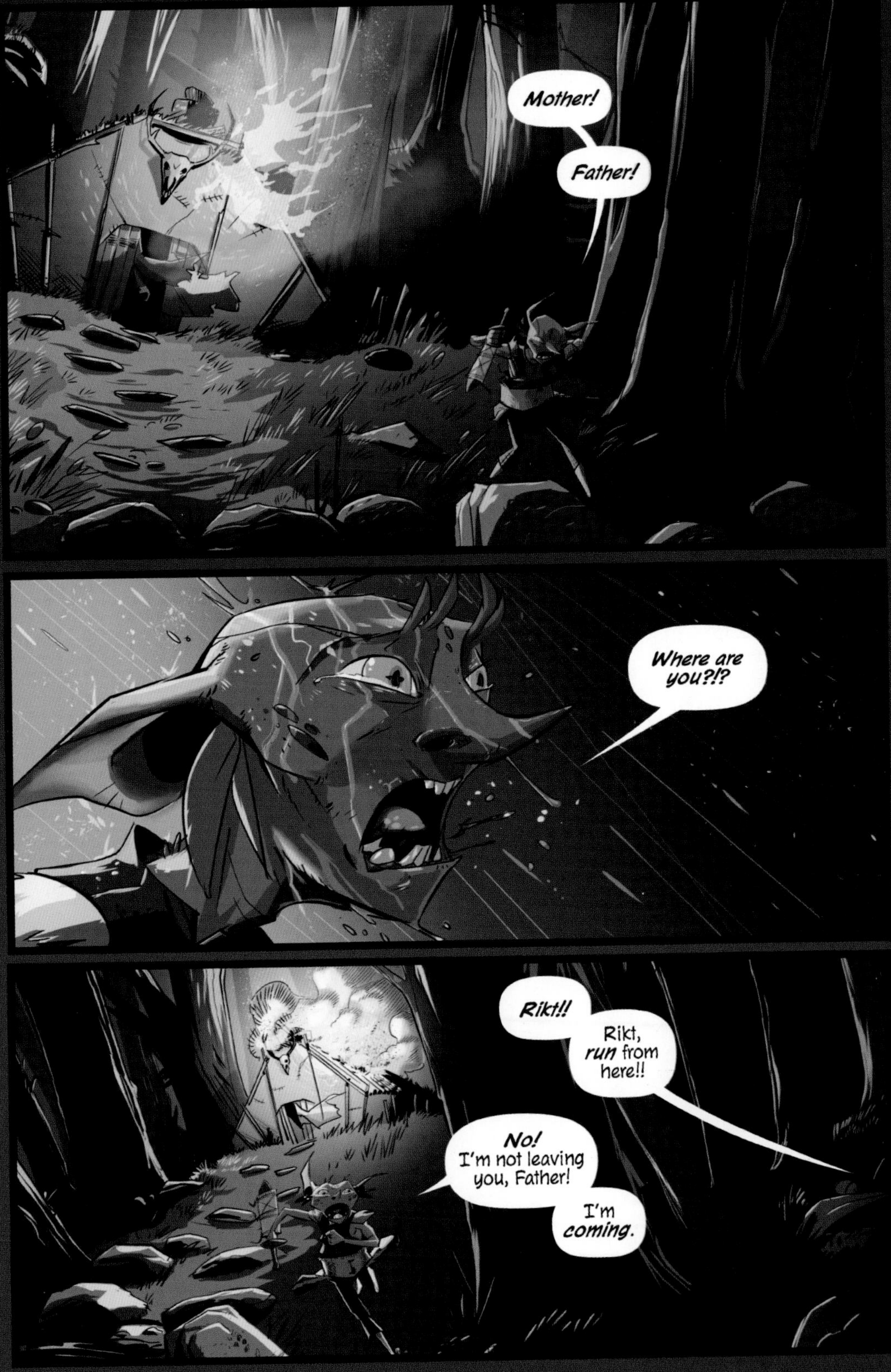
Mother!
Father!
Where are you?!?
Rikt!!
Rikt, run from here!!
No! I'm not leaving you, Father!
I'm coming.

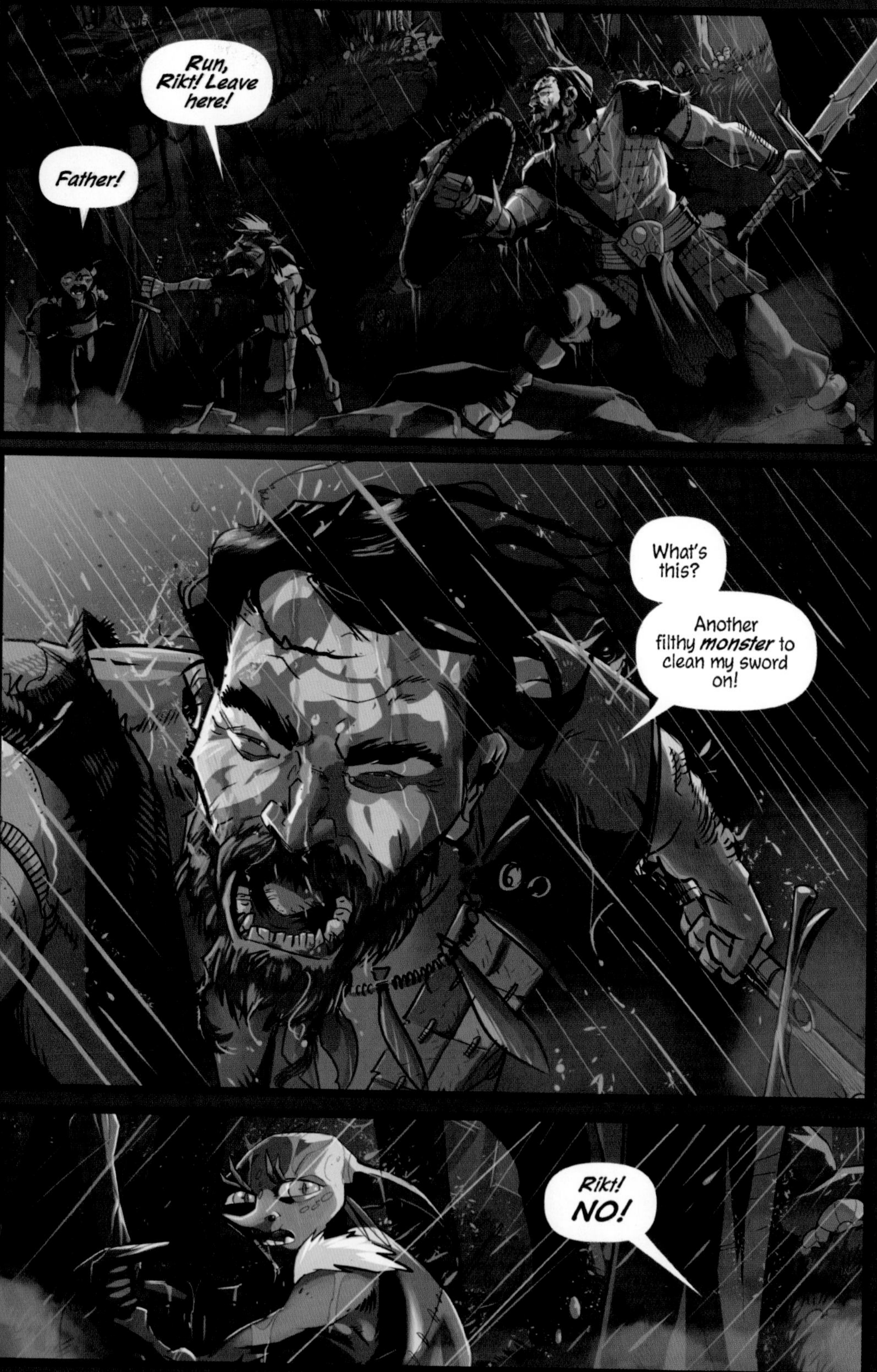
Father!
Run, Rikt! Leave here!
What's this?
Another filthy ***monster*** to clean my sword on!
Rikt! NO!

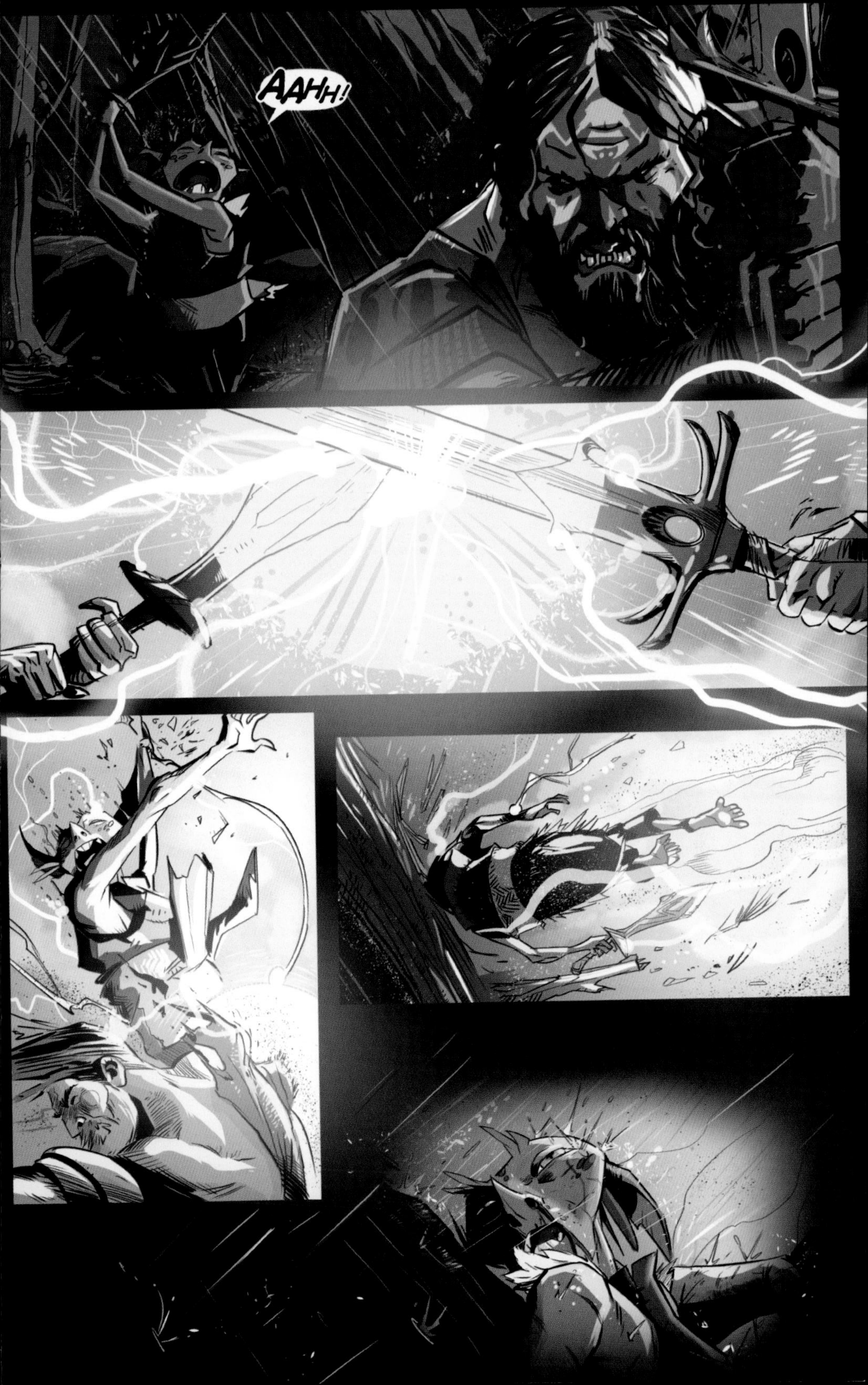
AAHH!

CHAPTER TWO
A CIRCLE GOLD

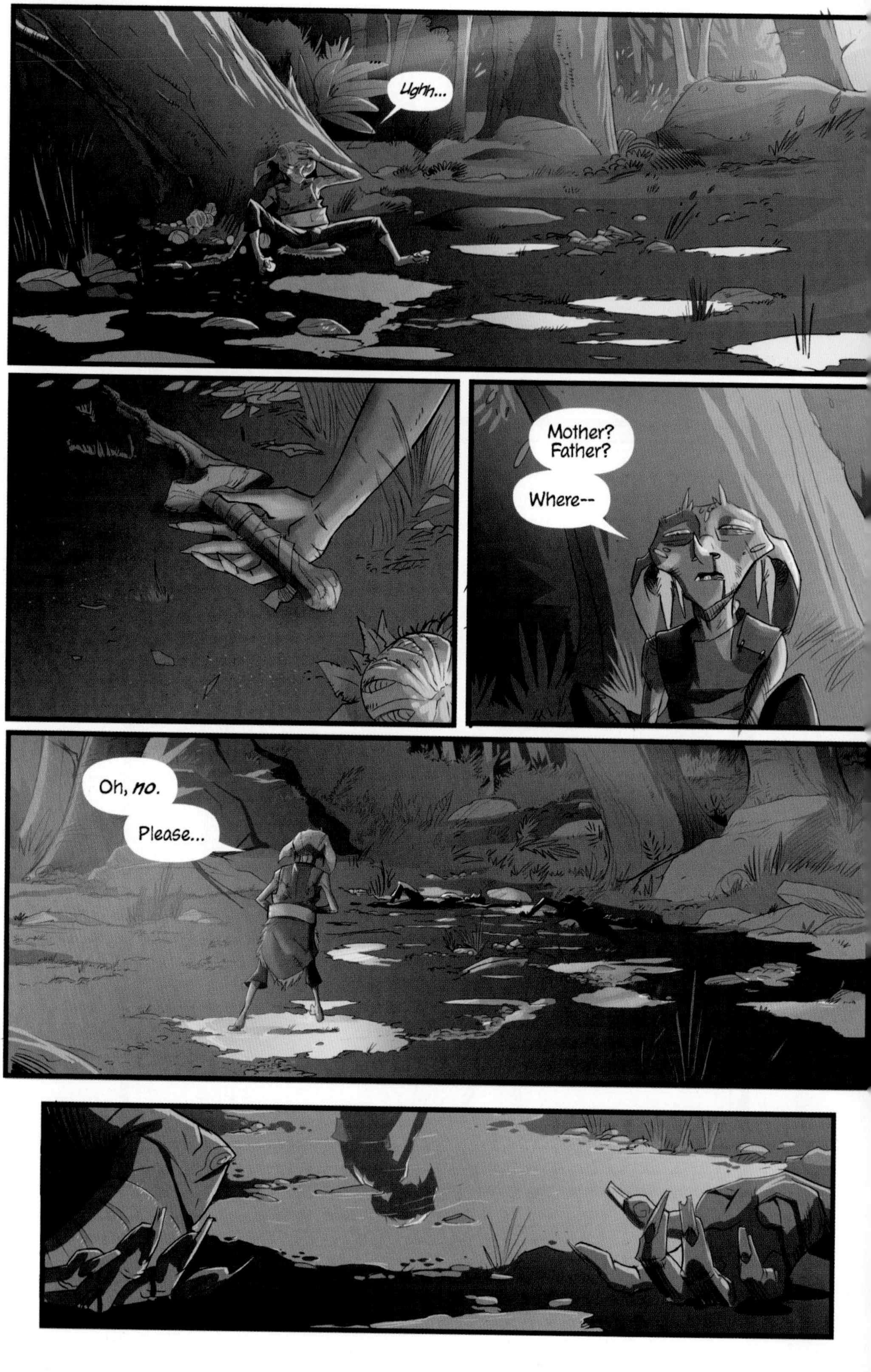
Ughh...
Mother? Father?
Where--
Oh, *no*.
Please...

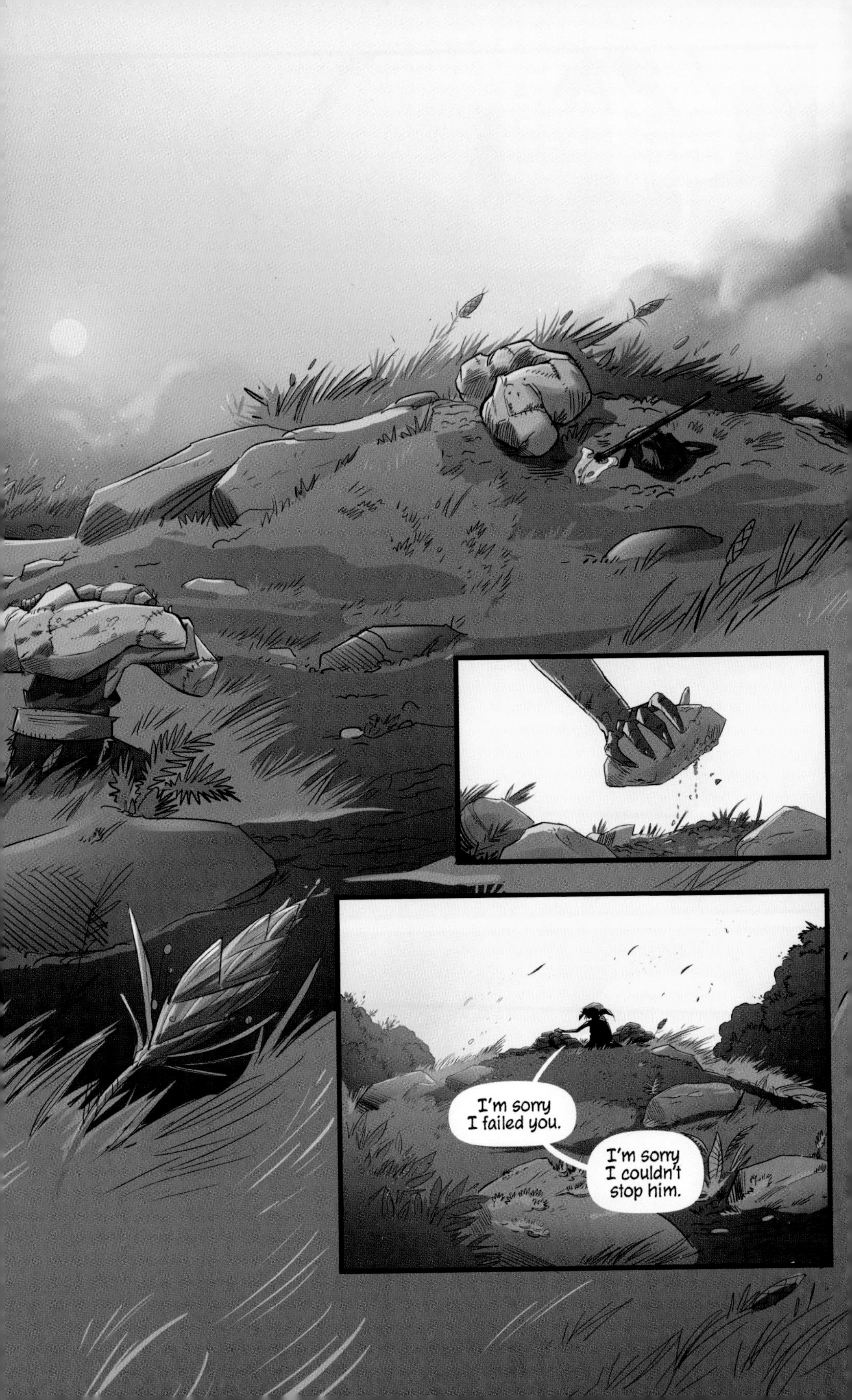
I'm sorry
I failed you.
I'm sorry
I couldn't
stop him.

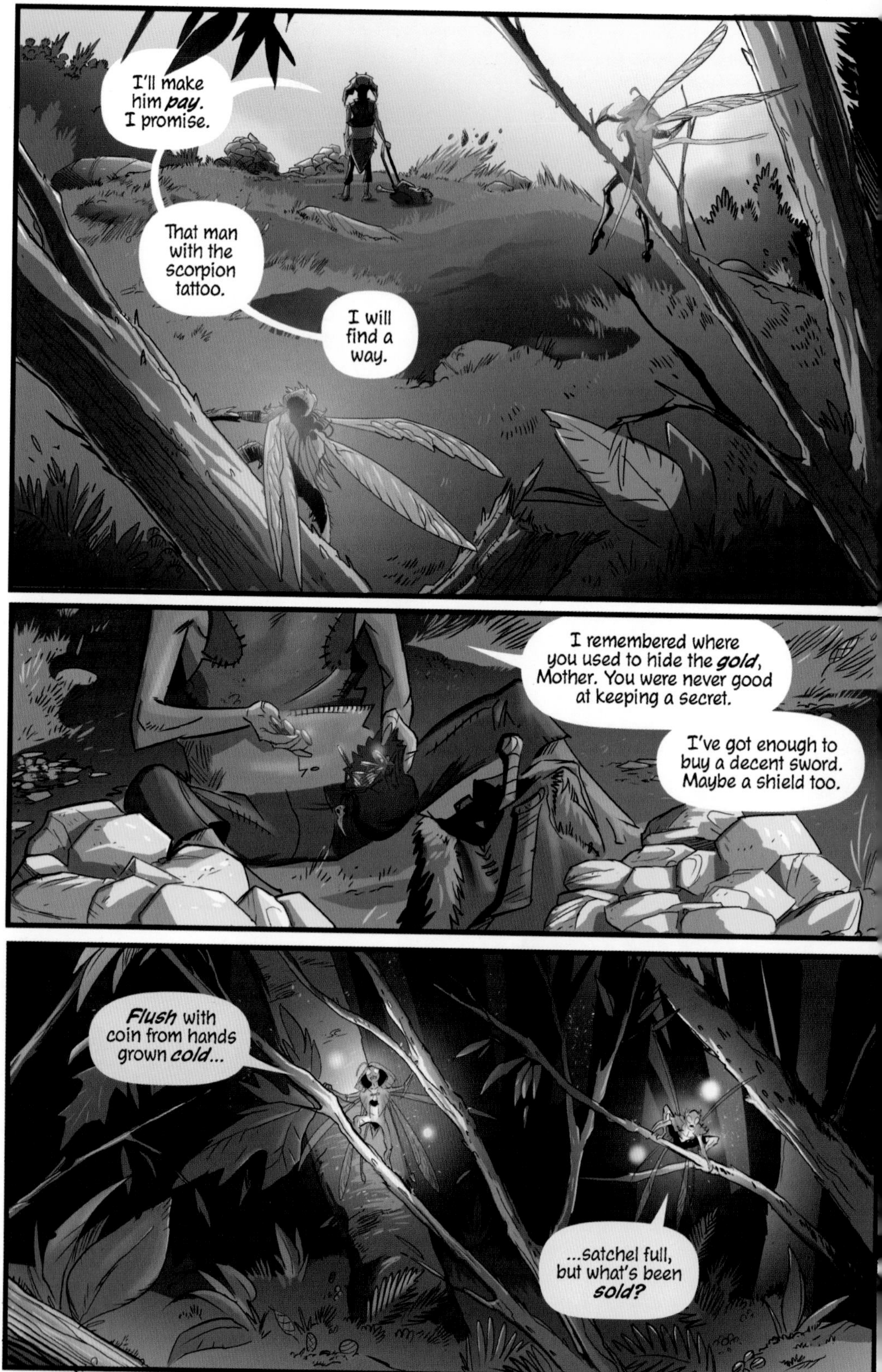
I'll make him *pay*. I promise.
That man with the scorpion tattoo.
I will find a way.
I remembered where you used to hide the *gold*, Mother. You were never good at keeping a secret.
I've got enough to buy a decent sword. Maybe a shield too.
Flush with coin from hands grown *cold*...
...satchel full, but what's been *sold?*

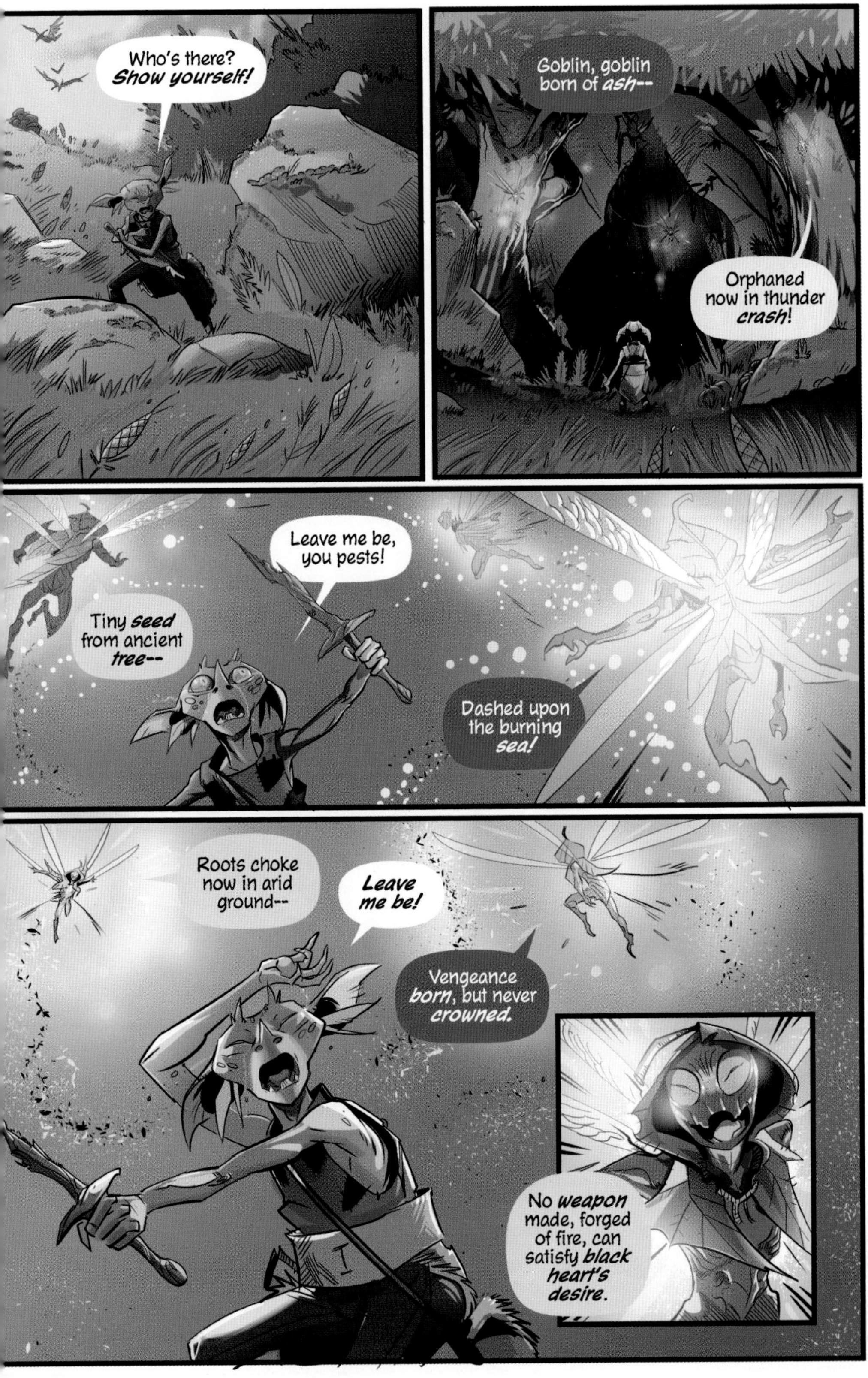
Who's there? *Show yourself!*
Goblin, goblin born of *ash*--
Orphaned now in thunder *crash*!
Tiny *seed* from ancient *tree*--
Leave me be, you pests!
Dashed upon the burning *sea!*
Roots choke now in arid ground--
Leave me be!
Vengeance *born*, but never *crowned.*
No *weapon* made, forged of fire, can satisfy *black heart's desire*.

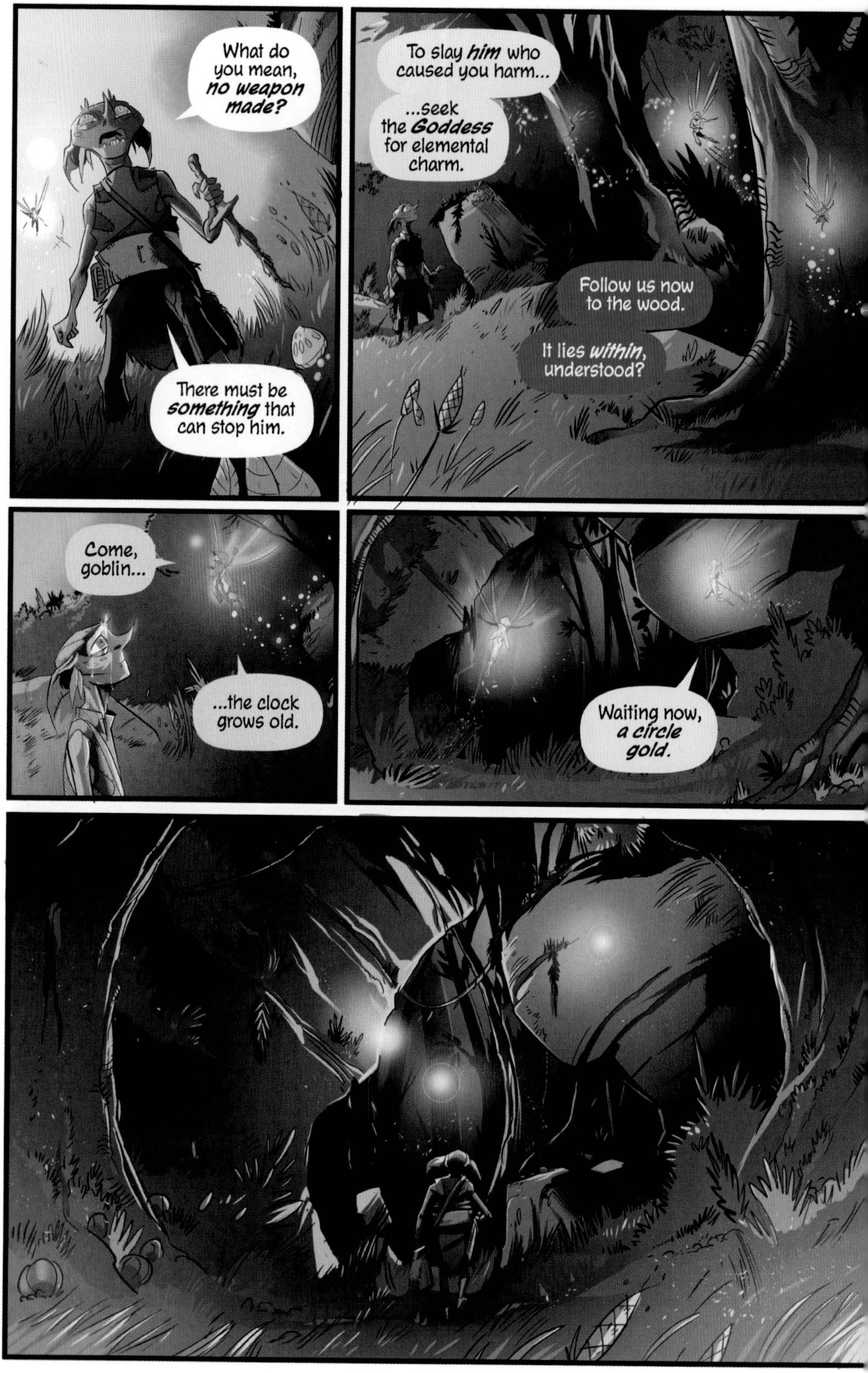
What do you mean, *no weapon made?*
There must be *something* that can stop him.
To slay *him* who caused you harm...
...seek the *Goddess* for elemental charm.
Follow us now to the wood.
It lies *within*, understood?
Come, goblin...
...the clock grows old.
Waiting now, *a circle gold*.

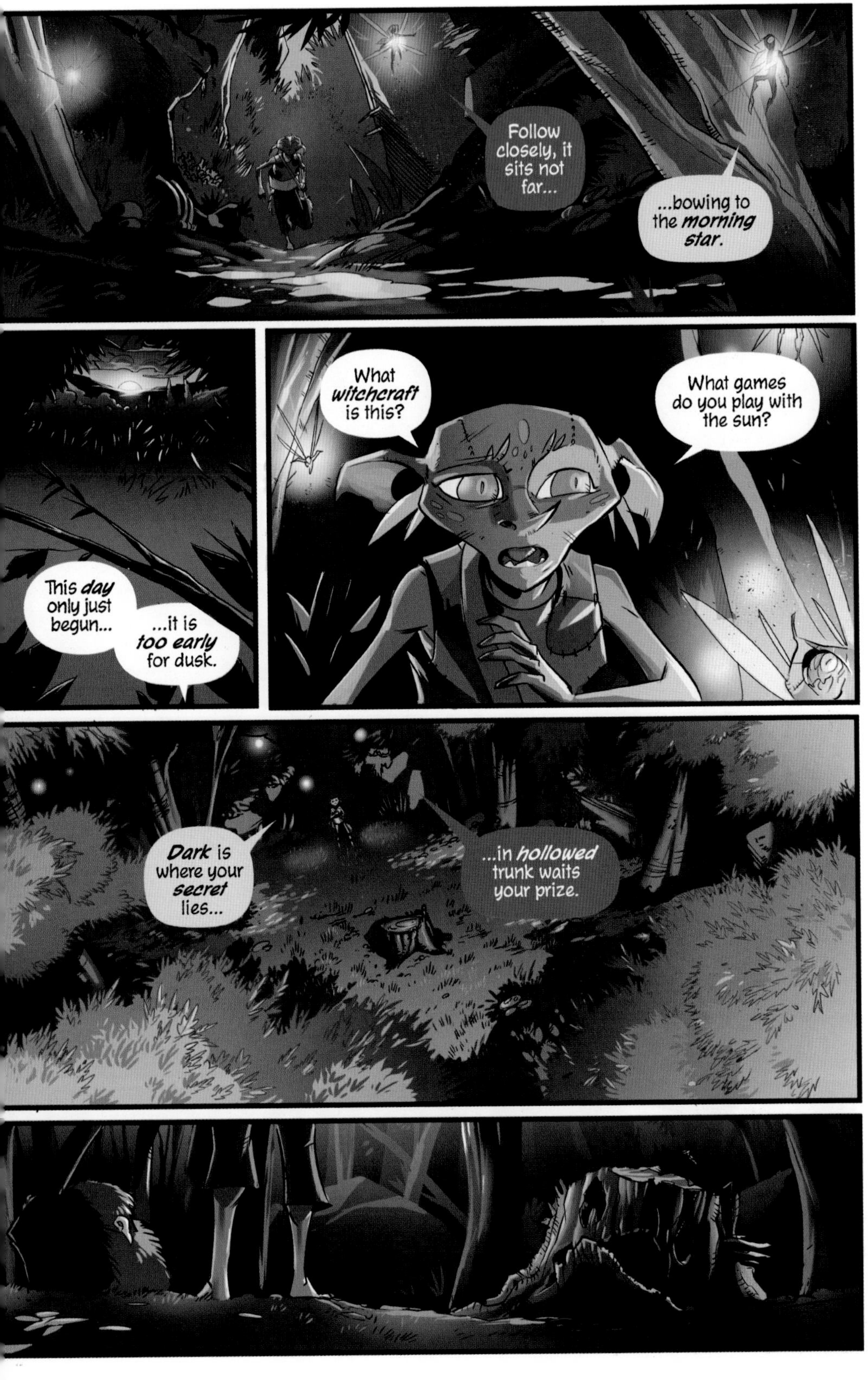
Follow closely, it sits not far...
...bowing to the *morning star.*
This *day* only just begun...
...it is *too early* for dusk.
What *witchcraft* is this?
What games do you play with the sun?
Dark is where your *secret* lies...
...in *hollowed* trunk waits your prize.

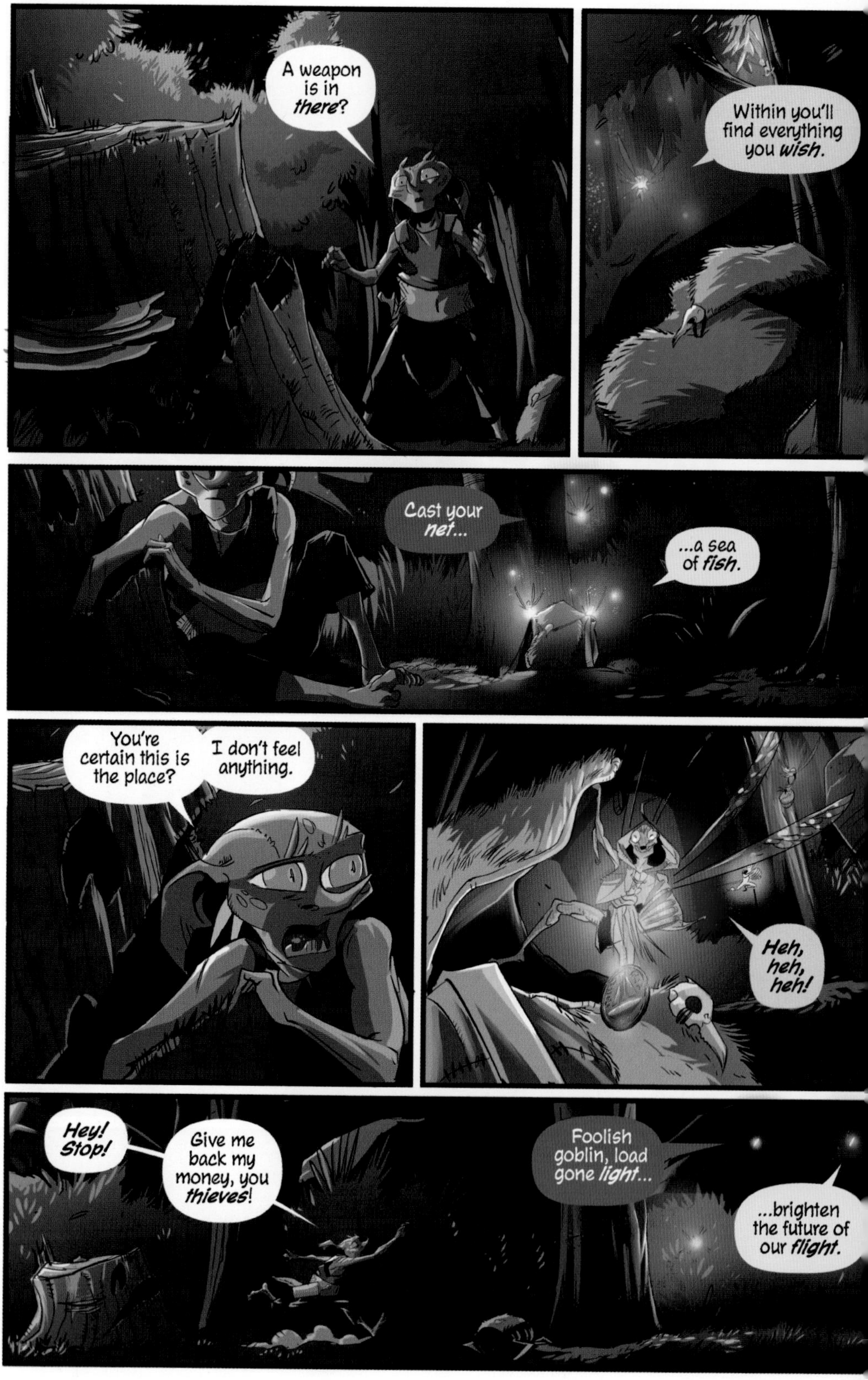
A weapon is in *there*?
Within you'll find everything you *wish*.
Cast your *net*...
...a sea of *fish*.
You're certain this is the place?
I don't feel anything.
Heh, heh, heh!
Hey! Stop!
Give me back my money, you *thieves*!
Foolish goblin, load gone *light*...
...brighten the future of our *flight*.

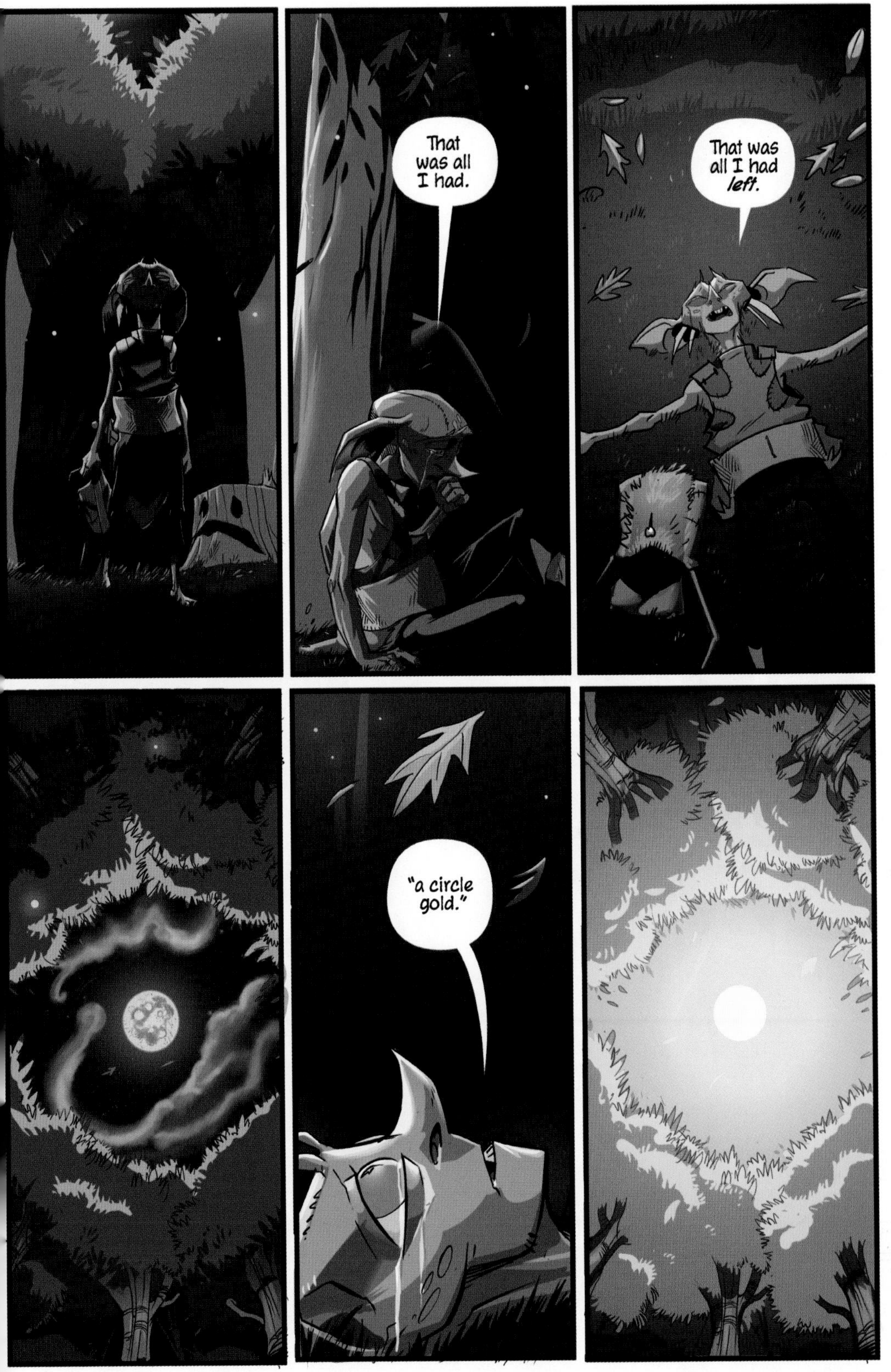
That was all I had.
That was all I had *left*.
"a circle gold."

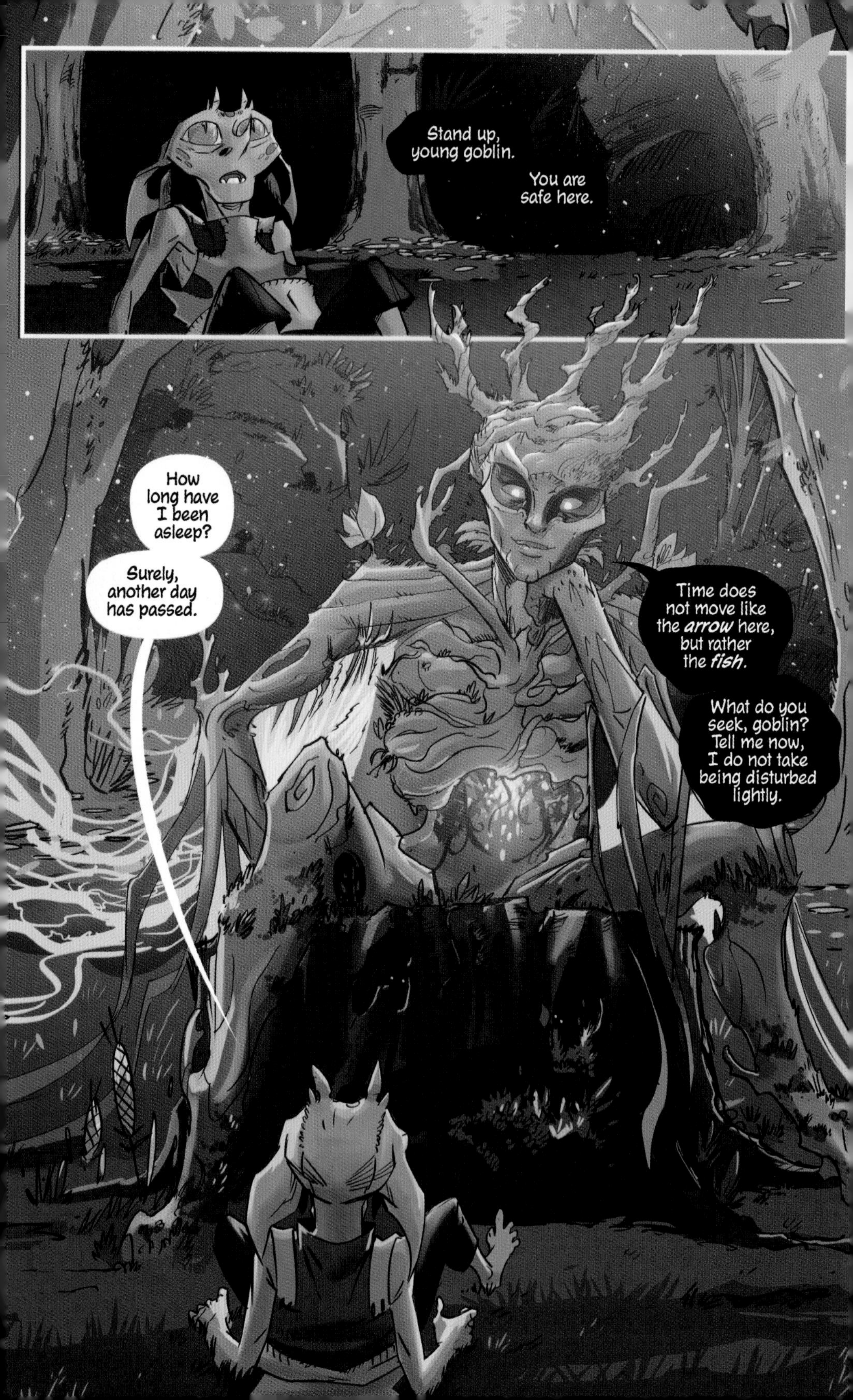
Stand up, young goblin.
You are safe here.
How long have I been asleep?
Surely, another day has passed.
Time does not move like the *arrow* here, but rather the *fish*.
What do you seek, goblin? Tell me now, I do not take being disturbed lightly.

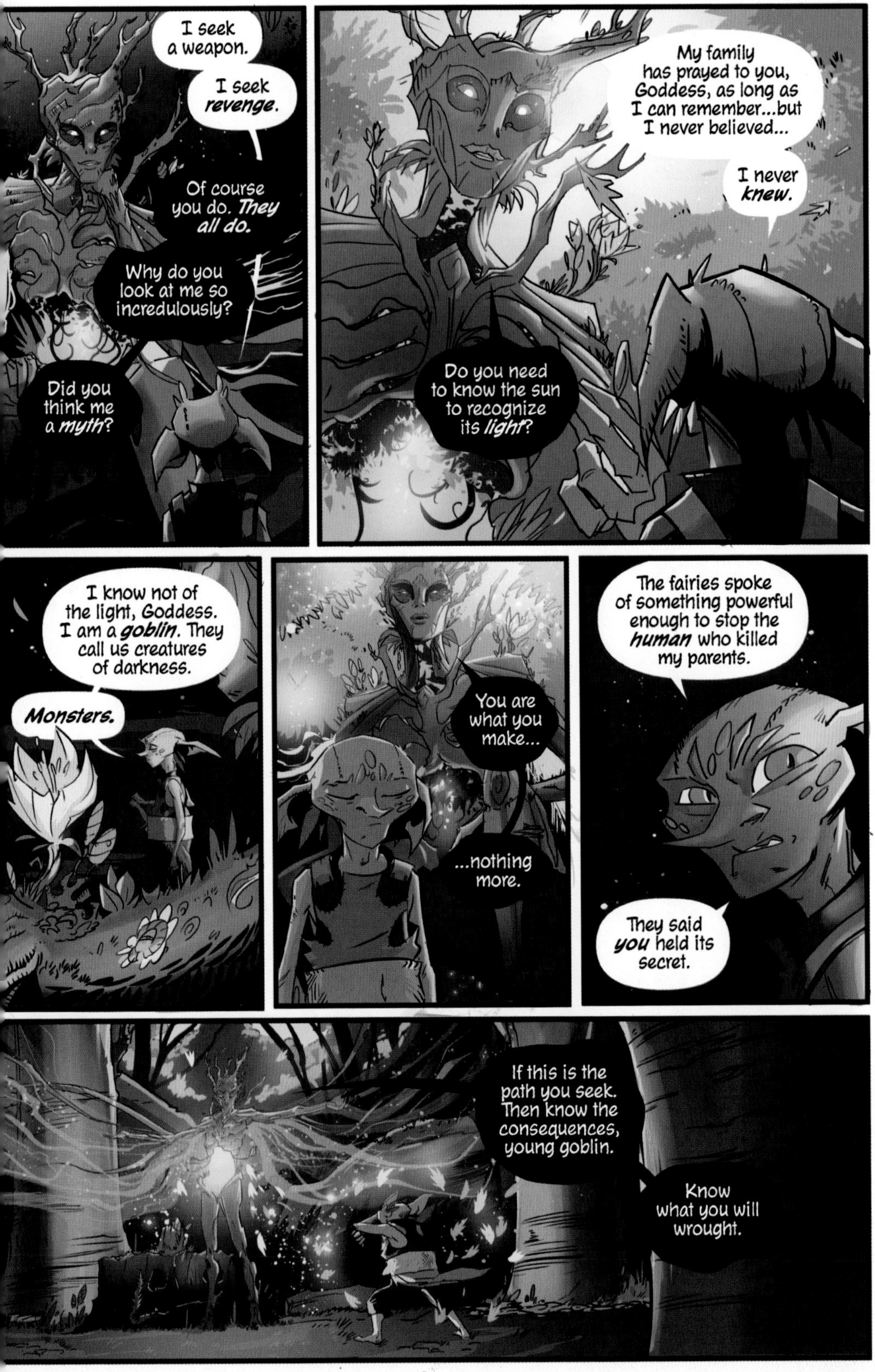
I seek a weapon.
I seek *revenge*.
Of course you do. *They all do.*
Why do you look at me so incredulously?
Did you think me a *myth*?
My family has prayed to you, Goddess, as long as I can remember...but I never believed...
I never *knew*.
Do you need to know the sun to recognize its *light*?
I know not of the light, Goddess. I am a *goblin*. They call us creatures of darkness.
Monsters.
You are what you make...
...nothing more.
The fairies spoke of something powerful enough to stop the *human* who killed my parents.
They said *you* held its secret.
If this is the path you seek. Then know the consequences, young goblin.
Know what you will wrought.

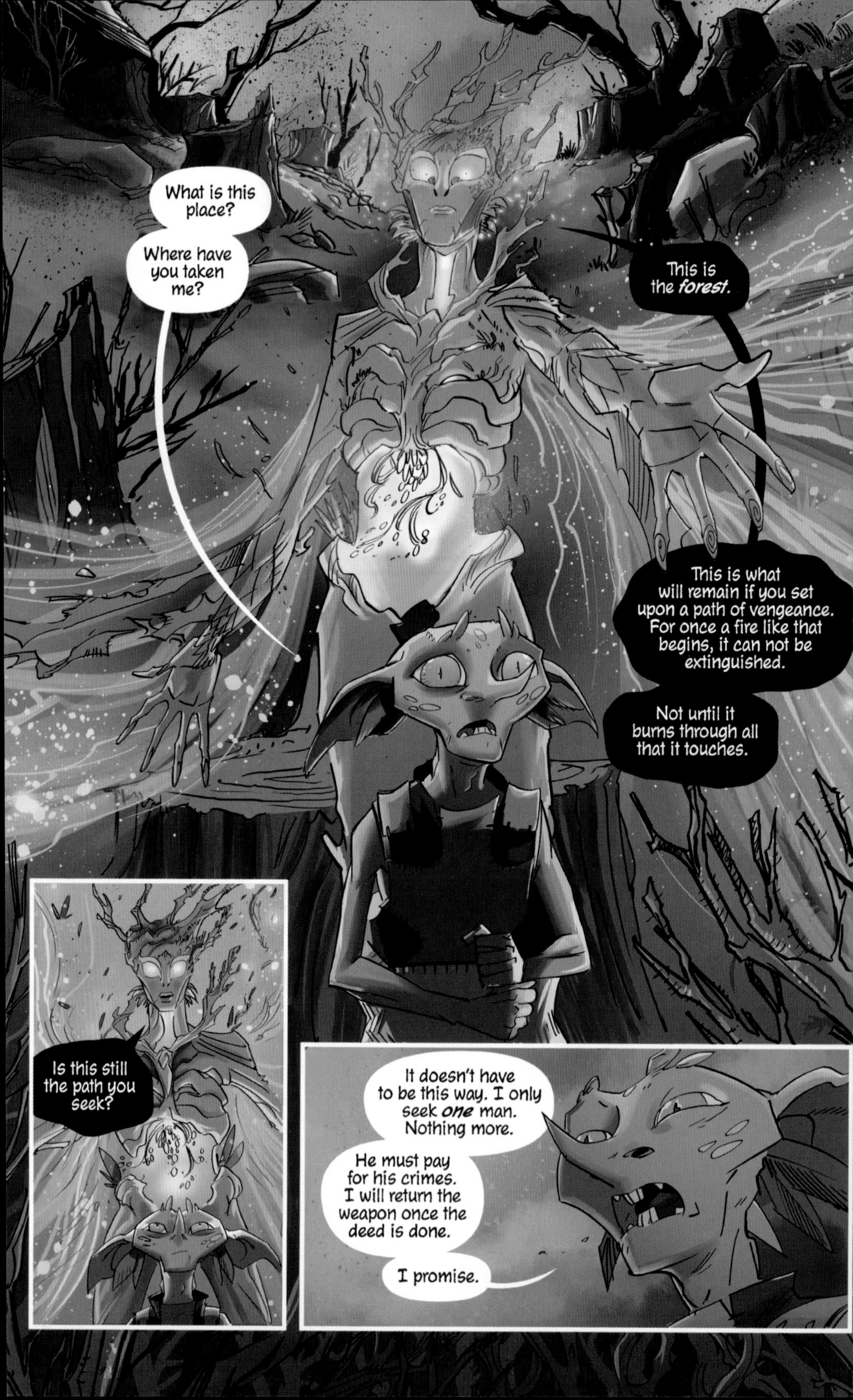
What is this place?
Where have you taken me?
This is the *forest.*
This is what will remain if you set upon a path of vengeance. For once a fire like that begins, it can not be extinguished.
Not until it burns through all that it touches.
Is this still the path you seek?
It doesn't have to be this way. I only seek *one* man. Nothing more.
He must pay for his crimes. I will return the weapon once the deed is done.
I promise.

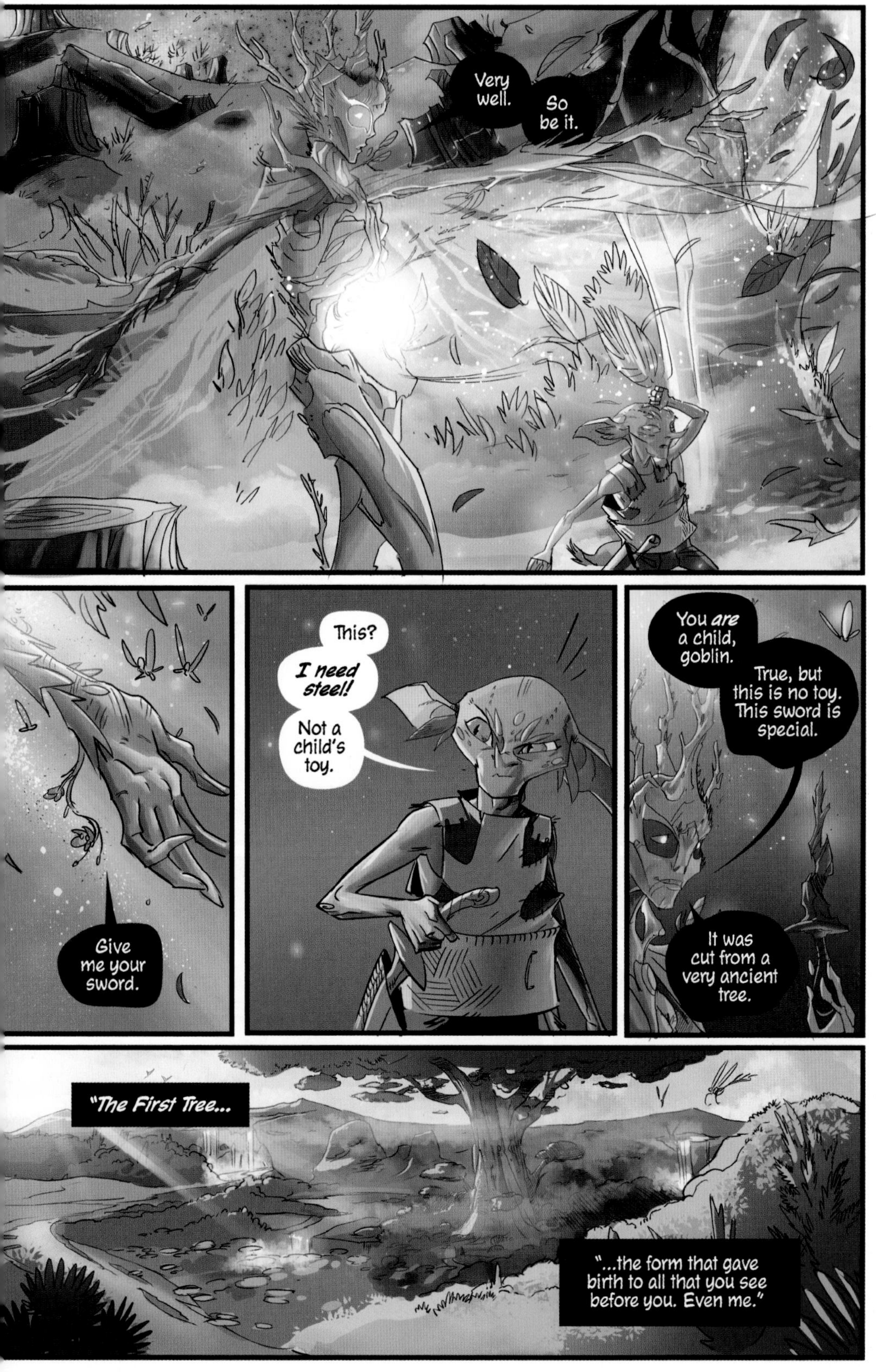
Very well.
So be it.
Give me your sword.
This?
I need steel!
Not a child's toy.
You *are* a child, goblin.
True, but this is no toy. This sword is special.
It was cut from a very ancient tree.
"*The First Tree...*
"...the form that gave birth to all that you see before you. Even me."

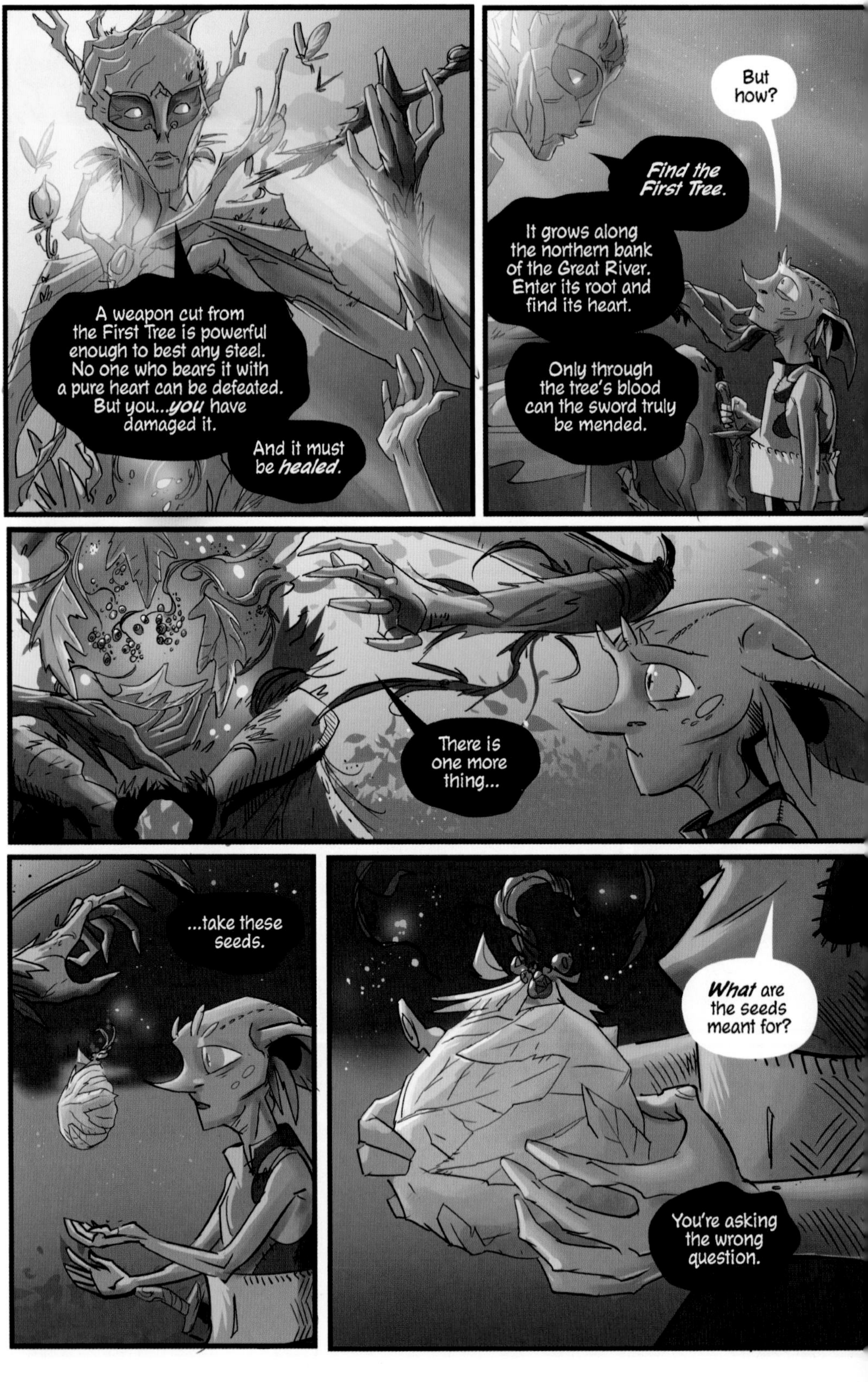
A weapon cut from the First Tree is powerful enough to best any steel. No one who bears it with a pure heart can be defeated. But you...*you* have damaged it.
And it must be *healed*.
But how?
Find the First Tree.
It grows along the northern bank of the Great River. Enter its root and find its heart.
Only through the tree's blood can the sword truly be mended.
There is one more thing...
...take these seeds.
What are the seeds meant for?
You're asking the wrong question.

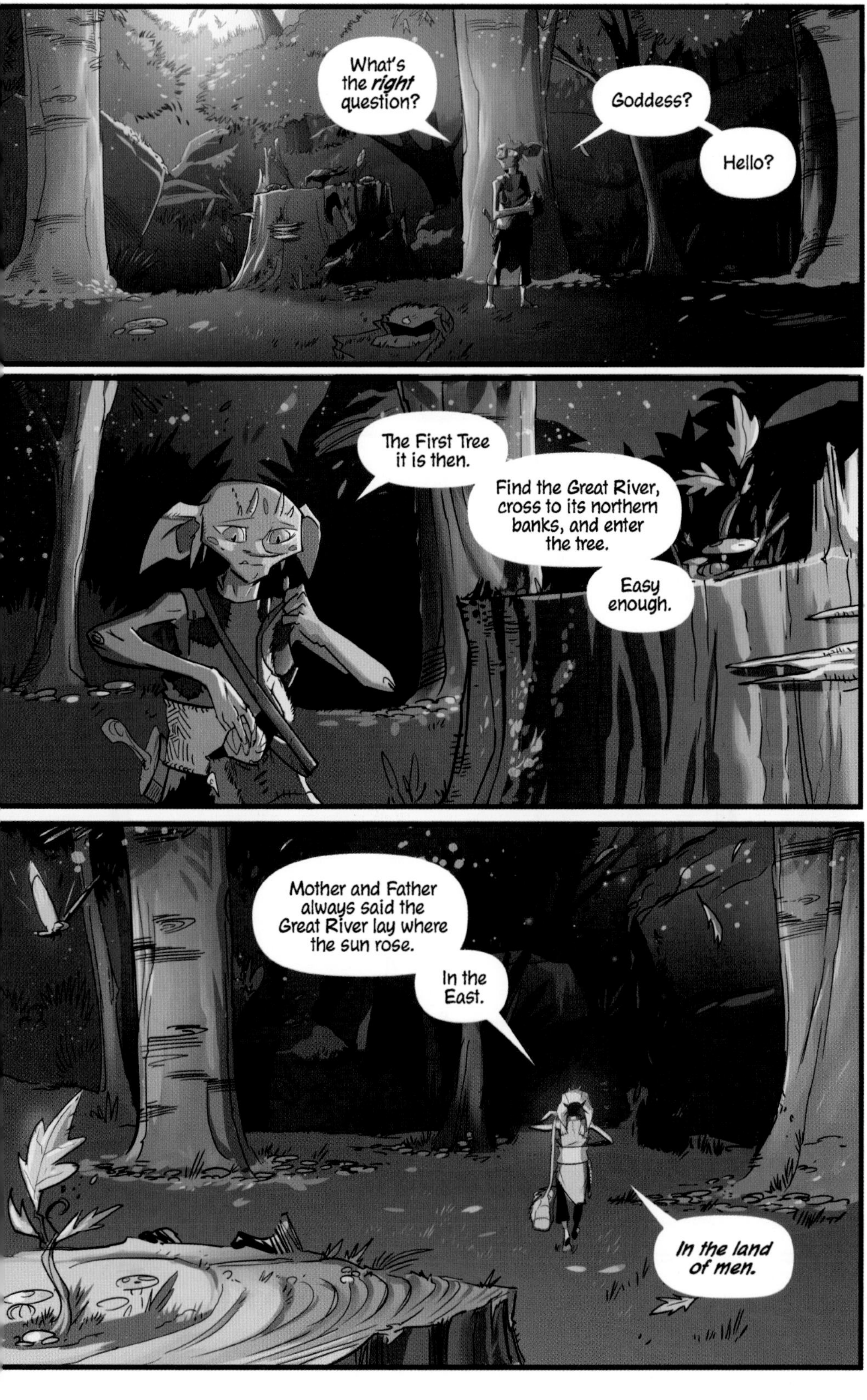

What's the *right* question?
Goddess?
Hello?
The First Tree it is then.
Find the Great River, cross to its northern banks, and enter the tree.
Easy enough.
Mother and Father always said the Great River lay where the sun rose.
In the East.
In the land of men.

CHAPTER THREE
A CHANCE ENCOUNTER

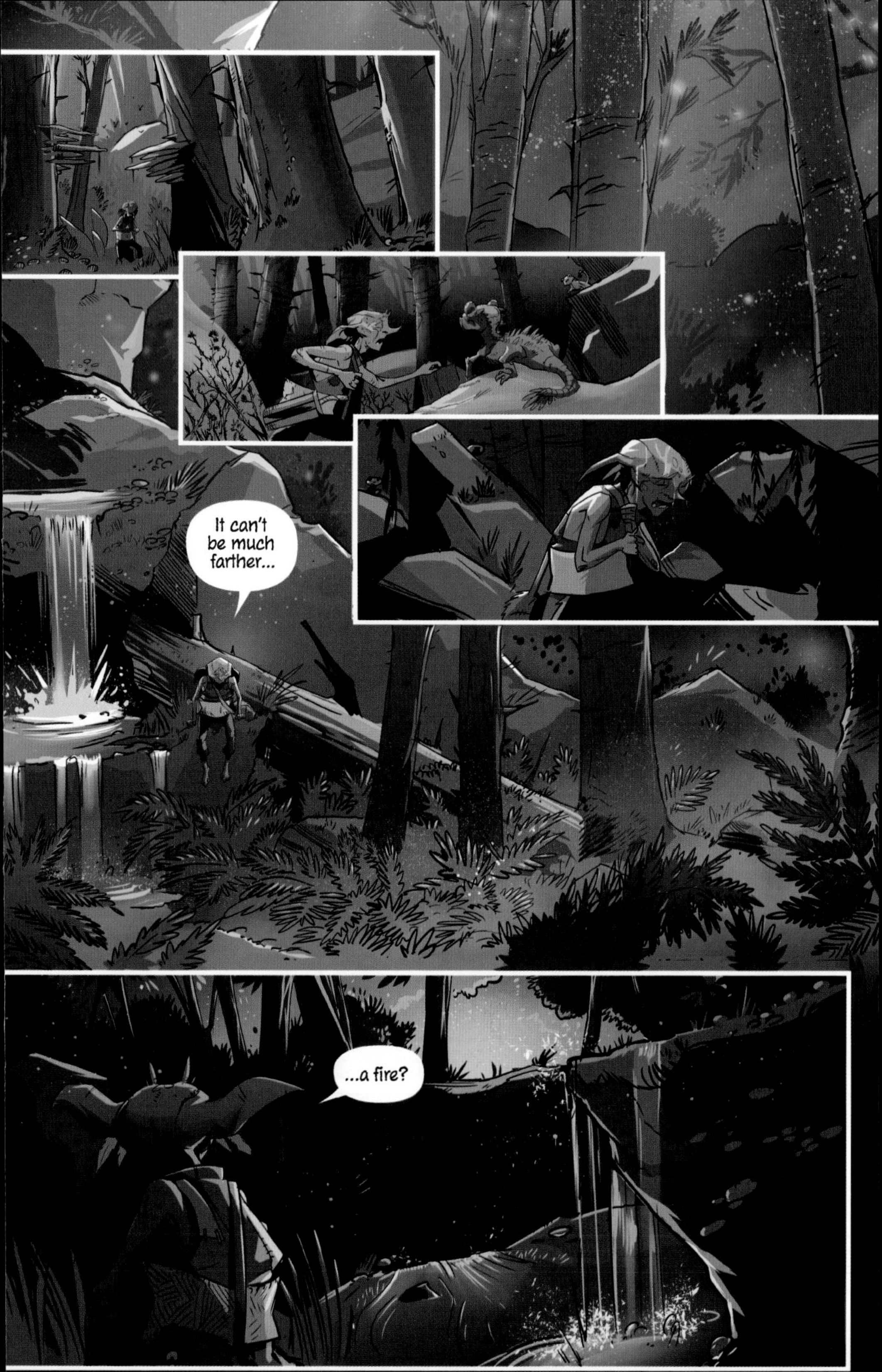
It can't be much farther...
...a fire?

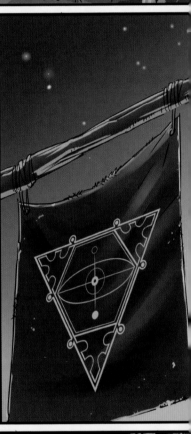

That's from *our* home.

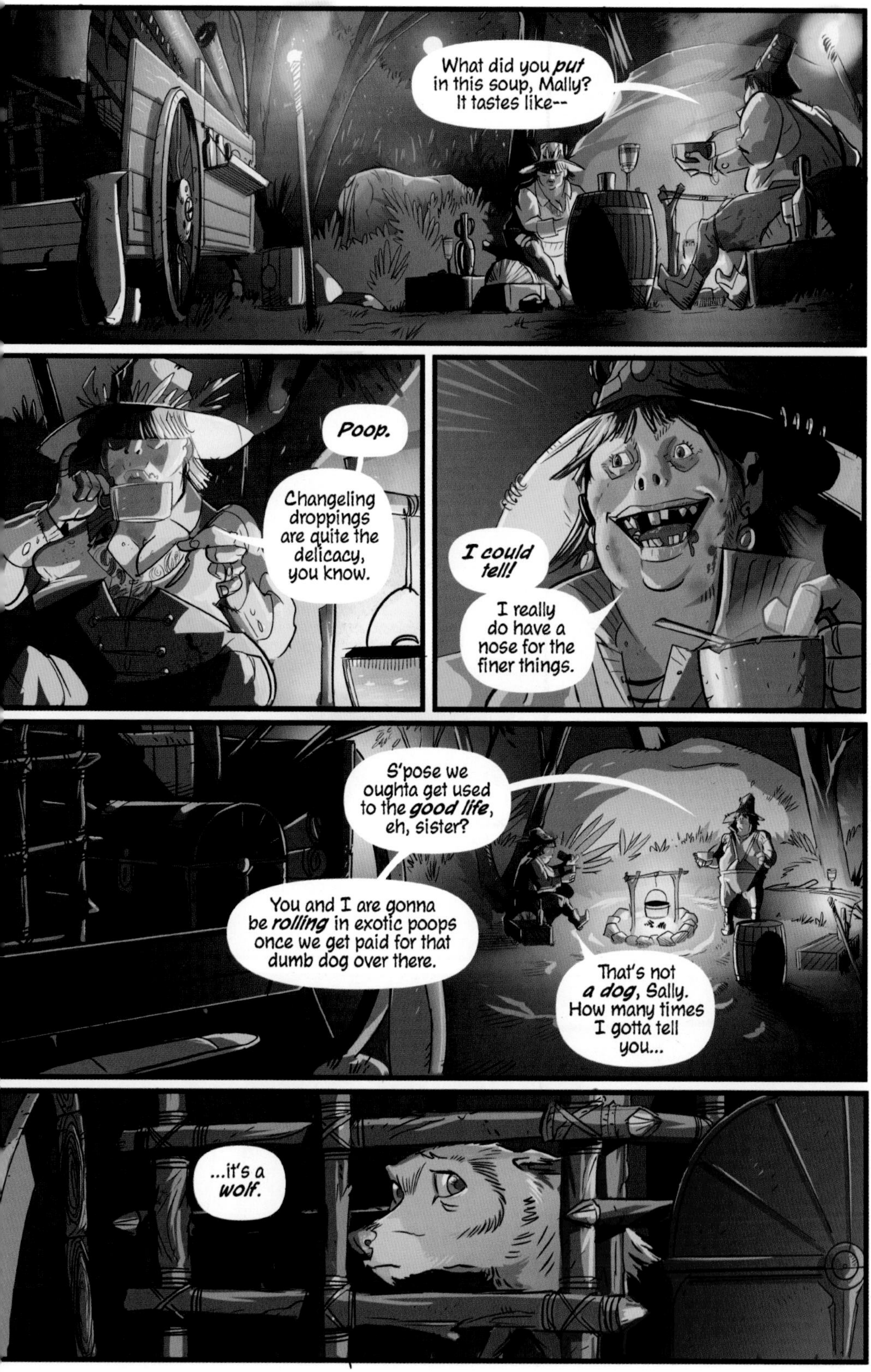
What did you *put* in this soup, Mally? It tastes like--
Poop.
Changeling droppings are quite the delicacy, you know.
I could tell!
I really do have a nose for the finer things.
S'pose we oughta get used to the *good life*, eh, sister?
You and I are gonna be *rolling* in exotic poops once we get paid for that dumb dog over there.
That's not *a dog*, Sally. How many times I gotta tell you...
...it's a *wolf*.

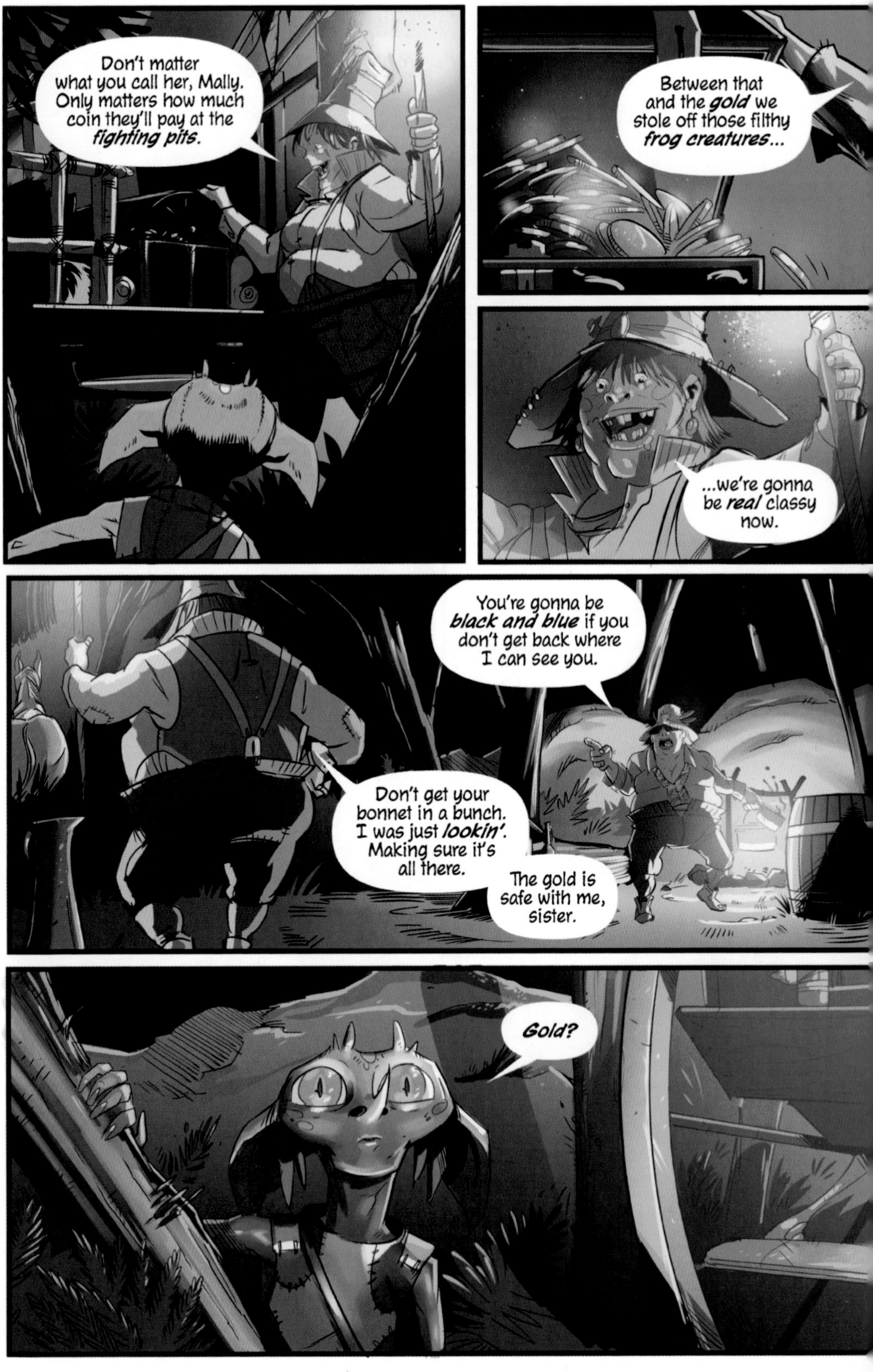
Don't matter what you call her, Mally. Only matters how much coin they'll pay at the *fighting pits*.
Between that and the *gold* we stole off those filthy *frog creatures*...
...we're gonna be *real* classy now.
You're gonna be *black and blue* if you don't get back where I can see you.
Don't get your bonnet in a bunch. I was just *lookin'*. Making sure it's all there.
The gold is safe with me, sister.
Gold?

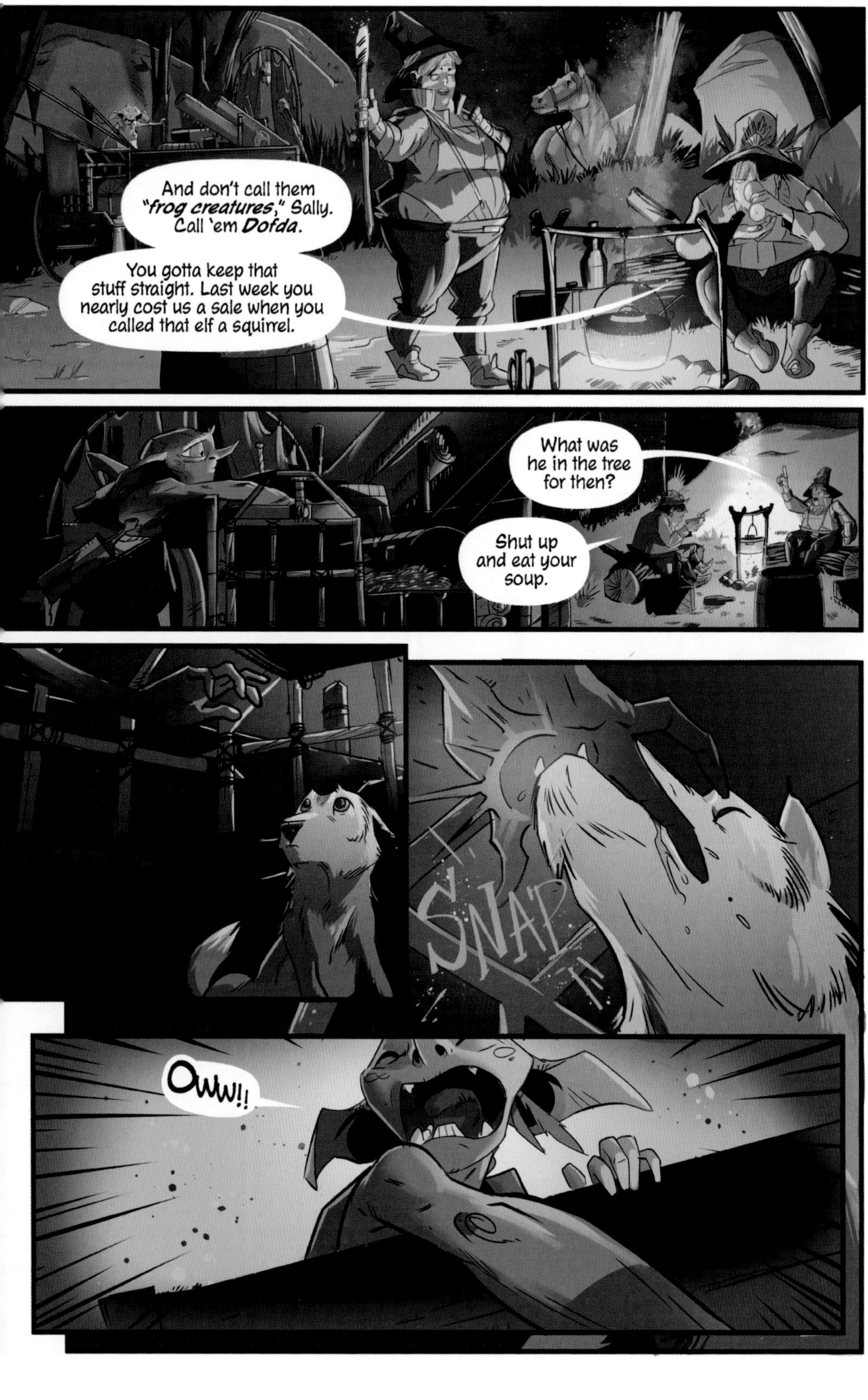
And don't call them "*frog creatures*," Sally. Call 'em ***Dofda***.
You gotta keep that stuff straight. Last week you nearly cost us a sale when you called that elf a squirrel.
What was he in the tree for then?
Shut up and eat your soup.
SNAP
OWW!!

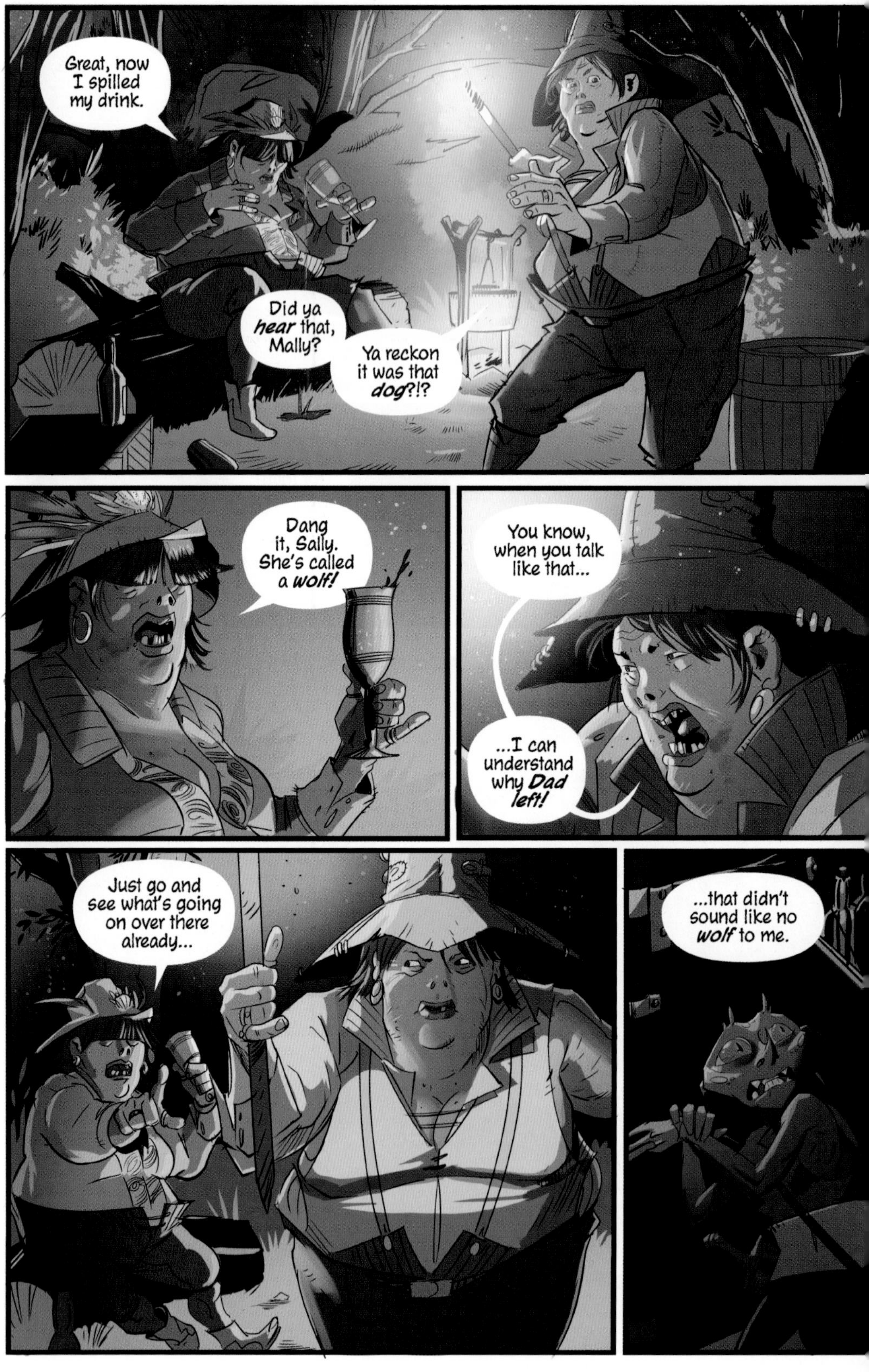
Great, now I spilled my drink.
Did ya *hear* that, Mally?
Ya reckon it was that *dog*?!?
Dang it, Sally. She's called a *wolf!*
You know, when you talk like that...
...I can understand why *Dad left!*
Just go and see what's going on over there already...
...that didn't sound like no *wolf* to me.

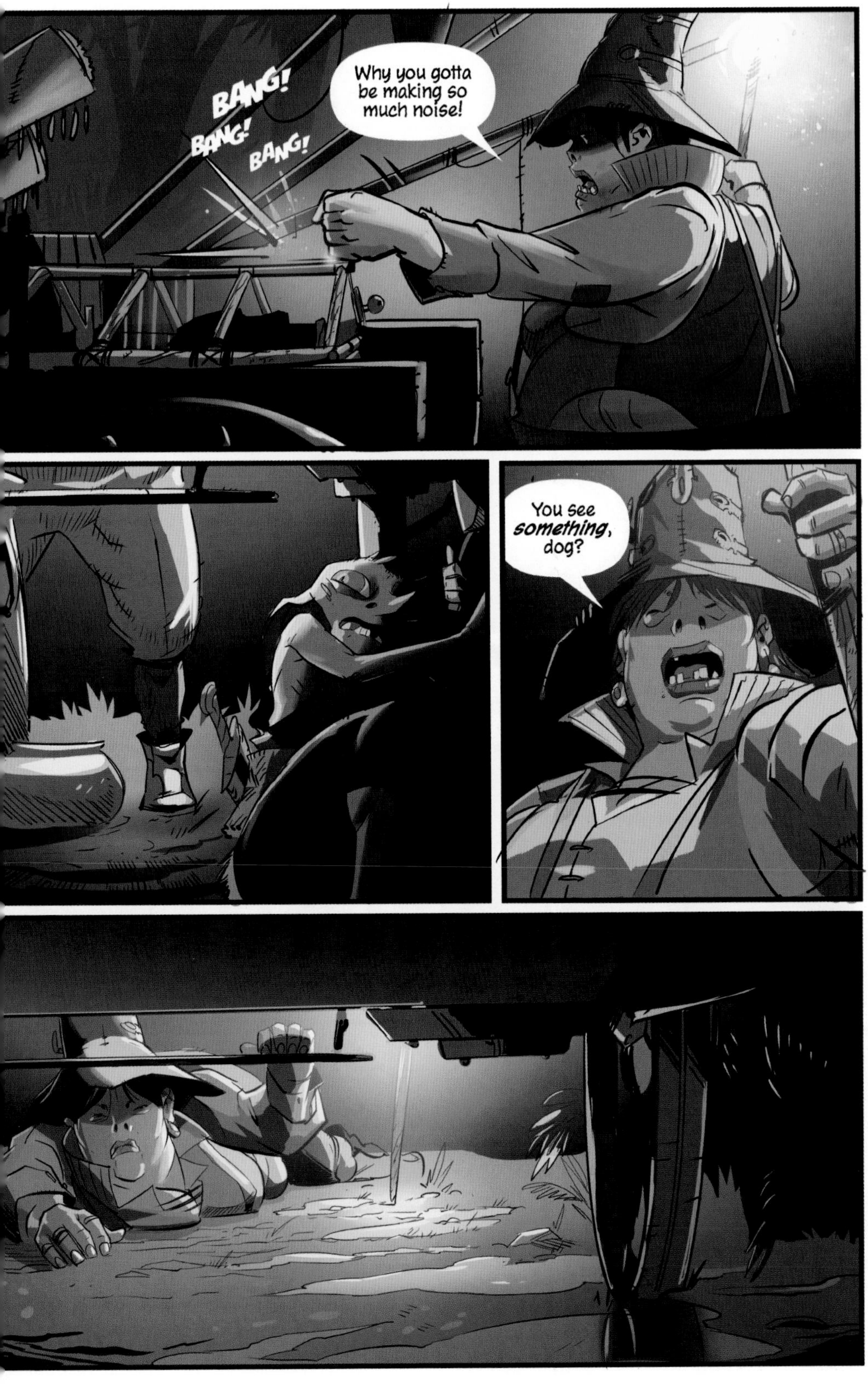
BANG!
BANG!
BANG!
Why you gotta be making so much noise!
You see *something*, dog?

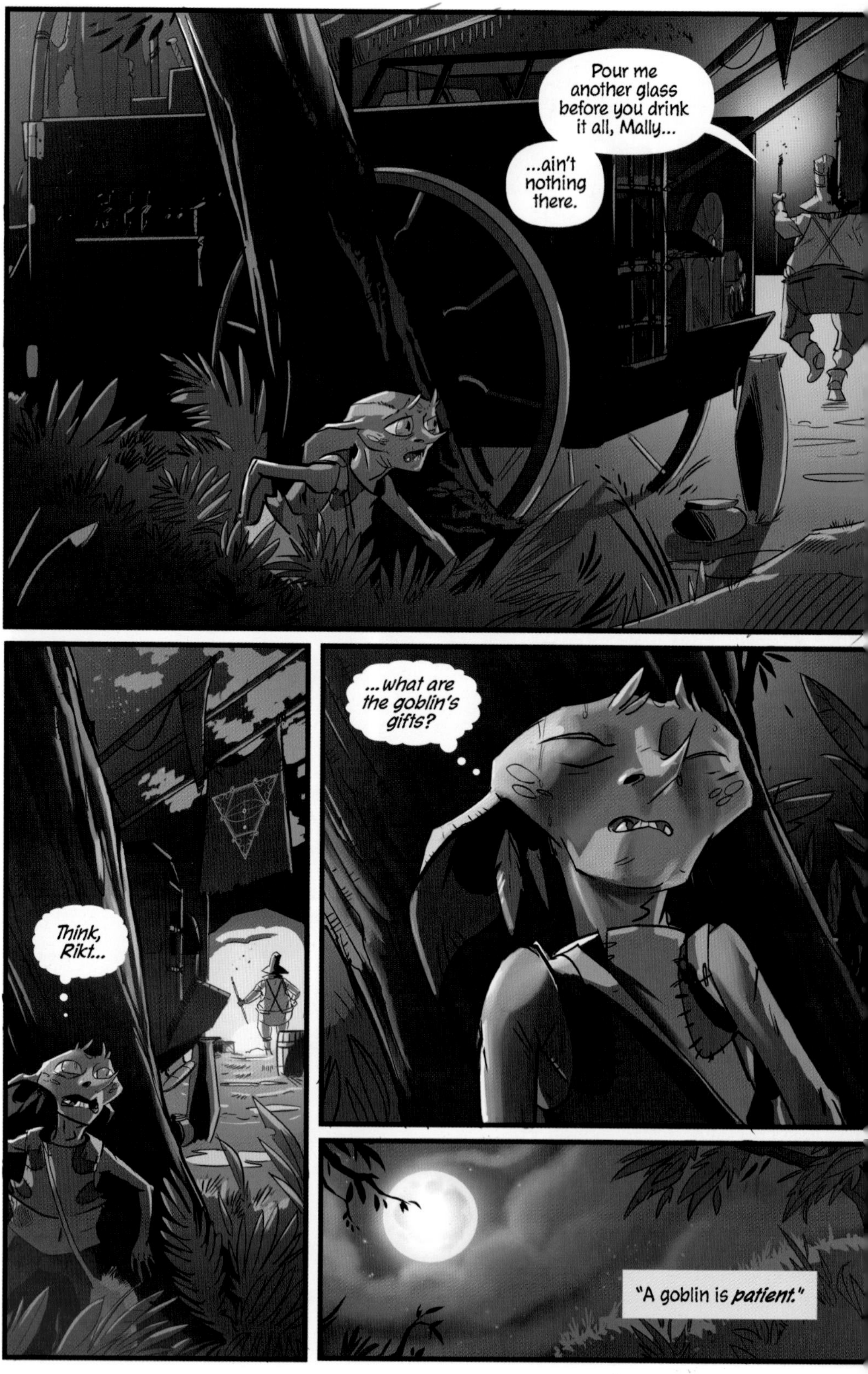
Pour me another glass before you drink it all, Mally...
...ain't nothing there.
Think, Rikt...
...what are the goblin's gifts?
"A goblin is *patient.*"

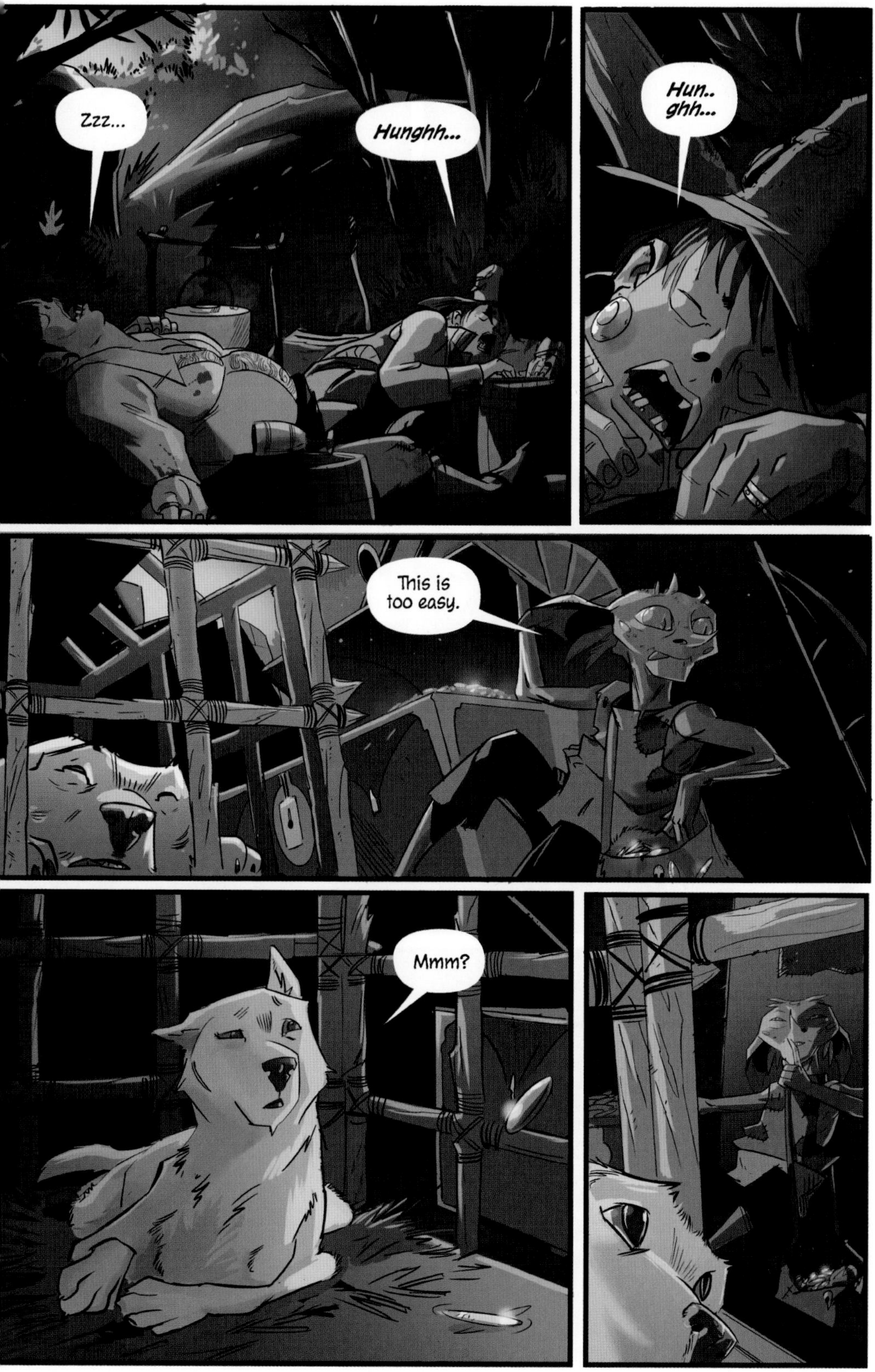
Zzz...
Hunghh...
Hun.. ghh...
This is too easy.
Mmm?

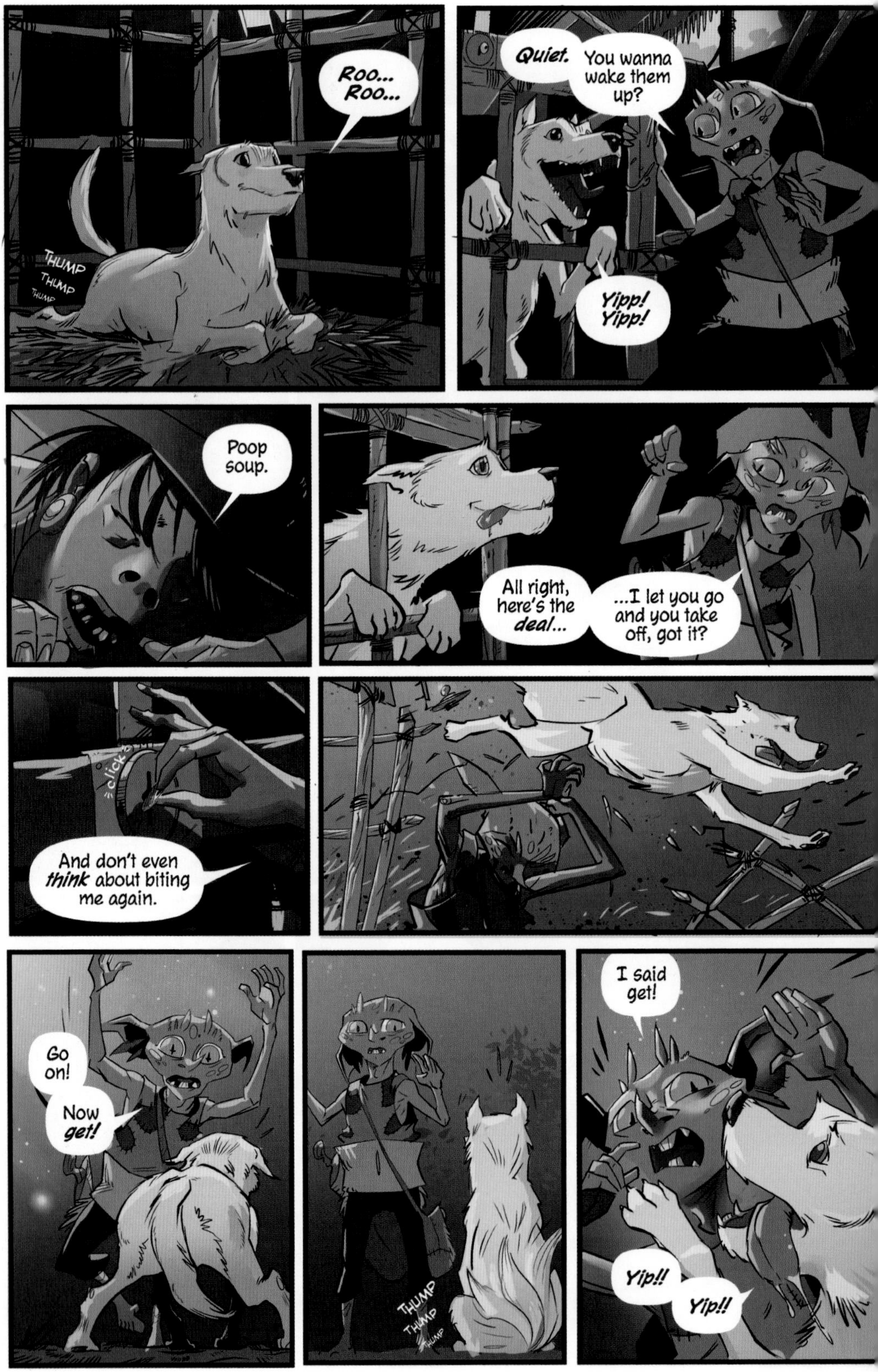
Roo... Roo...
THUMP
THUMP
THUMP
Quiet.
You wanna wake them up?
Yipp! Yipp!
Poop soup.
All right, here's the deal...
...I let you go and you take off, got it?
click
And don't even think about biting me again.
Go on!
Now get!
THUMP
THUMP
THUMP
I said get!
Yip!!
Yip!!

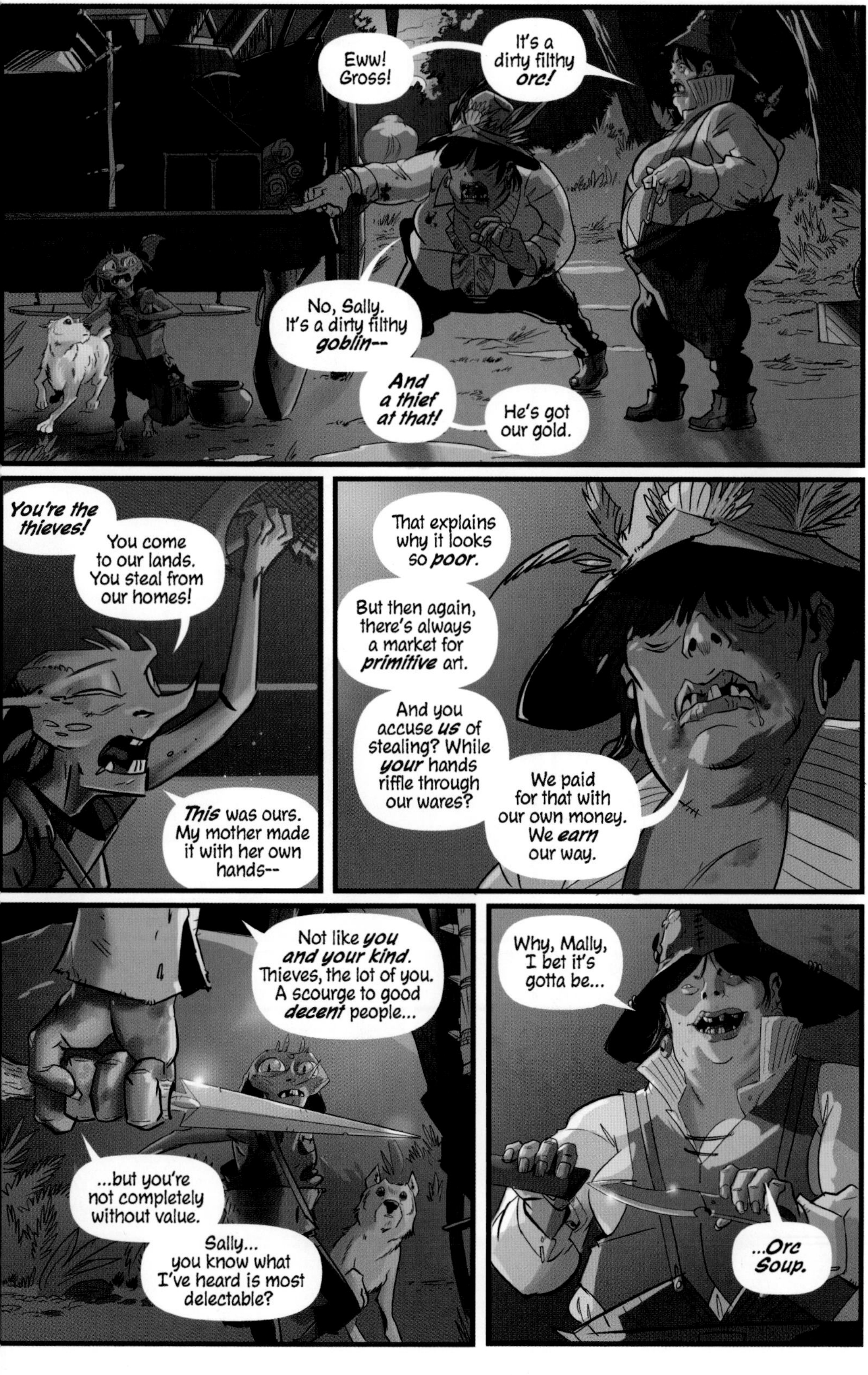
It's a dirty filthy *orc!*
Eww! Gross!
No, Sally. It's a dirty filthy *goblin--*
And a thief at that!
He's got our gold.
You're the thieves!
You come to our lands. You steal from our homes!
This was ours. My mother made it with her own hands--
That explains why it looks so *poor*.
But then again, there's always a market for *primitive* art.
And you accuse *us* of stealing? While *your* hands riffle through our wares?
We paid for that with our own money. We *earn* our way.
Not like *you and your kind*. Thieves, the lot of you. A scourge to good *decent* people...
...but you're not completely without value.
Sally... you know what I've heard is most delectable?
Why, Mally, I bet it's gotta be...
...Orc Soup.

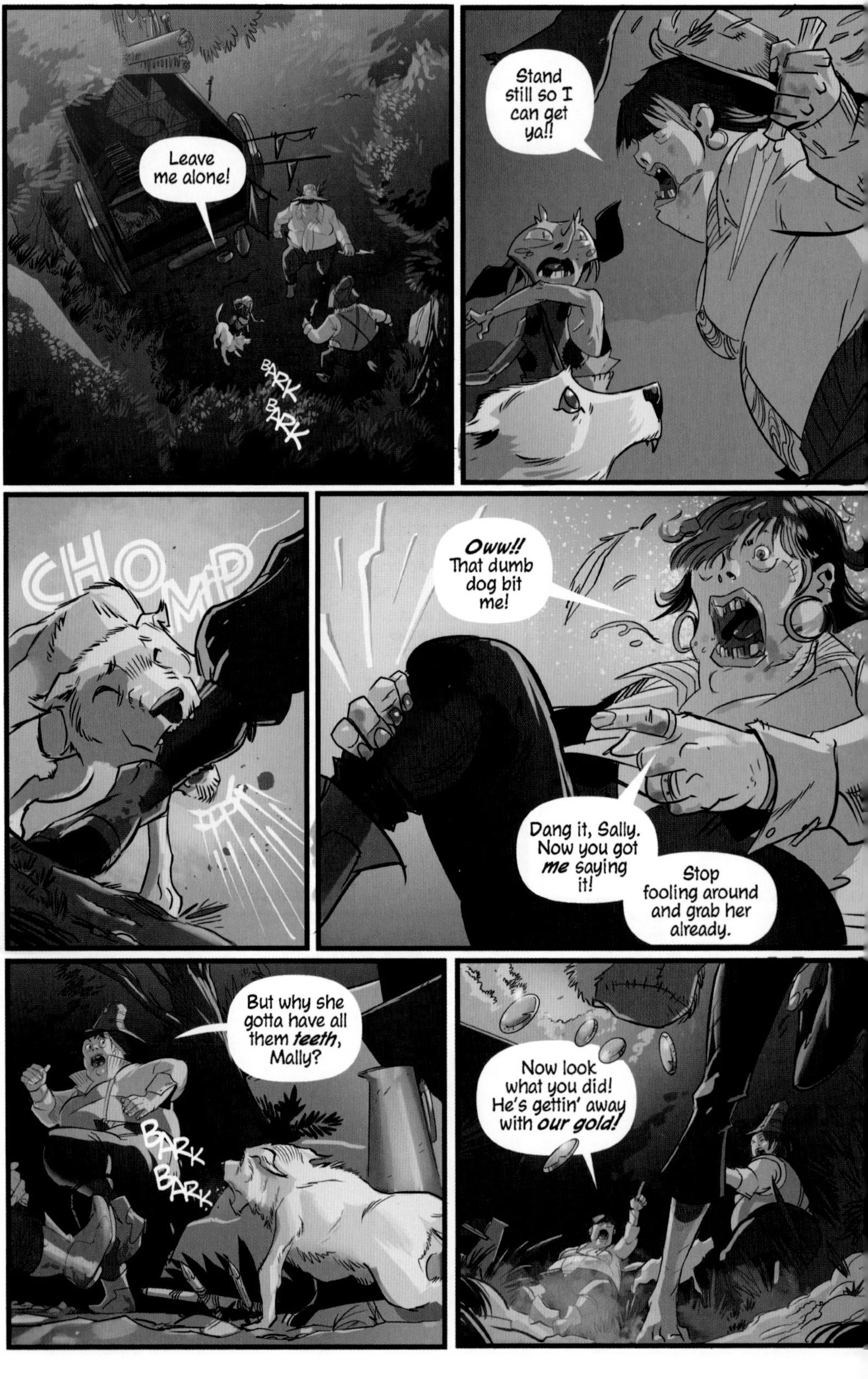
Leave me alone!
BARK
BARK
Stand still so I can get ya!!
CHOMP
Oww!! That dumb dog bit me!
Dang it, Sally. Now you got *me* saying it!
Stop fooling around and grab her already.
But why she gotta have all them *teeth*, Mally?
BARK
BARK
Now look what you did! He's gettin' away with *our gold!*

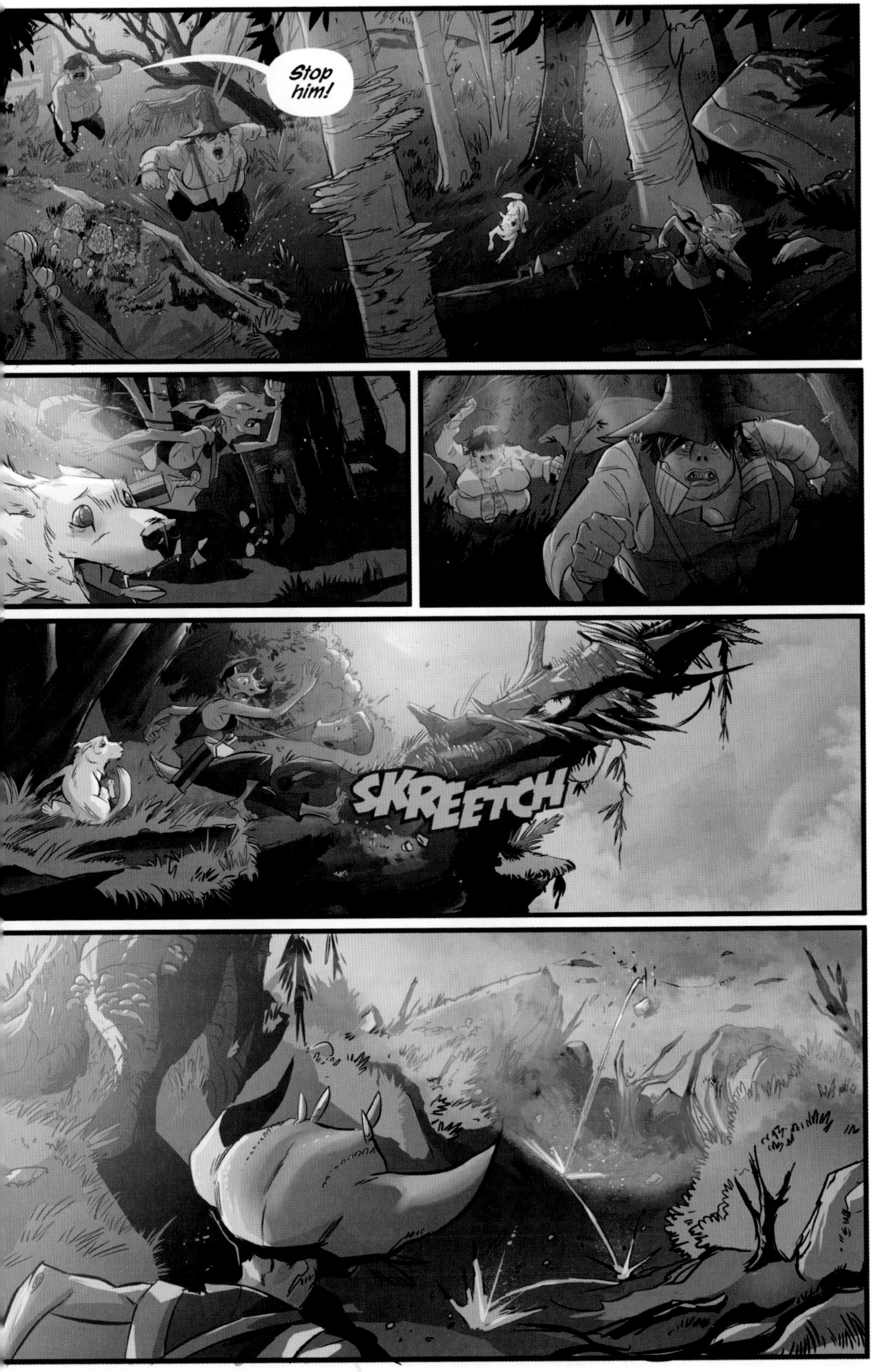
Stop him!
SKREETCH

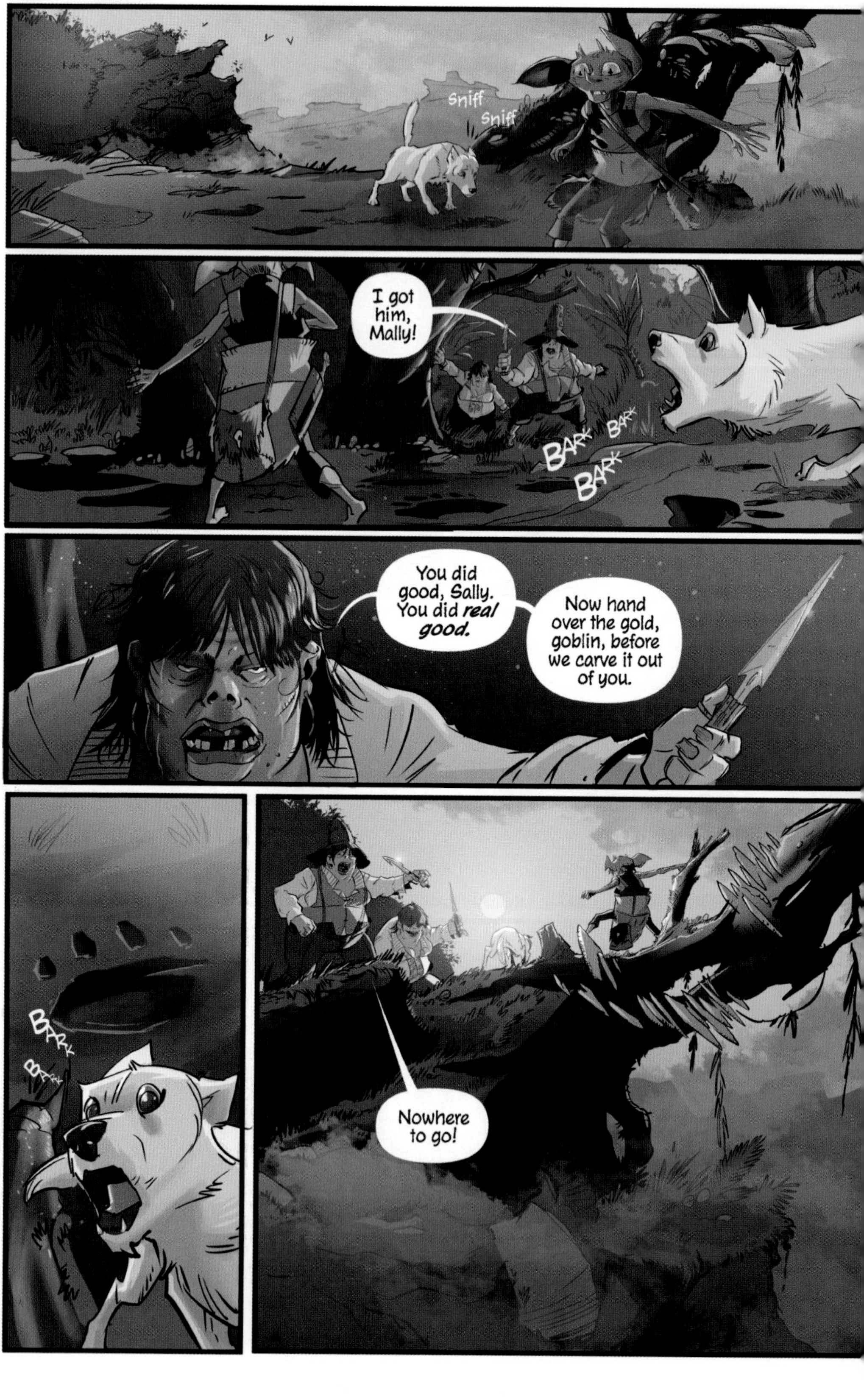
Sniff
Sniff
I got him, Mally!
BARK
BARK
BARK
You did good, Sally. You did *real good.*
Now hand over the gold, goblin, before we carve it out of you.
BARK
BARK
Nowhere to go!

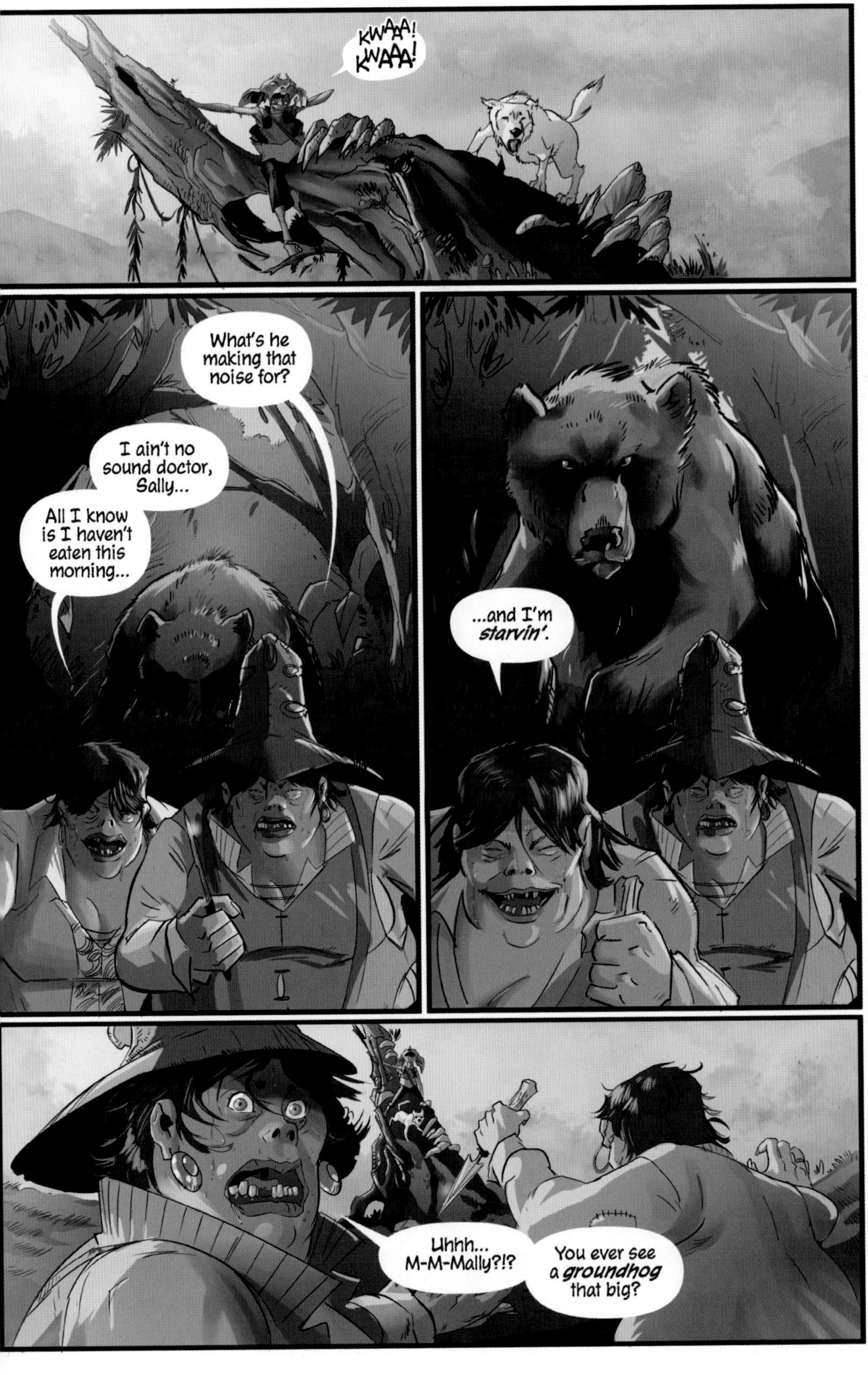
KWAAA! KWAAA!
What's he making that noise for?
I ain't no sound doctor, Sally...
All I know is I haven't eaten this morning...
...and I'm *starvin'.*
Uhhh... M-M-Mally?!?
You ever see a **groundhog** that big?

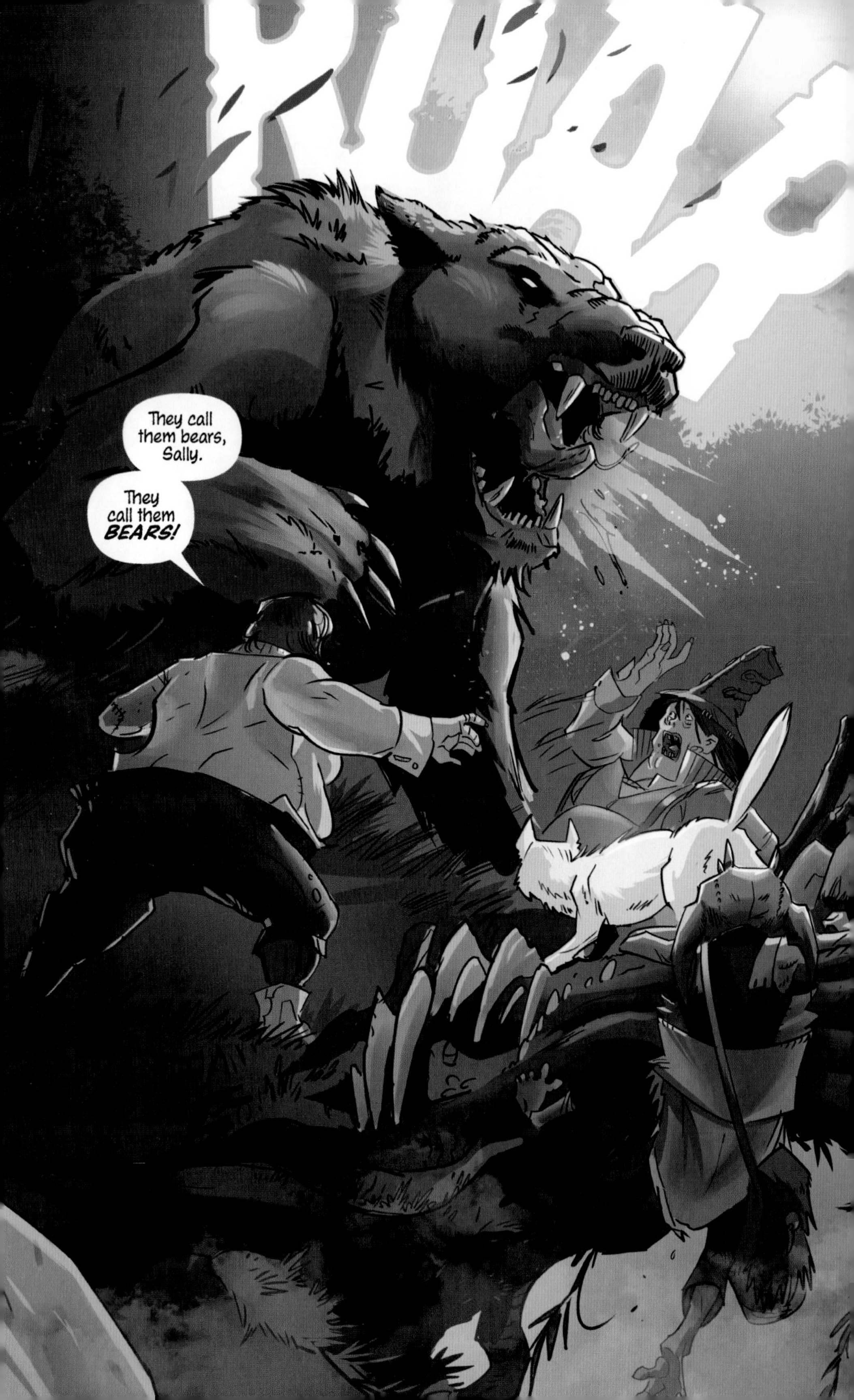
They call them bears, Sally.
They call them **BEARS!**

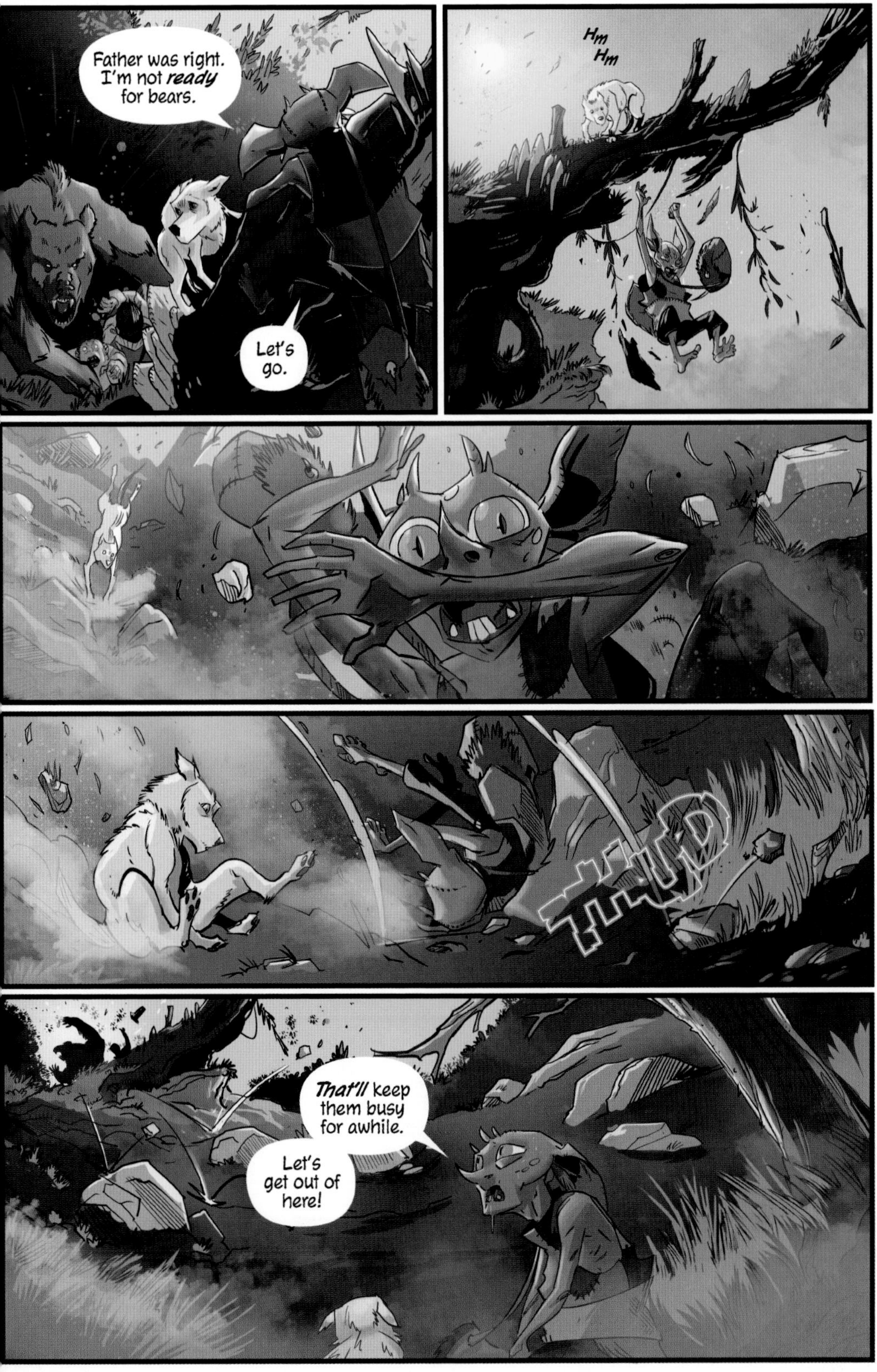
Father was right. I'm not *ready* for bears.
Let's go.
Hm Hm
THUD
That'll keep them busy for awhile.
Let's get out of here!

Chapter Four
The Sound of Water

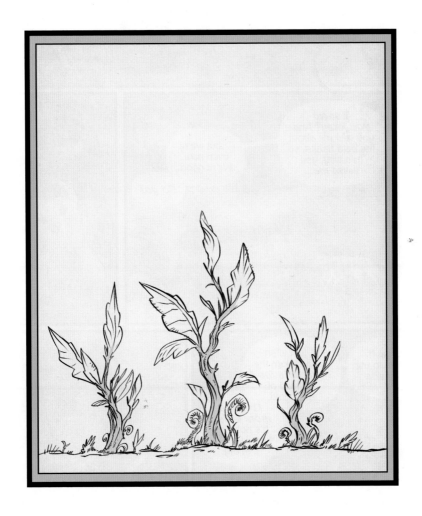

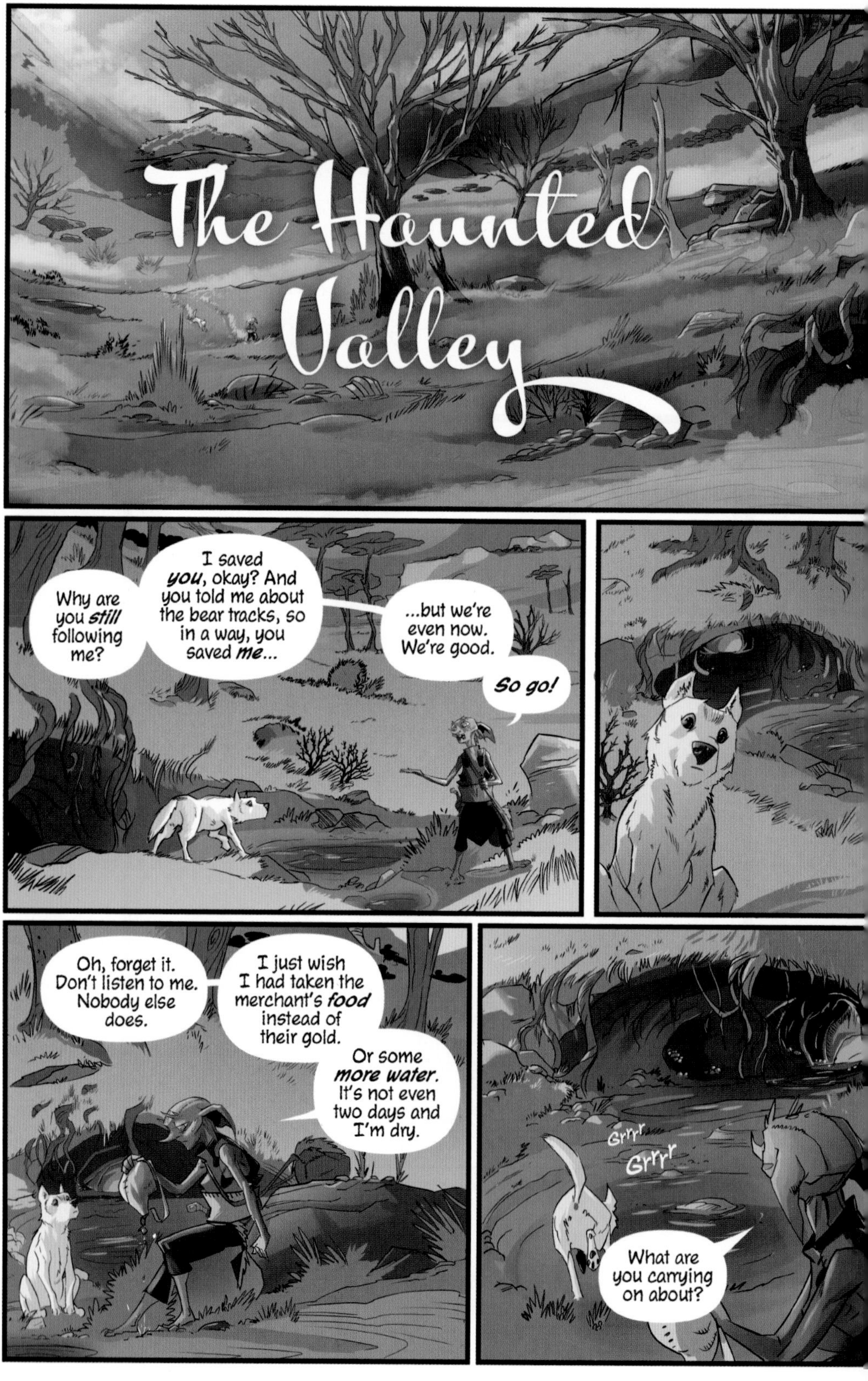
The Haunted Valley
Why are you *still* following me?
I saved *you*, okay? And you told me about the bear tracks, so in a way, you saved *me*...
...but we're even now. We're good.
So go!
Oh, forget it. Don't listen to me. Nobody else does.
I just wish I had taken the merchant's *food* instead of their gold.
Or some *more water*. It's not even two days and I'm dry.
Grrr
Grrr
What are you carrying on about?

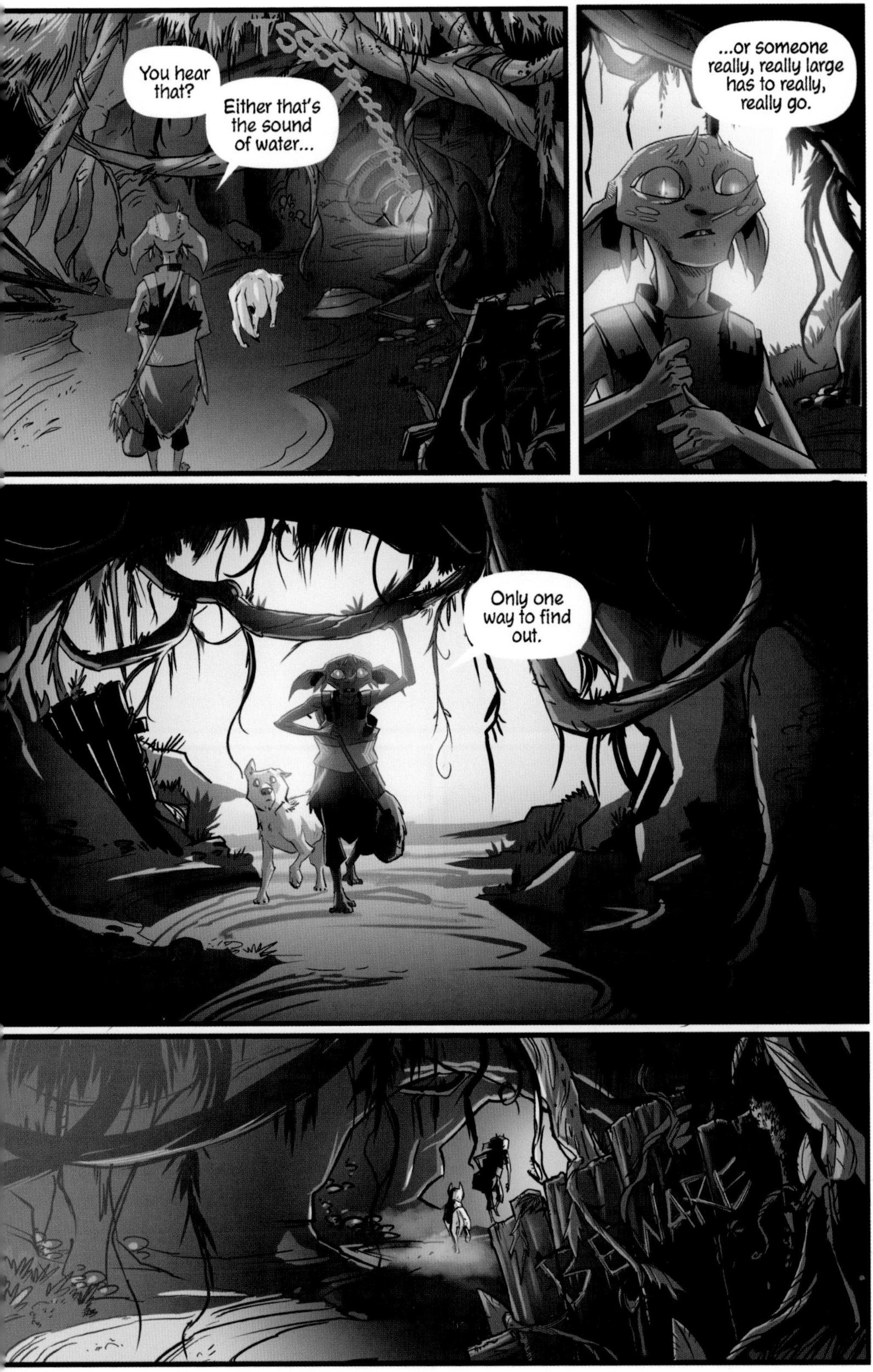
You hear that?
Either that's the sound of water...
...or someone really, really large has to really, really go.
Only one way to find out.

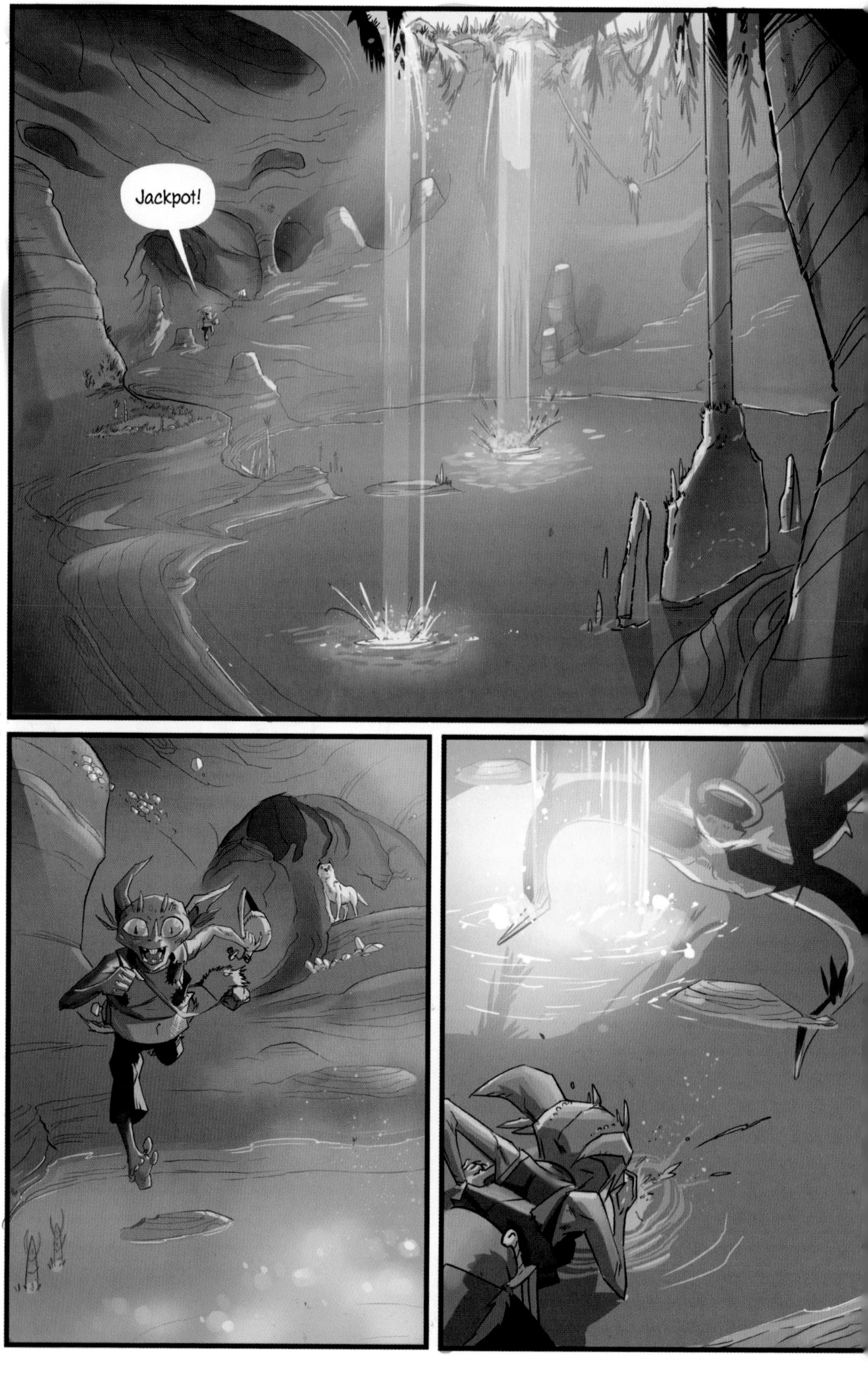
Jackpot!

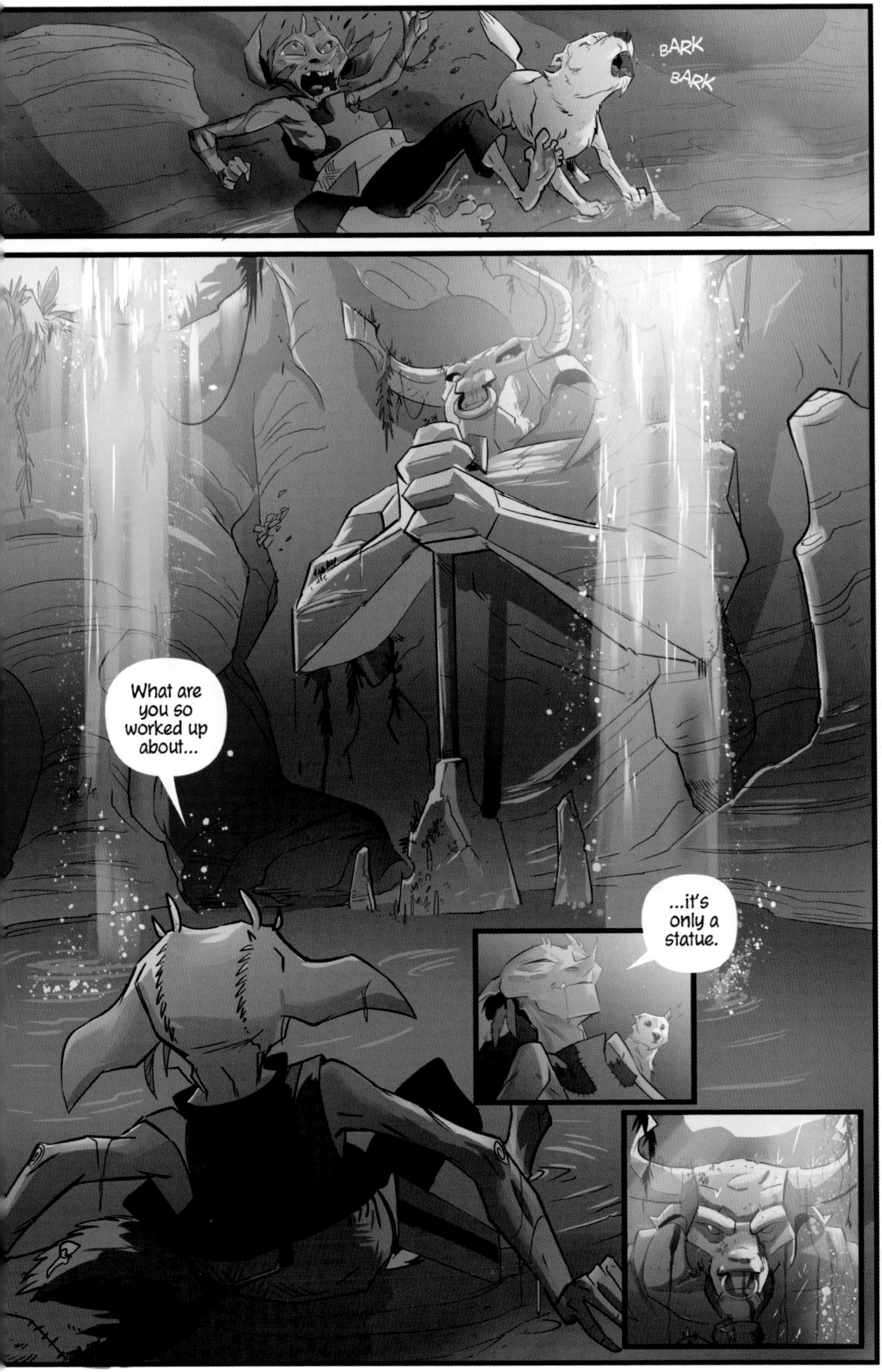
BARK
BARK
What are you so worked up about...
...it's only a statue.

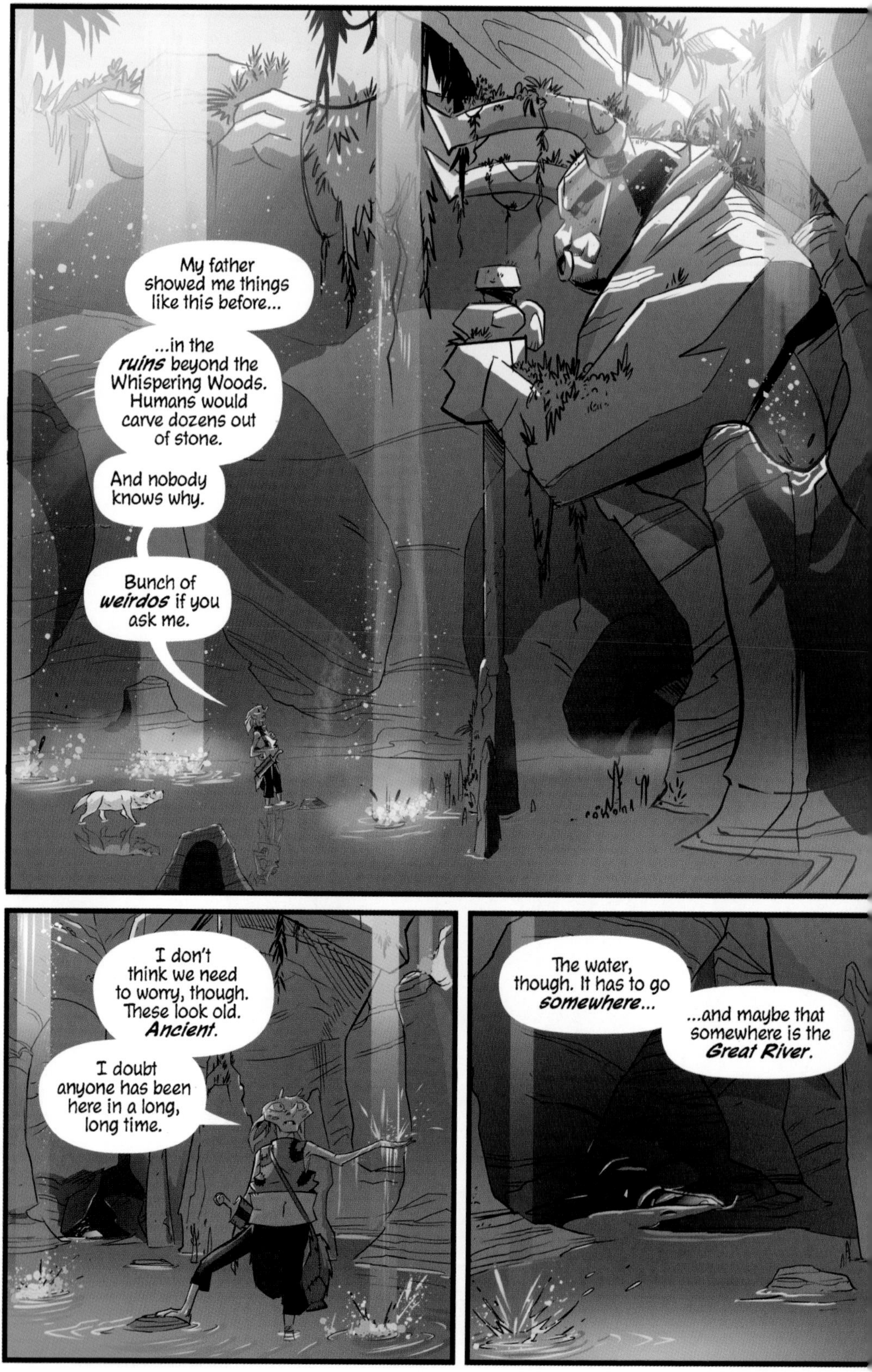
My father showed me things like this before...
...in the *ruins* beyond the Whispering Woods. Humans would carve dozens out of stone.
And nobody knows why.
Bunch of *weirdos* if you ask me.
I don't think we need to worry, though. These look old. *Ancient*.
I doubt anyone has been here in a long, long time.
The water, though. It has to go *somewhere*...
...and maybe that somewhere is the *Great River*.

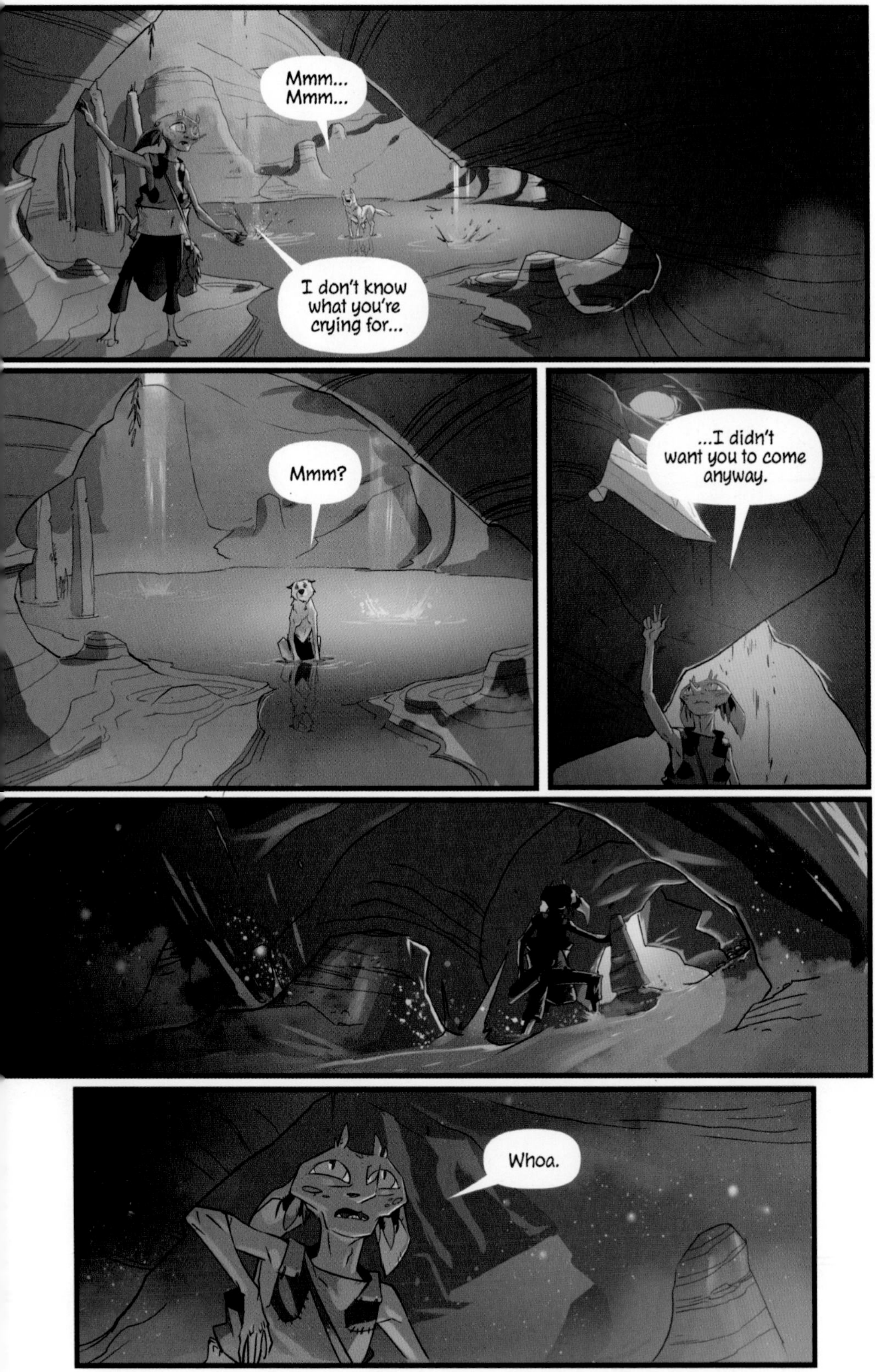
Mmm...
Mmm...
I don't know what you're crying for...
Mmm?
...I didn't want you to come anyway.
Whoa.

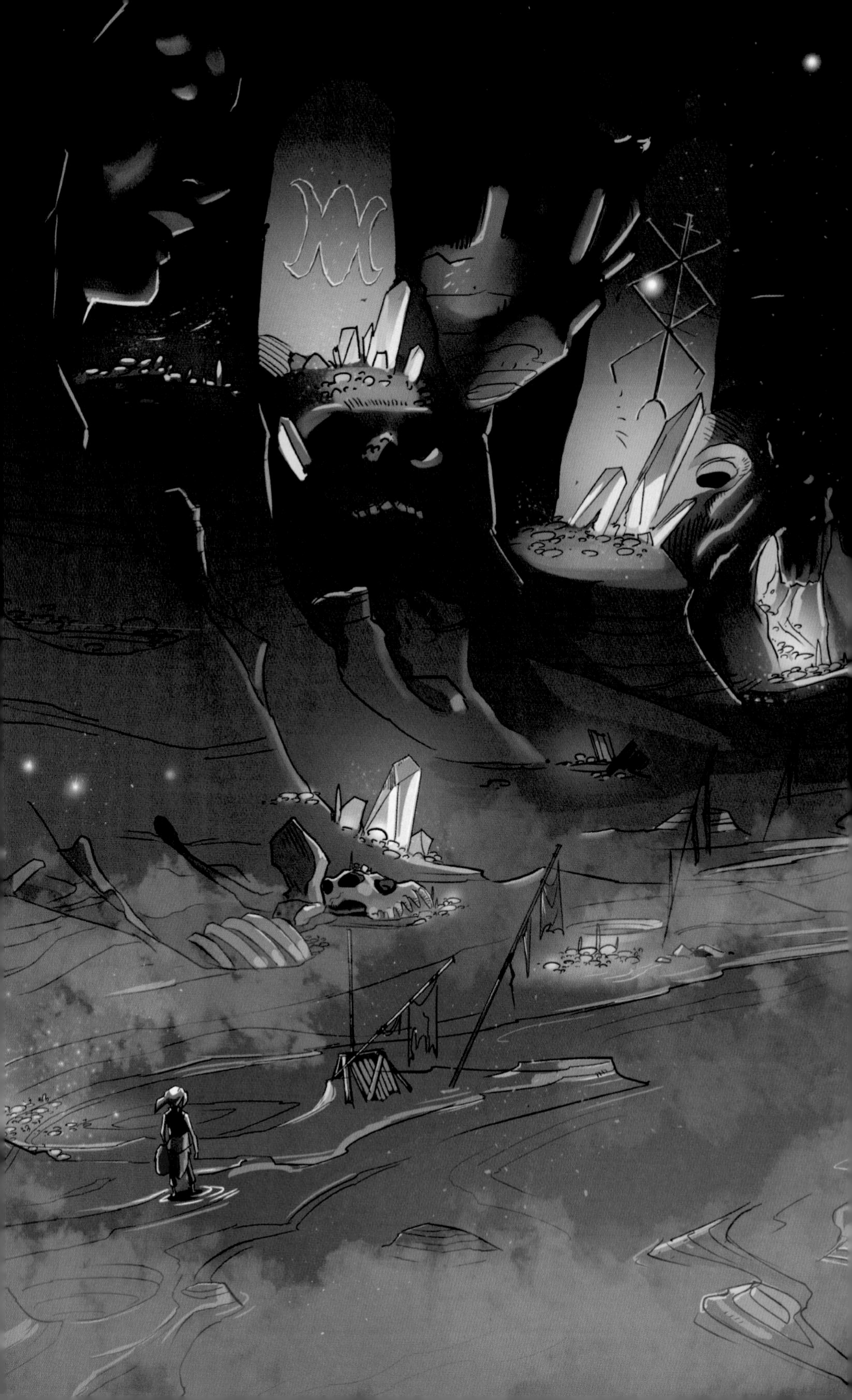

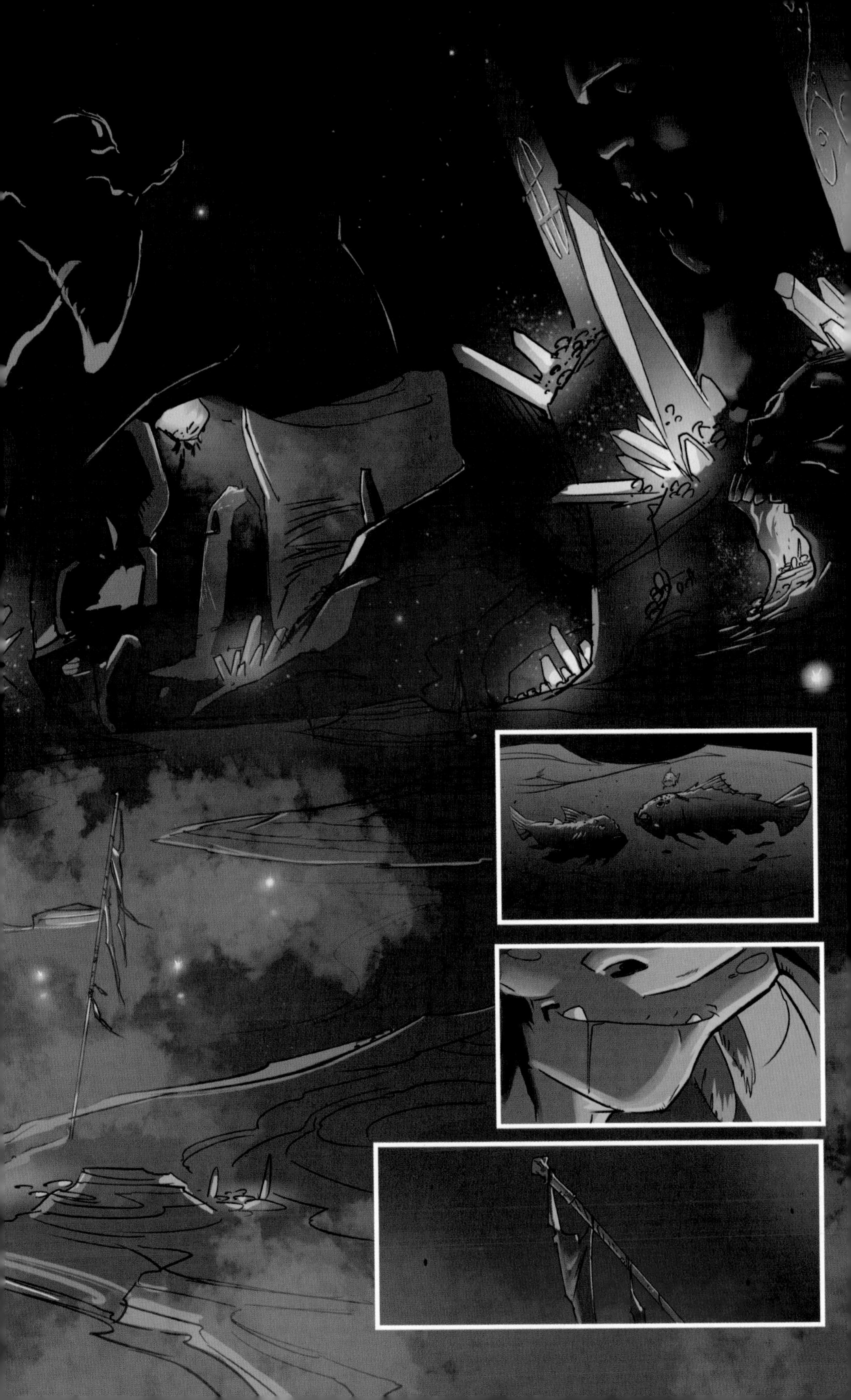

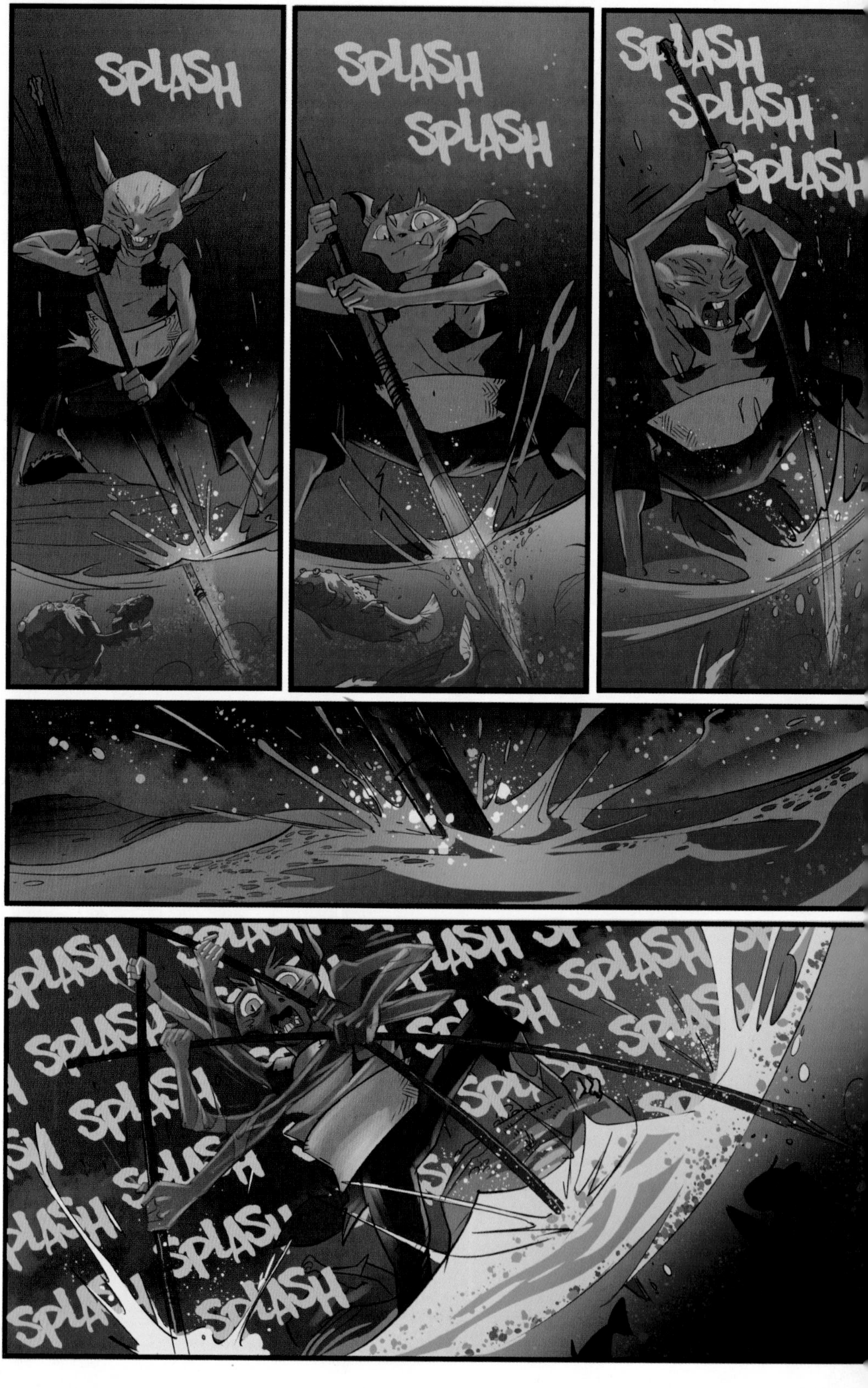
SPLASH
SPLASH
SPLASH
SPLASH
SPLASH
SPLASH
SPLASH
SPLASH
SPLASH
SPLASH

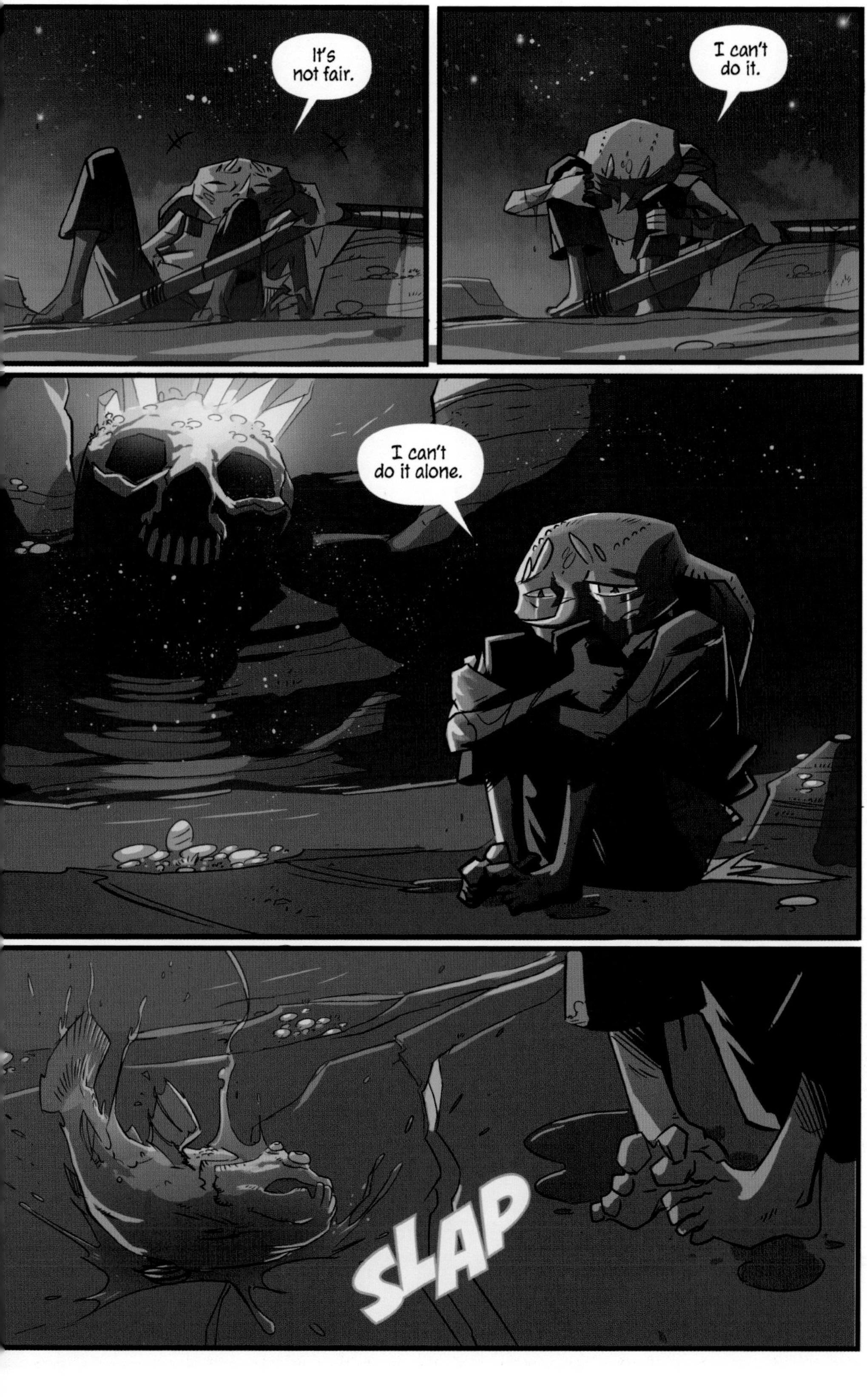
It's not fair.
I can't do it.
I can't do it alone.
SLAP

THUMP
THUMP
THUMP

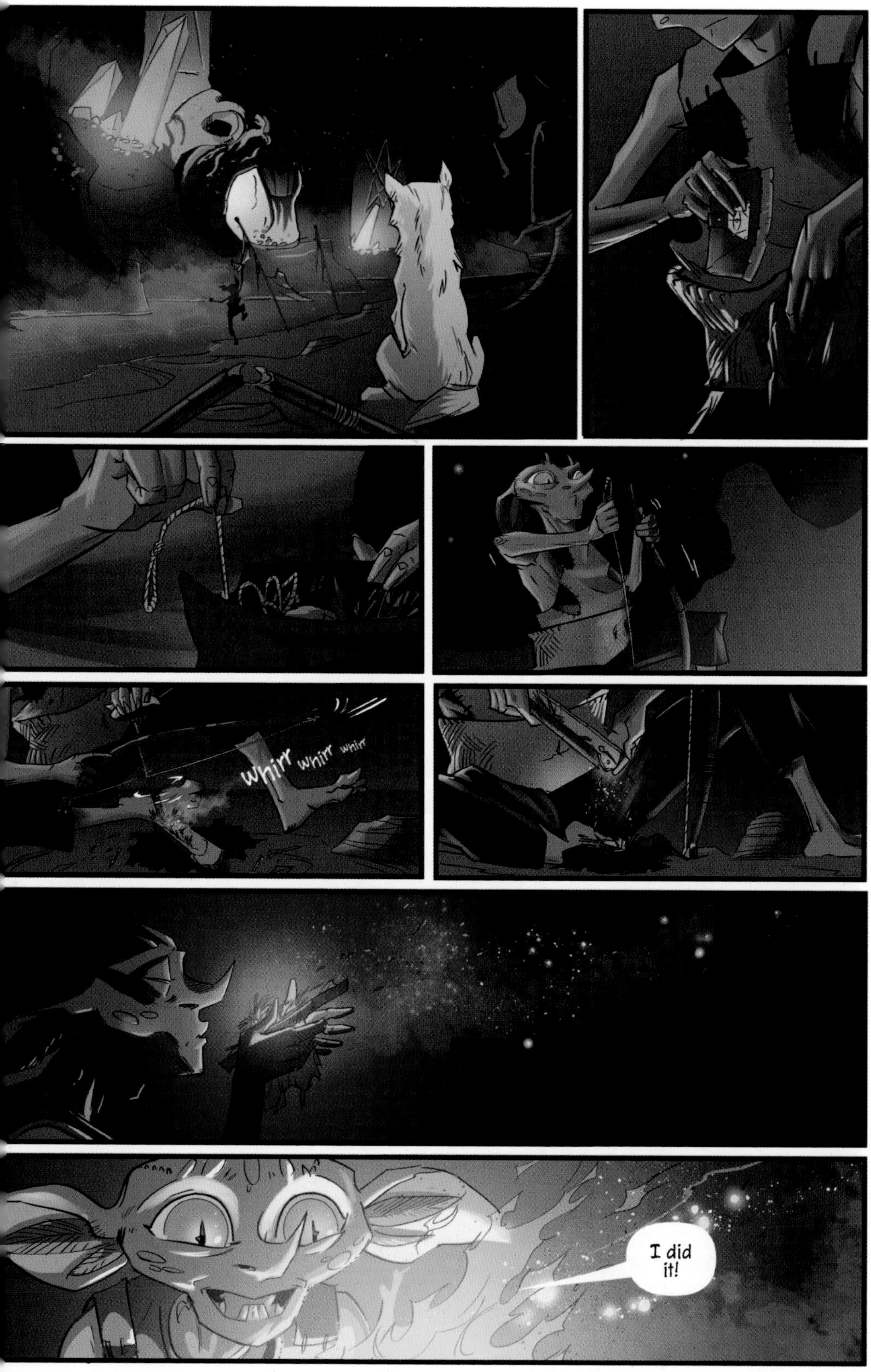
whirr whirr whirr
I did it!

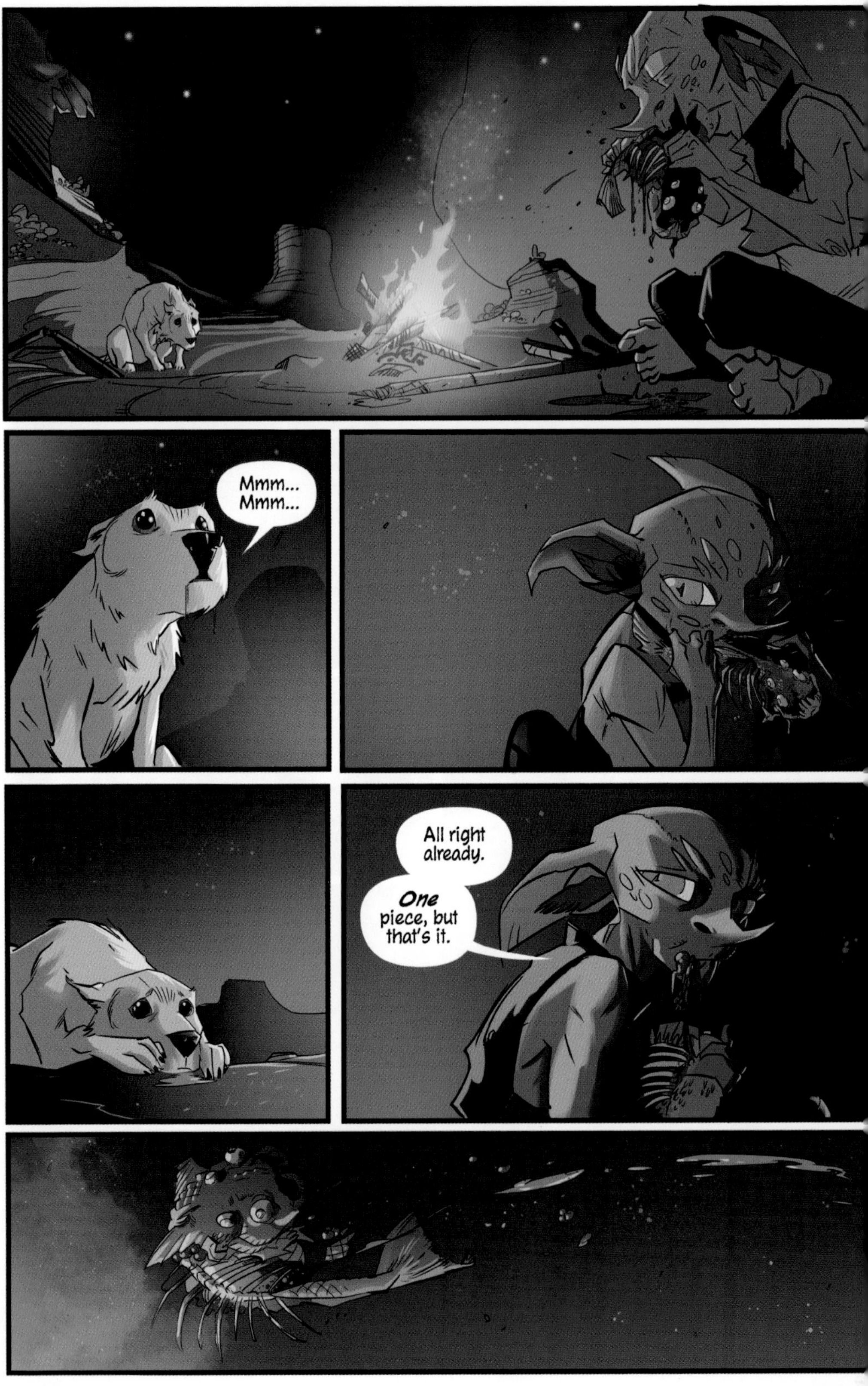
Mmm...
Mmm...
All right already.
One piece, but that's it.

And don't get any ideas that we're sticking together.

You're on your own in the morning.

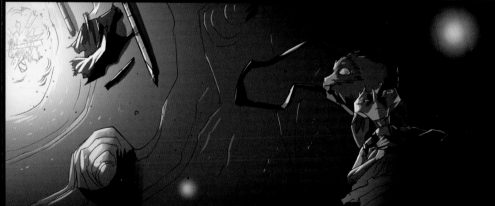

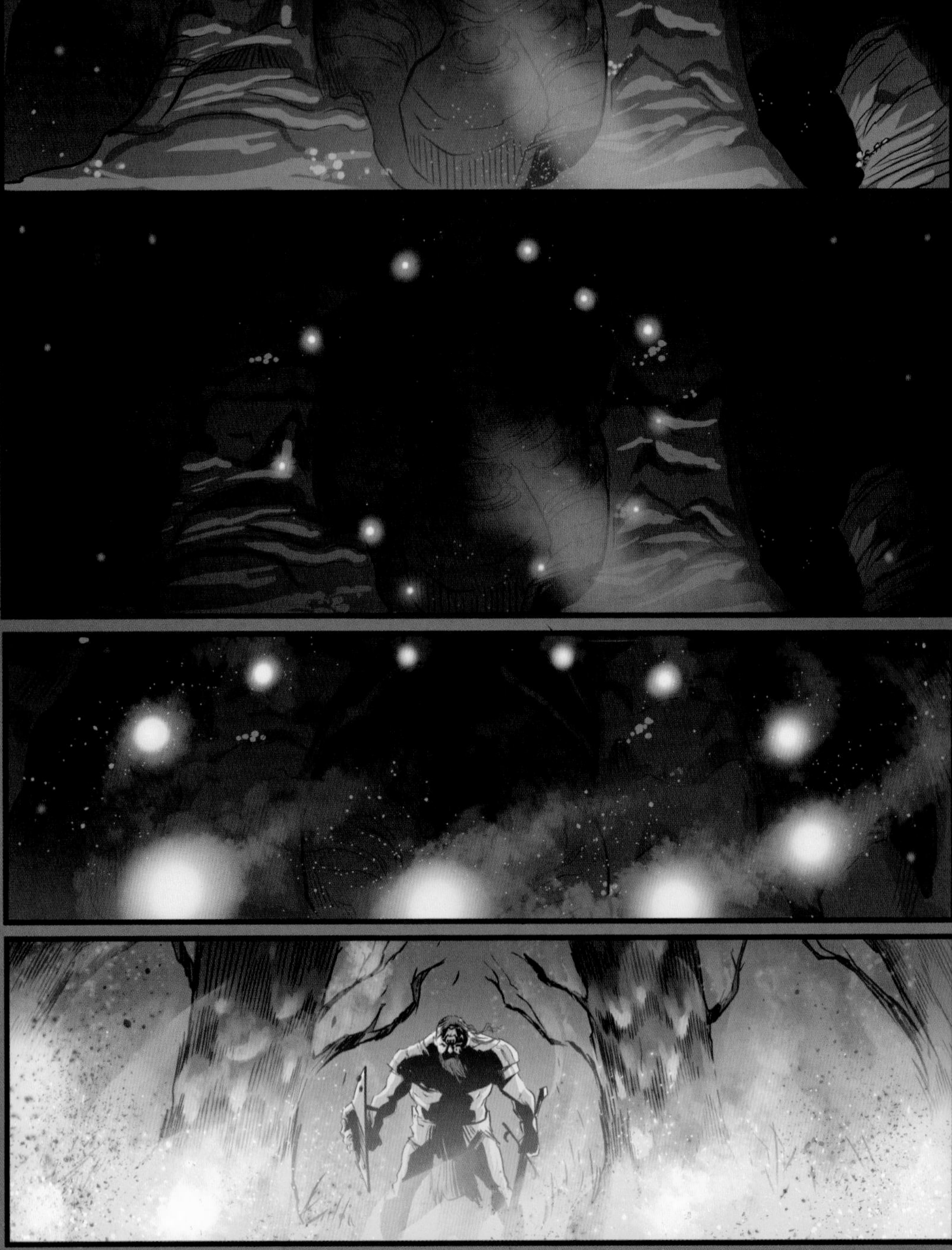

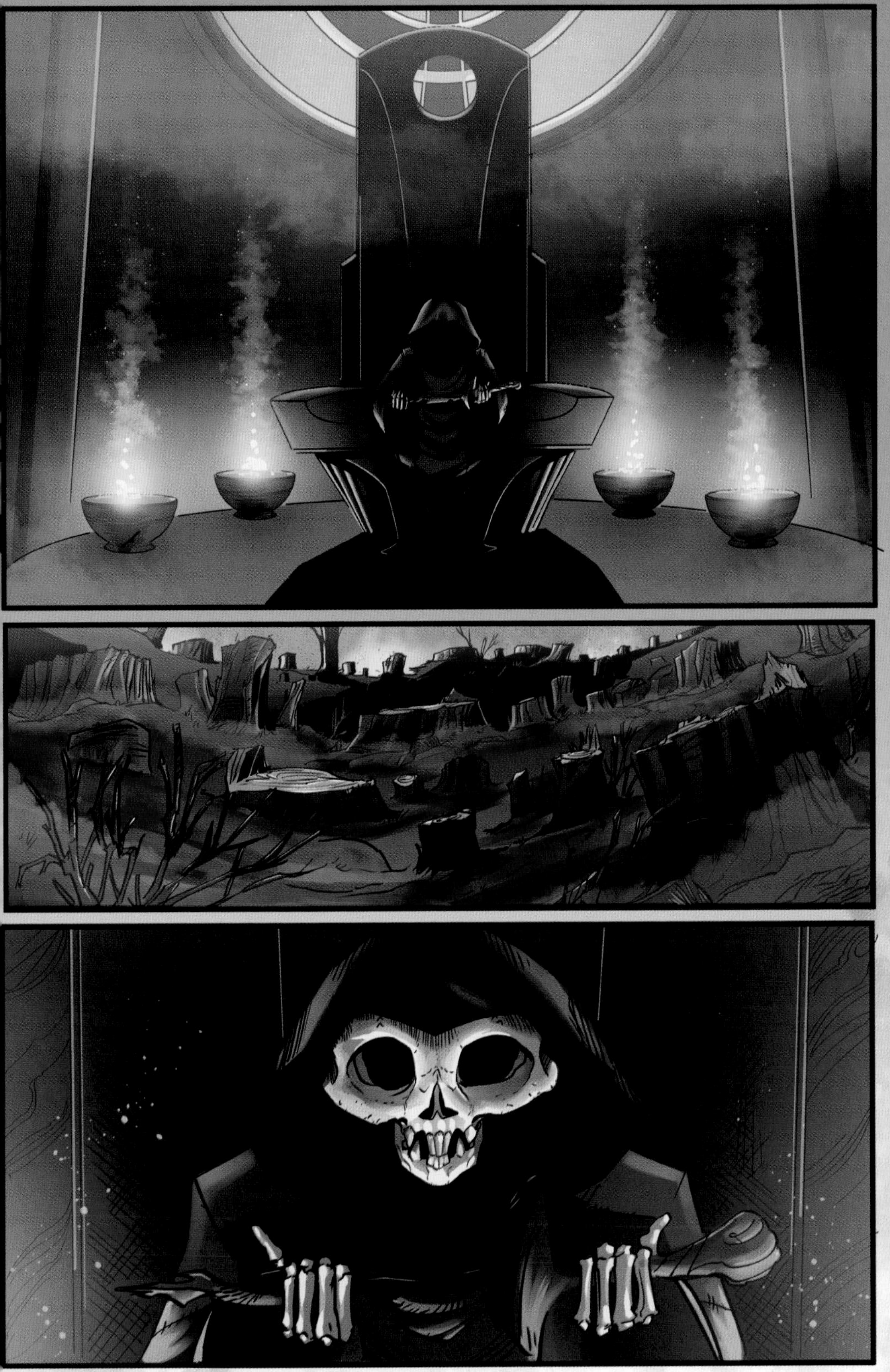

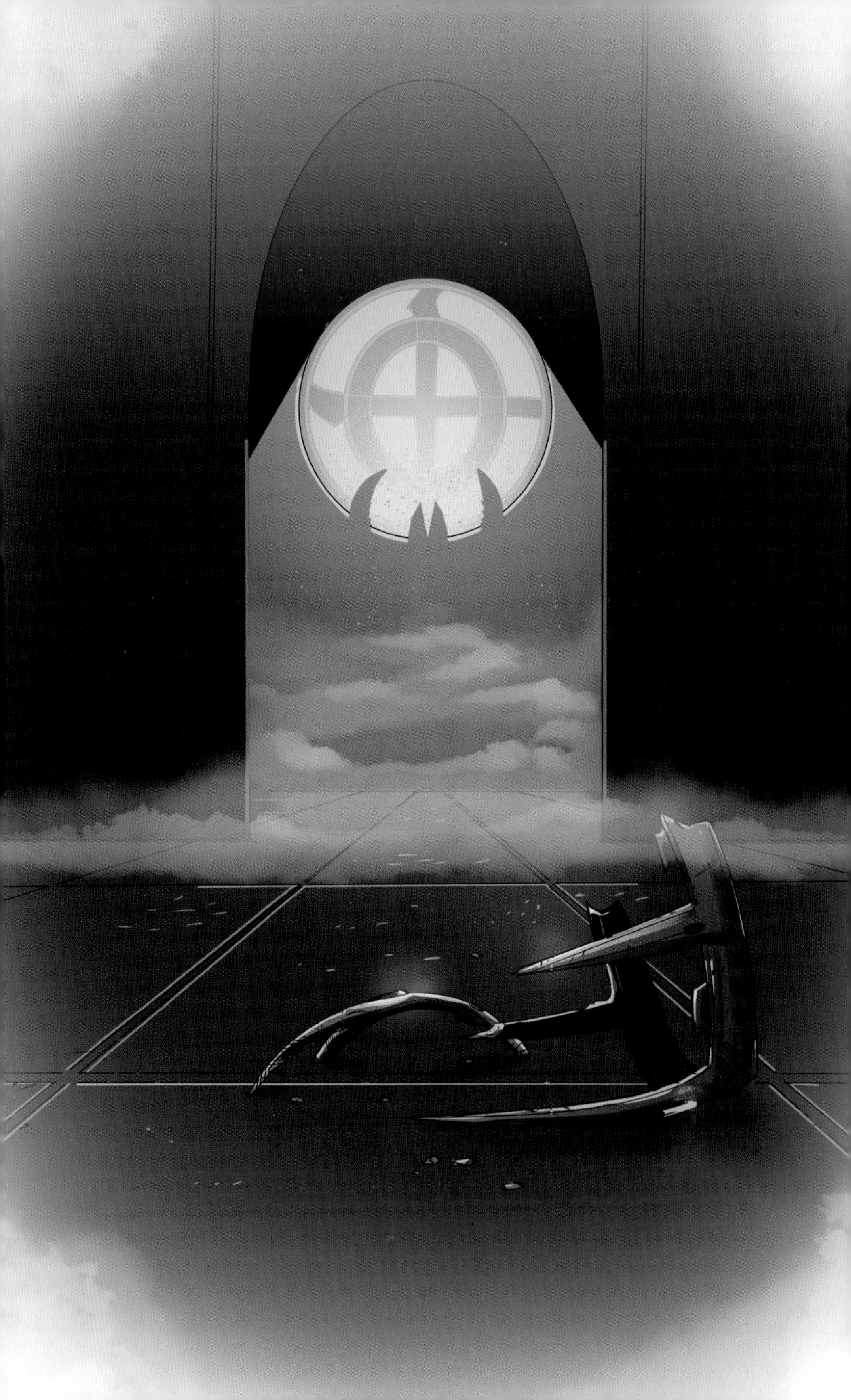

CHAPTER FIVE
THE GOBLIN'S HEART

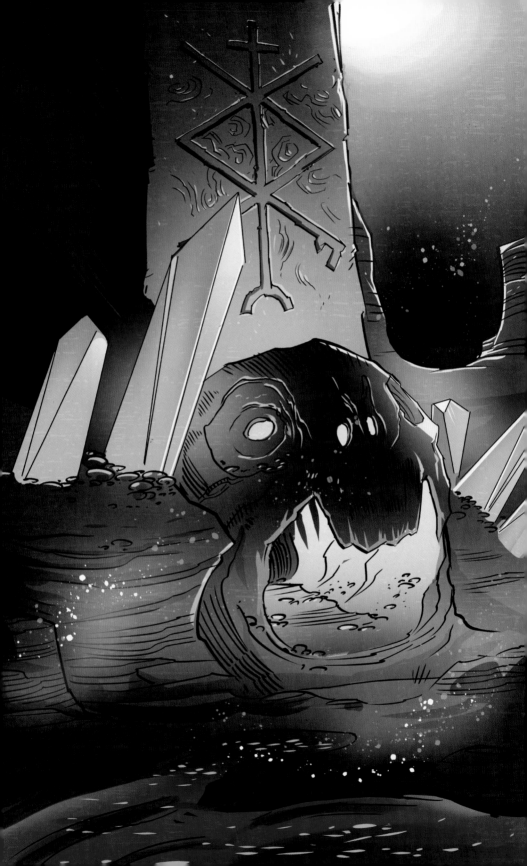

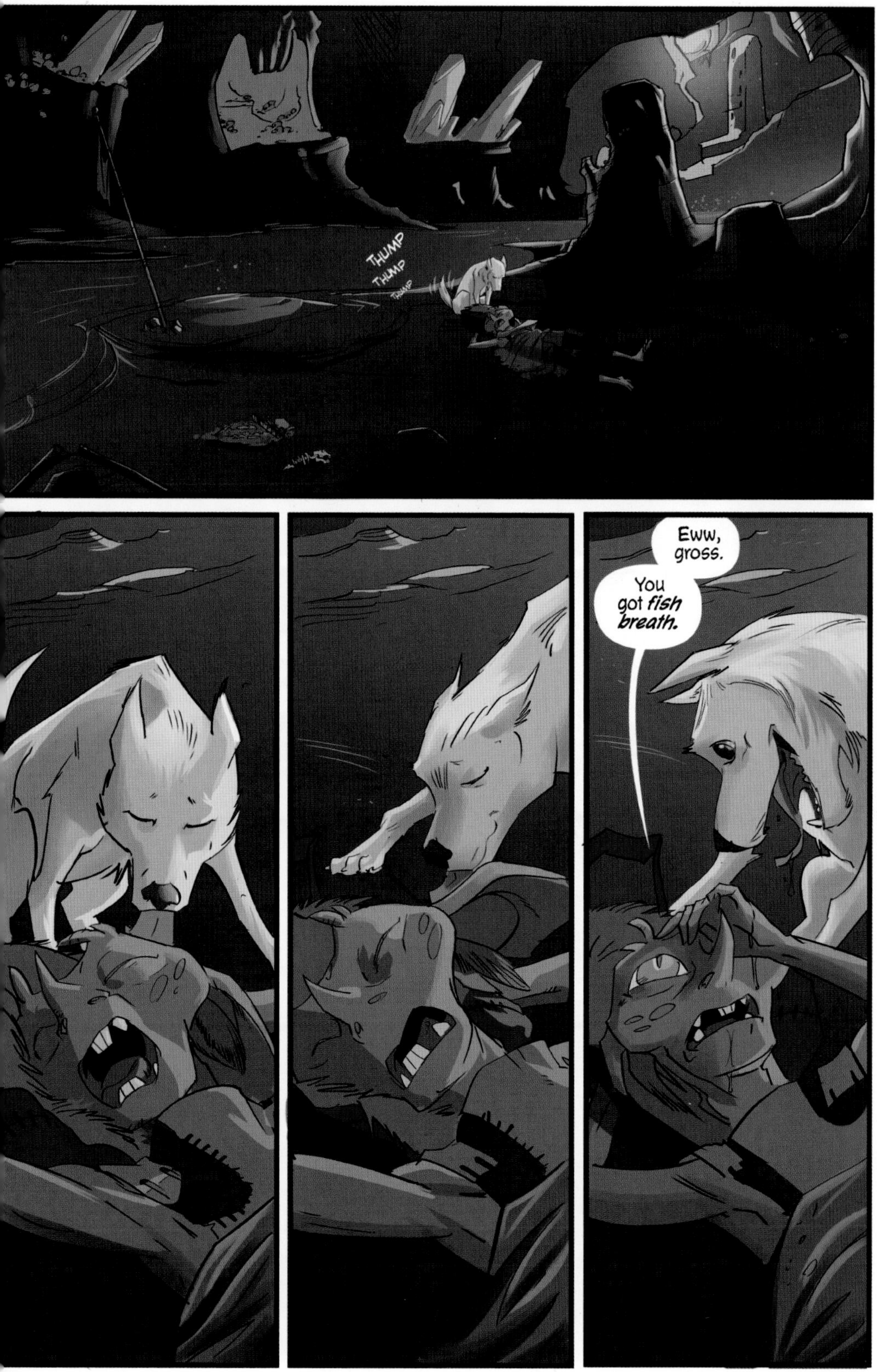

THUMP
THUMP
THUMP
Eww, gross.
You got fish breath.

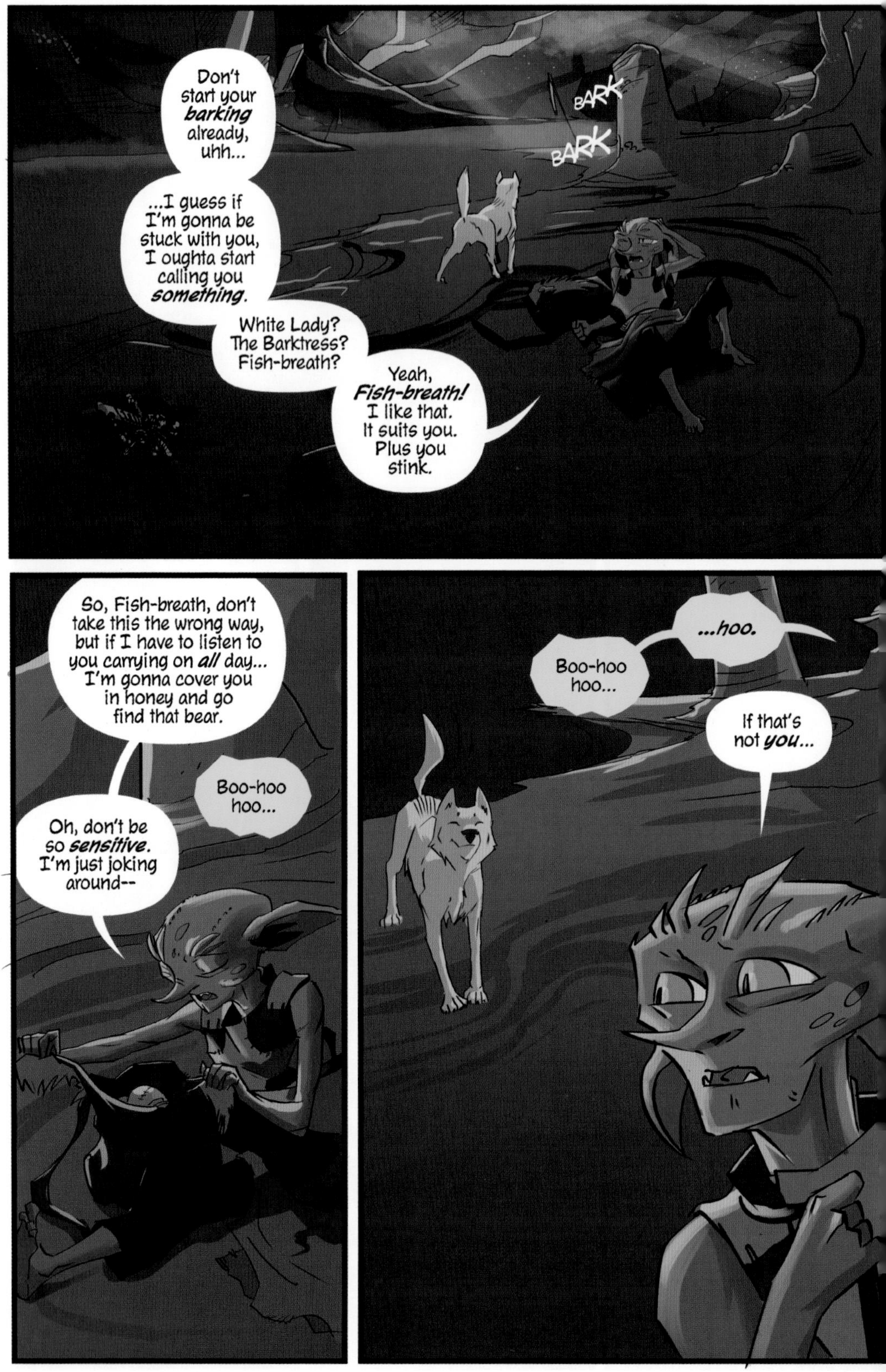
Don't start your barking already, uhh...
BARK
BARK
...I guess if I'm gonna be stuck with you, I oughta start calling you something.
White Lady? The Barktress? Fish-breath?
Yeah, Fish-breath! I like that. It suits you. Plus you stink.
So, Fish-breath, don't take this the wrong way, but if I have to listen to you carrying on all day... I'm gonna cover you in honey and go find that bear.
Boo-hoo hoo...
Oh, don't be so sensitive. I'm just joking around--
Boo-hoo hoo...
...hoo.
If that's not you...

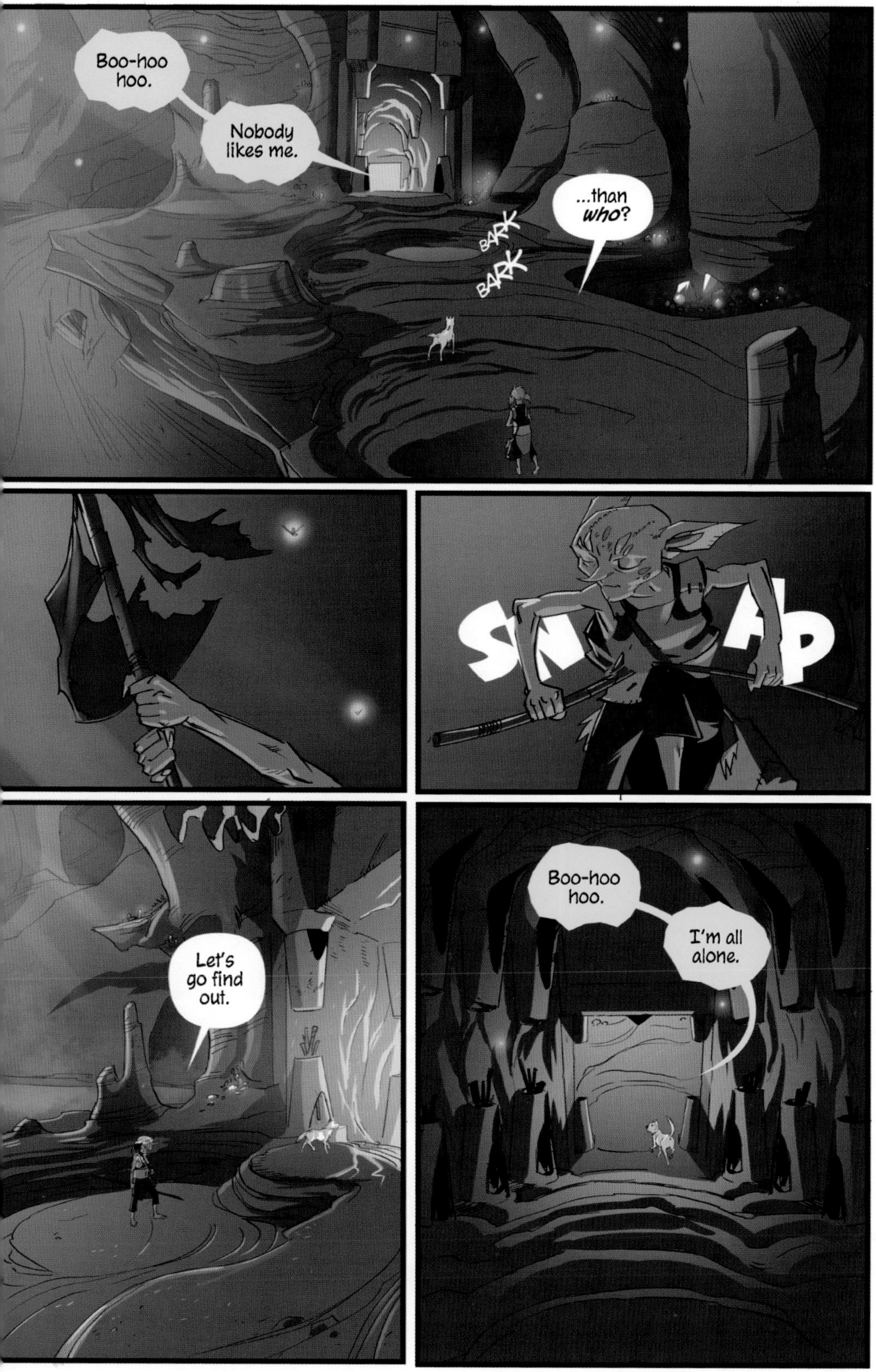
Boo-hoo
hoo.
Nobody
likes me.
BARK
BARK
...than
who?
SNAP
Let's
go find
out.
Boo-hoo
hoo.
I'm all
alone.

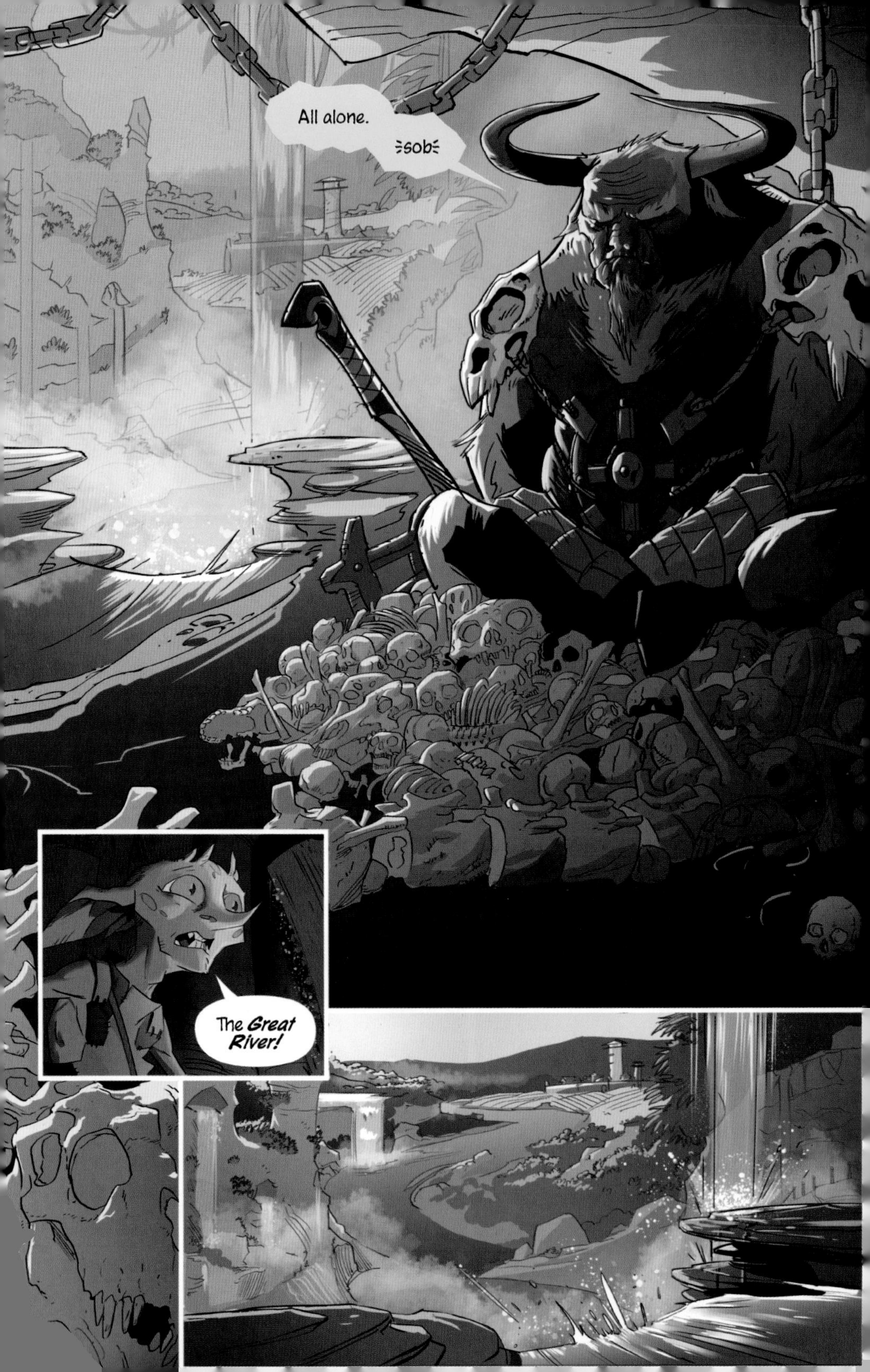
All alone.
sob
The *Great River!*

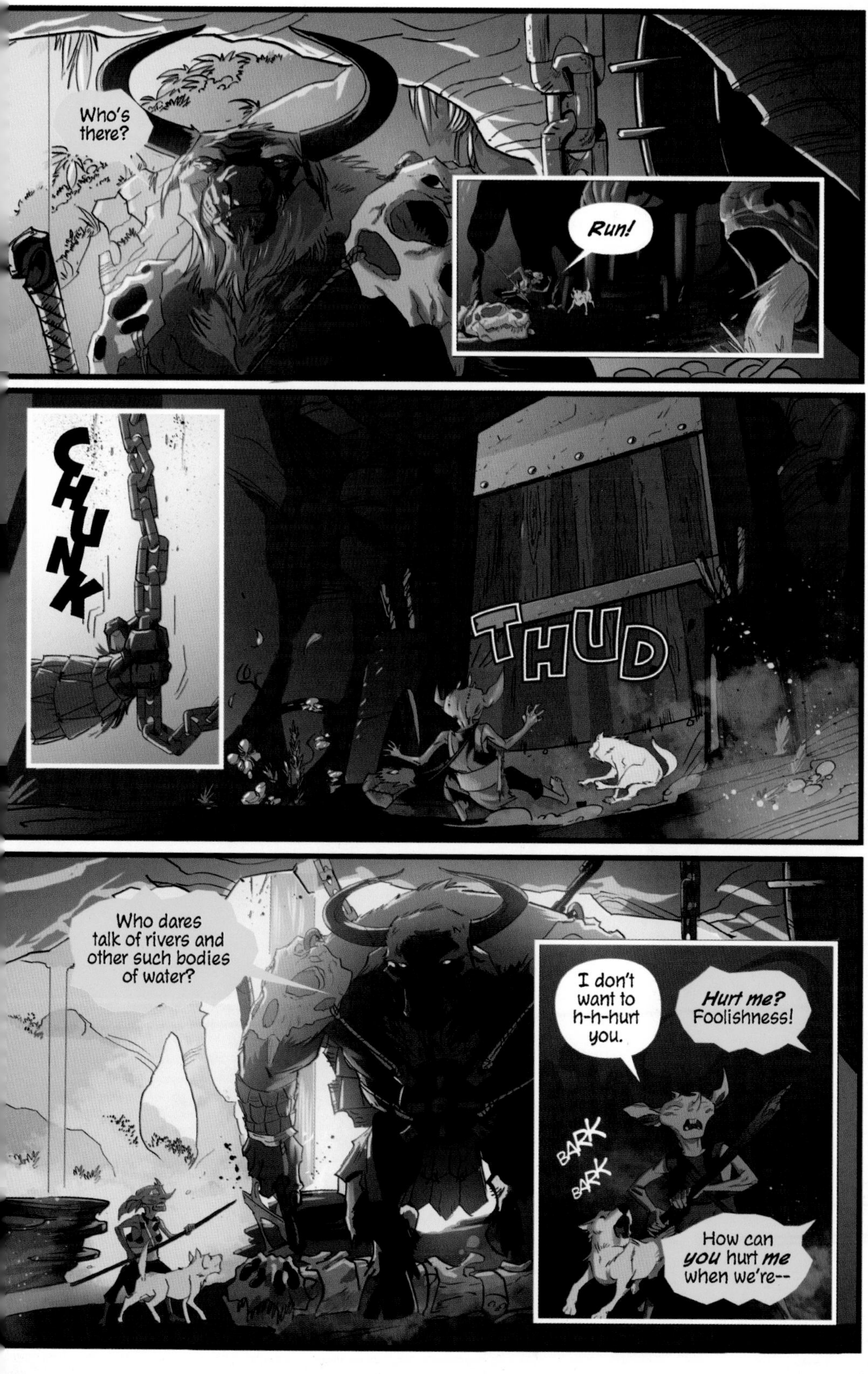
Who's there?
Run!
CHUNK
THUD
Who dares talk of rivers and other such bodies of water?
I don't want to h-h-hurt you.
Hurt me? Foolishness!
BARK
BARK
How can you hurt me when we're--

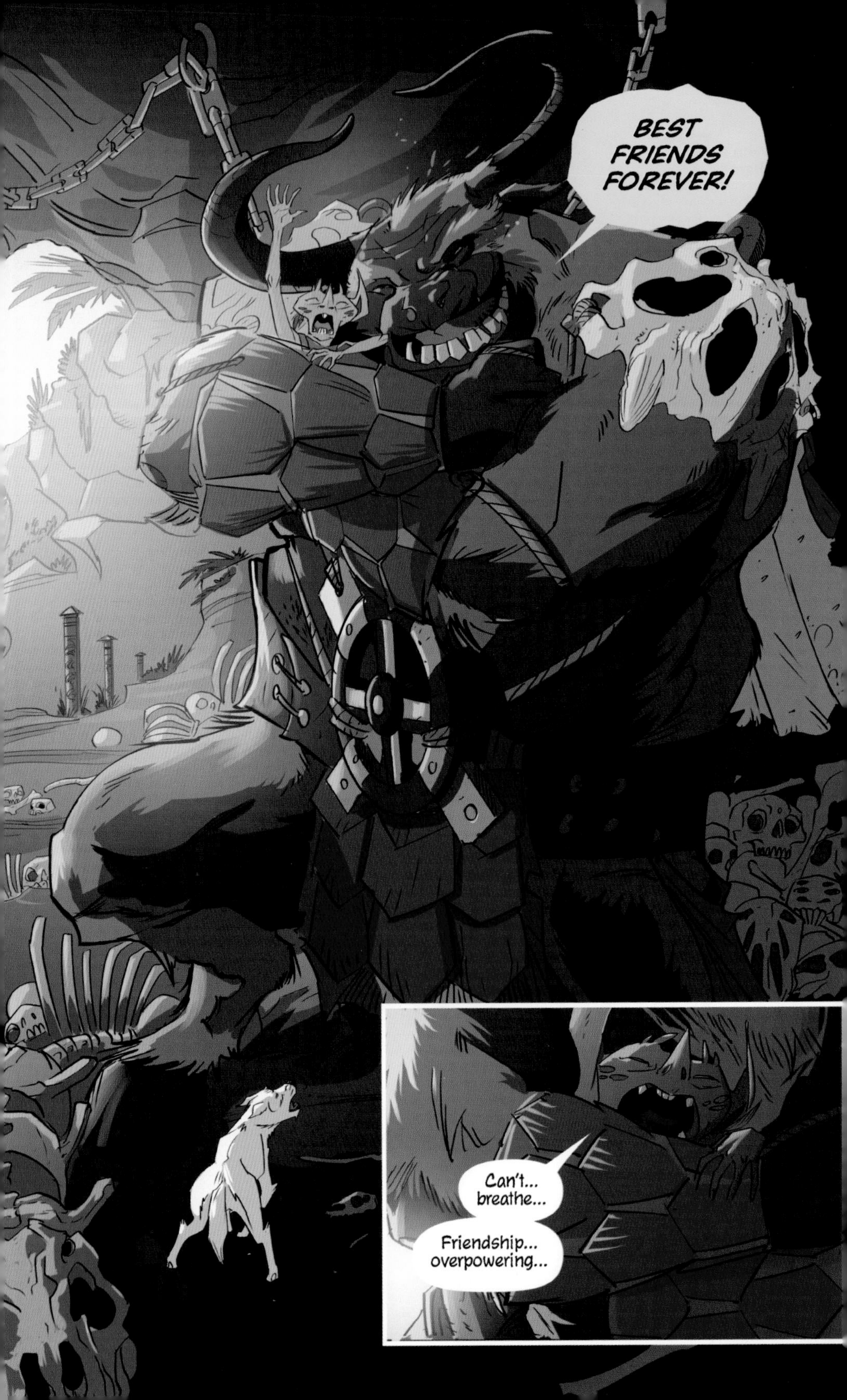
BEST FRIENDS FOREVER!
Can't... breathe...
Friendship... overpowering...

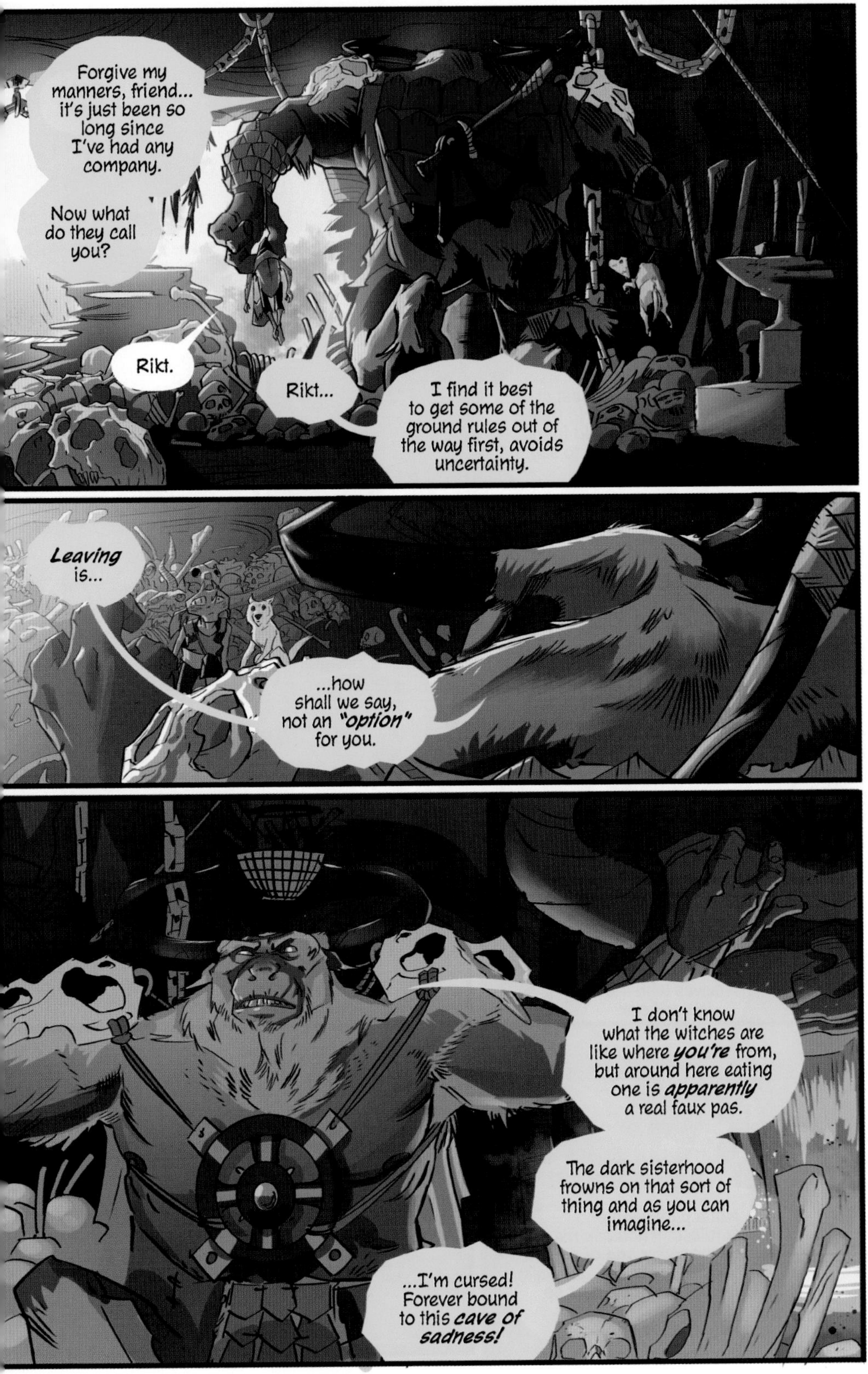
Forgive my manners, friend... it's just been so long since I've had any company.
Now what do they call you?
Rikt.
Rikt...
I find it best to get some of the ground rules out of the way first, avoids uncertainty.
Leaving is...
...how shall we say, not an "option" for you.
I don't know what the witches are like where you're from, but around here eating one is apparently a real faux pas.
The dark sisterhood frowns on that sort of thing and as you can imagine...
...I'm cursed! Forever bound to this cave of sadness!

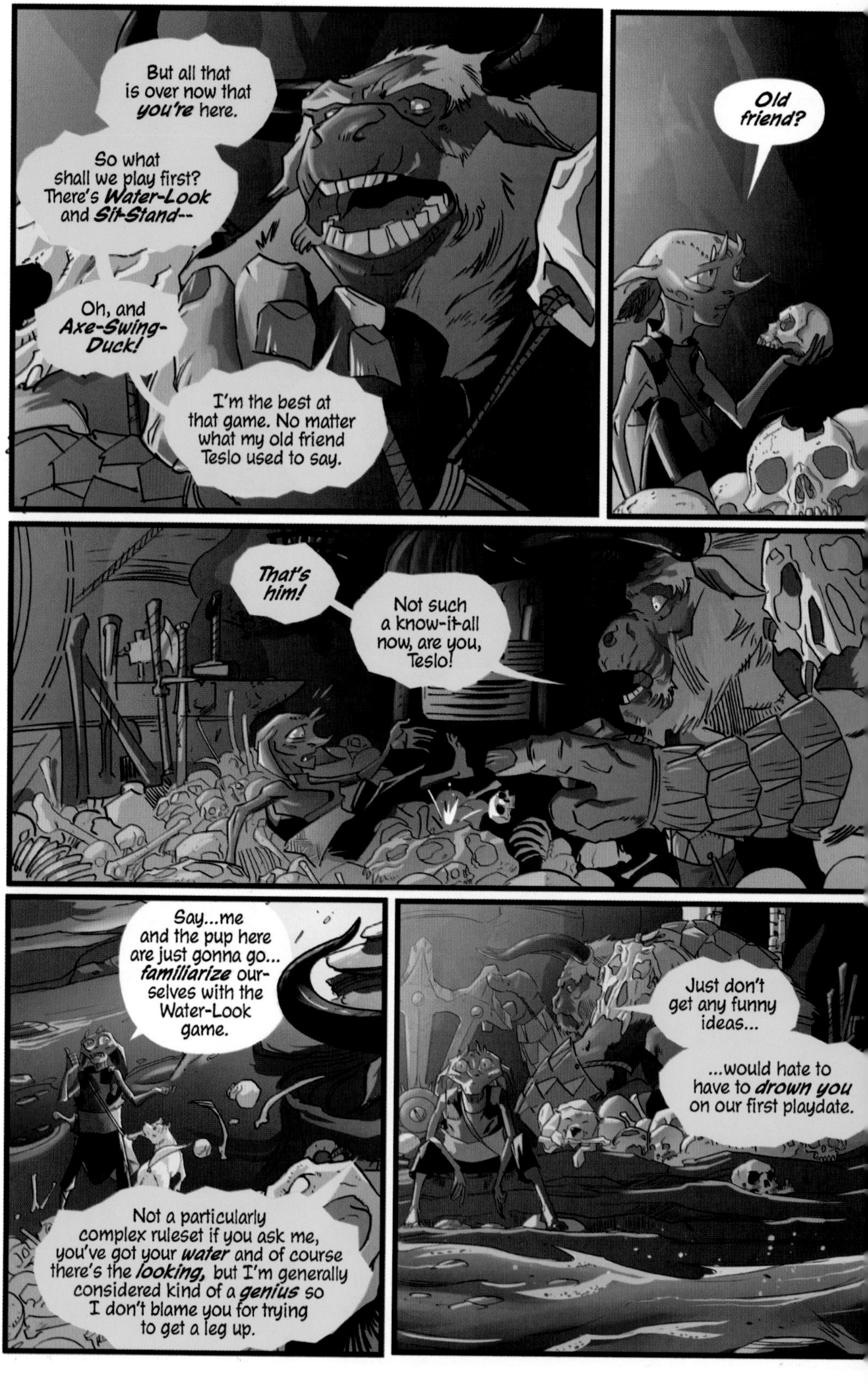
But all that is over now that *you're* here.
So what shall we play first? There's ***Water-Look*** and ***Sit-Stand***--
Oh, and ***Axe-Swing-Duck!***
I'm the best at that game. No matter what my old friend Teslo used to say.
Old friend?
That's him!
Not such a know-it-all now, are you, Teslo!
Say...me and the pup here are just gonna go... ***familiarize*** our-selves with the Water-Look game.
Not a particularly complex ruleset if you ask me, you've got your ***water*** and of course there's the ***looking,*** but I'm generally considered kind of a ***genius*** so I don't blame you for trying to get a leg up.
Just don't get any funny ideas...
...would hate to have to ***drown you*** on our first playdate.

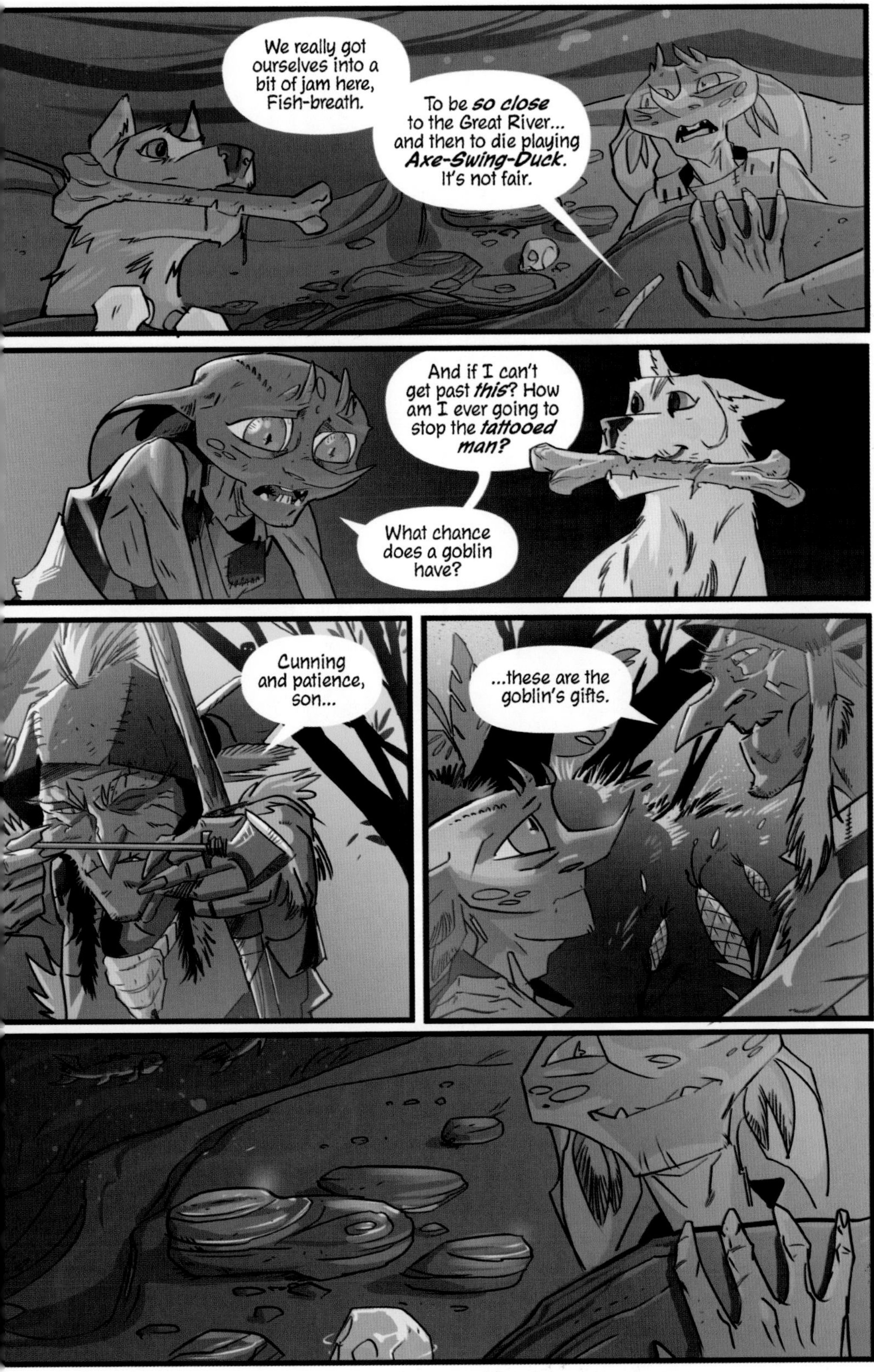
We really got ourselves into a bit of jam here, Fish-breath.
To be *so close* to the Great River... and then to die playing *Axe-Swing-Duck*. It's not fair.
And if I can't get past *this*? How am I ever going to stop the *tattooed man?*
What chance does a goblin have?
Cunning and patience, son...
...these are the goblin's gifts.

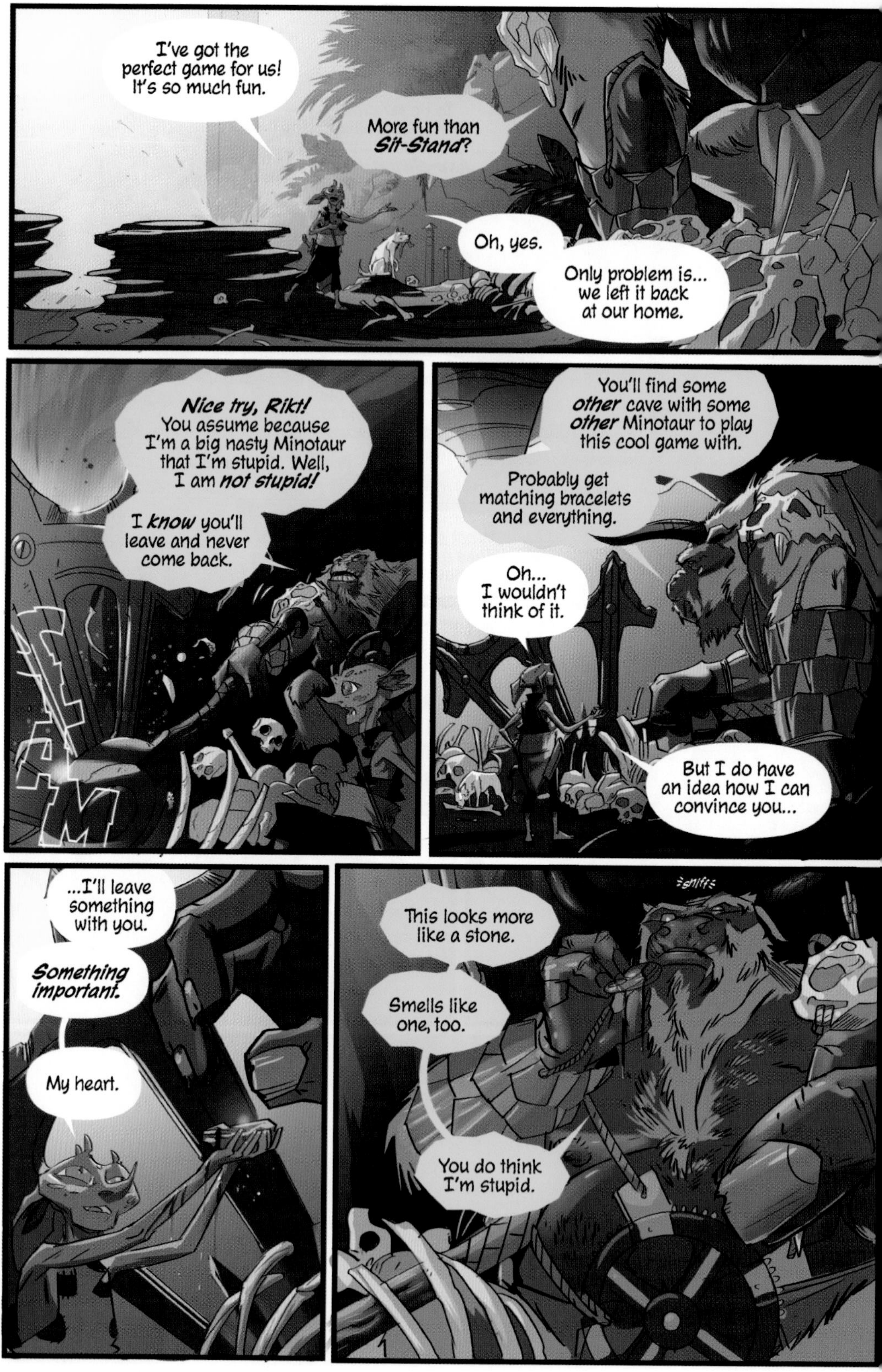
I've got the perfect game for us! It's so much fun.
More fun than *Sit-Stand*?
Oh, yes.
Only problem is... we left it back at our home.
Nice try, Rikt! You assume because I'm a big nasty Minotaur that I'm stupid. Well, I am *not stupid!*
I *know* you'll leave and never come back.
You'll find some *other* cave with some *other* Minotaur to play this cool game with.
Probably get matching bracelets and everything.
Oh... I wouldn't think of it.
But I do have an idea how I can convince you...
...I'll leave something with you.
Something important.
My heart.
sniff
This looks more like a stone.
Smells like one, too.
You do think I'm stupid.

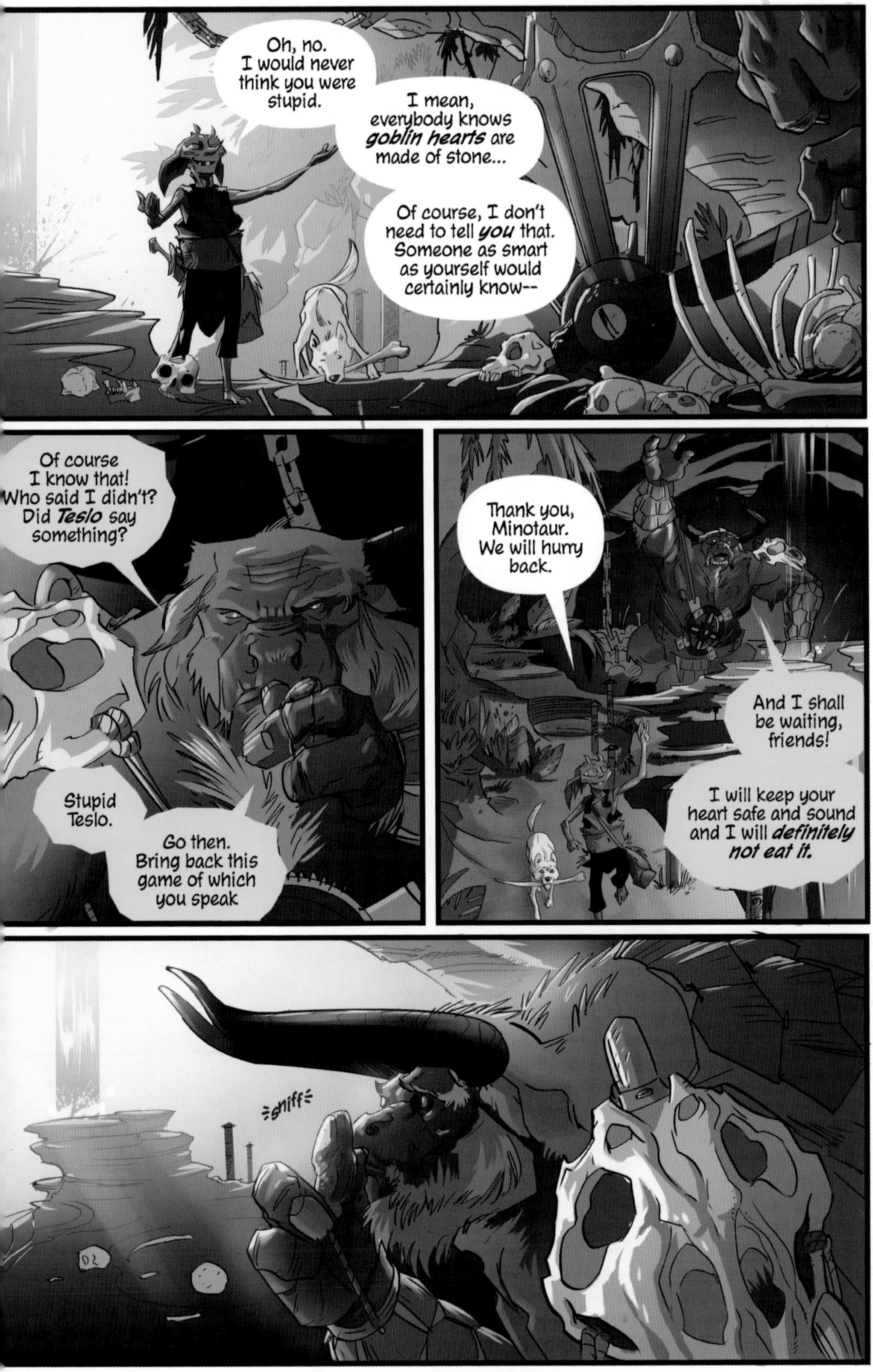
Oh, no. I would never think you were stupid.
I mean, everybody knows goblin hearts are made of stone...
Of course, I don't need to tell you that. Someone as smart as yourself would certainly know--
Of course I know that! Who said I didn't? Did Teslo say something?
Stupid Teslo.
Go then. Bring back this game of which you speak
Thank you, Minotaur. We will hurry back.
And I shall be waiting, friends!
I will keep your heart safe and sound and I will definitely not eat it.
sniff

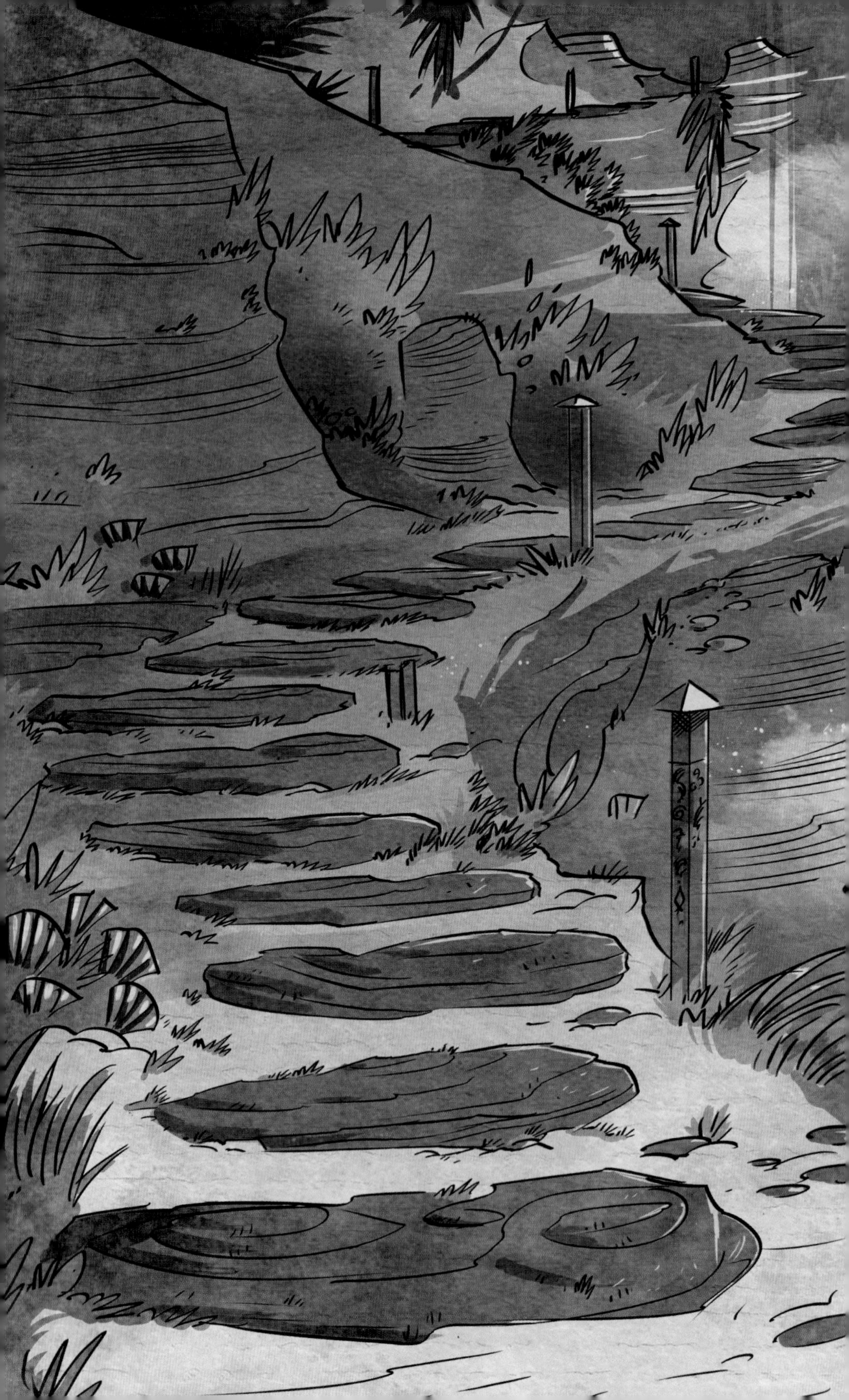

CHAPTER SIX
THE SCORPION'S STING

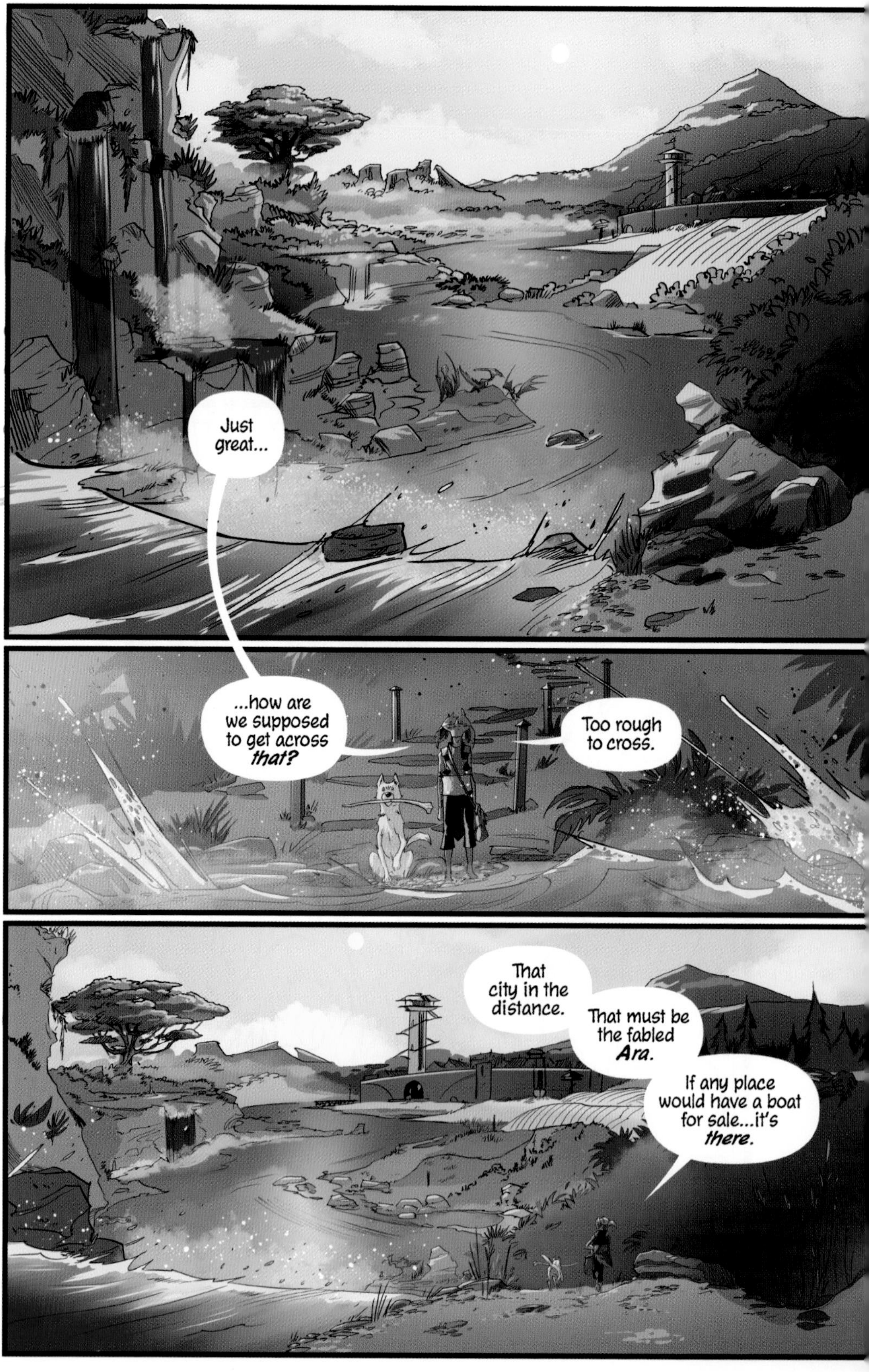
Just great...
...how are we supposed to get across *that?*
Too rough to cross.
That city in the distance.
That must be the fabled *Ara*.
If any place would have a boat for sale...it's *there*.

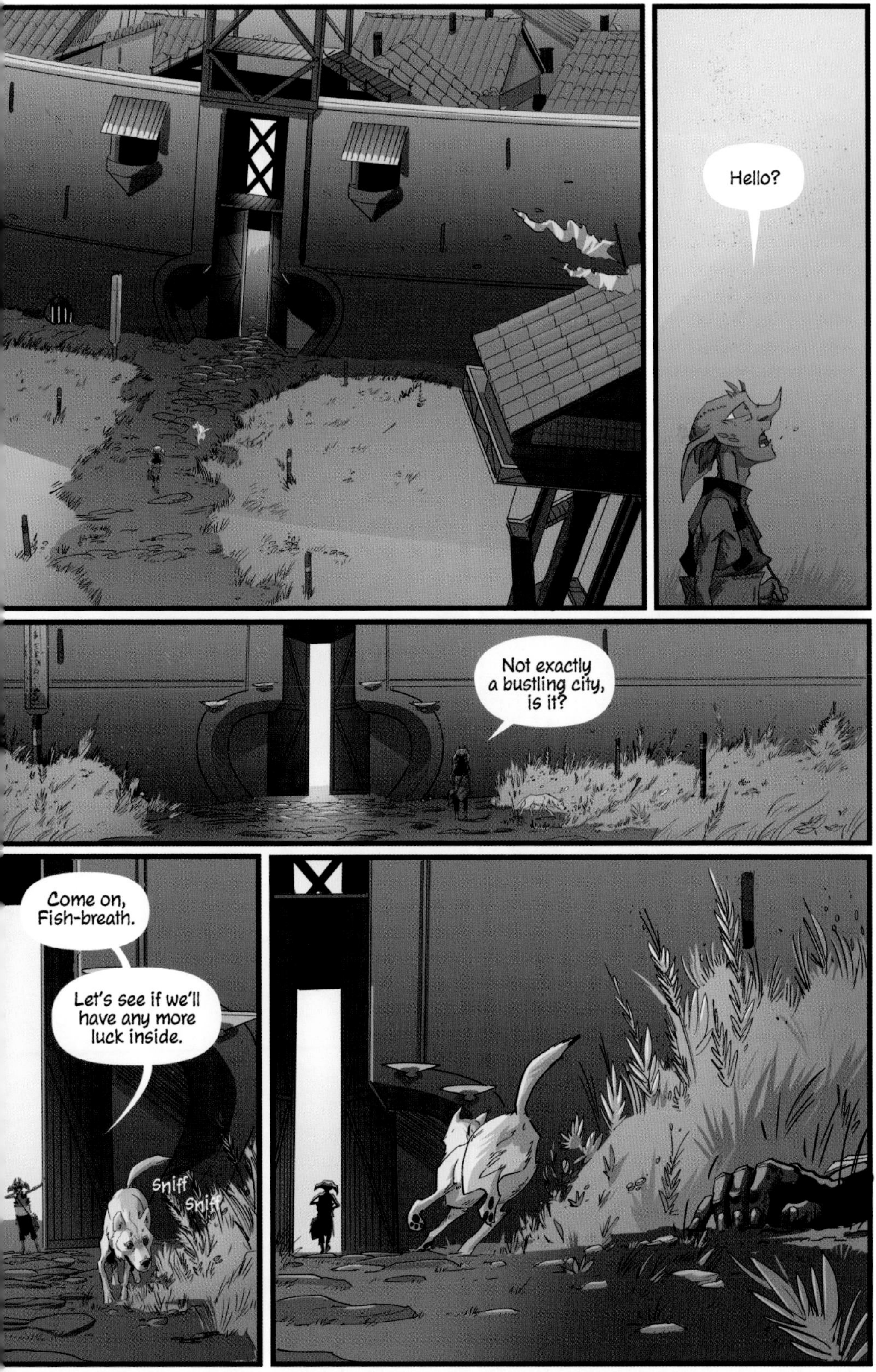
Hello?
Not exactly a bustling city, is it?
Come on, Fish-breath.
Let's see if we'll have any more luck inside.
Sniff
Sniff

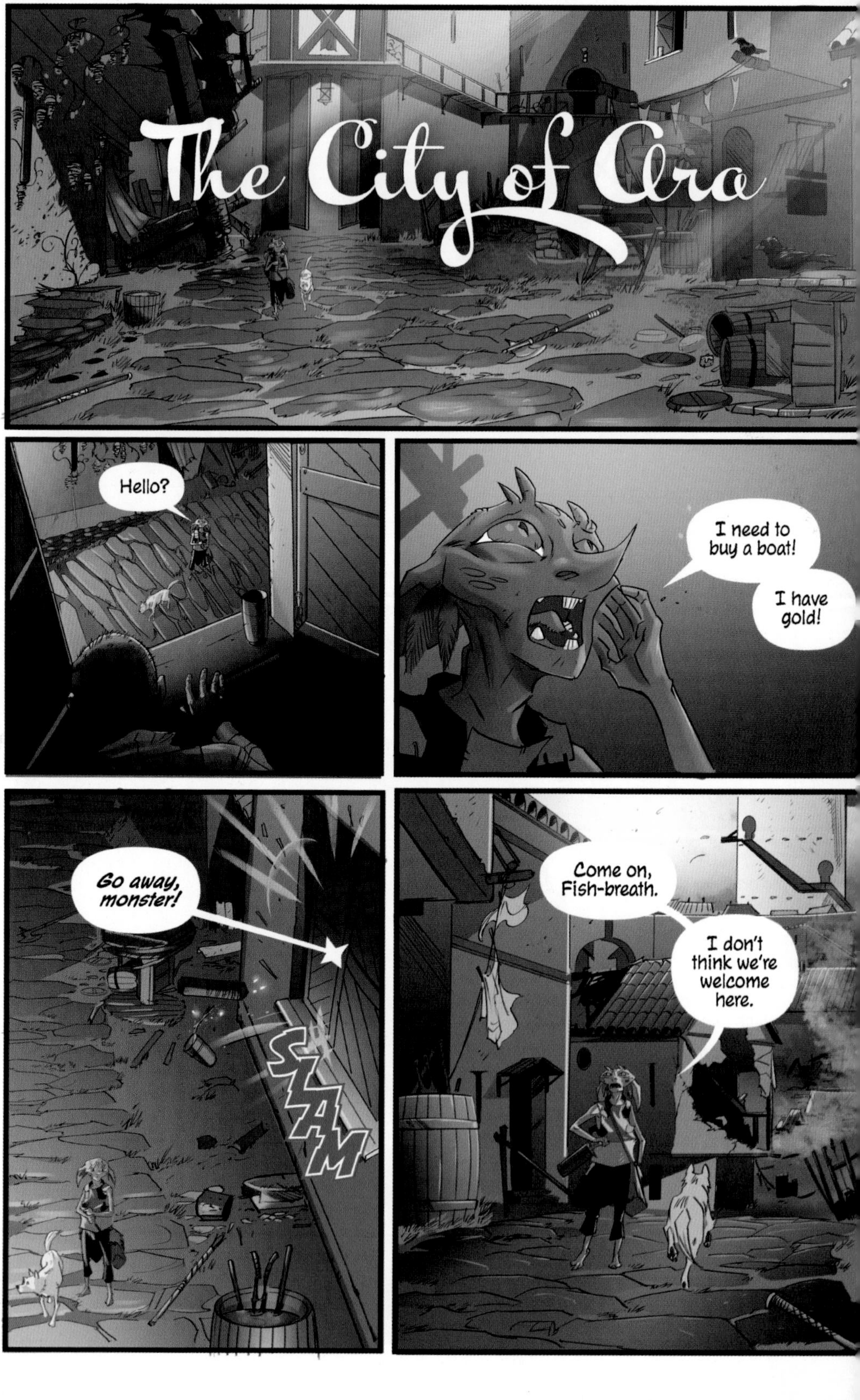
The City of Ara
Hello?
I need to buy a boat!
I have gold!
Go away, monster!
SLAM
Come on, Fish-breath.
I don't think we're welcome here.

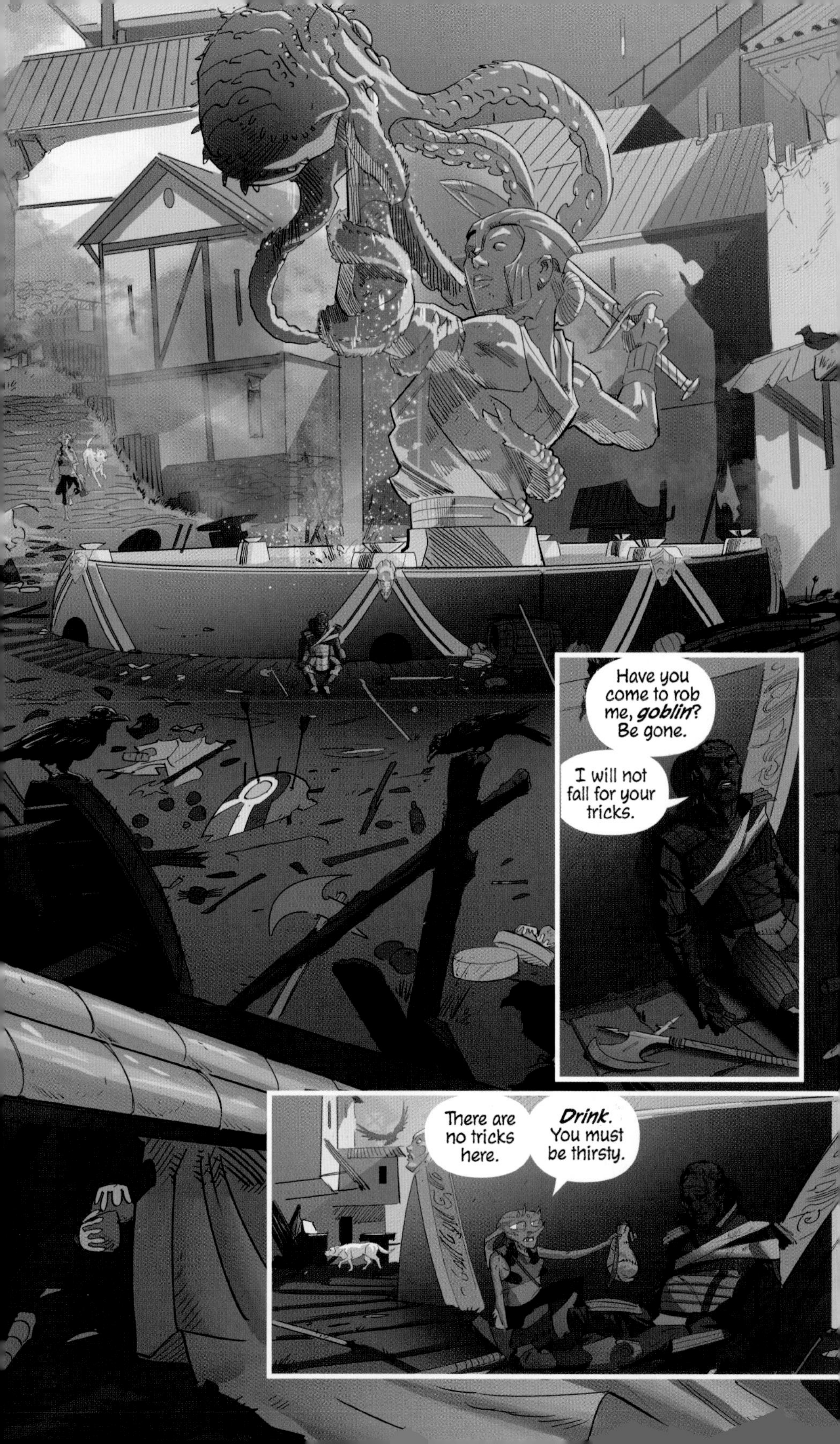
Have you come to rob me, ***goblin***? Be gone.
I will not fall for your tricks.
There are no tricks here.
Drink. You must be thirsty.

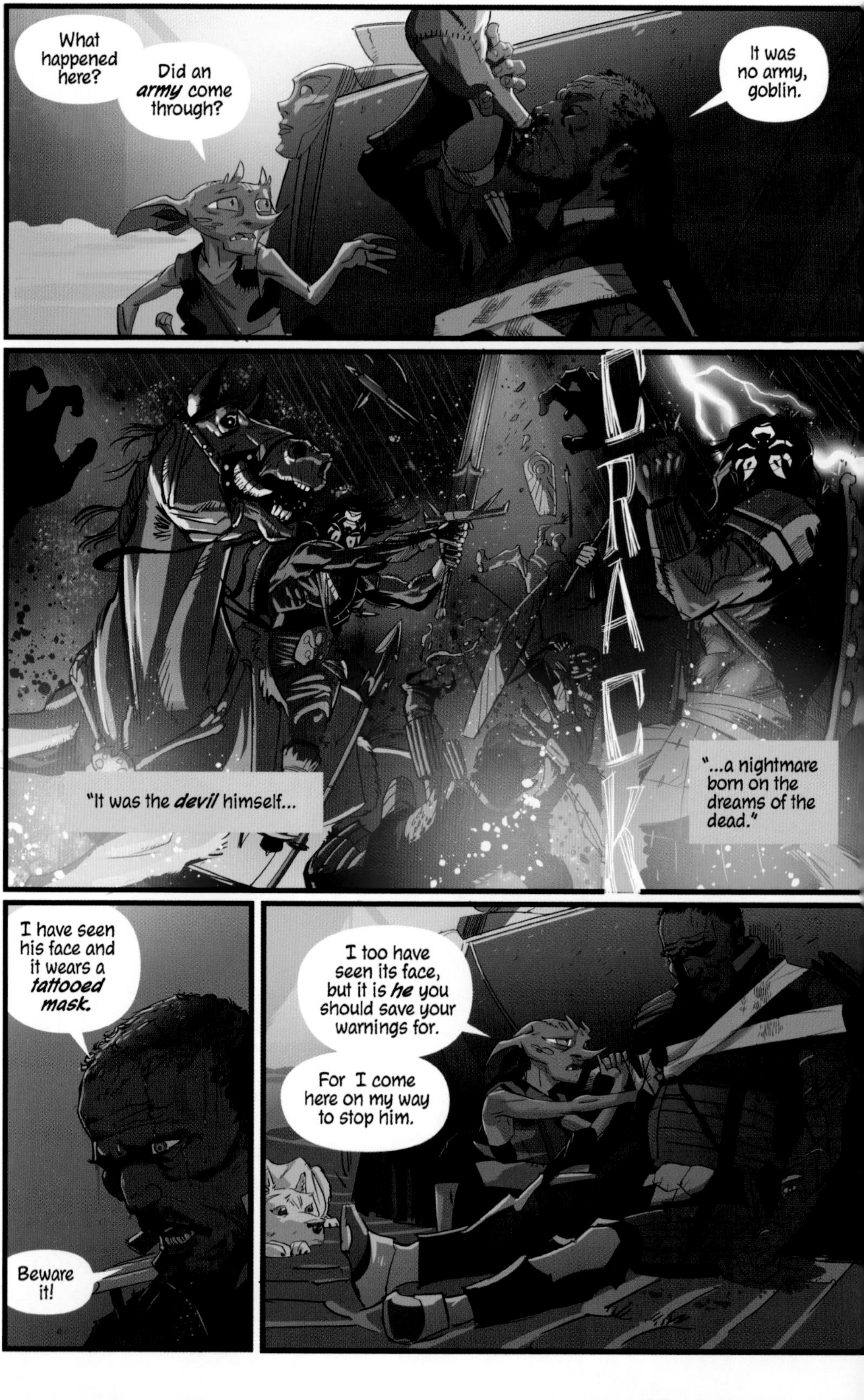
What happened here?
Did an *army* come through?
It was no army, goblin.
CRRACK
"It was the *devil* himself...
"...a nightmare born on the dreams of the dead."
I have seen his face and it wears a *tattooed mask.*
Beware it!
I too have seen its face, but it is *he* you should save your warnings for.
For I come here on my way to stop him.

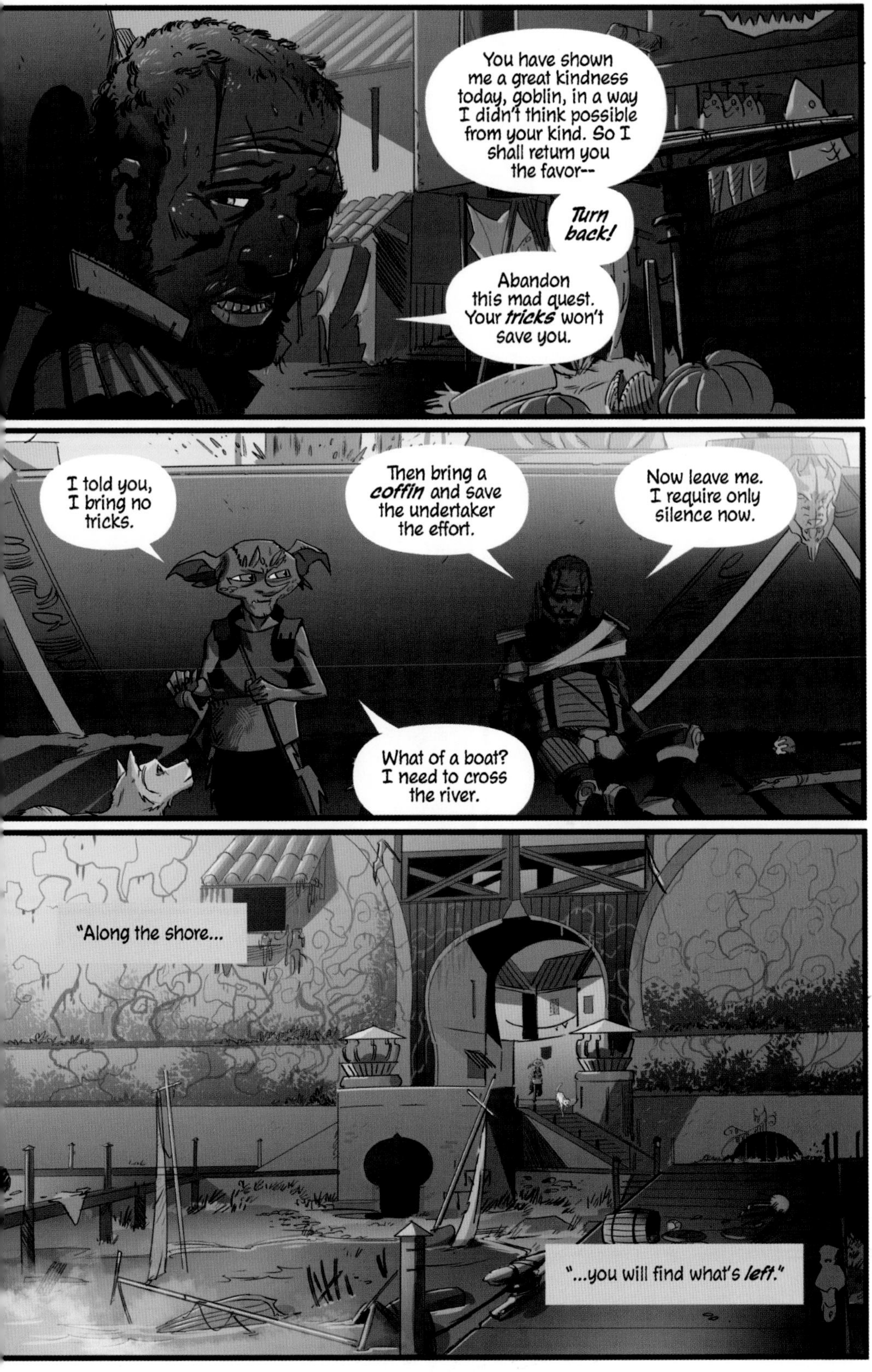
You have shown me a great kindness today, goblin, in a way I didn't think possible from your kind. So I shall return you the favor--
Turn back!
Abandon this mad quest. Your *tricks* won't save you.
I told you, I bring no tricks.
Then bring a *coffin* and save the undertaker the effort.
Now leave me. I require only silence now.
What of a boat? I need to cross the river.
"Along the shore...
"...you will find what's *left*."

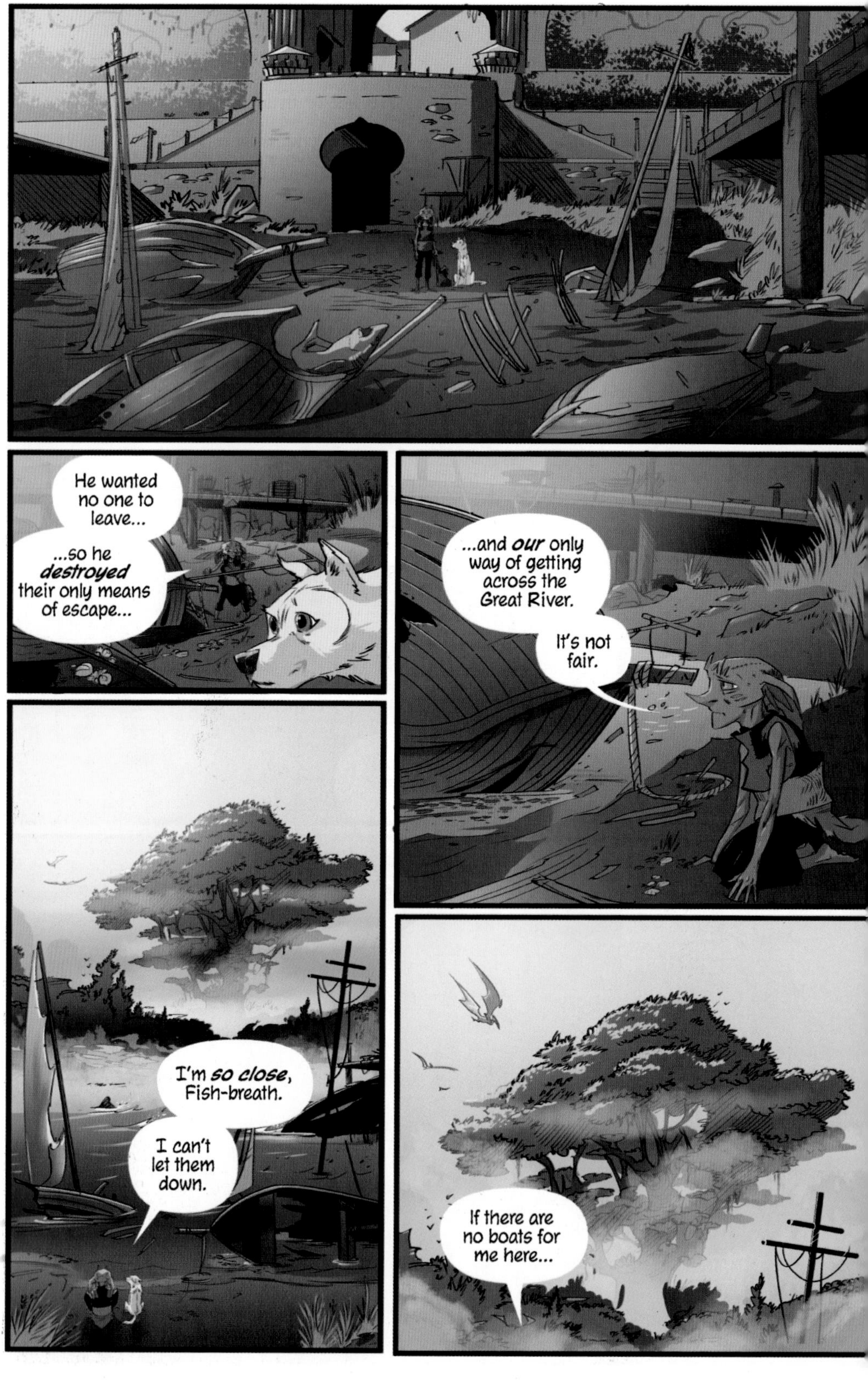
He wanted no one to leave...
...so he destroyed their only means of escape...
...and our only way of getting across the Great River.
It's not fair.
I'm so close, Fish-breath.
I can't let them down.
If there are no boats for me here...

"...then I shall *build* my own."

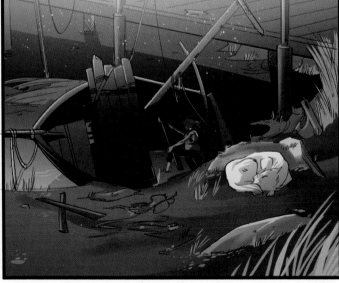

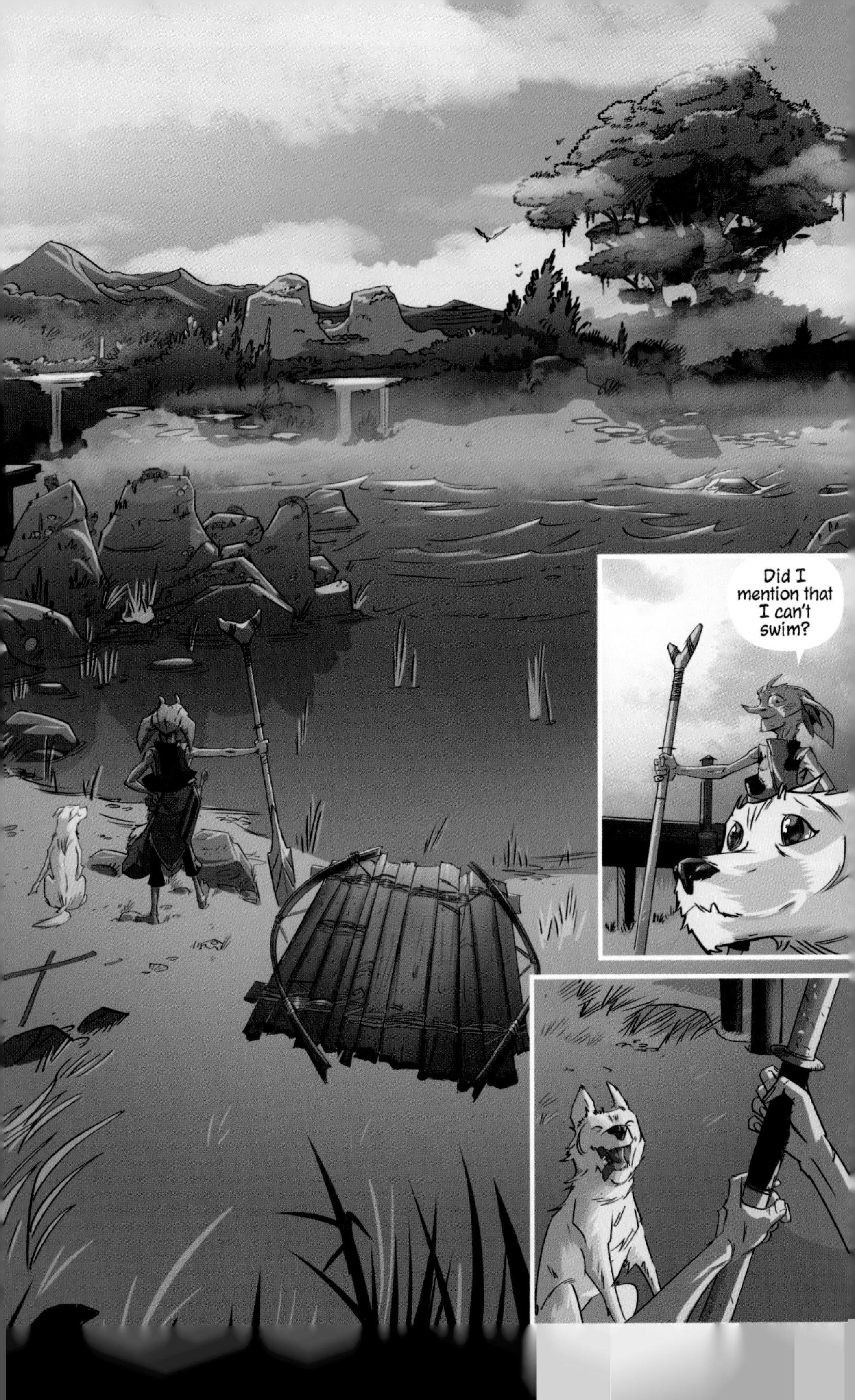
Did I mention that I can't swim?

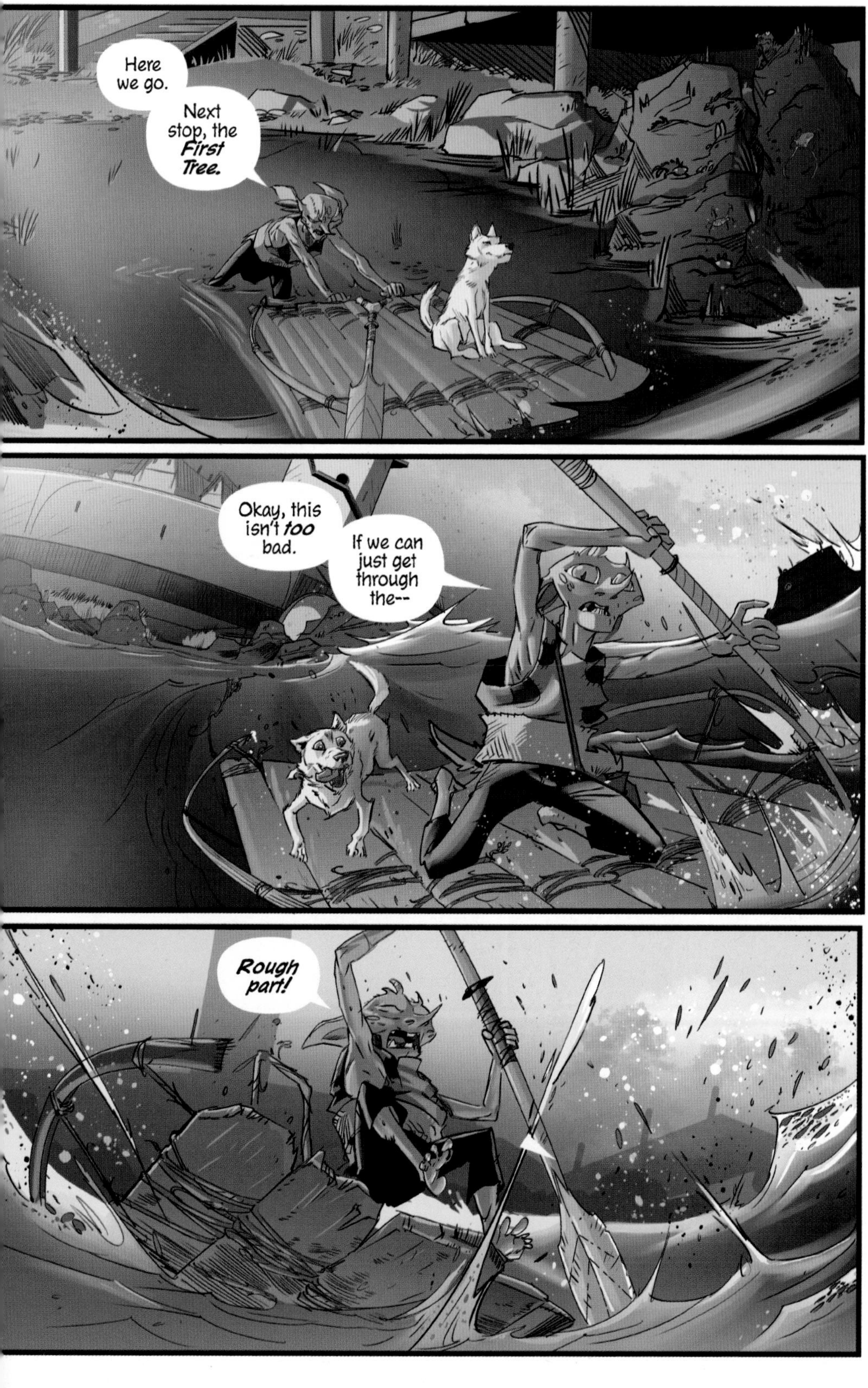
Here we go.
Next stop, the *First Tree.*
Okay, this isn't *too* bad.
If we can just get through the--
Rough part!

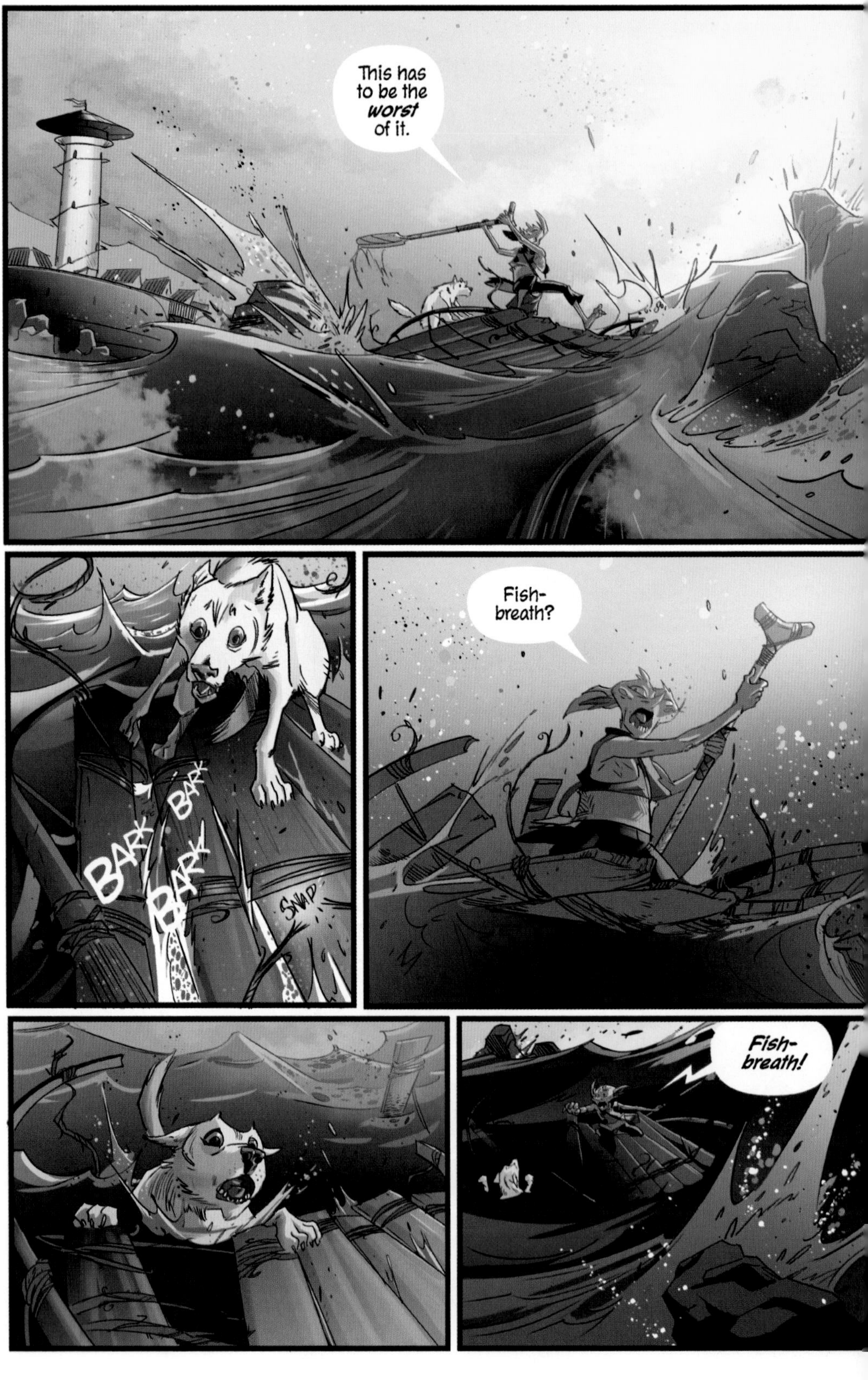
This has to be the *worst* of it.
BARK BARK BARK BARK
SNAP
Fish-breath?
Fish-breath!

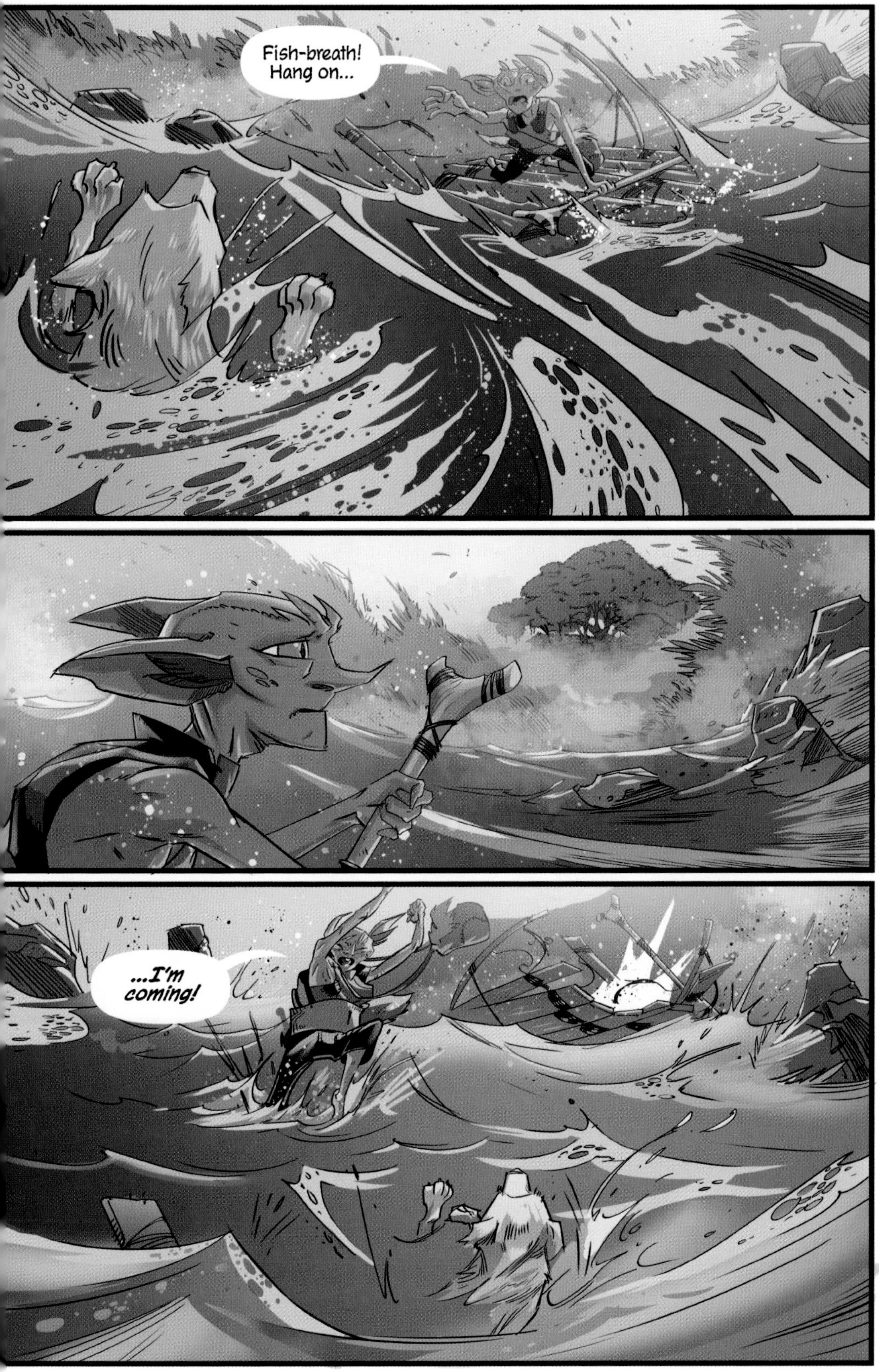
Fish-breath! Hang on...
...I'm coming!

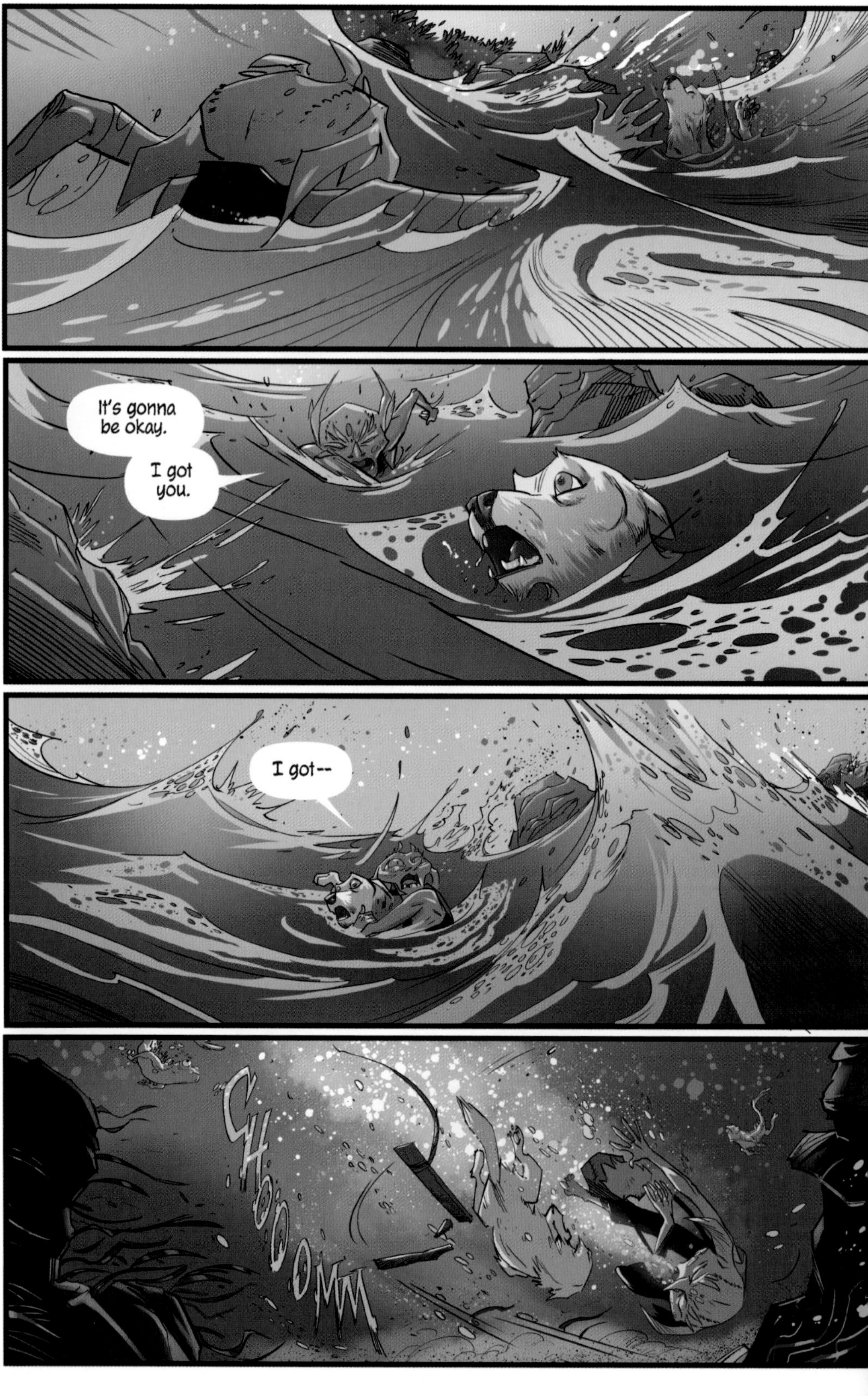
It's gonna be okay.
I got you.
I got--
CHOOOMM

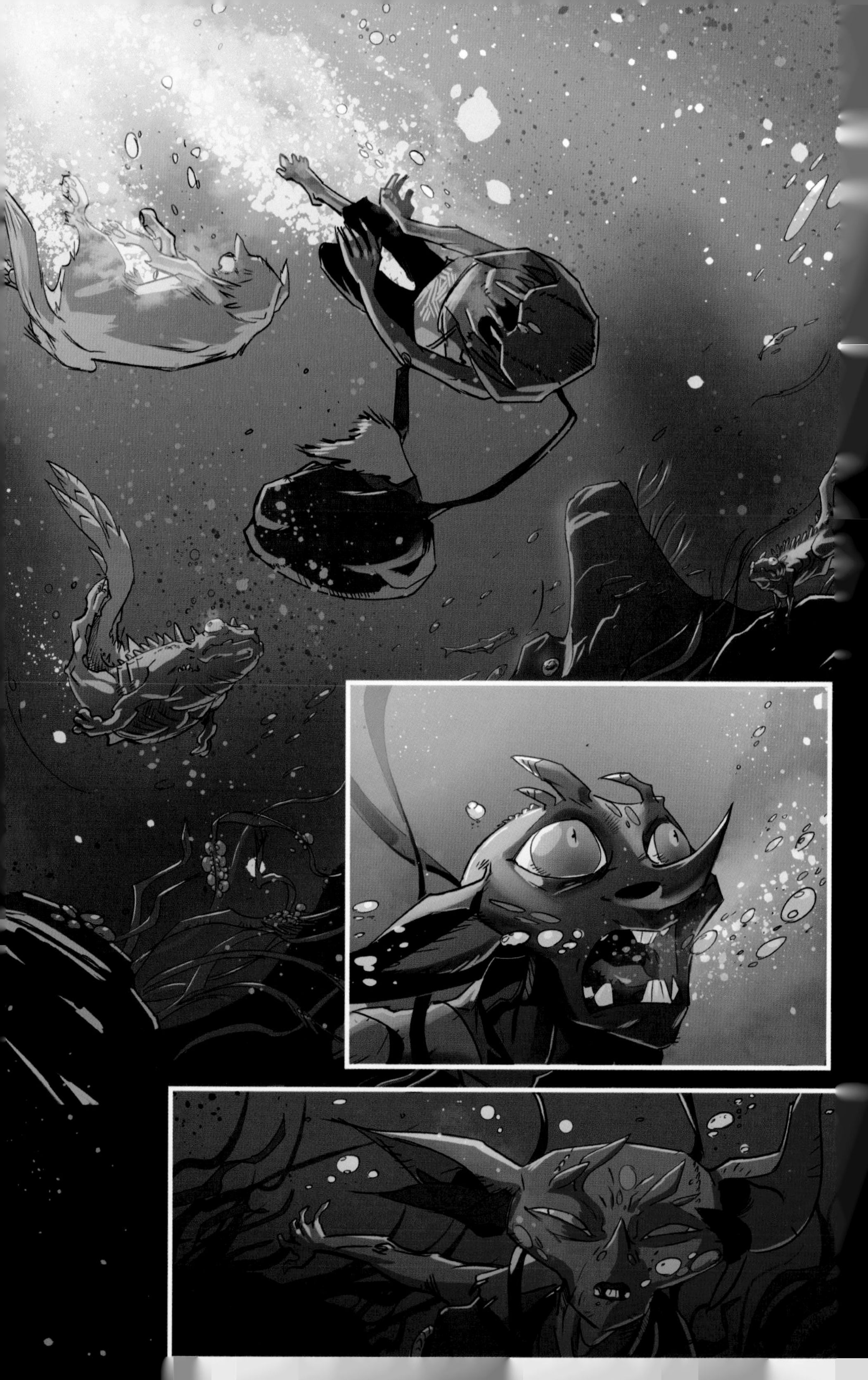

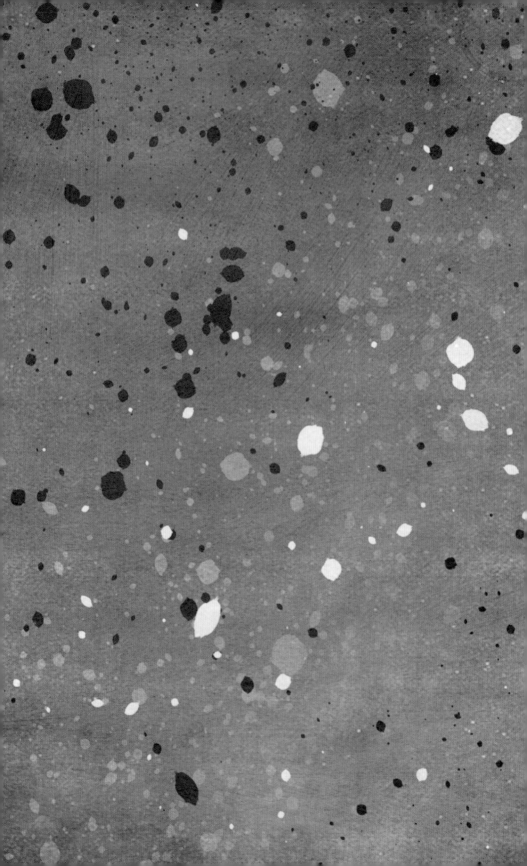

CHAPTER SEVEN
LITTLE BOY LOST

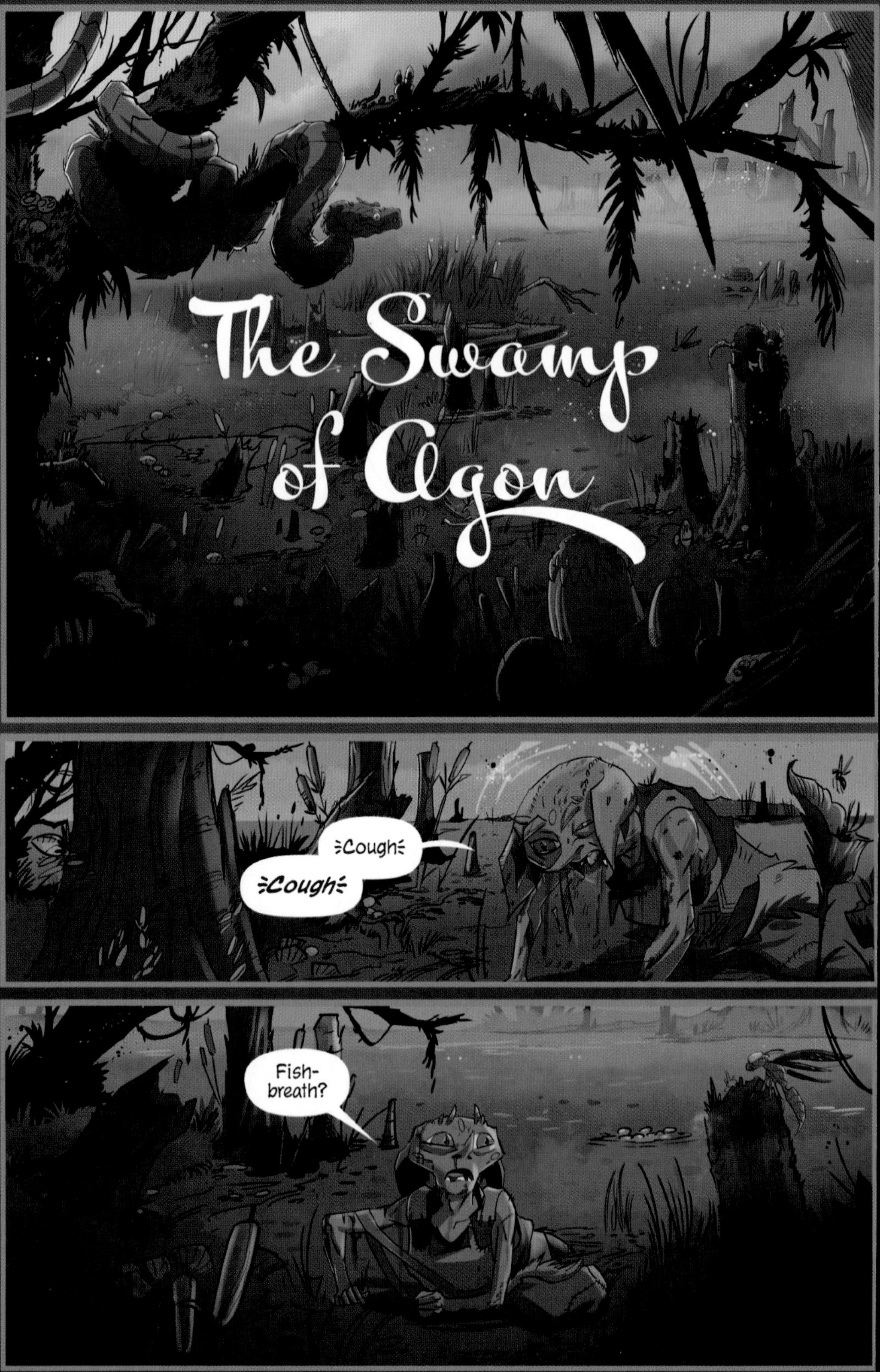
The Swamp of Agon
Cough
Cough
Fish-breath?

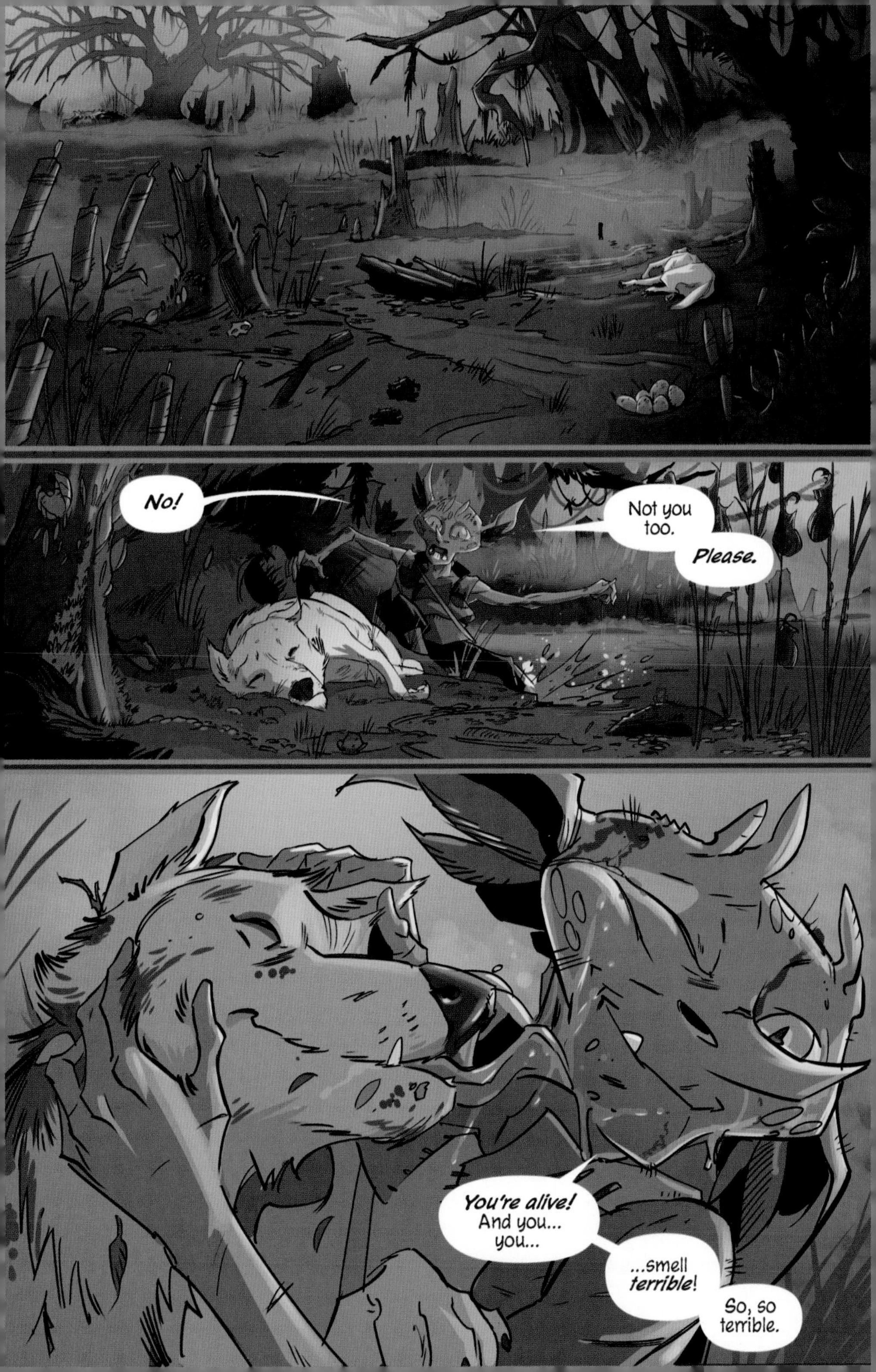

No!
Not you too.
Please.
You're alive! And you... you...
...smell ***terrible***!
So, so terrible.

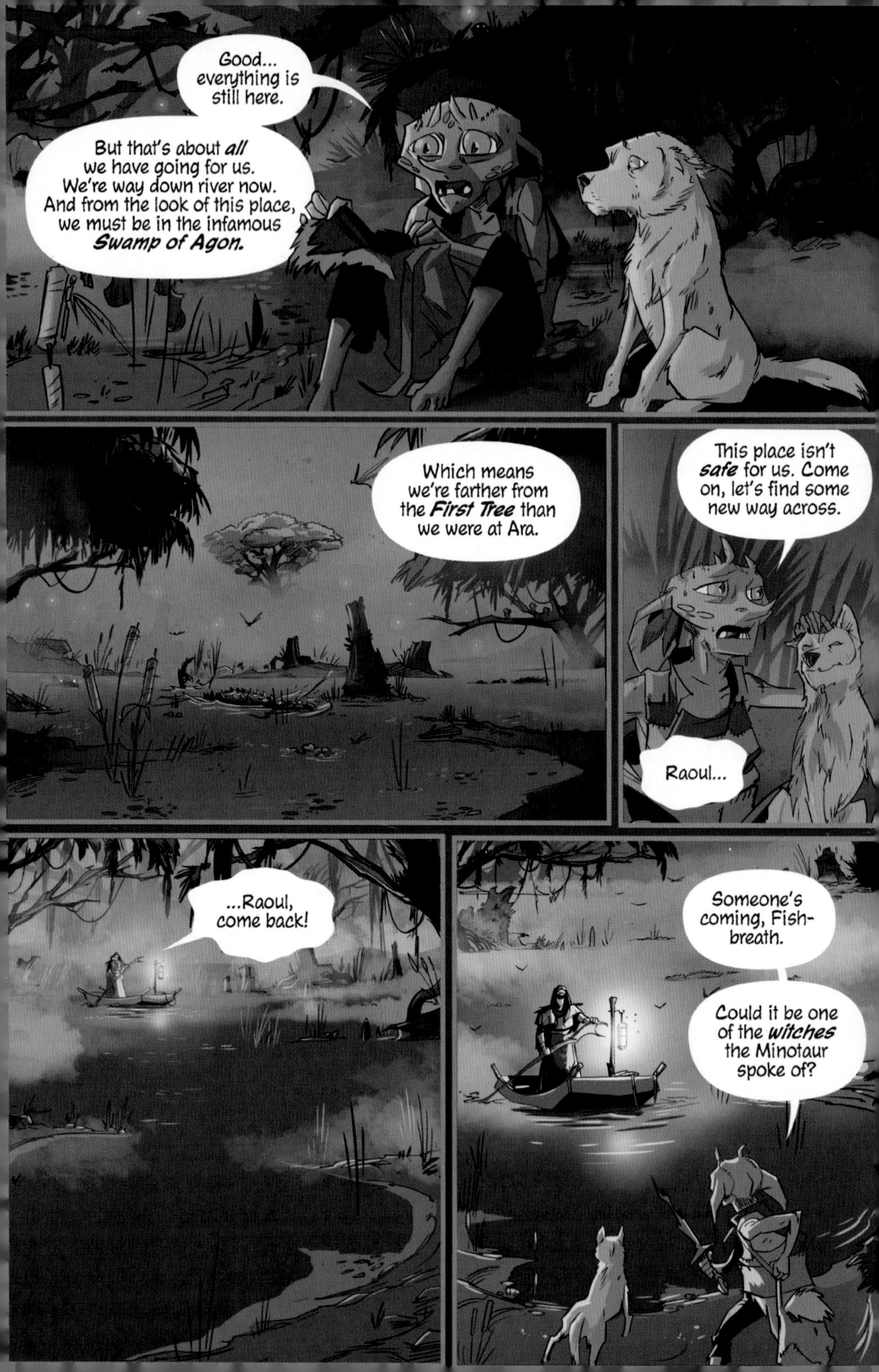
Good... everything is still here.
But that's about *all* we have going for us. We're way down river now. And from the look of this place, we must be in the infamous ***Swamp of Agon.***
Which means we're farther from the ***First Tree*** than we were at Ara.
This place isn't ***safe*** for us. Come on, let's find some new way across.
Raoul...
...Raoul, come back!
Someone's coming, Fish-breath.
Could it be one of the ***witches*** the Minotaur spoke of?

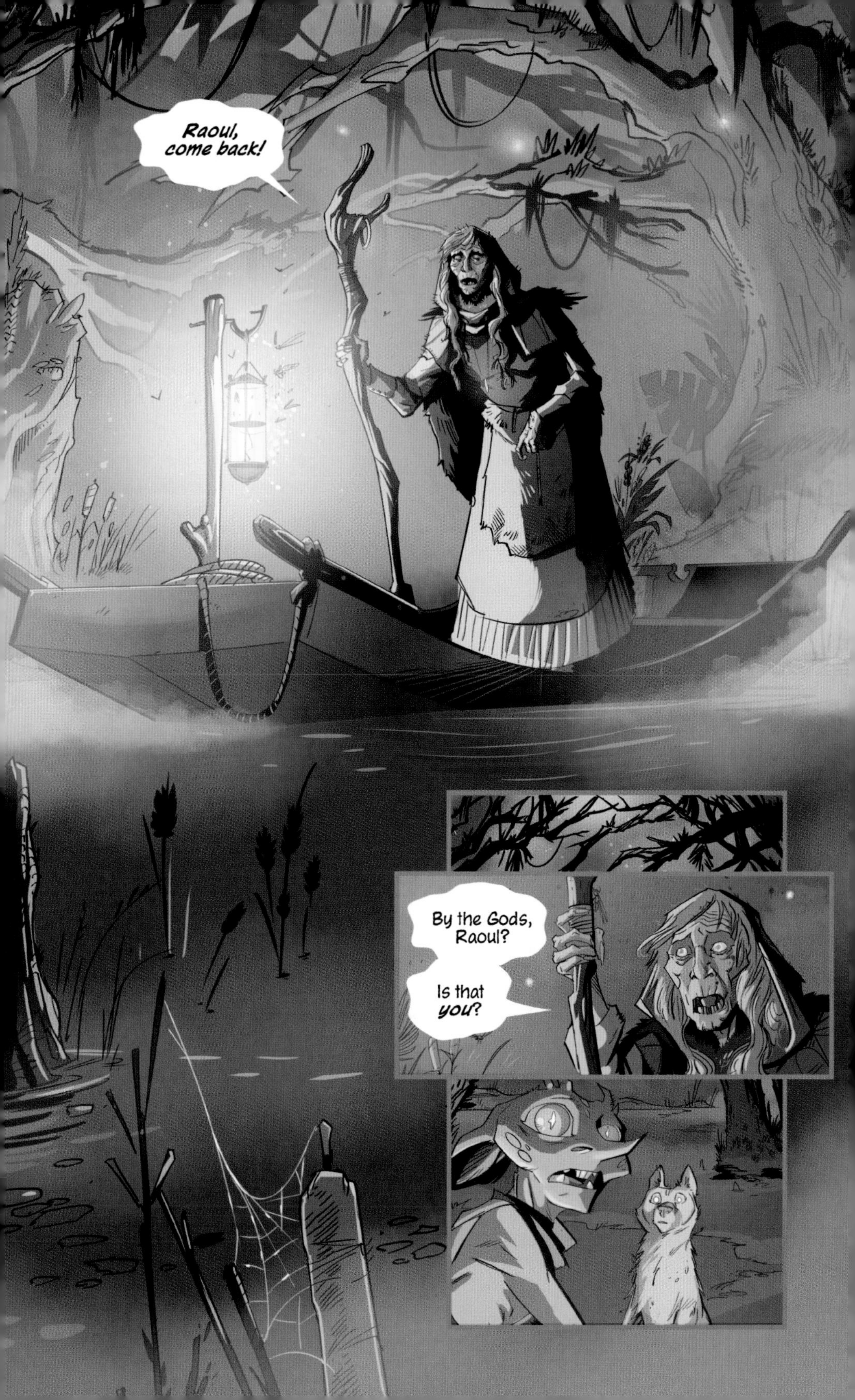
Raoul, come back!
By the Gods, Raoul?
Is that you?

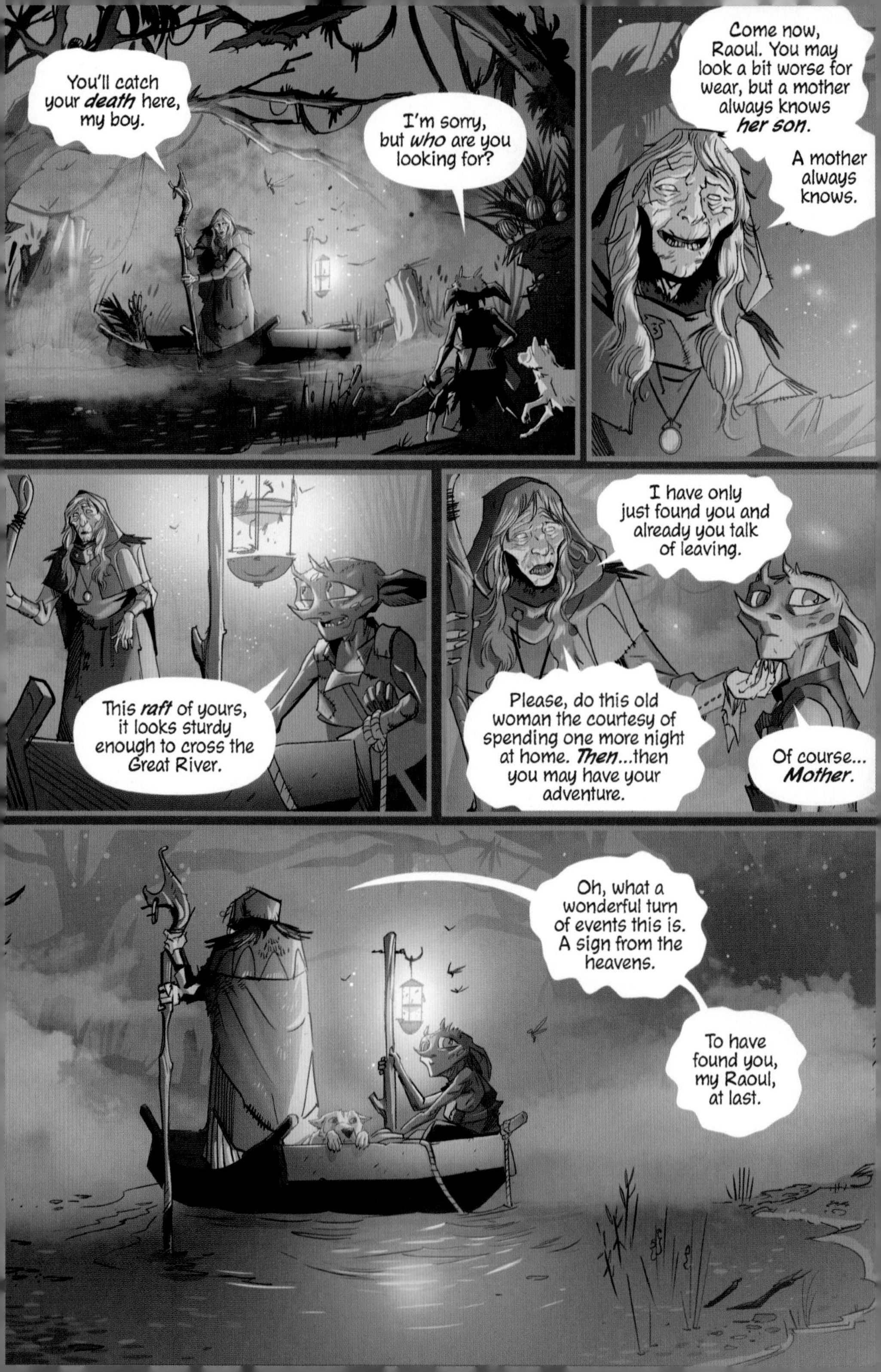
You'll catch your *death* here, my boy.
I'm sorry, but *who* are you looking for?
Come now, Raoul. You may look a bit worse for wear, but a mother always knows ***her son***.
A mother always knows.
This *raft* of yours, it looks sturdy enough to cross the Great River.
I have only just found you and already you talk of leaving.
Please, do this old woman the courtesy of spending one more night at home. ***Then***...then you may have your adventure.
Of course... ***Mother***.
Oh, what a wonderful turn of events this is. A sign from the heavens.
To have found you, my Raoul, at last.

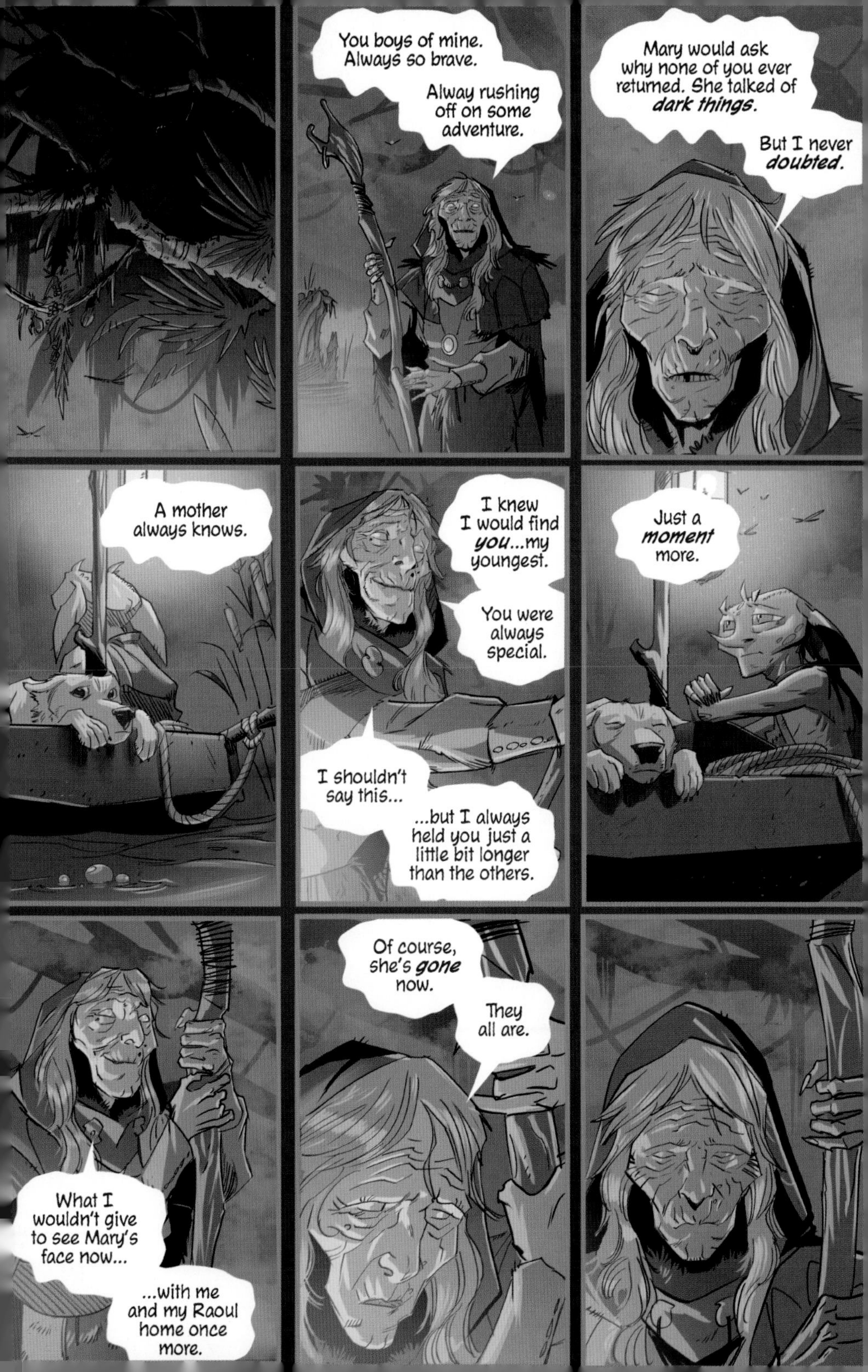
You boys of mine. Always so brave.
Alway rushing off on some adventure.
Mary would ask why none of you ever returned. She talked of *dark things*.
But I never *doubted.*
A mother always knows.
I knew I would find *you*...my youngest.
You were always special.
I shouldn't say this...
...but I always held you just a little bit longer than the others.
Just a *moment* more.
What I wouldn't give to see Mary's face now...
...with me and my Raoul home once more.
Of course, she's *gone* now.
They all are.

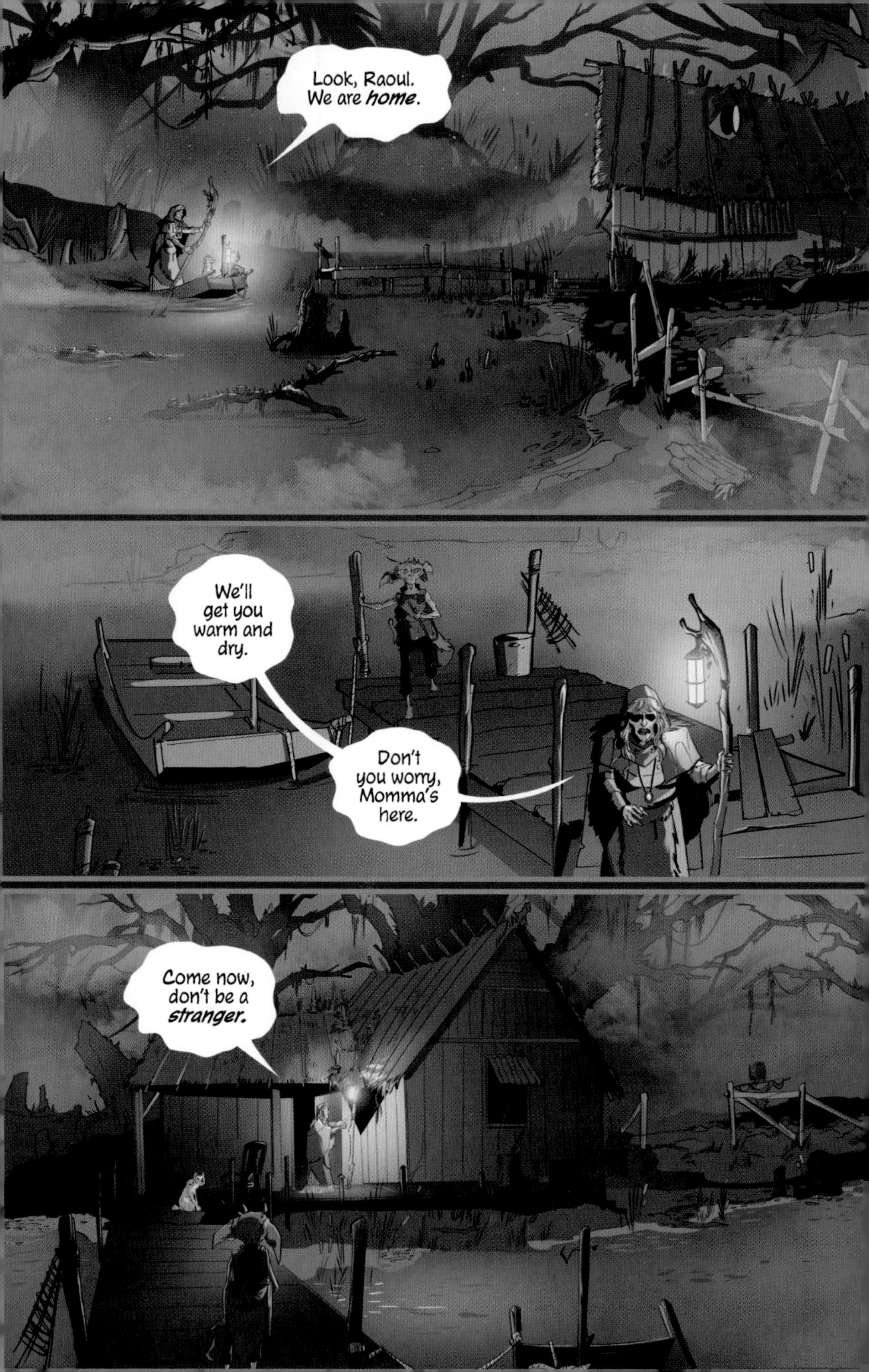

Look, Raoul. We are *home*.
We'll get you warm and dry.
Don't you worry, Momma's here.
Come now, don't be a *stranger.*

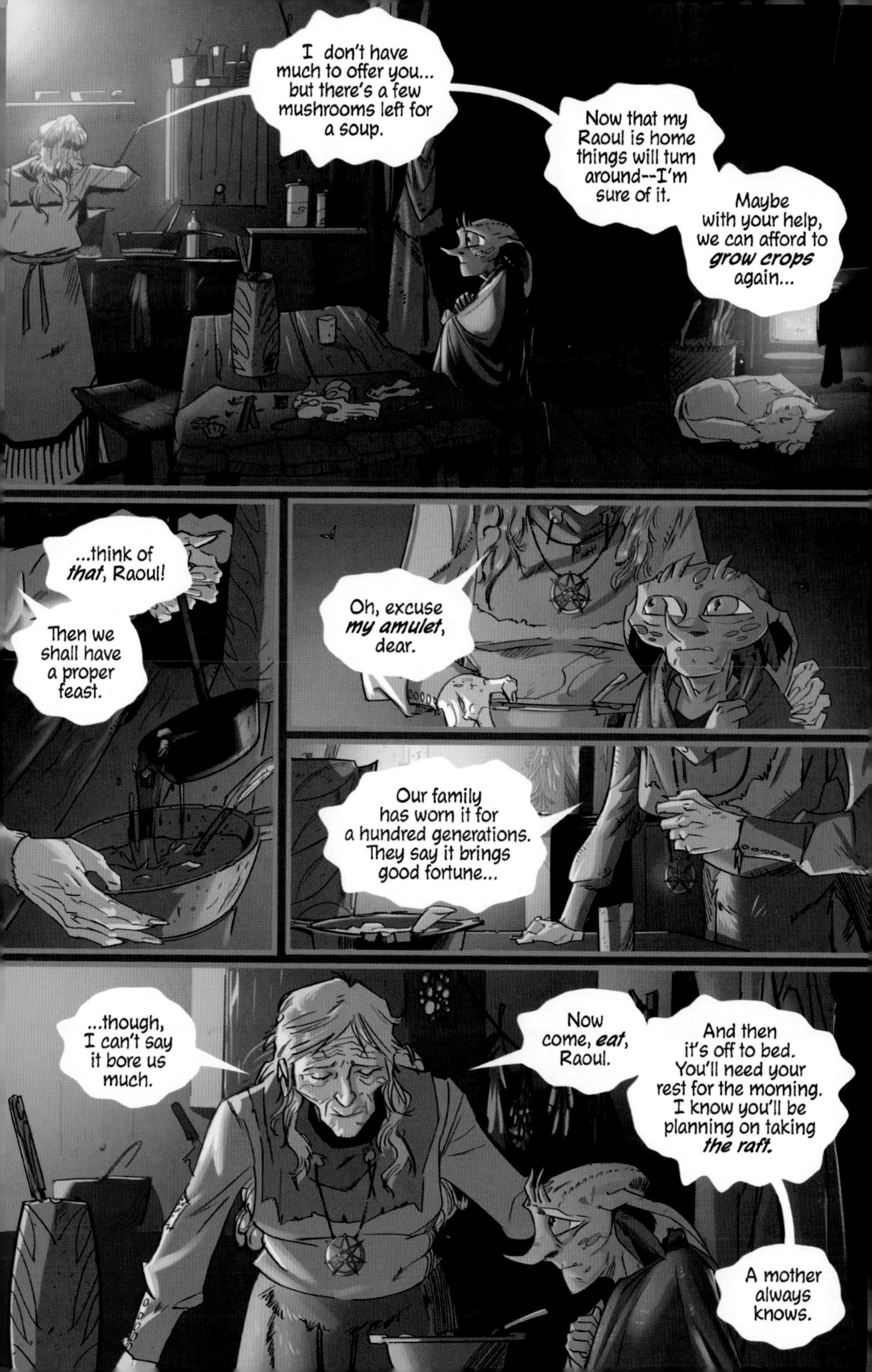
I don't have much to offer you... but there's a few mushrooms left for a soup.
Now that my Raoul is home things will turn around--I'm sure of it.
Maybe with your help, we can afford to *grow crops* again...
...think of *that*, Raoul!
Then we shall have a proper feast.
Oh, excuse *my amulet*, dear.
Our family has worn it for a hundred generations. They say it brings good fortune...
...though, I can't say it bore us much.
Now come, *eat*, Raoul.
And then it's off to bed. You'll need your rest for the morning. I know you'll be planning on taking *the raft.*
A mother always knows.

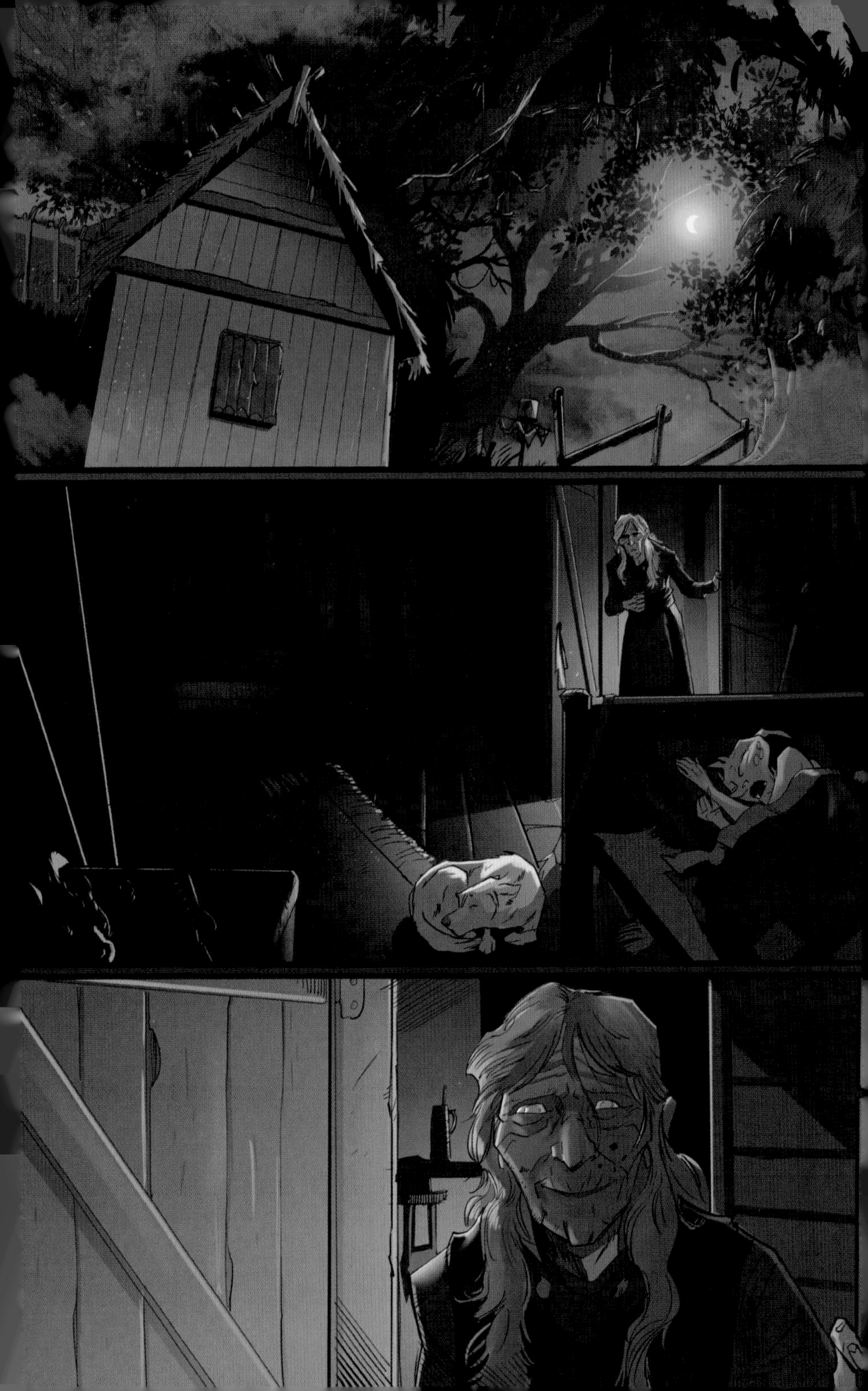

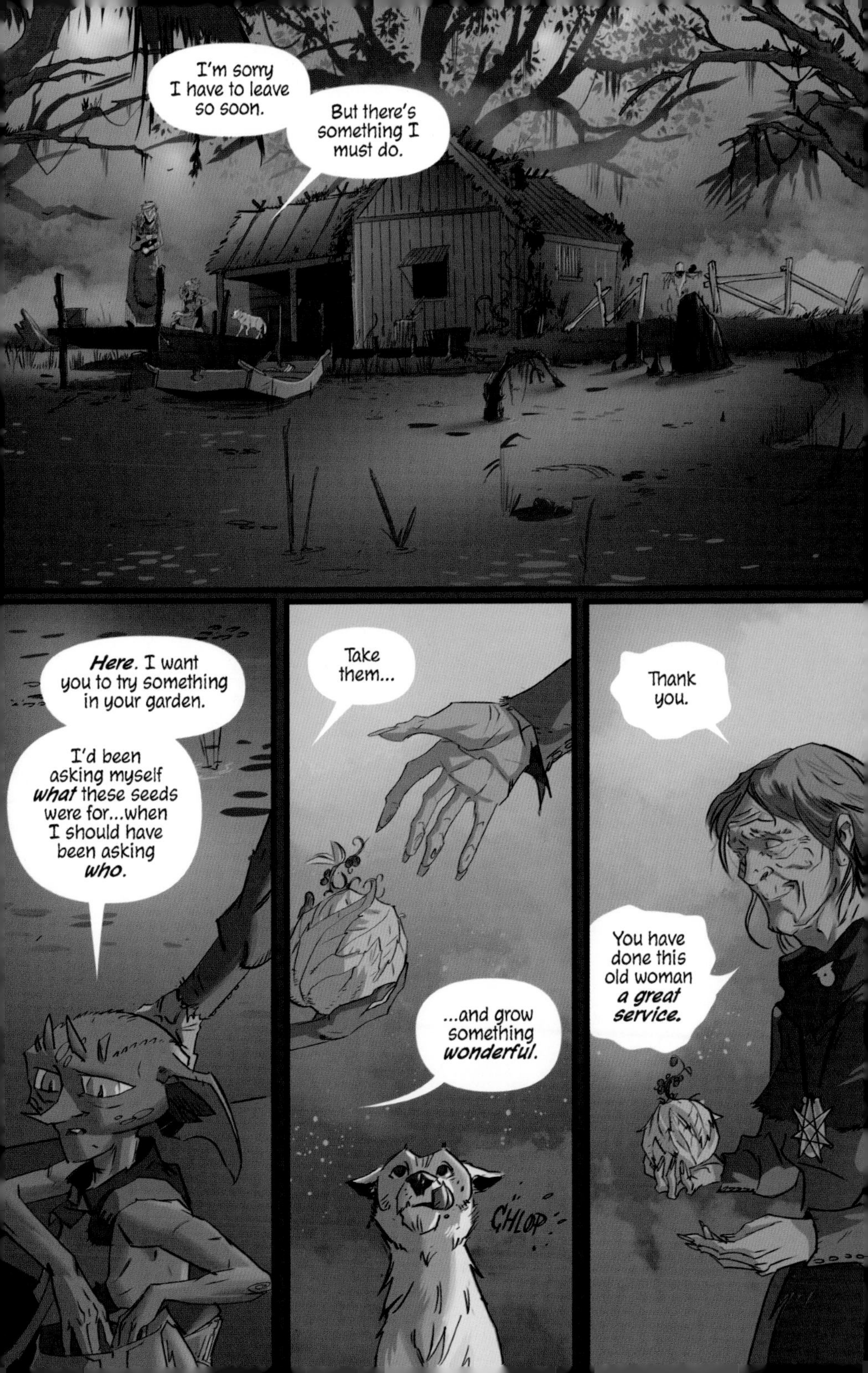
I'm sorry I have to leave so soon.
But there's something I must do.
Here. I want you to try something in your garden.
I'd been asking myself ***what*** these seeds were for...when I should have been asking ***who***.
Take them...
...and grow something ***wonderful***.
CHLOP
Thank you.
You have done this old woman ***a great service.***

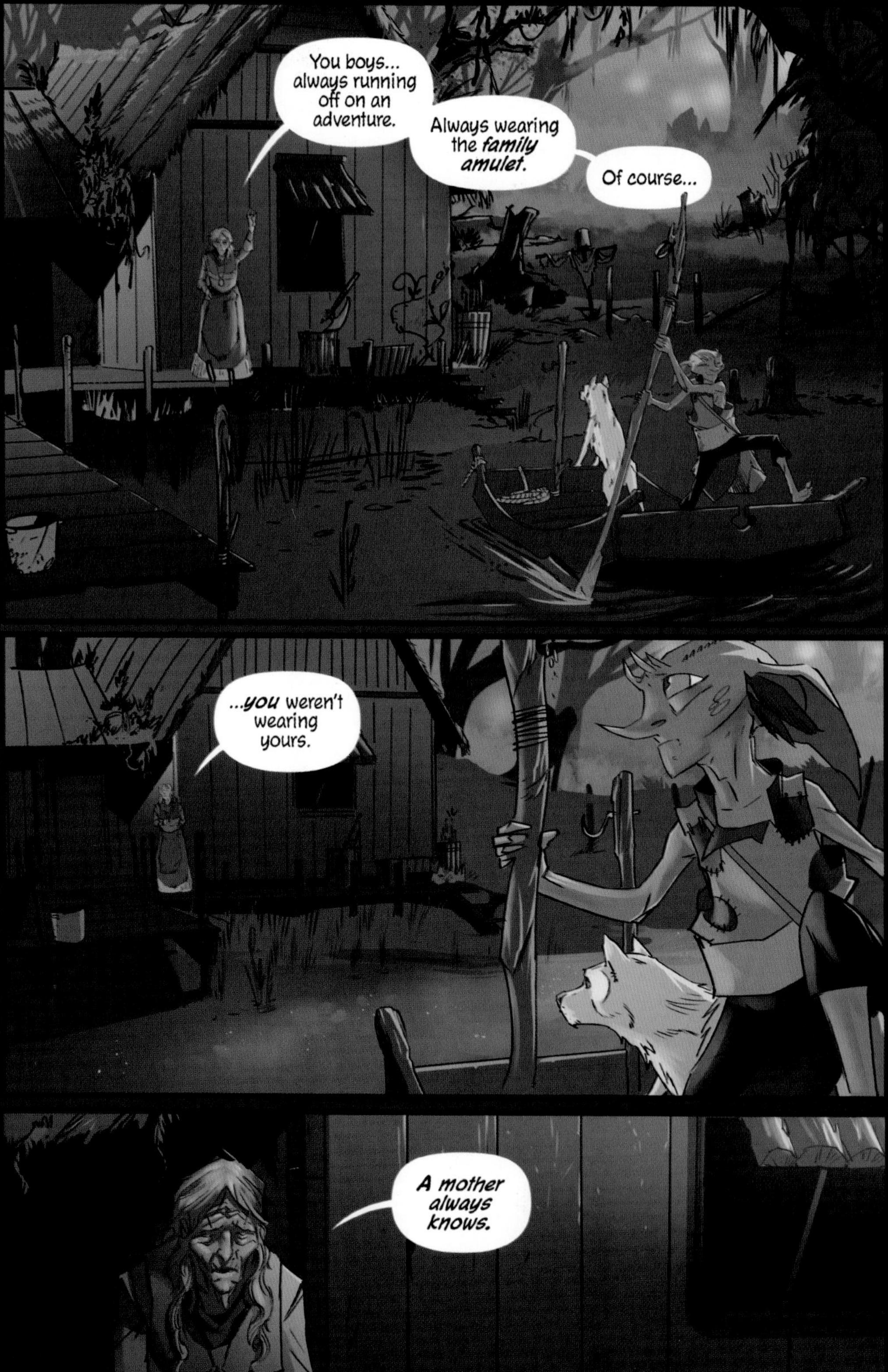
You boys... always running off on an adventure.
Always wearing the *family amulet*.
Of course...
...*you* weren't wearing yours.
A mother always knows.

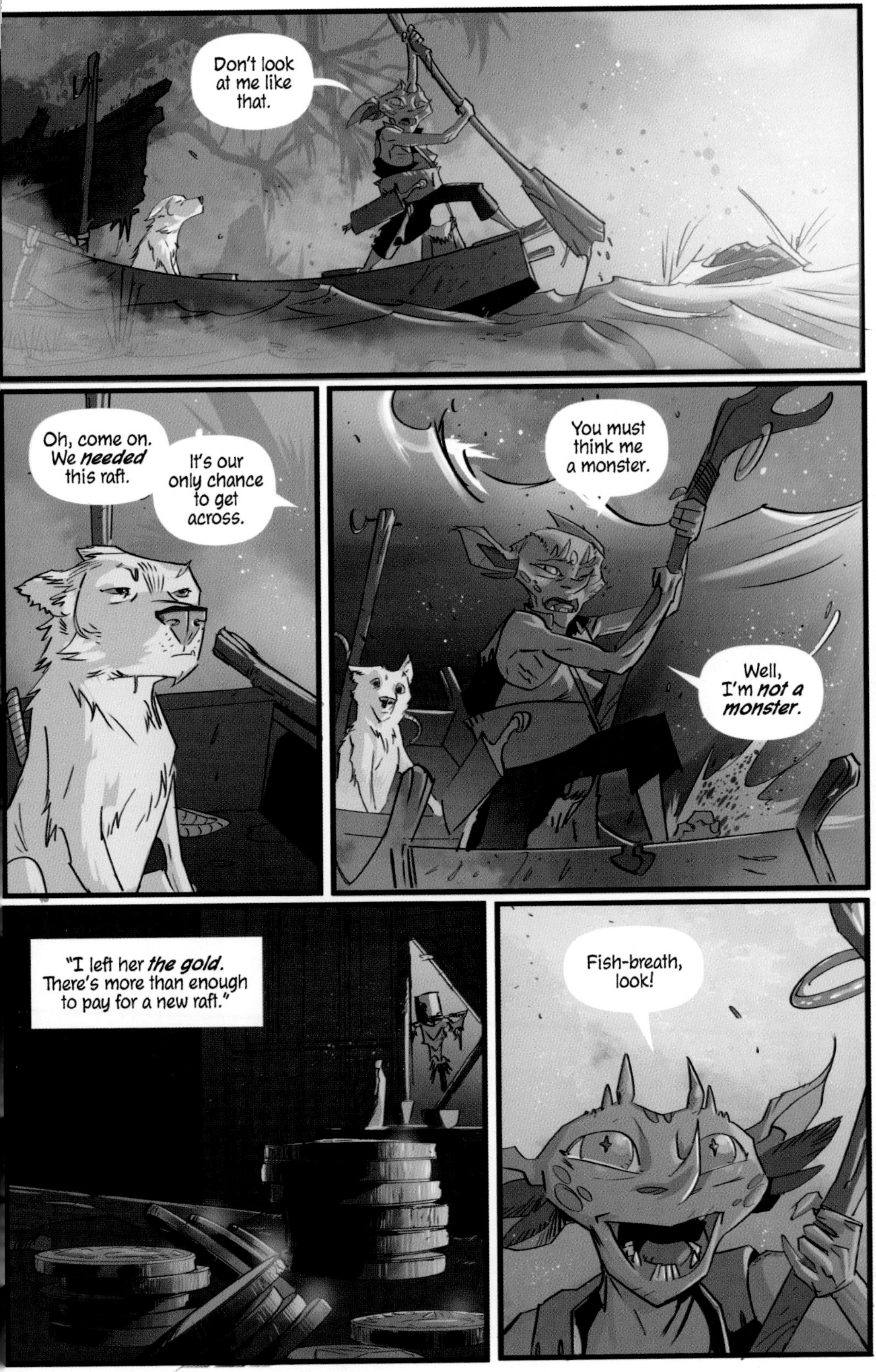
Don't look at me like that.
Oh, come on. We ***needed*** this raft.
It's our only chance to get across.
You must think me a monster.
Well, I'm ***not a monster***.
"I left her ***the gold***. There's more than enough to pay for a new raft."
Fish-breath, look!

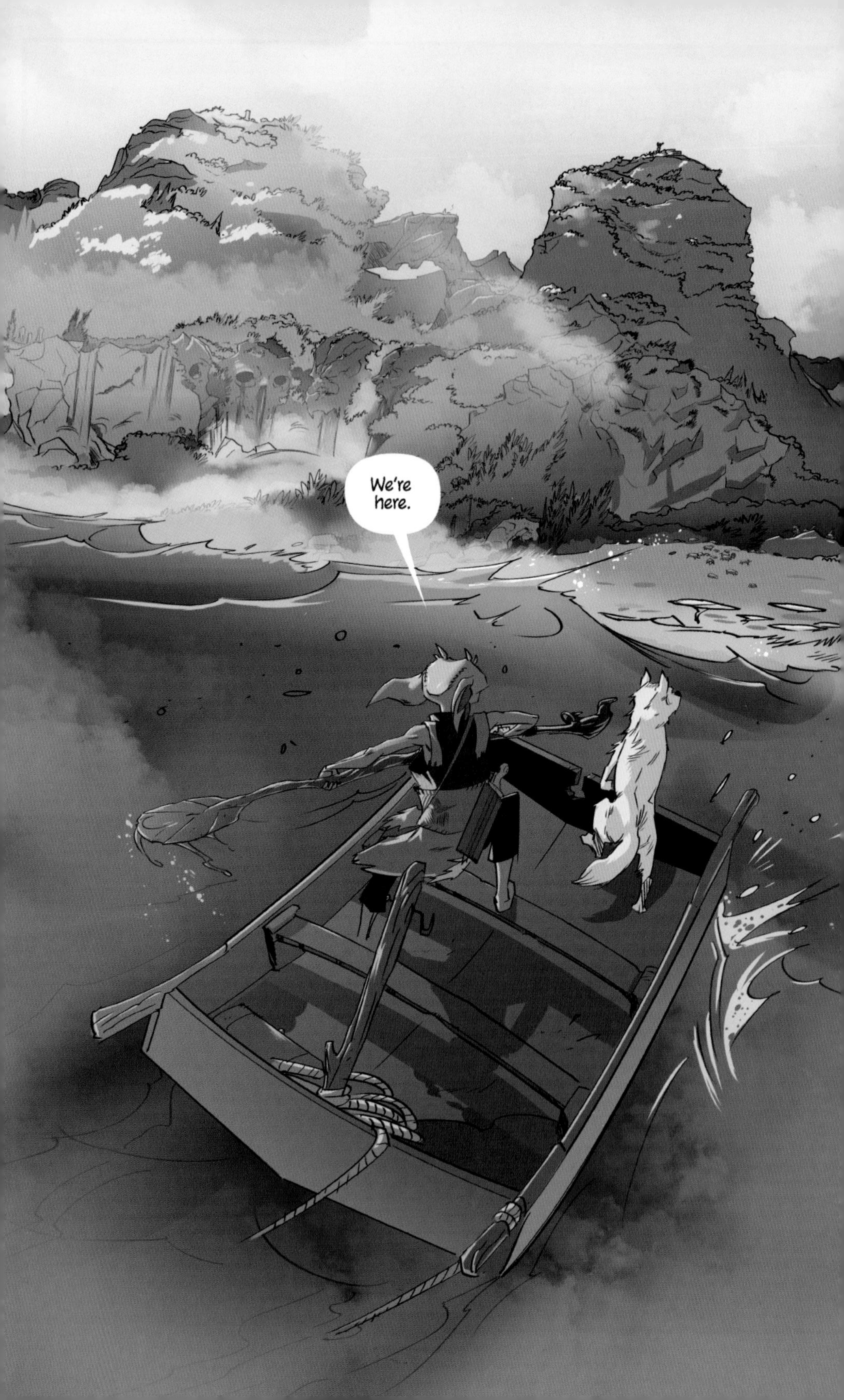
We're here.

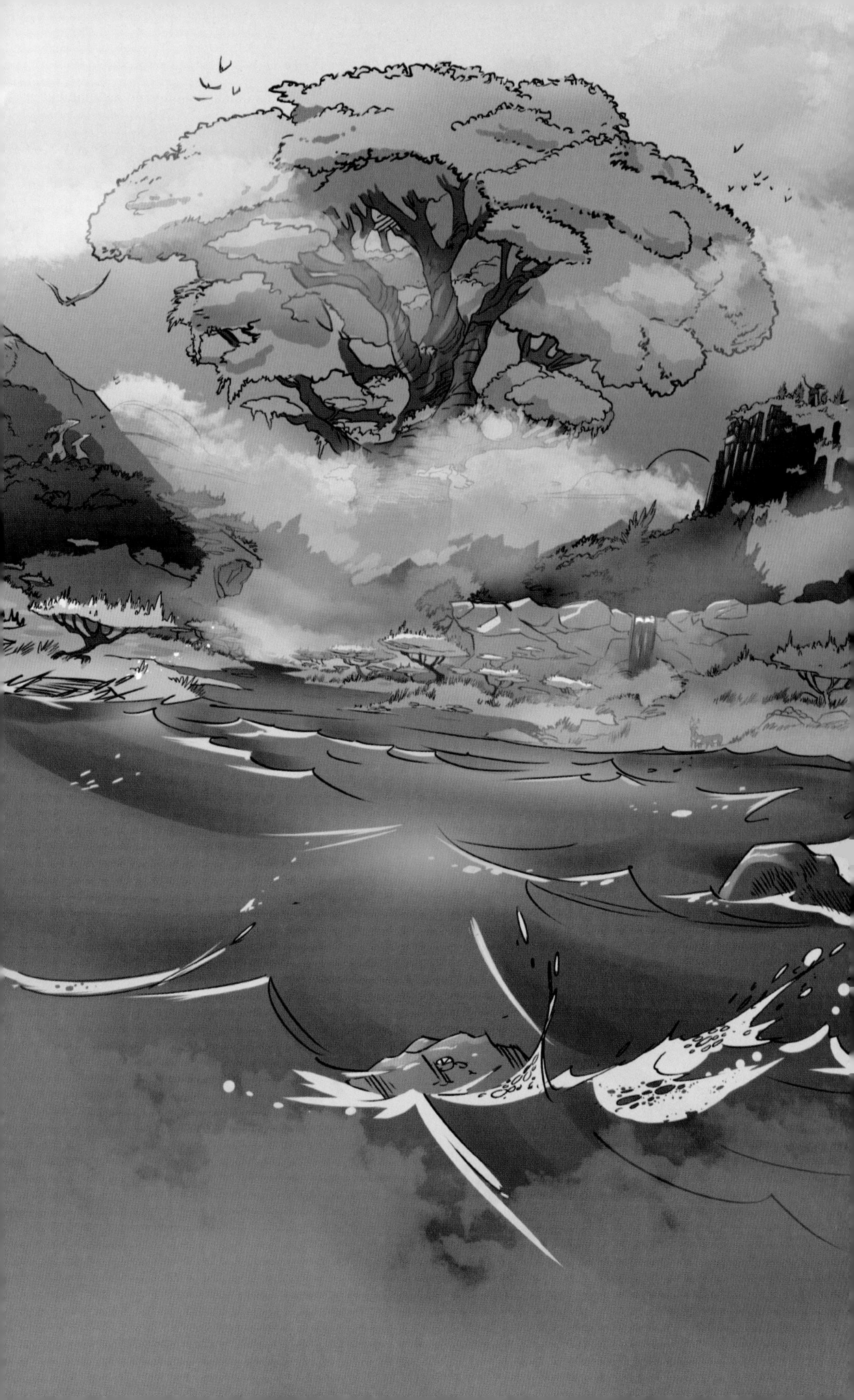

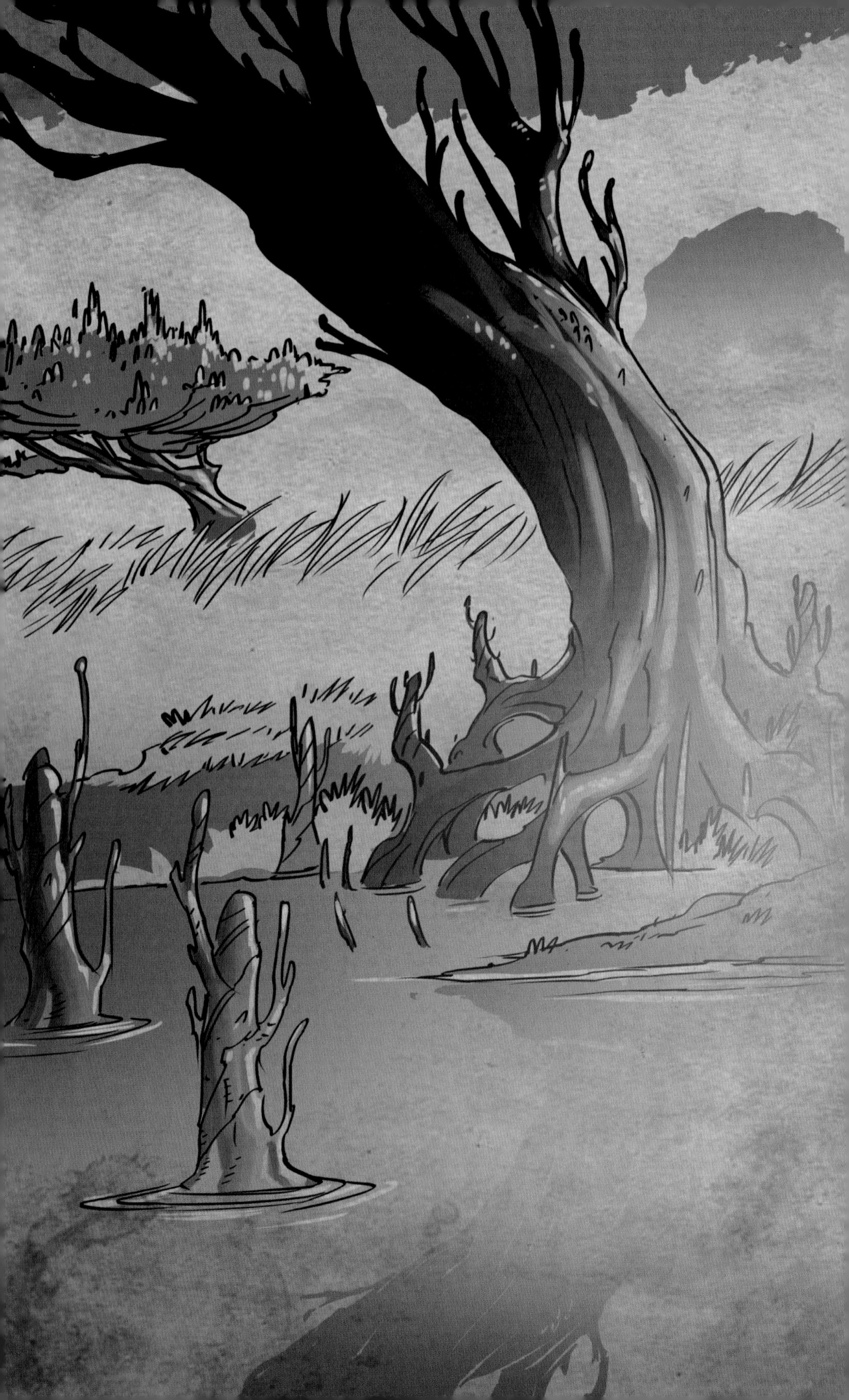

CHAPTER EIGHT
THE TRIAL OF THE GOBLIN

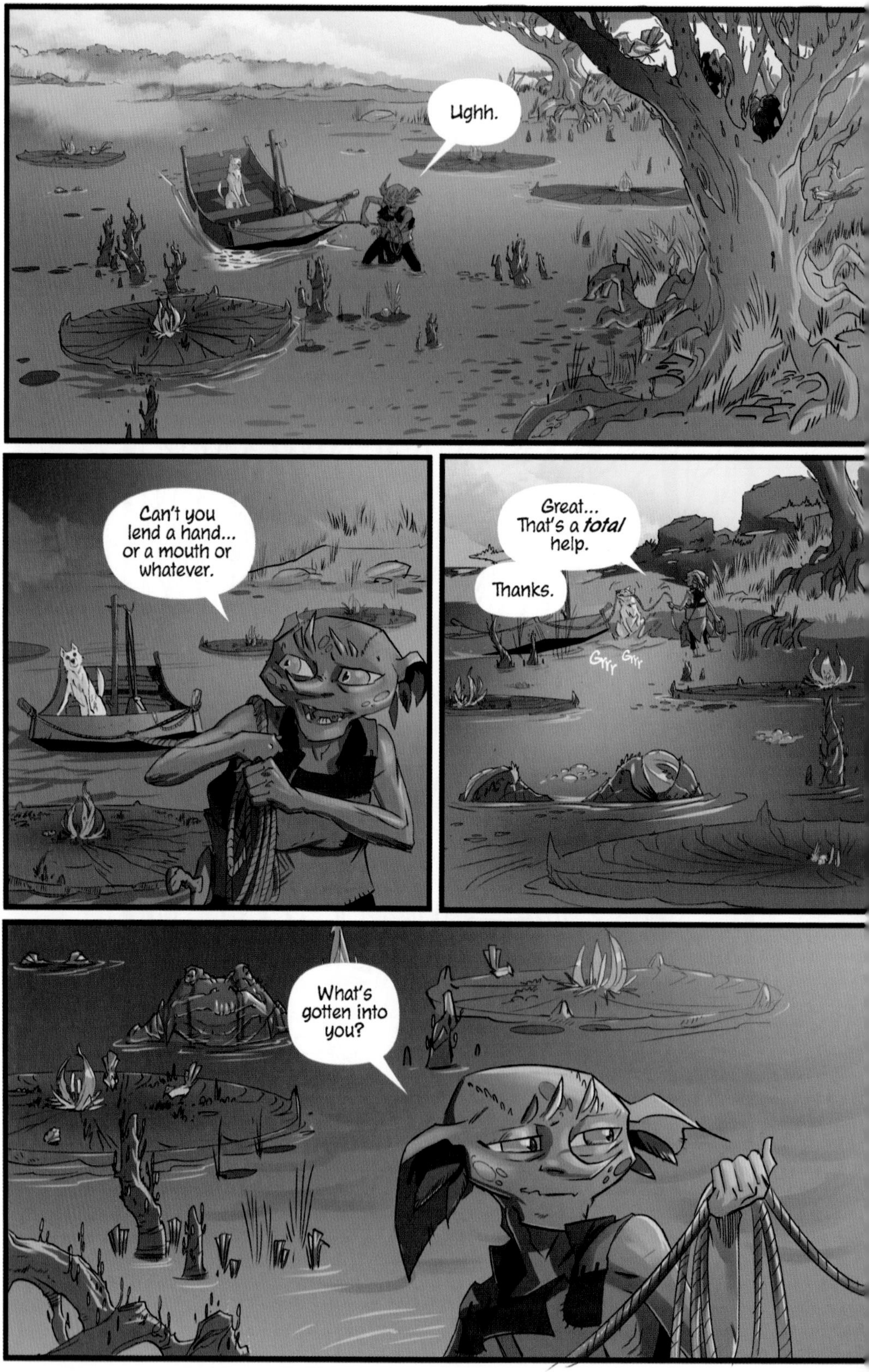
Ughh.
Can't you lend a hand... or a mouth or whatever.
Great... That's a *total* help.
Thanks.
Grrr Grrr
What's gotten into you?

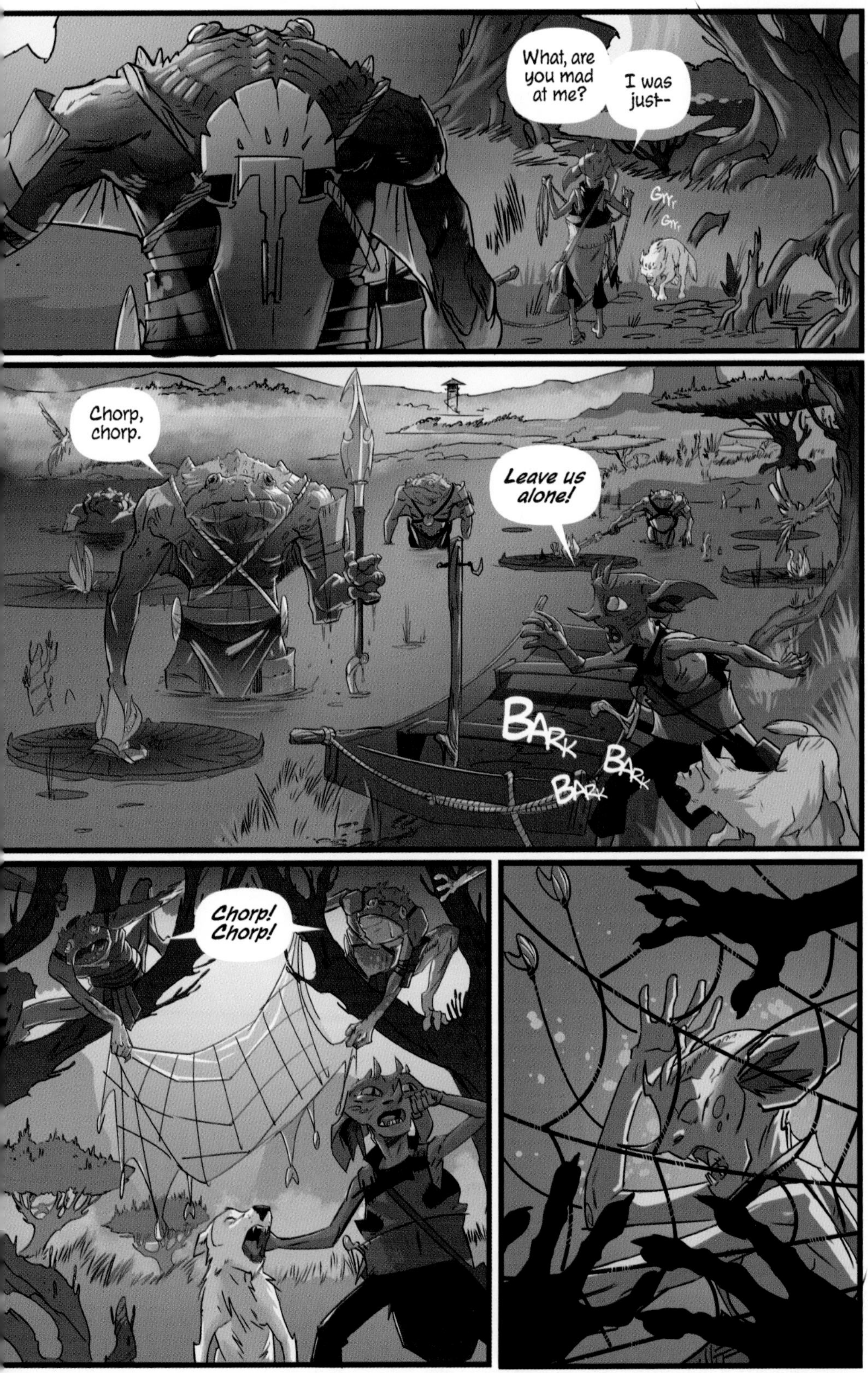
What, are you mad at me?
I was just-
Grrr
Grrr
Chorp, chorp.
Leave us alone!
BARK
BARK
BARK
Chorp! Chorp!

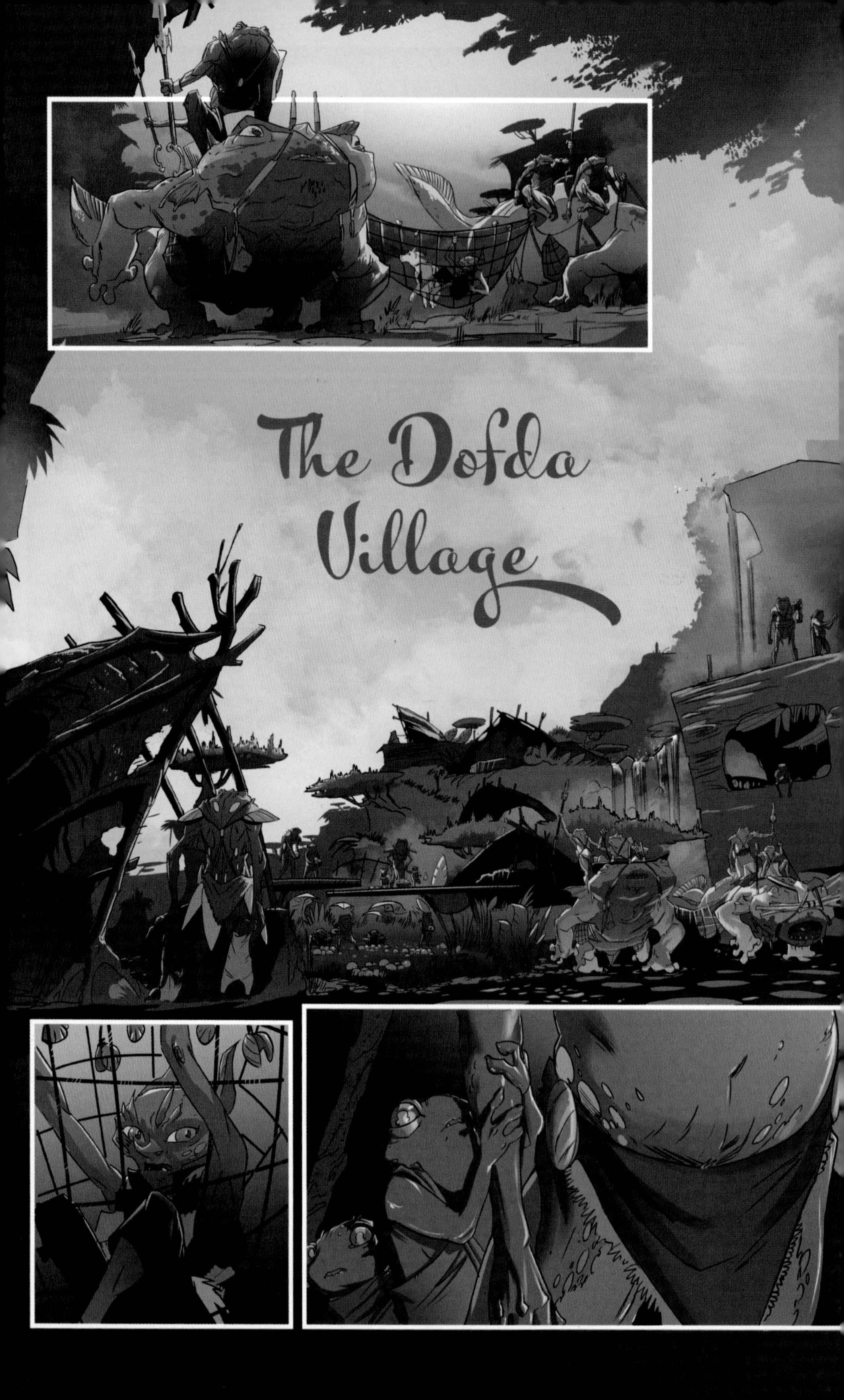
The Dofda Village

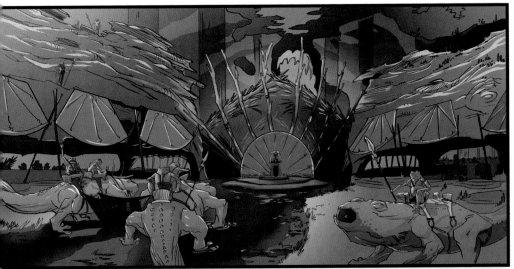

Chorp.

SNIP
SNIP
SNIP

I knew it, Fish-breath!

There must have been some kind of mis-understanding.

They're *freeing* us!

THUD

Whoa, take it easy! Would someone mind telling us what the heck it is that you want?

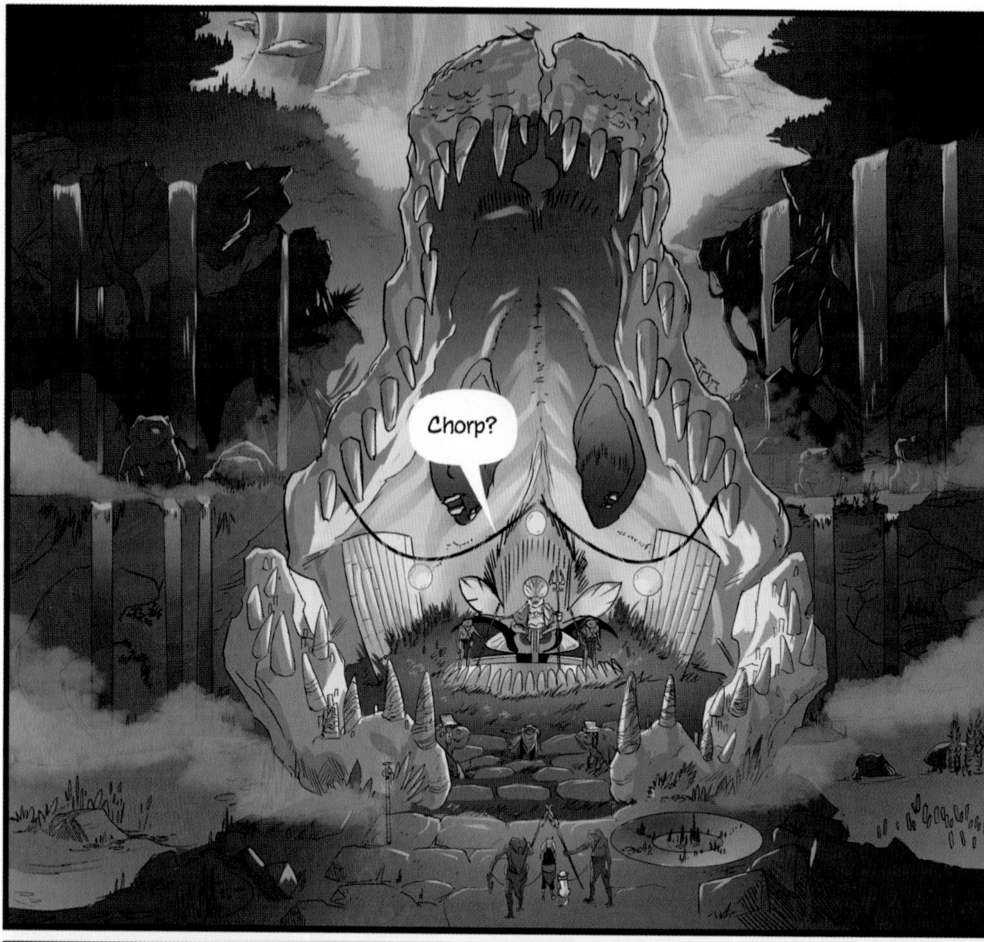
Chorp?

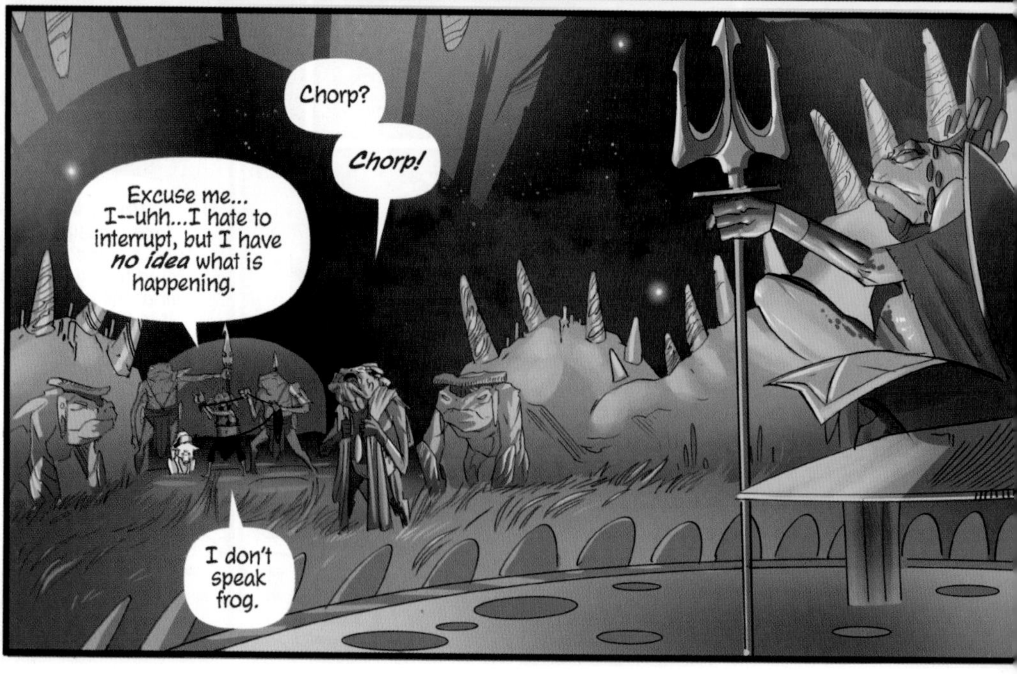
Chorp?
Chorp!
Excuse me... I--uhh...I hate to interrupt, but I have ***no idea*** what is happening.
I don't speak frog.

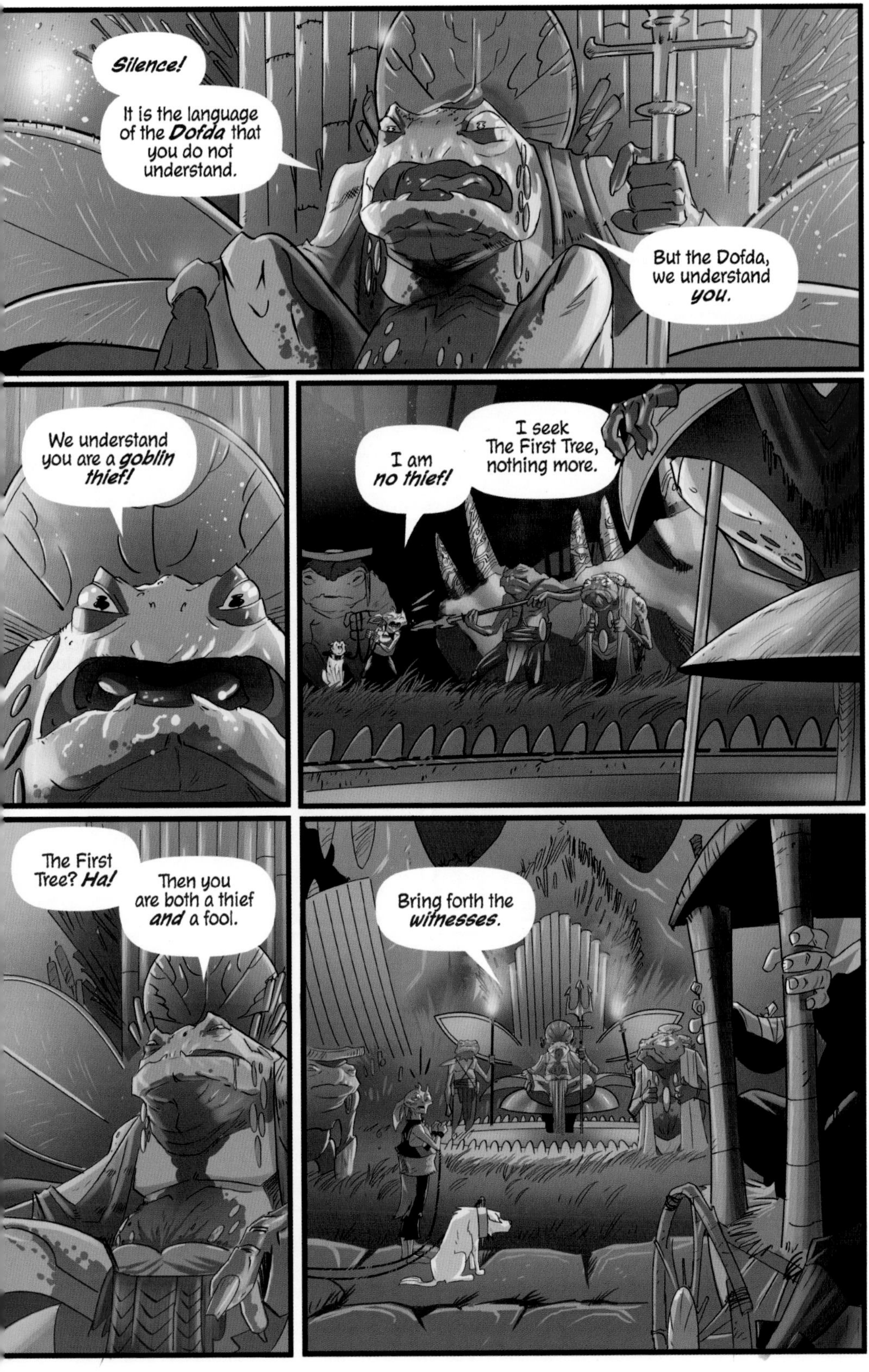

Silence!
It is the language of the Dofda that you do not understand.
But the Dofda, we understand you.
We understand you are a goblin thief!
I am no thief!
I seek The First Tree, nothing more.
The First Tree? Ha!
Then you are both a thief and a fool.
Bring forth the witnesses.

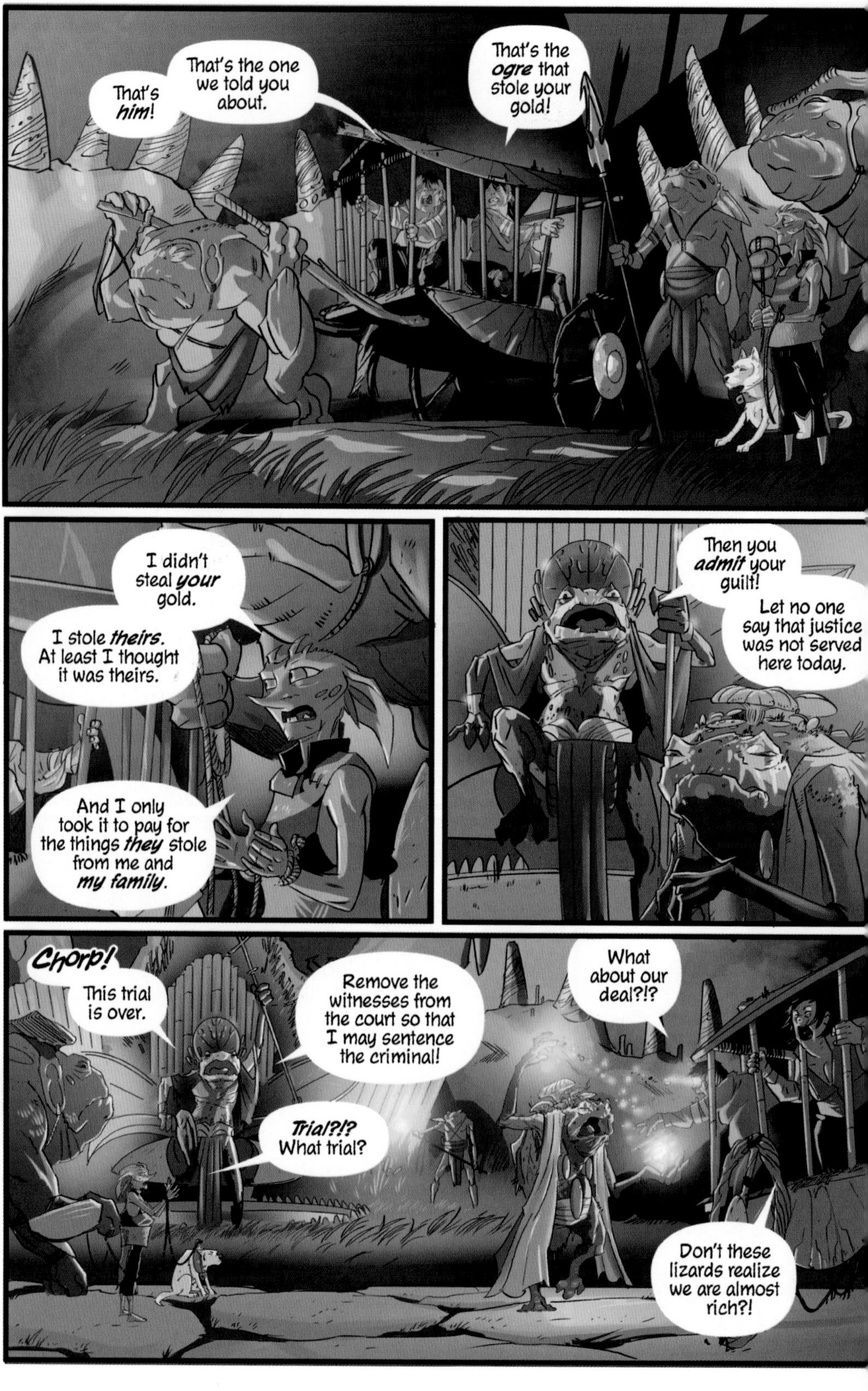
That's *him*!
That's the one we told you about.
That's the *ogre* that stole your gold!
I didn't steal *your* gold.
I stole *theirs.* At least I thought it was theirs.
And I only took it to pay for the things *they* stole from me and *my family*.
Then you *admit* your guilt!
Let no one say that justice was not served here today.
Chorp!
This trial is over.
Remove the witnesses from the court so that I may sentence the criminal!
Trial?!? What trial?
What about our deal?!?
Don't these lizards realize we are almost rich?!

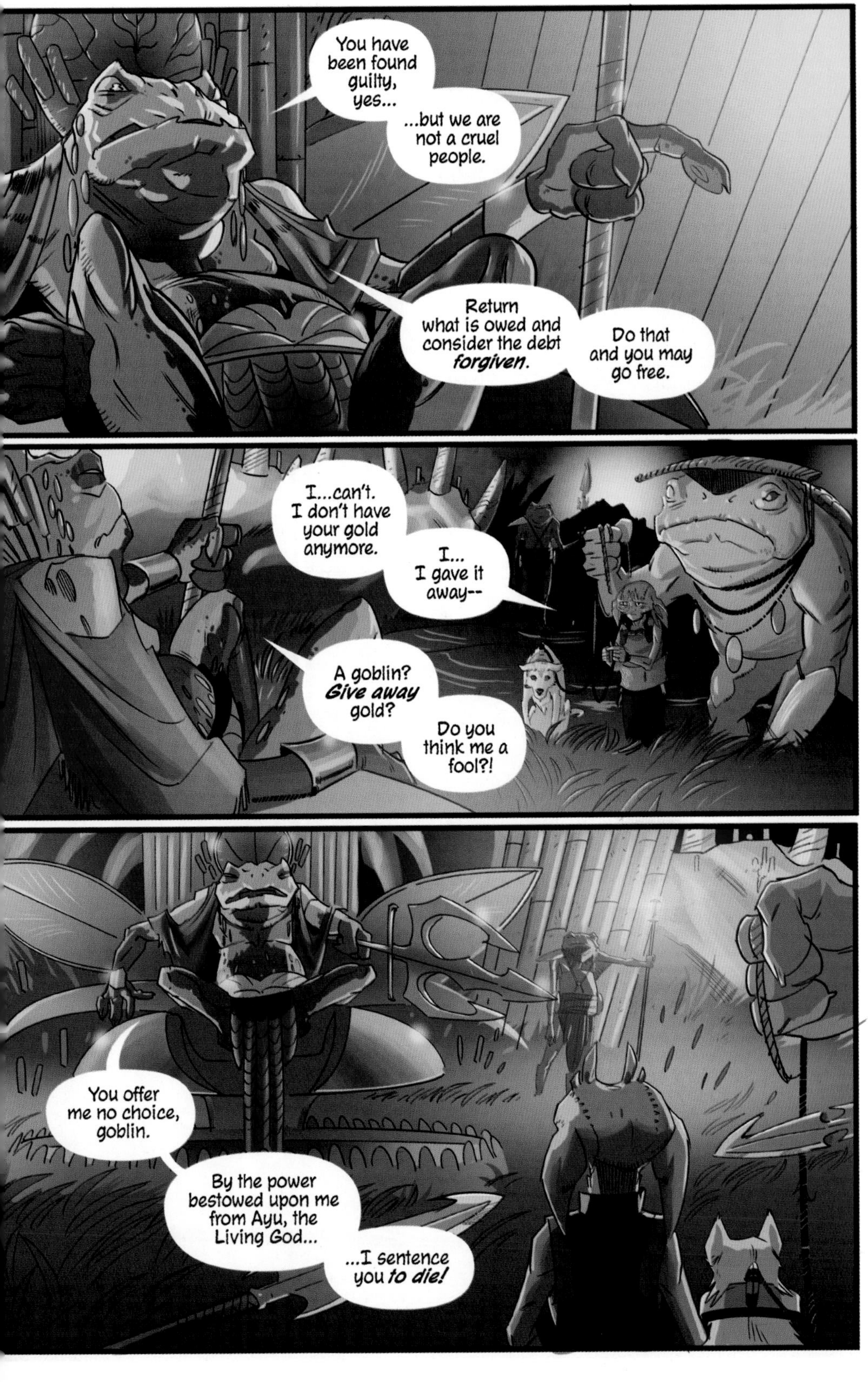
You have been found guilty, yes...
...but we are not a cruel people.
Return what is owed and consider the debt *forgiven*.
Do that and you may go free.
I...can't. I don't have your gold anymore.
I... I gave it away--
A goblin? *Give away* gold?
Do you think me a fool?!
You offer me no choice, goblin.
By the power bestowed upon me from Ayu, the Living God...
...I sentence you *to die!*

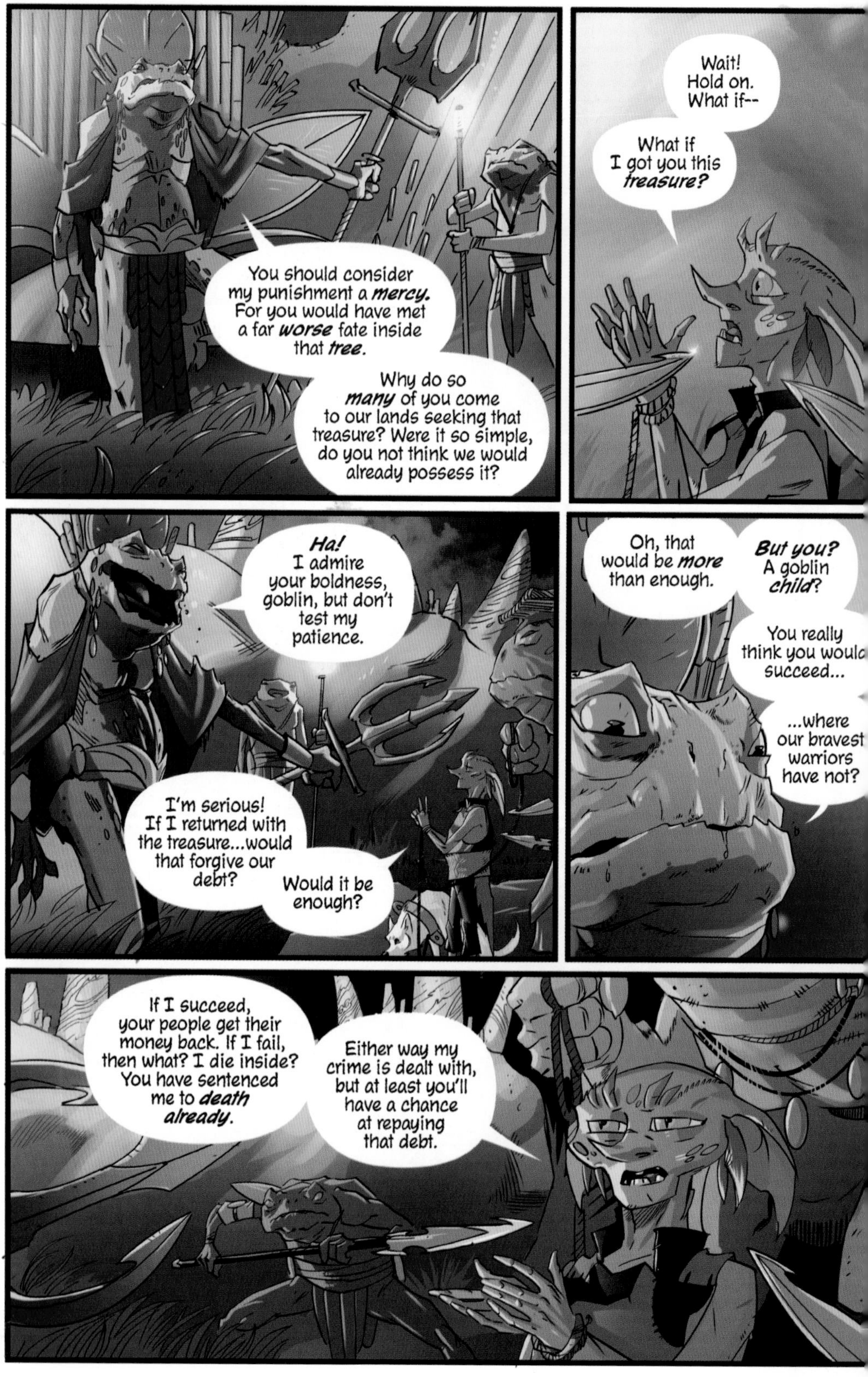
You should consider my punishment a *mercy.* For you would have met a far *worse* fate inside that *tree*.
Why do so *many* of you come to our lands seeking that treasure? Were it so simple, do you not think we would already possess it?
Wait! Hold on. What if--
What if I got you this *treasure?*
Ha! I admire your boldness, goblin, but don't test my patience.
I'm serious! If I returned with the treasure...would that forgive our debt?
Would it be enough?
Oh, that would be *more* than enough.
But you? A goblin *child*?
You really think you would succeed...
...where our bravest warriors have not?
If I succeed, your people get their money back. If I fail, then what? I die inside? You have sentenced me to *death already*.
Either way my crime is dealt with, but at least you'll have a chance at repaying that debt.

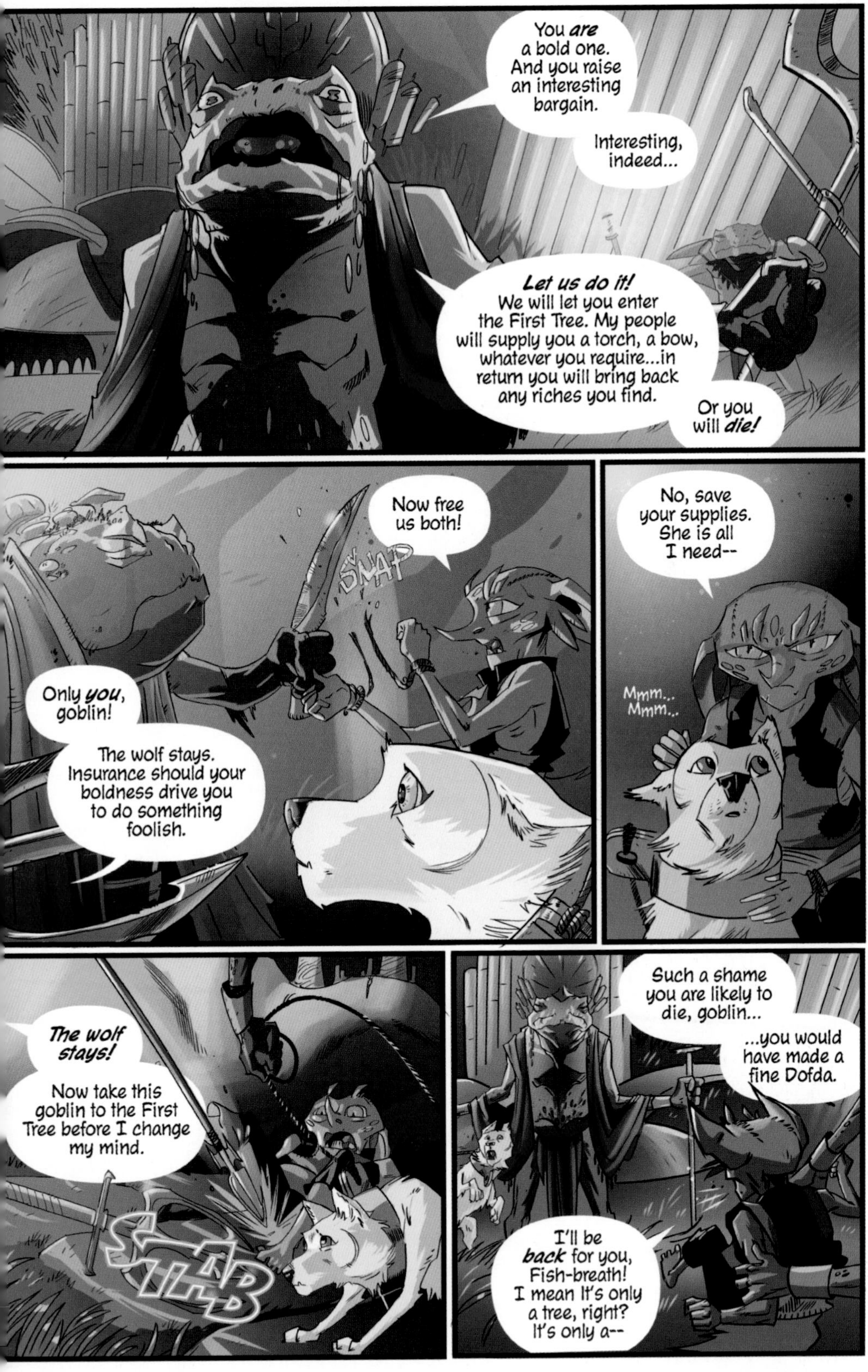
You *are* a bold one. And you raise an interesting bargain.
Interesting, indeed...
Let us do it! We will let you enter the First Tree. My people will supply you a torch, a bow, whatever you require...in return you will bring back any riches you find.
Or you will *die!*
Now free us both!
SNAP
Only *you*, goblin!
The wolf stays. Insurance should your boldness drive you to do something foolish.
No, save your supplies. She is all I need--
Mmm... Mmm...
The wolf stays!
Now take this goblin to the First Tree before I change my mind.
STAB
Such a shame you are likely to die, goblin...
...you would have made a fine Dofda.
I'll be *back* for you, Fish-breath! I mean It's only a tree, right? It's only a--

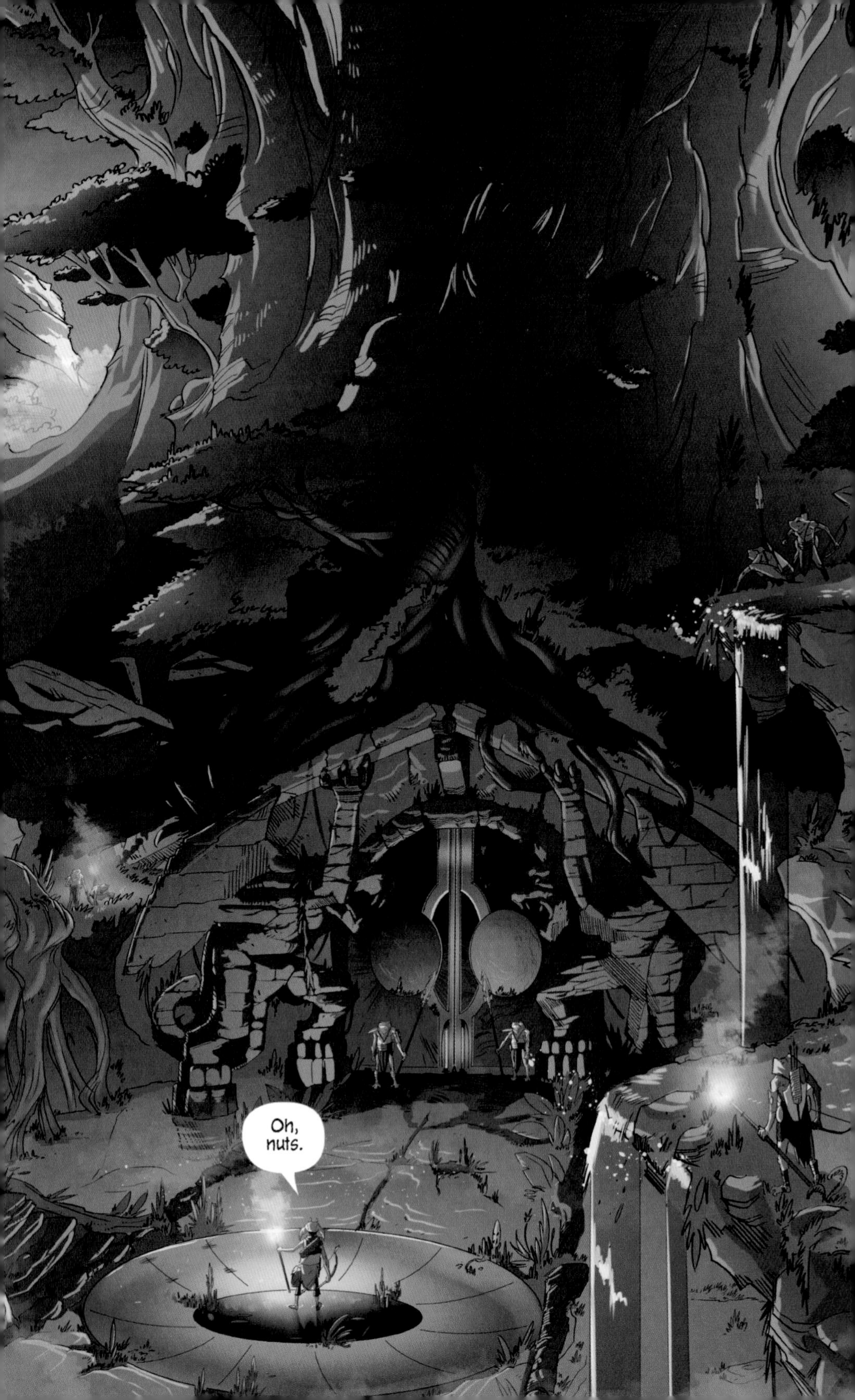
Oh, nuts.

CHAPTER NINE
THE UNDYING DEAD

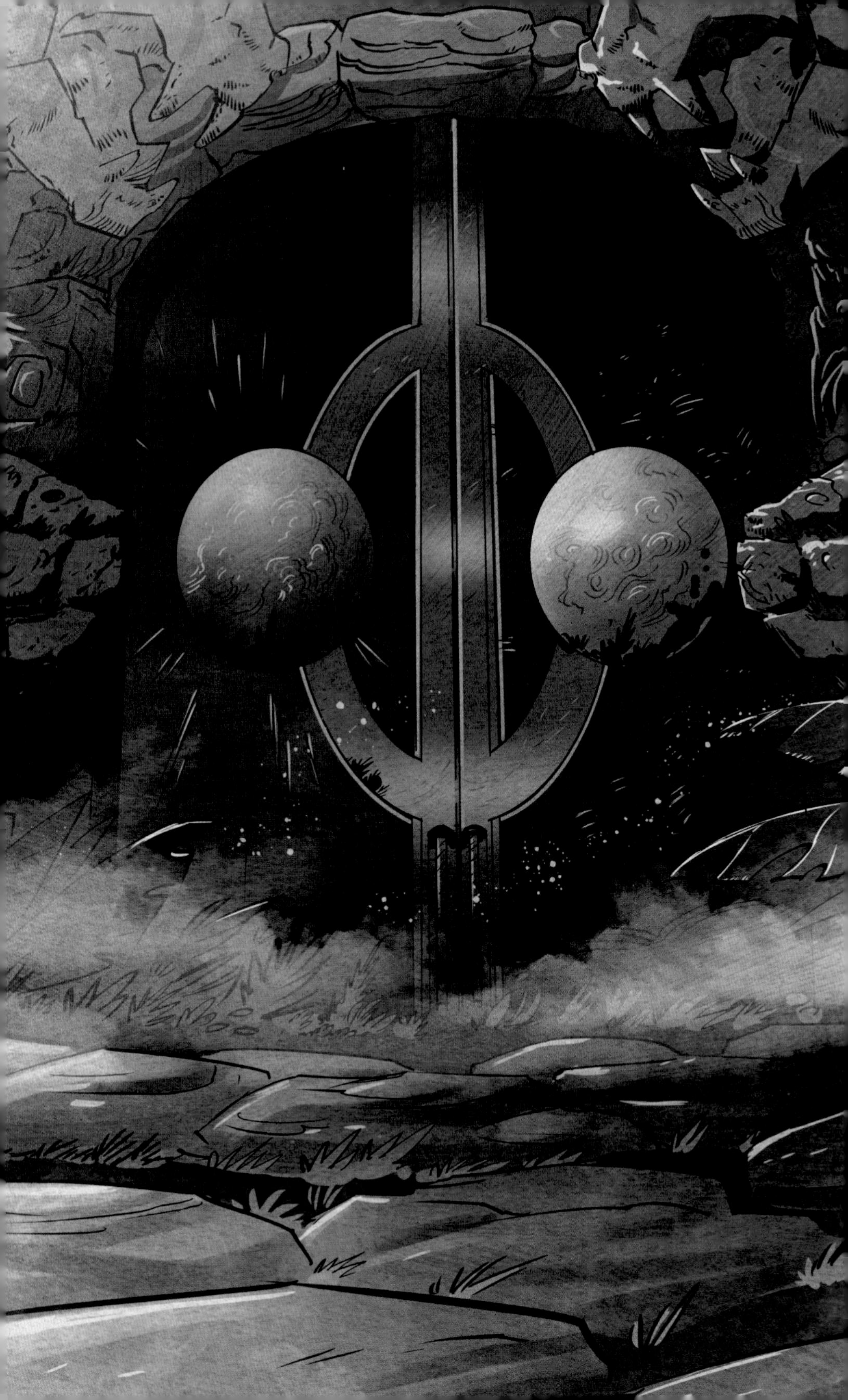

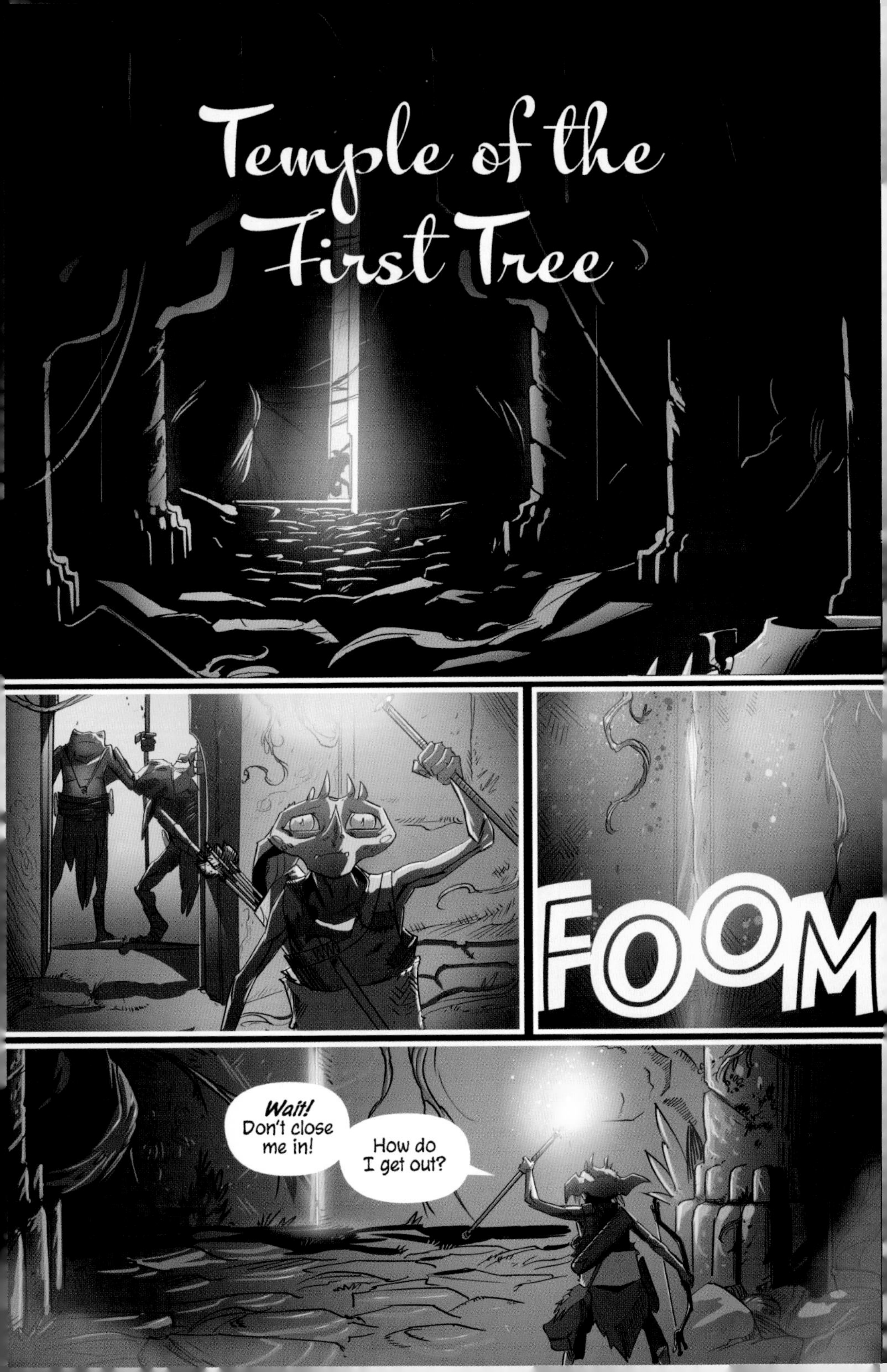
Temple of the First Tree
FOOM
Wait! Don't close me in!
How do I get out?

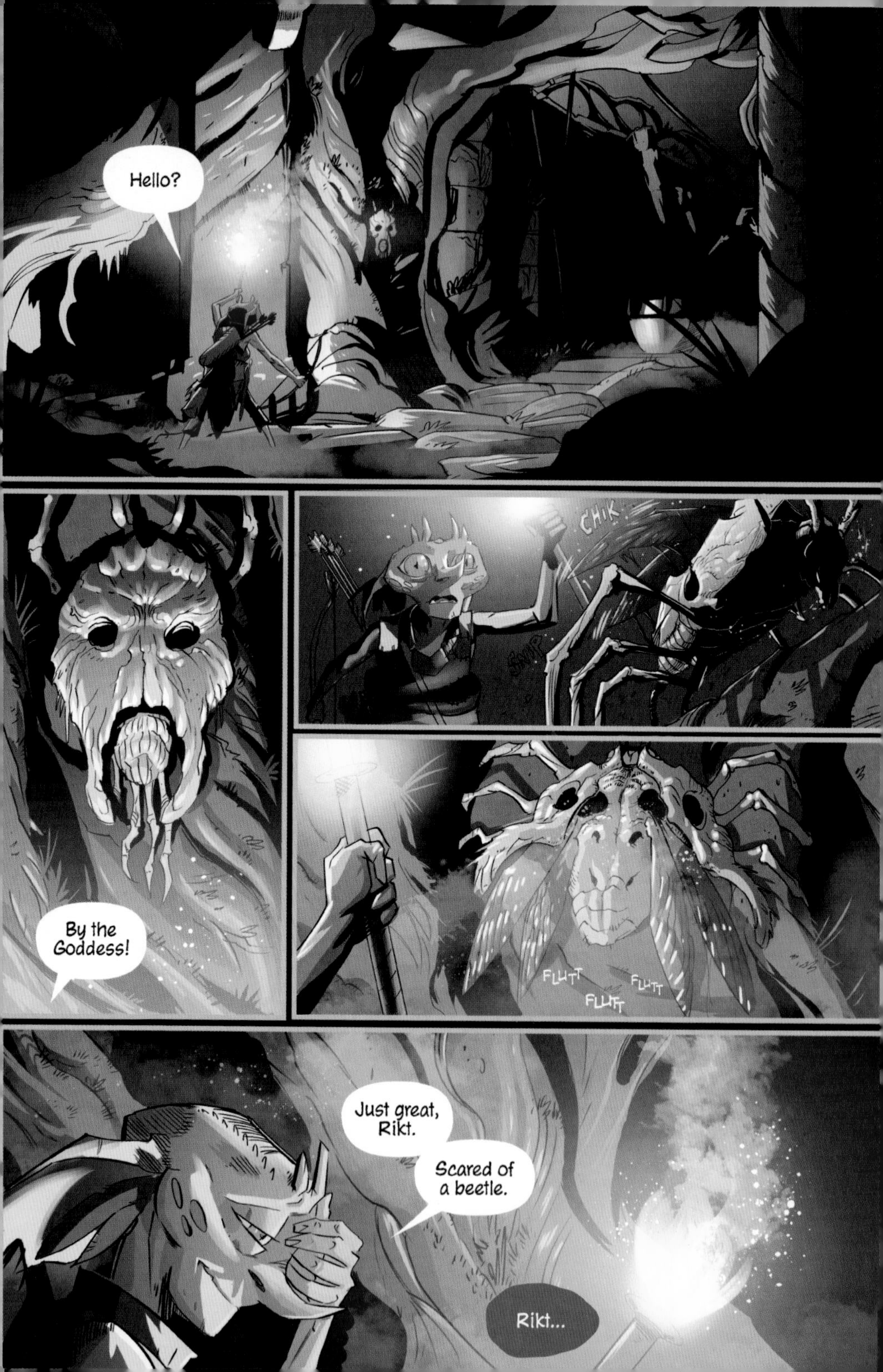
Hello?
By the Goddess!
CHIK
FLUTT
FLUTT
FLUTT
Just great, Rikt.
Scared of a beetle.
Rikt...

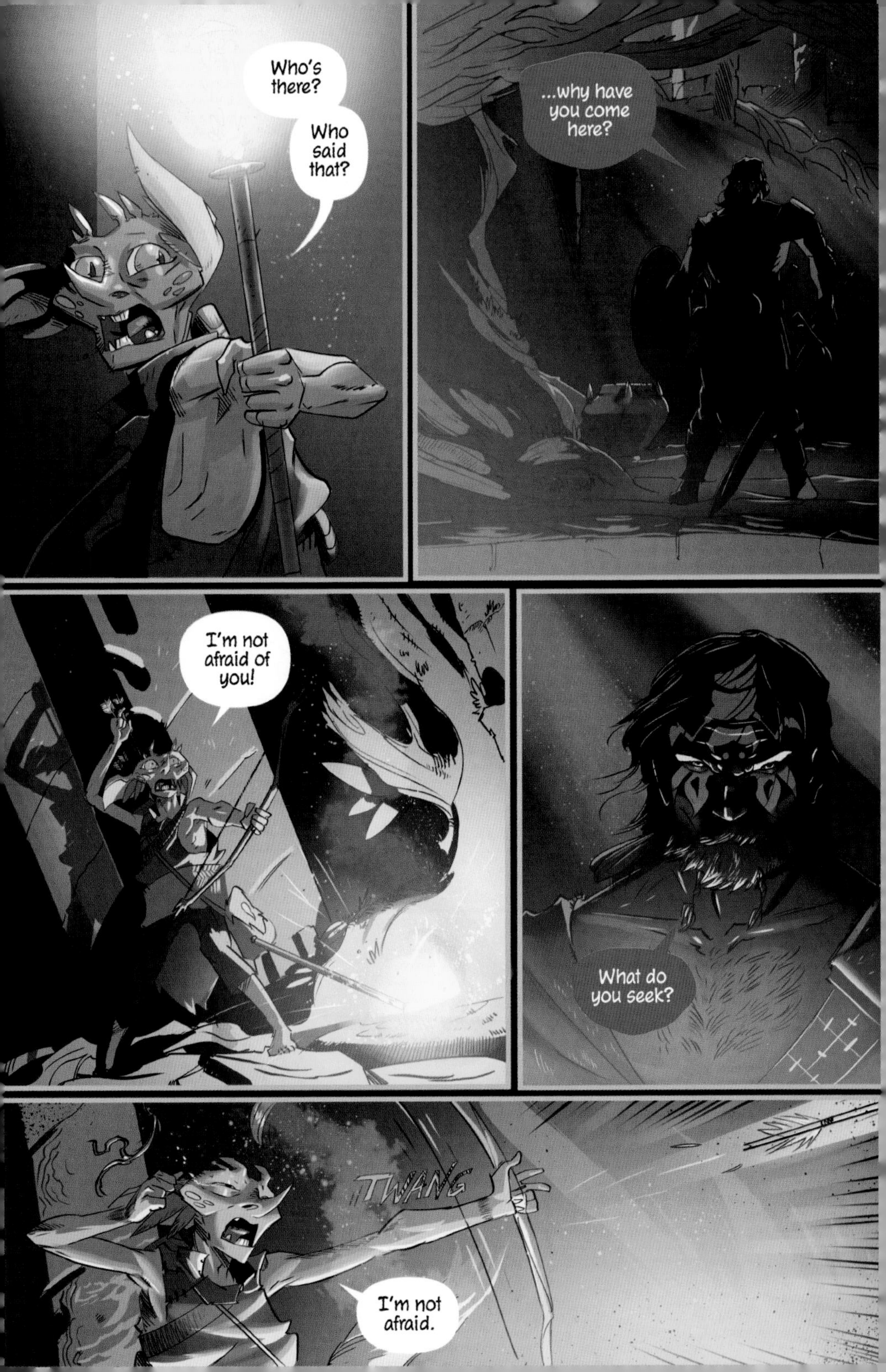
Who's there?
Who said that?
...why have you come here?
I'm not afraid of you!
What do you seek?
TWANG
I'm not afraid.

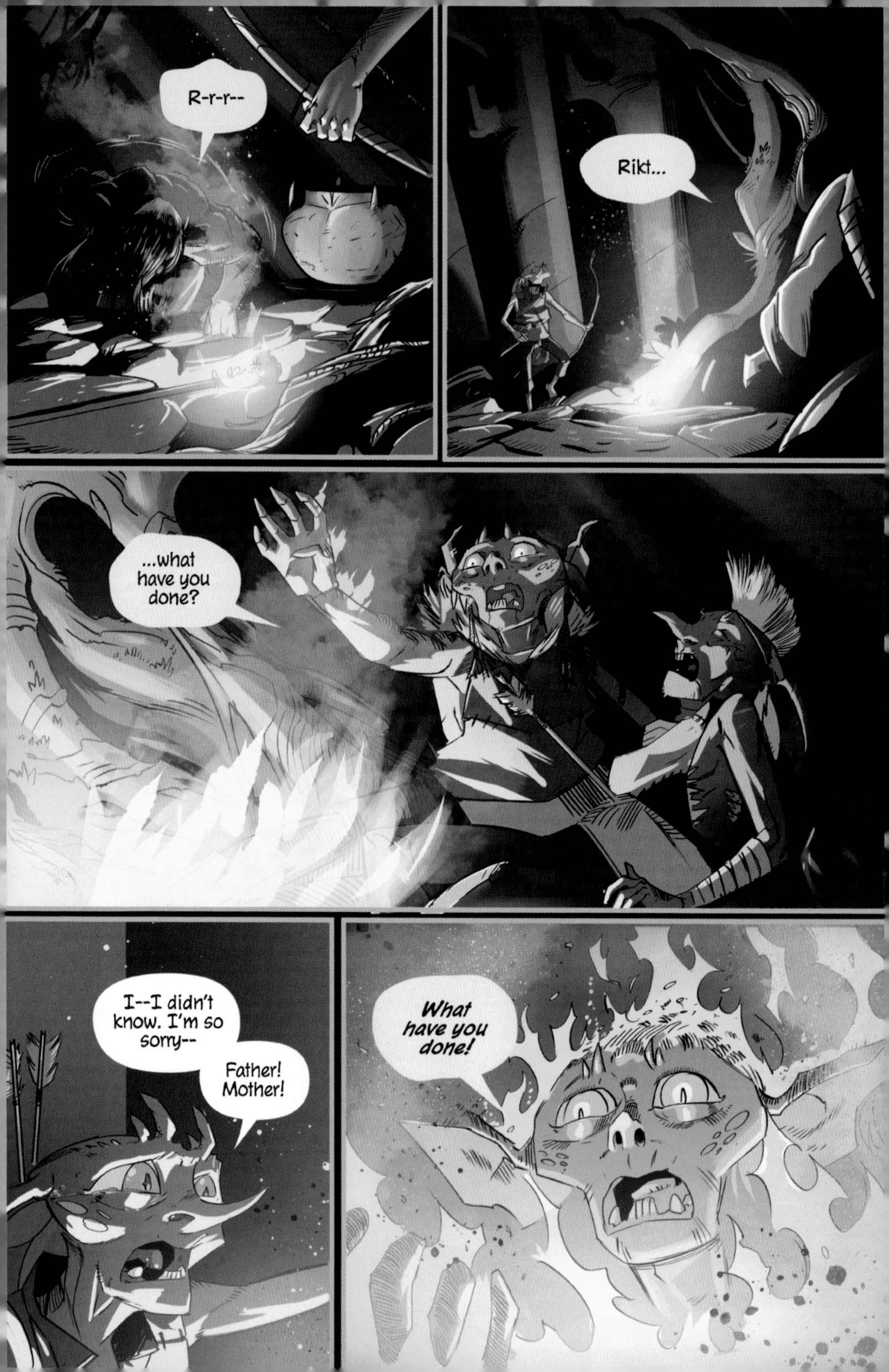
R-r-r--
Rikt...
...what have you done?
I--I didn't know. I'm so sorry--
Father! Mother!
What have you done!

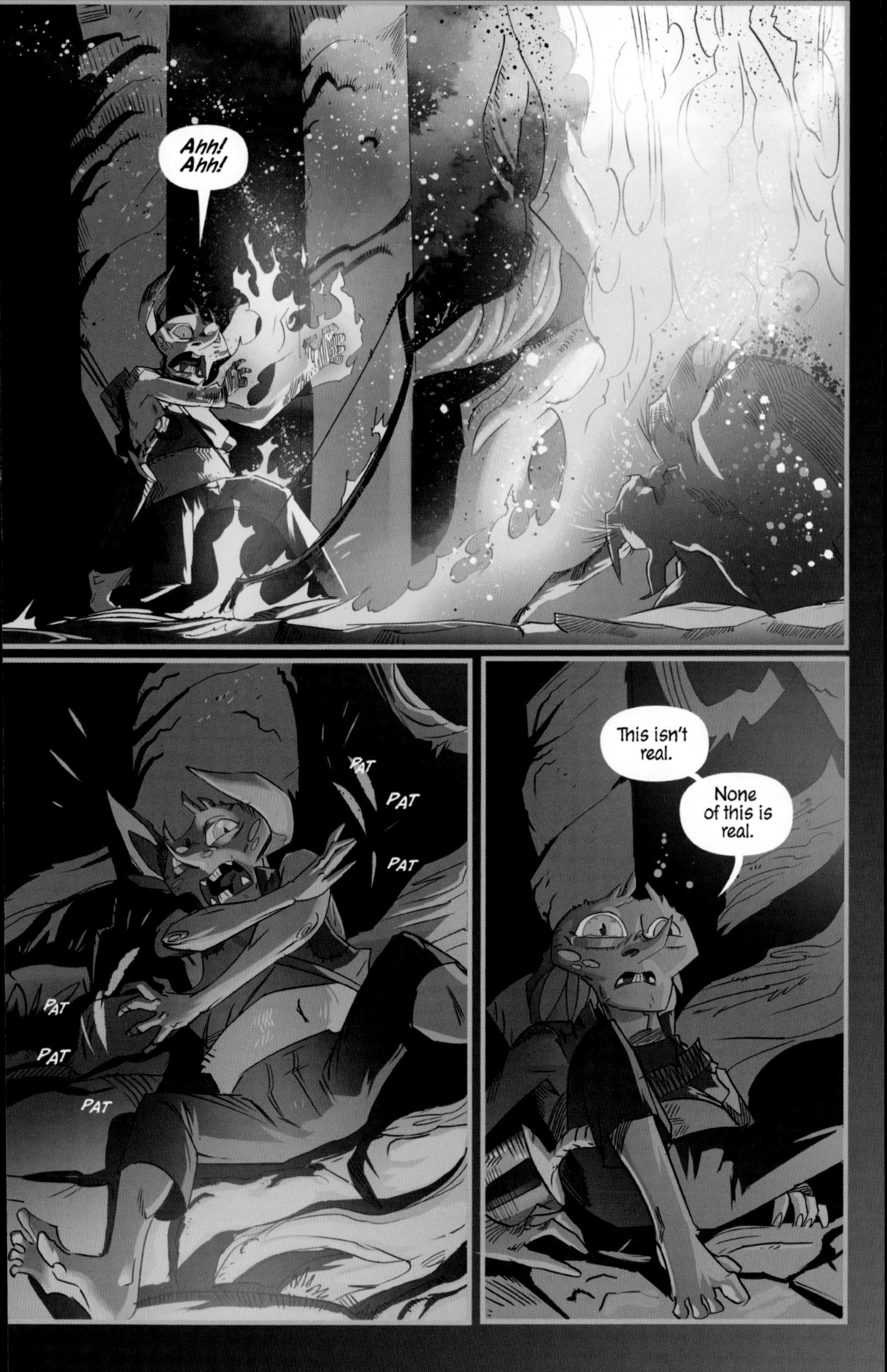
Ahh! Ahh!
PAT
PAT
PAT
PAT
PAT
PAT
This isn't real.
None of this is real.

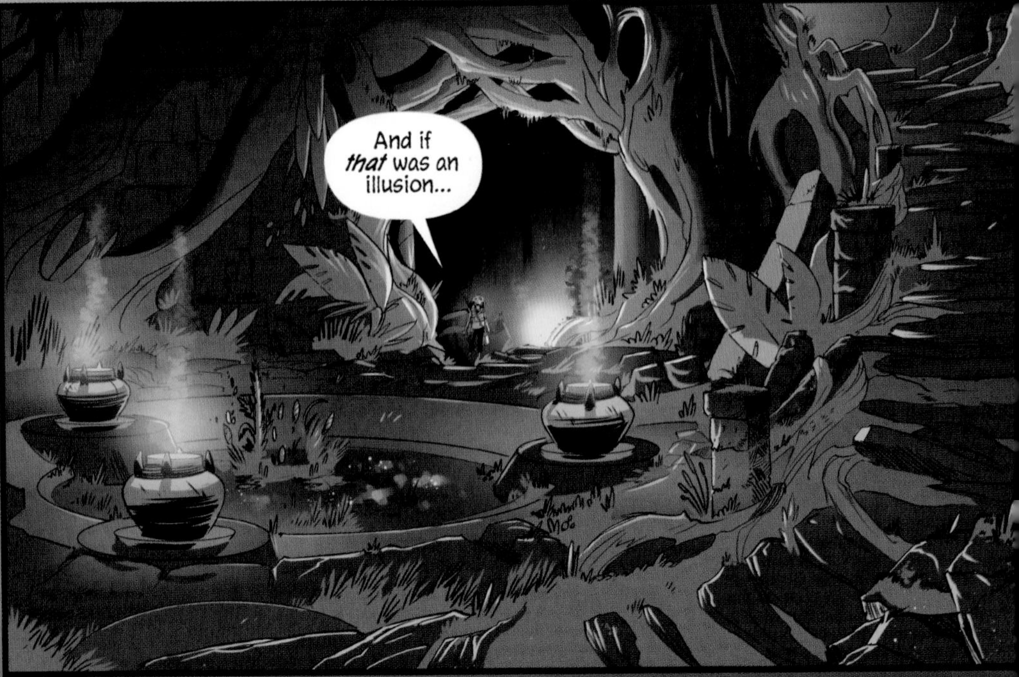
And if *that* was an illusion...

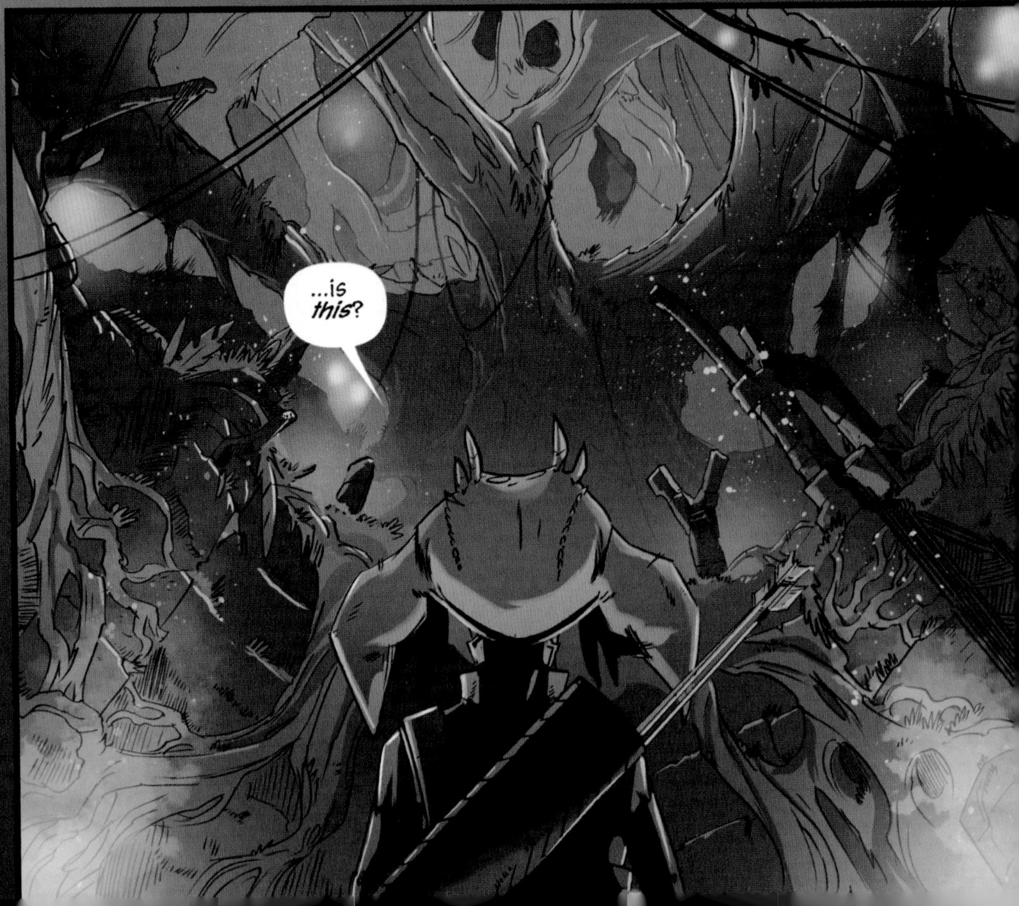
...is *this*?

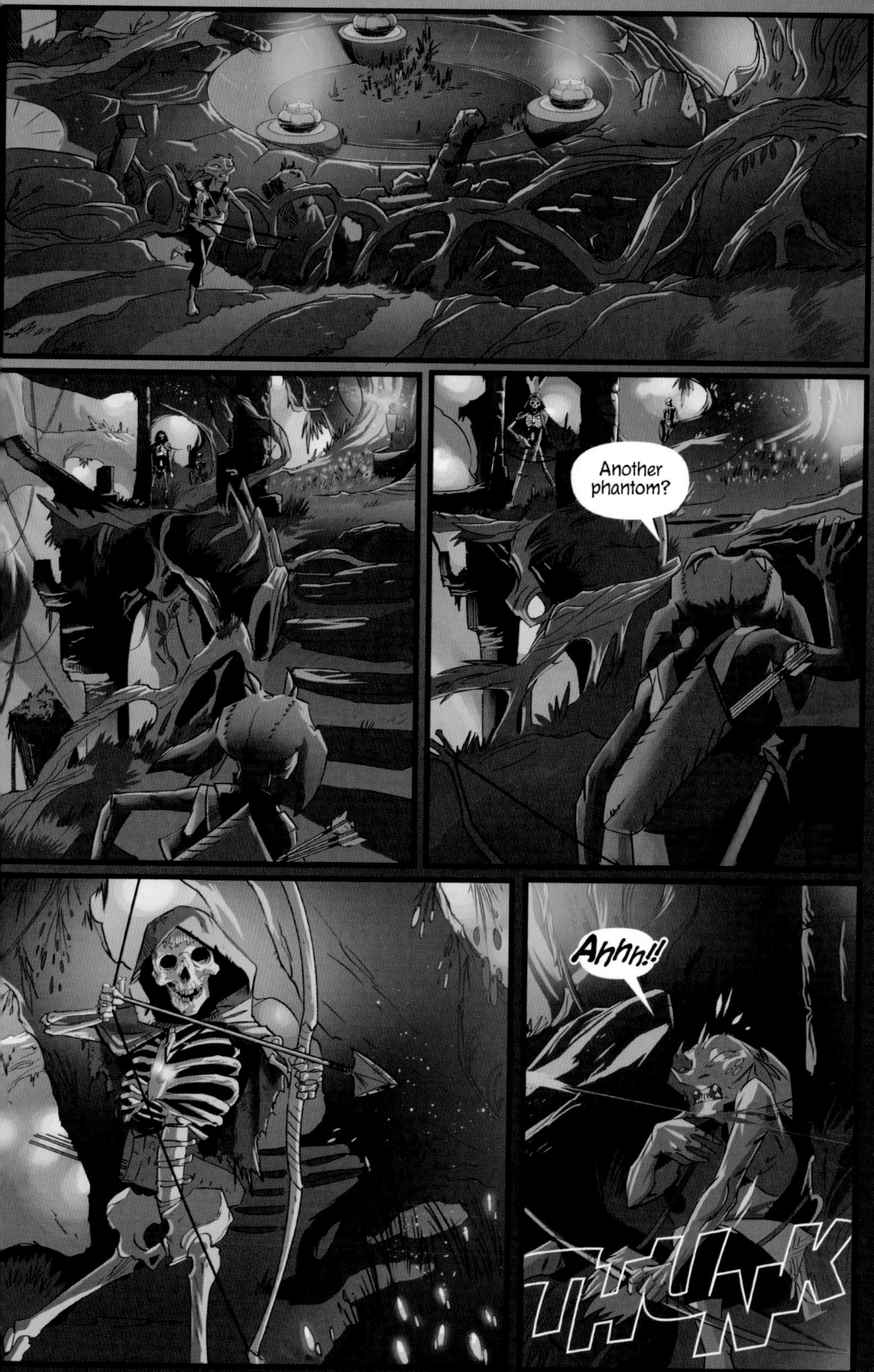
Another phantom?
Ahhn!!
THUNK

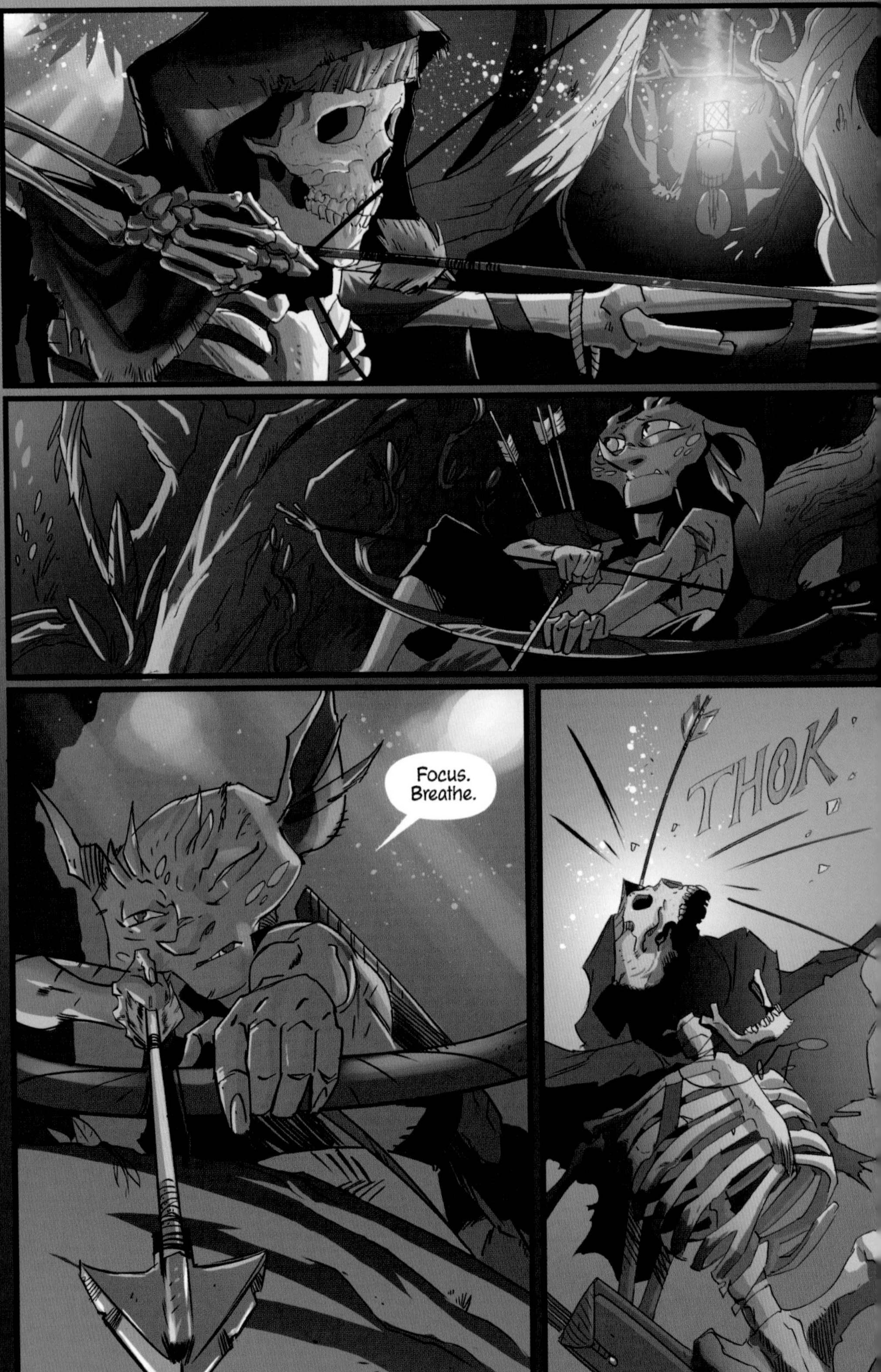
Focus.
Breathe.
THOK

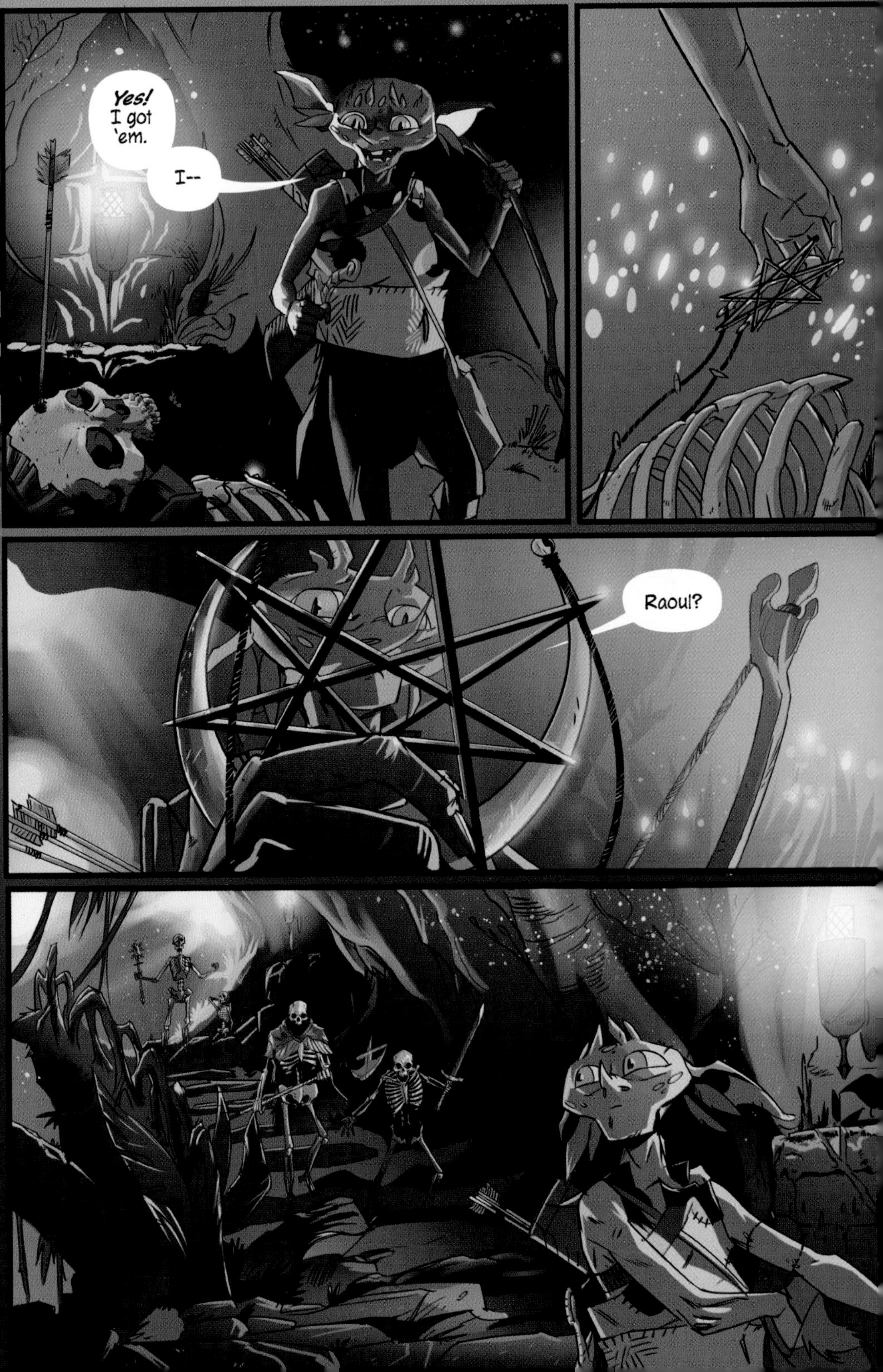
Yes! I got 'em.
I--
Raoul?

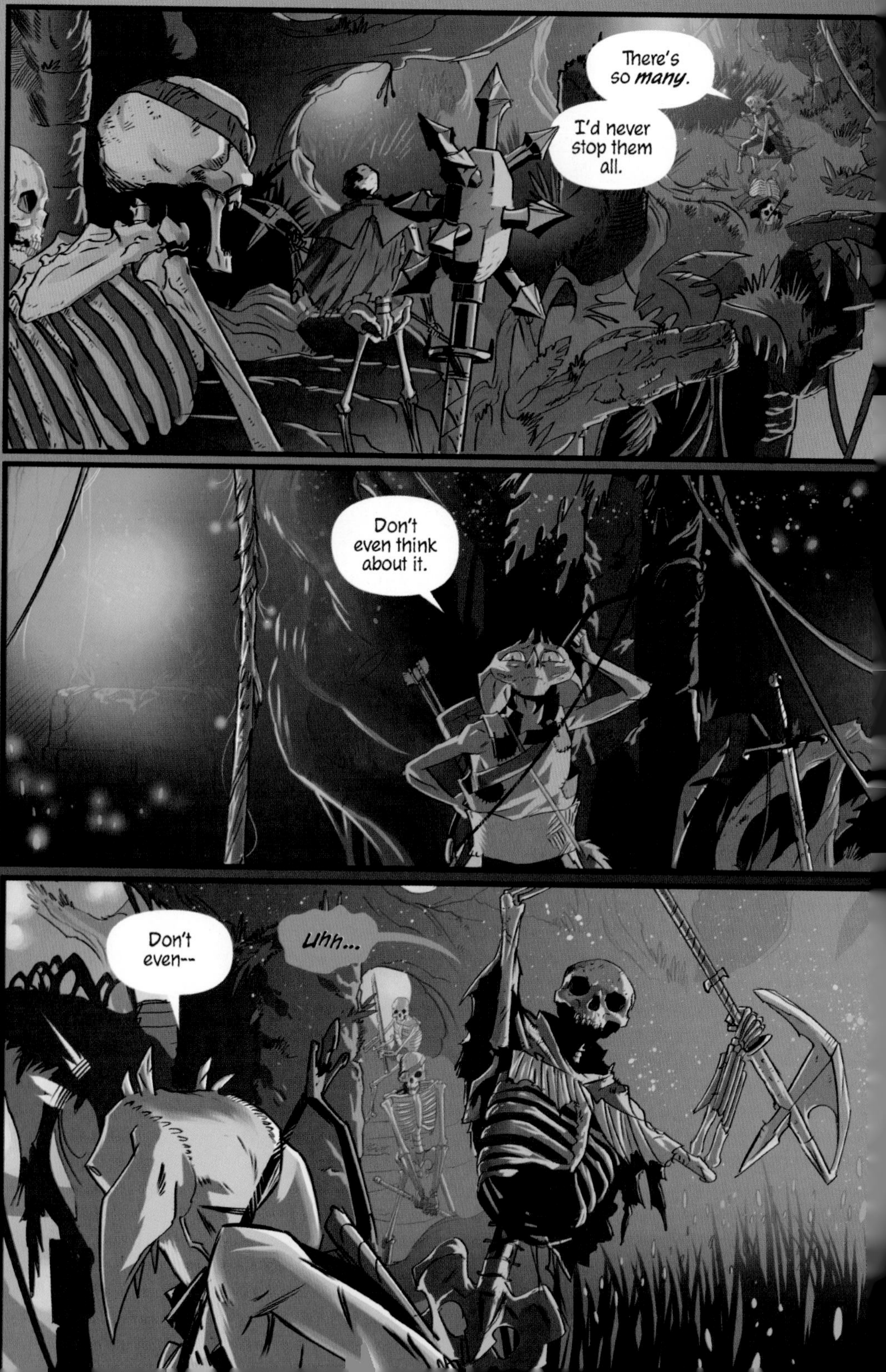
There's so *many*.
I'd never stop them all.
Don't even think about it.
Don't even--
Uhh...

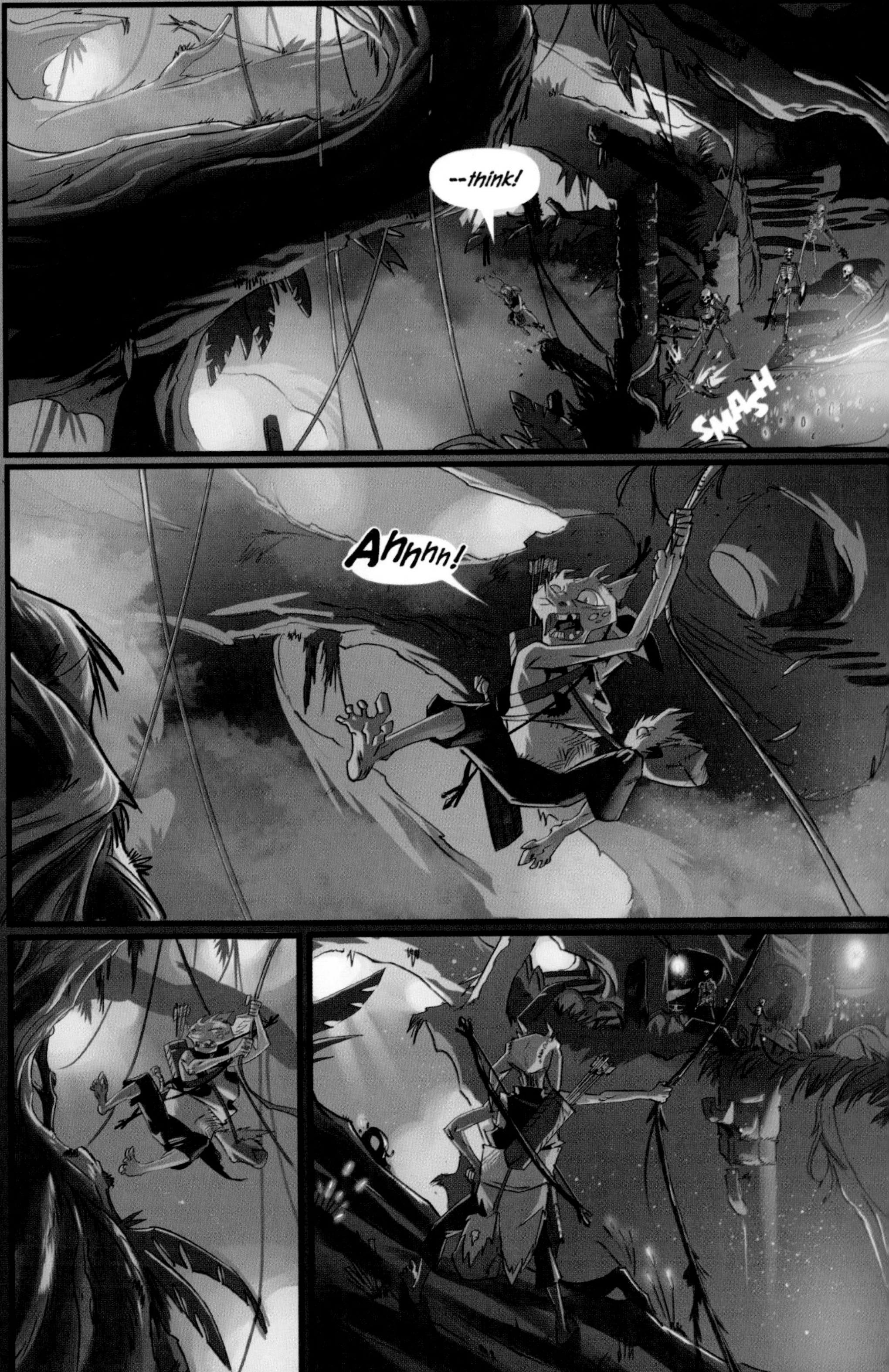
--think!
SMASH
Ahhhn!

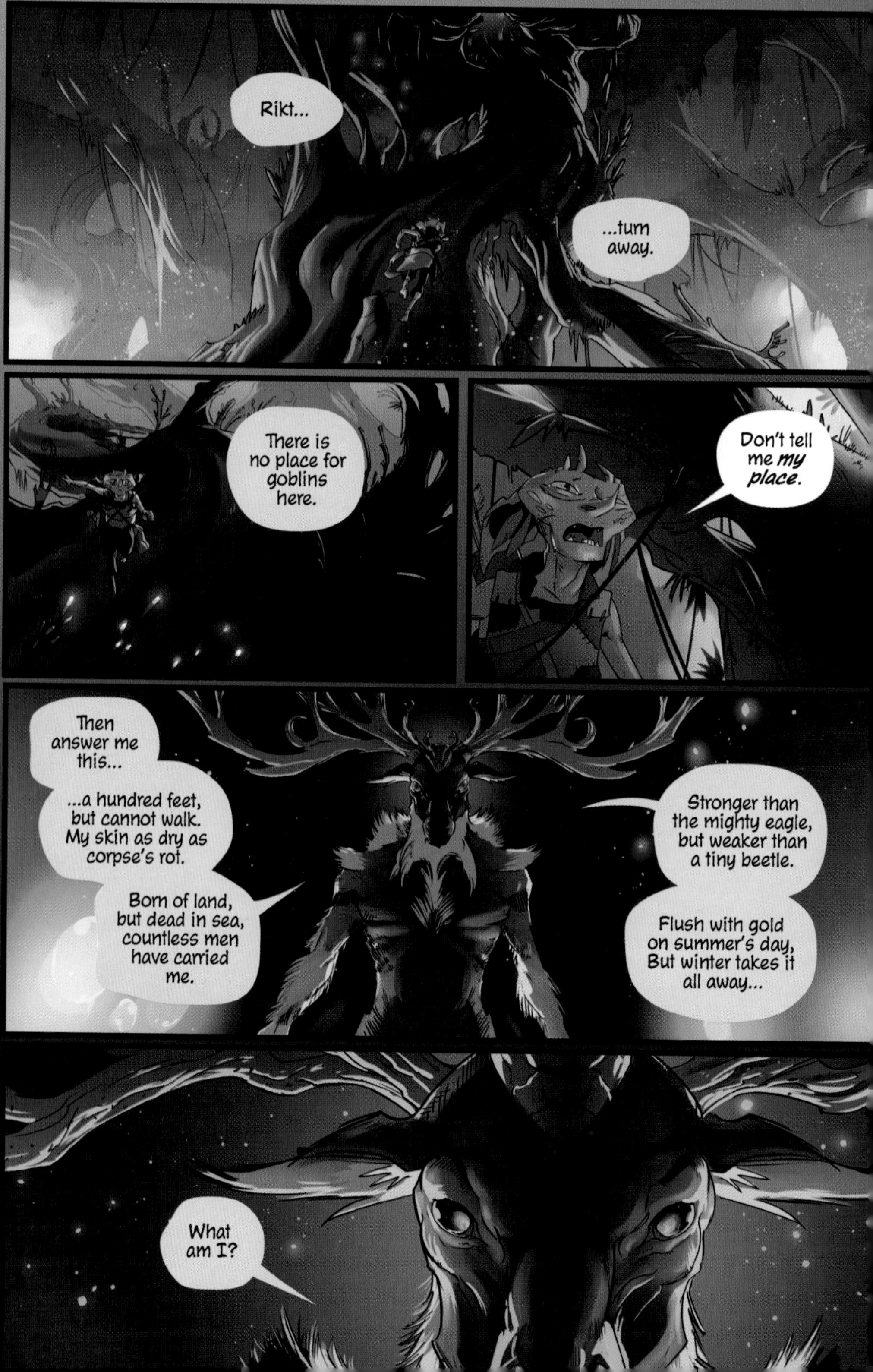
Rikt...
...turn away.
There is no place for goblins here.
Don't tell me ***my place***.
Then answer me this...
...a hundred feet, but cannot walk. My skin as dry as corpse's rot.
Born of land, but dead in sea, countless men have carried me.
Stronger than the mighty eagle, but weaker than a tiny beetle.
Flush with gold on summer's day, But winter takes it all away...
What am I?

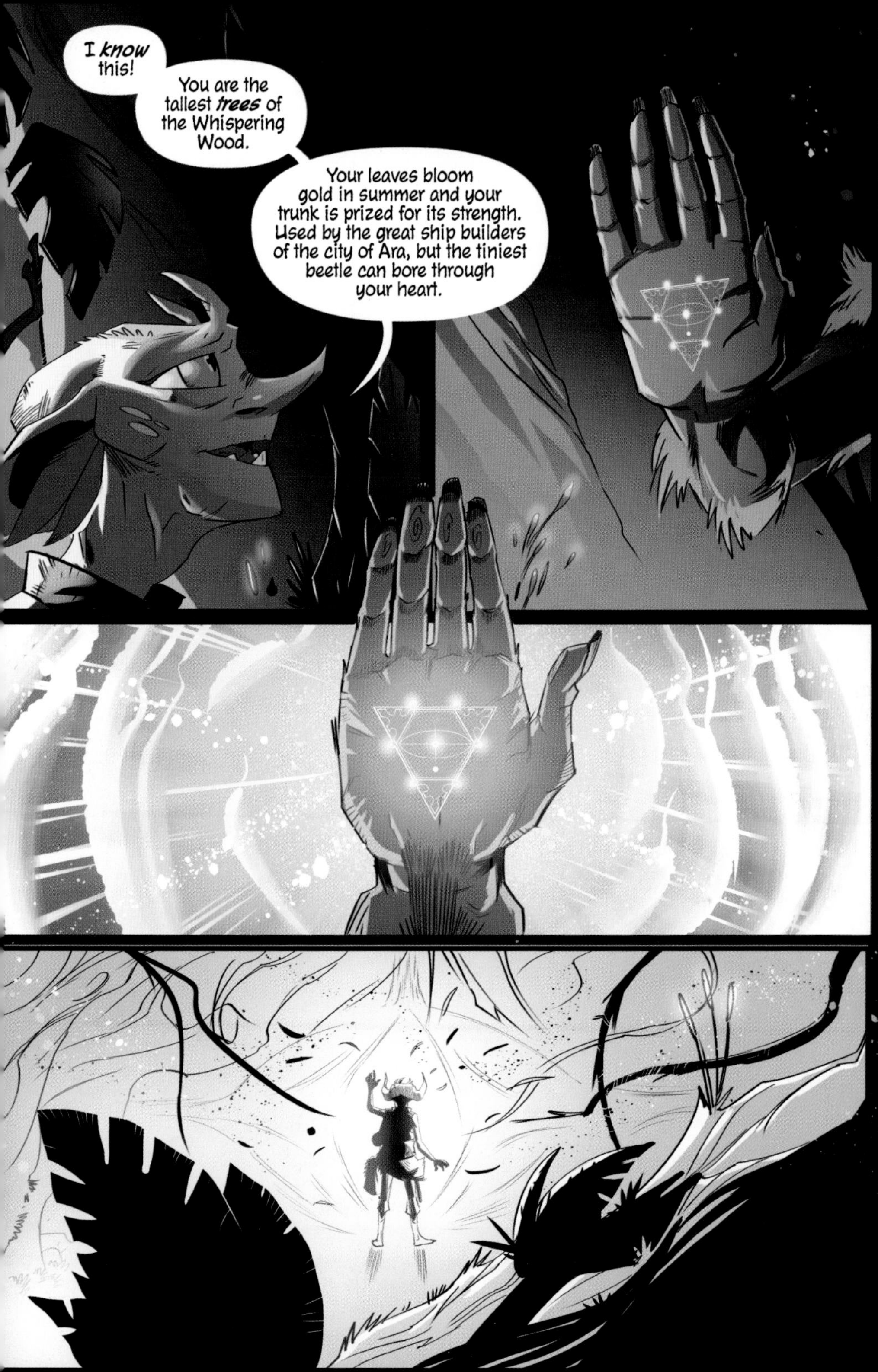
I *know* this!
You are the tallest *trees* of the Whispering Wood.
Your leaves bloom gold in summer and your trunk is prized for its strength. Used by the great ship builders of the city of Ara, but the tiniest beetle can bore through your heart.

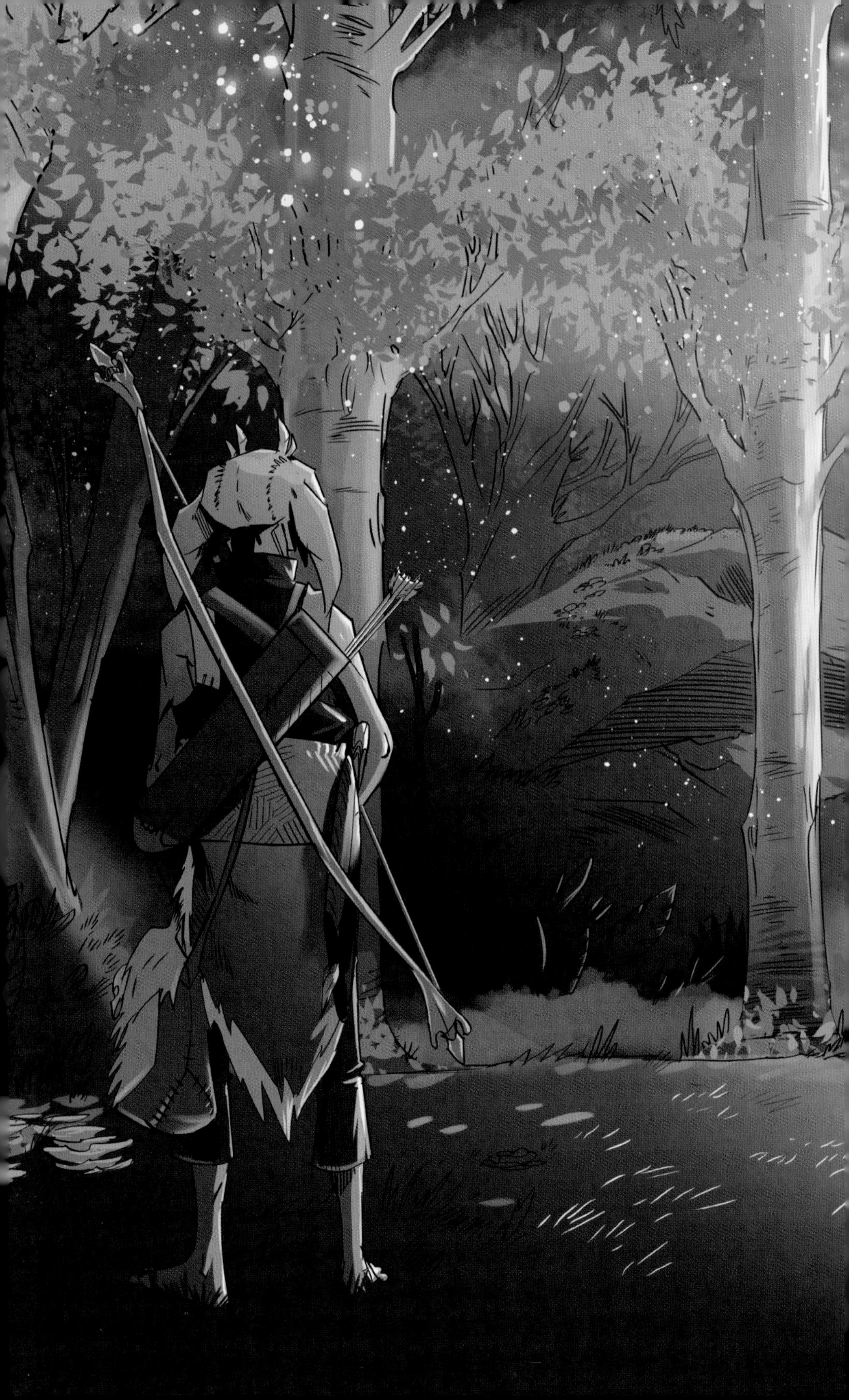

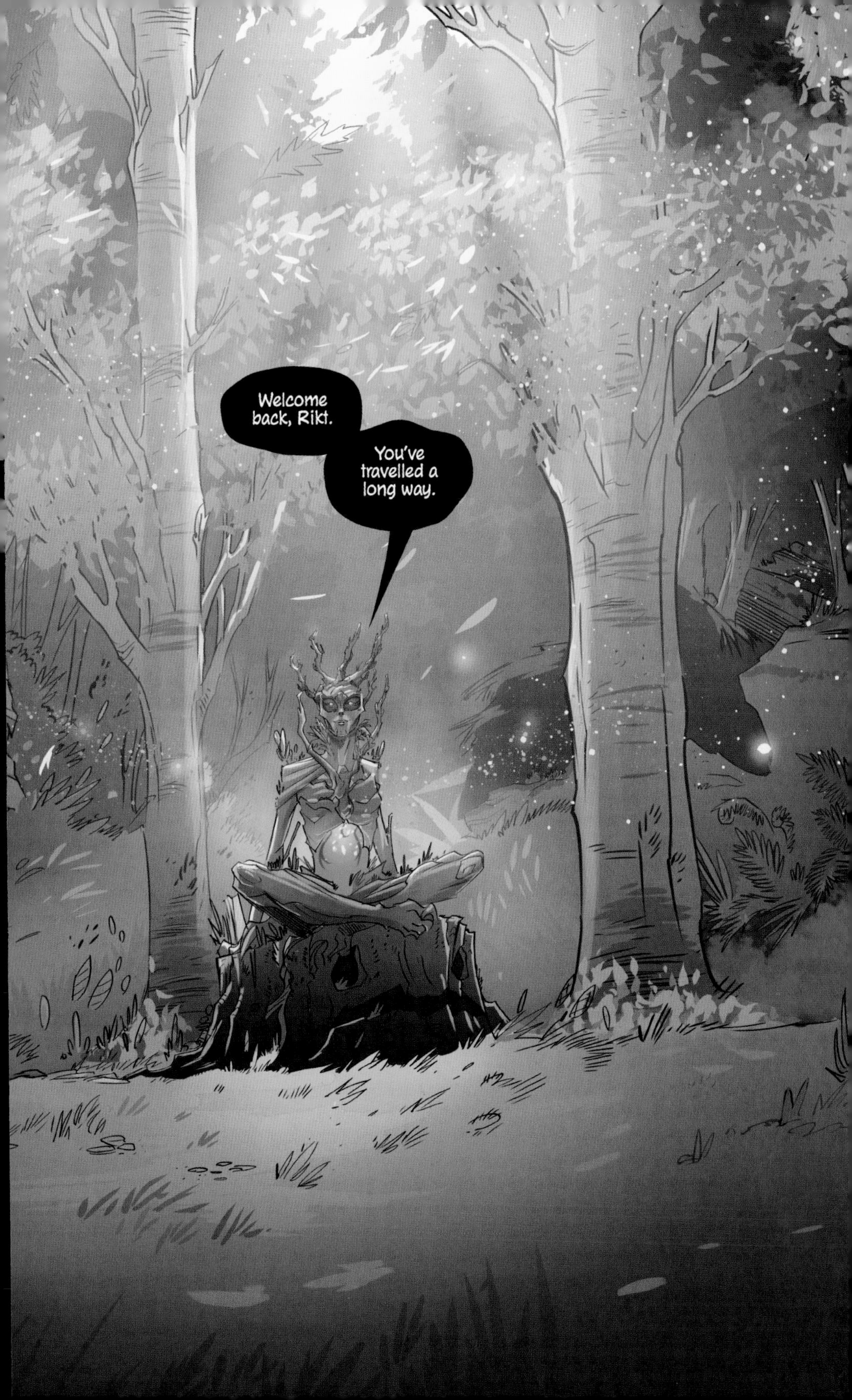
Welcome back, Rikt.
You've travelled a long way.

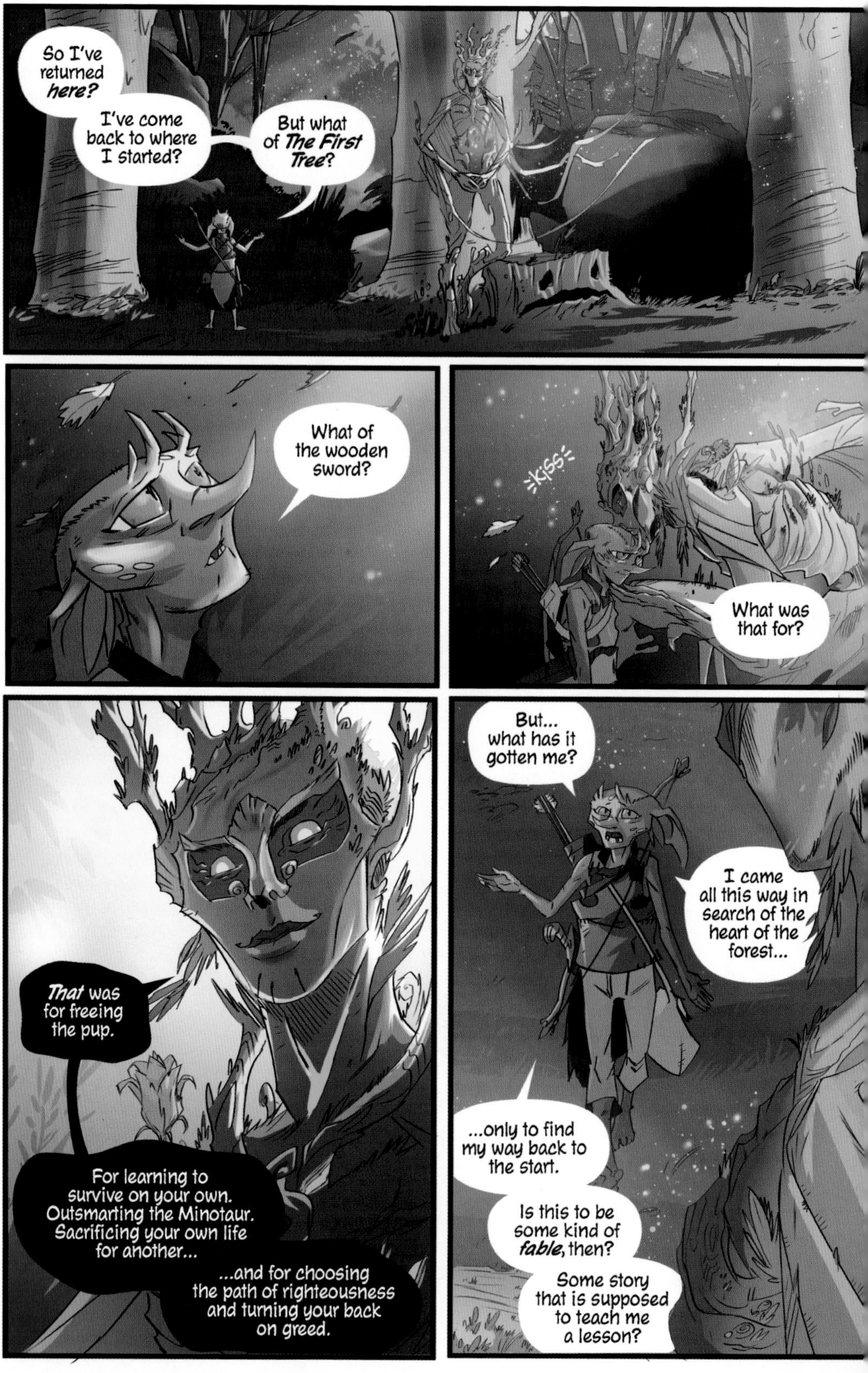
So I've returned *here?*
I've come back to where I started?
But what of *The First Tree*?
What of the wooden sword?
KISS
What was that for?
That was for freeing the pup.
For learning to survive on your own. Outsmarting the Minotaur. Sacrificing your own life for another...
...and for choosing the path of righteousness and turning your back on greed.
But... what has it gotten me?
I came all this way in search of the heart of the forest...
...only to find my way back to the start.
Is this to be some kind of *fable*, then?
Some story that is supposed to teach me a lesson?

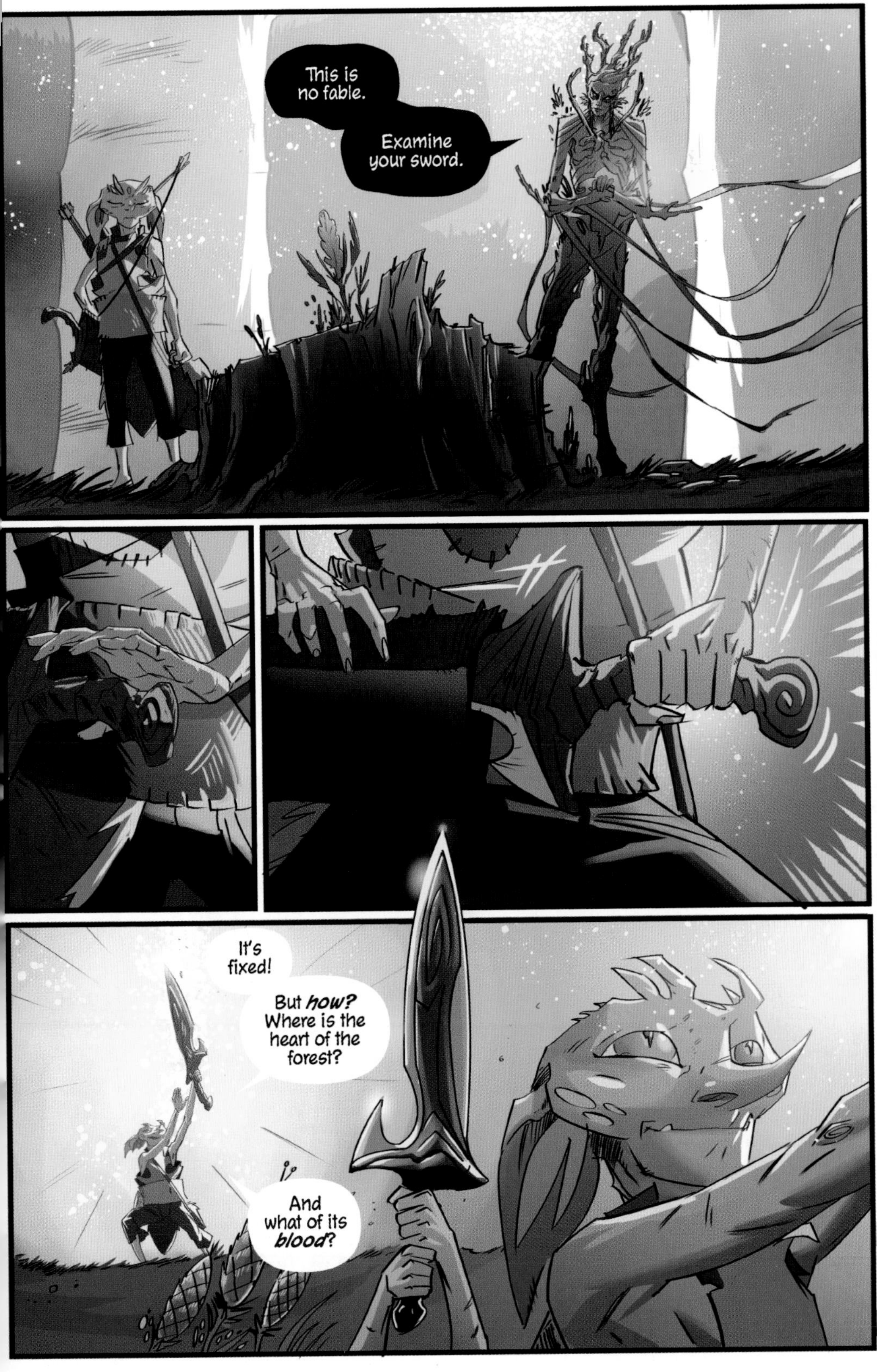
This is no fable.
Examine your sword.
It's fixed!
But *how?* Where is the heart of the forest?
And what of its *blood?*

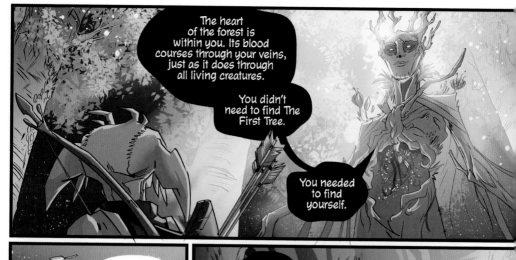

The heart of the forest is within you. Its blood courses through your veins, just as it does through all living creatures.

You didn't need to find The First Tree.

You needed to find yourself.

I knew this was some kind of fable!

If you see a lesson before you, *learn* from it.

I will, Goddess. I promise.

Know then that *time* is not as you left it. You are not the only thing that's changed.

The man you seek, the tattooed one, is now king over all the land.

His *castle* sits silent southeast of here. Your destiny lies there.

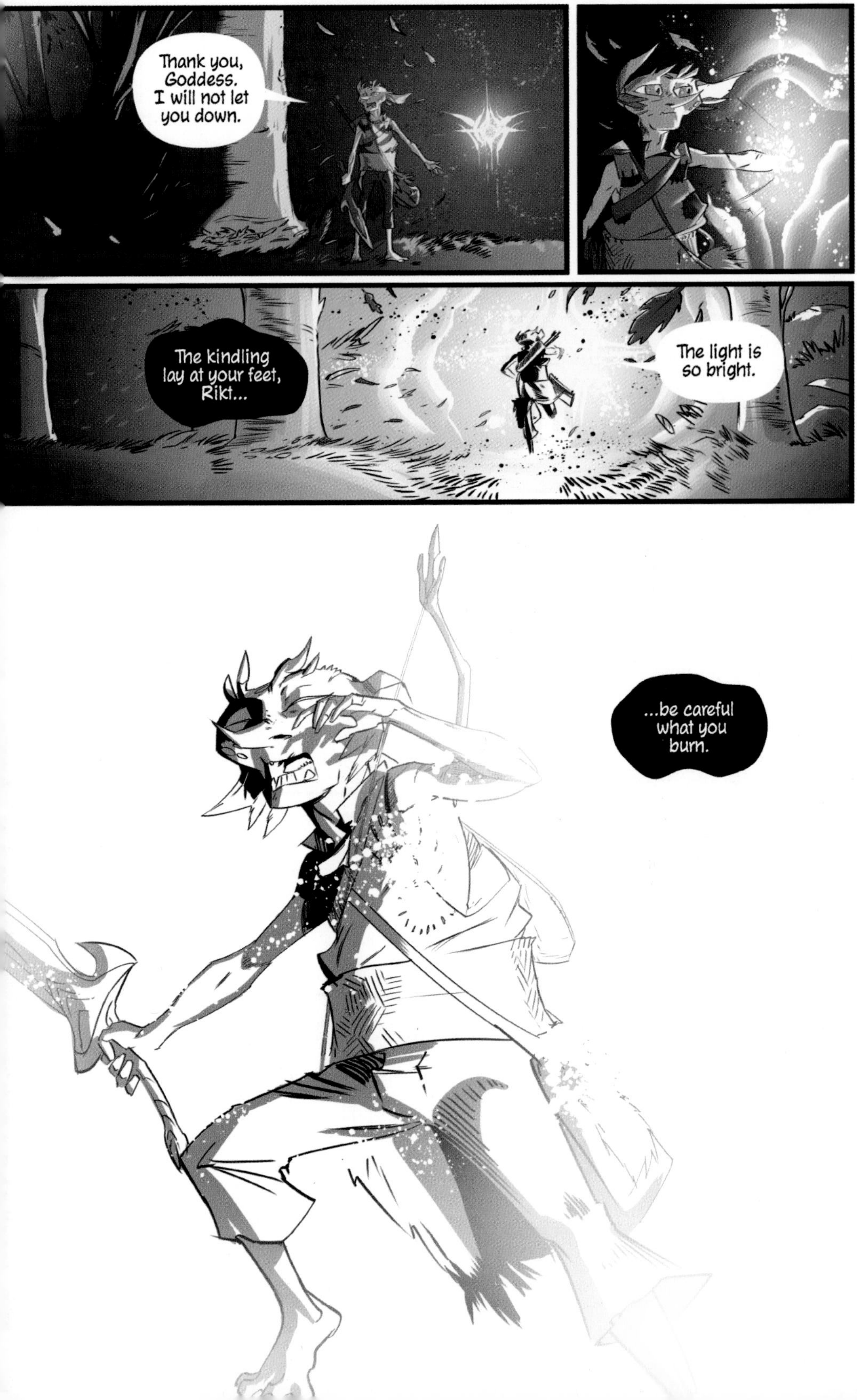
Thank you, Goddess. I will not let you down.
The kindling lay at your feet, Rikt...
The light is so bright.
...be careful what you burn.

Chapter Ten
Requiem

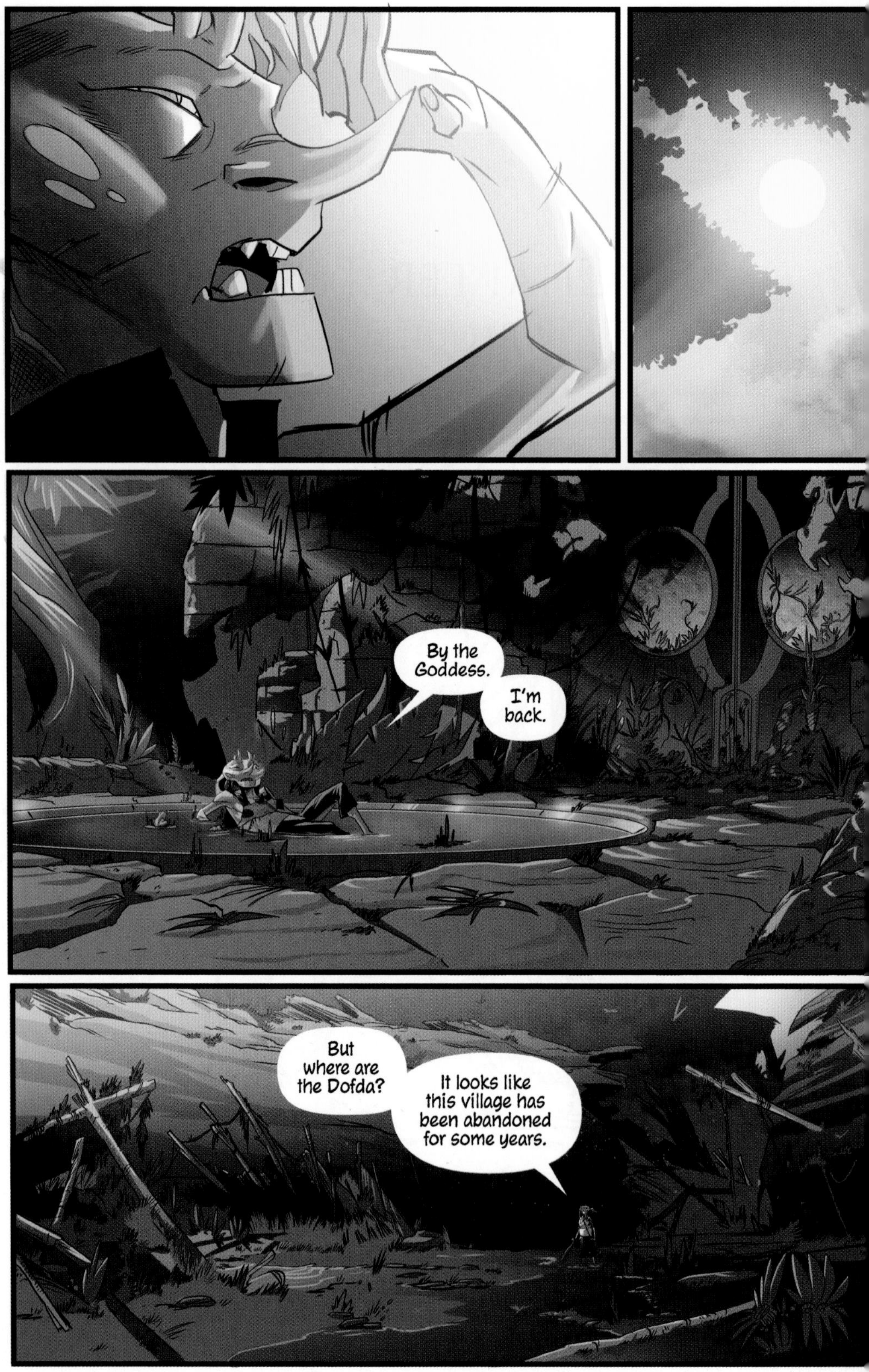
By the Goddess.
I'm back.
But where are the Dofda?
It looks like this village has been abandoned for some years.

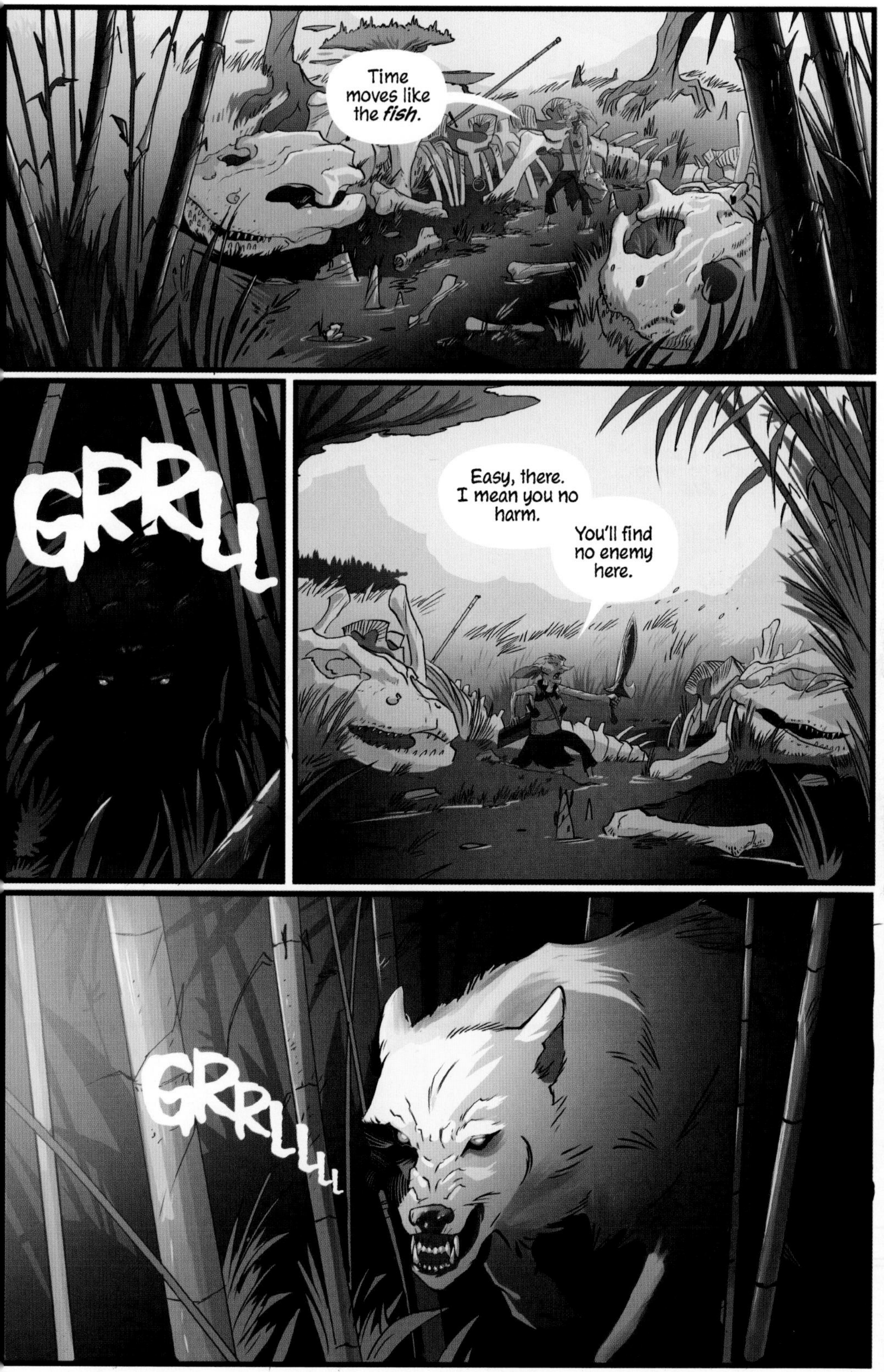
Time moves like the *fish*.
GRRL
Easy, there. I mean you no harm.
You'll find no enemy here.
GRRLLL

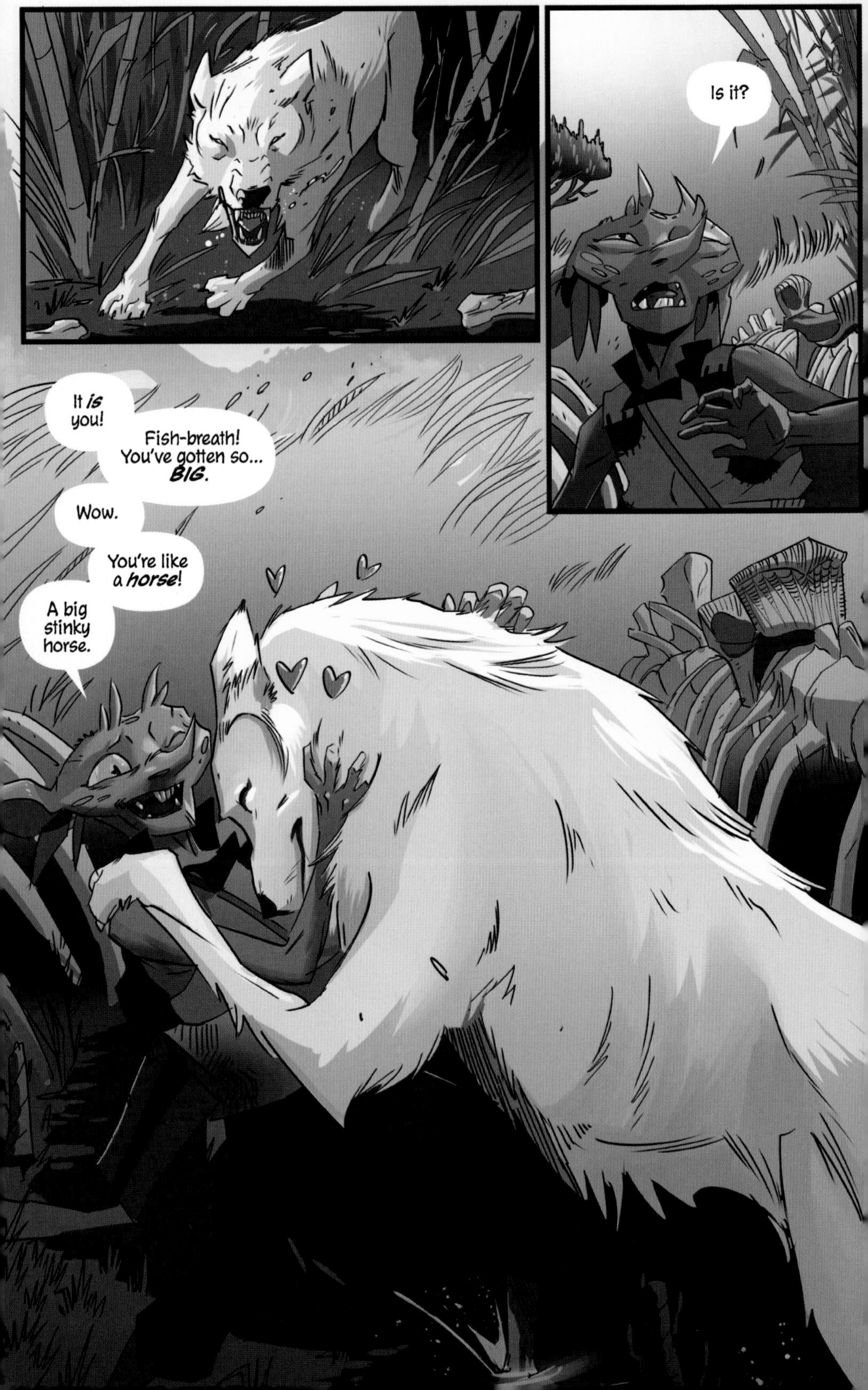

Is it?
It *is* you!
Fish-breath! You've gotten so... ***BIG***.
Wow.
You're like a ***horse***!
A big stinky horse.

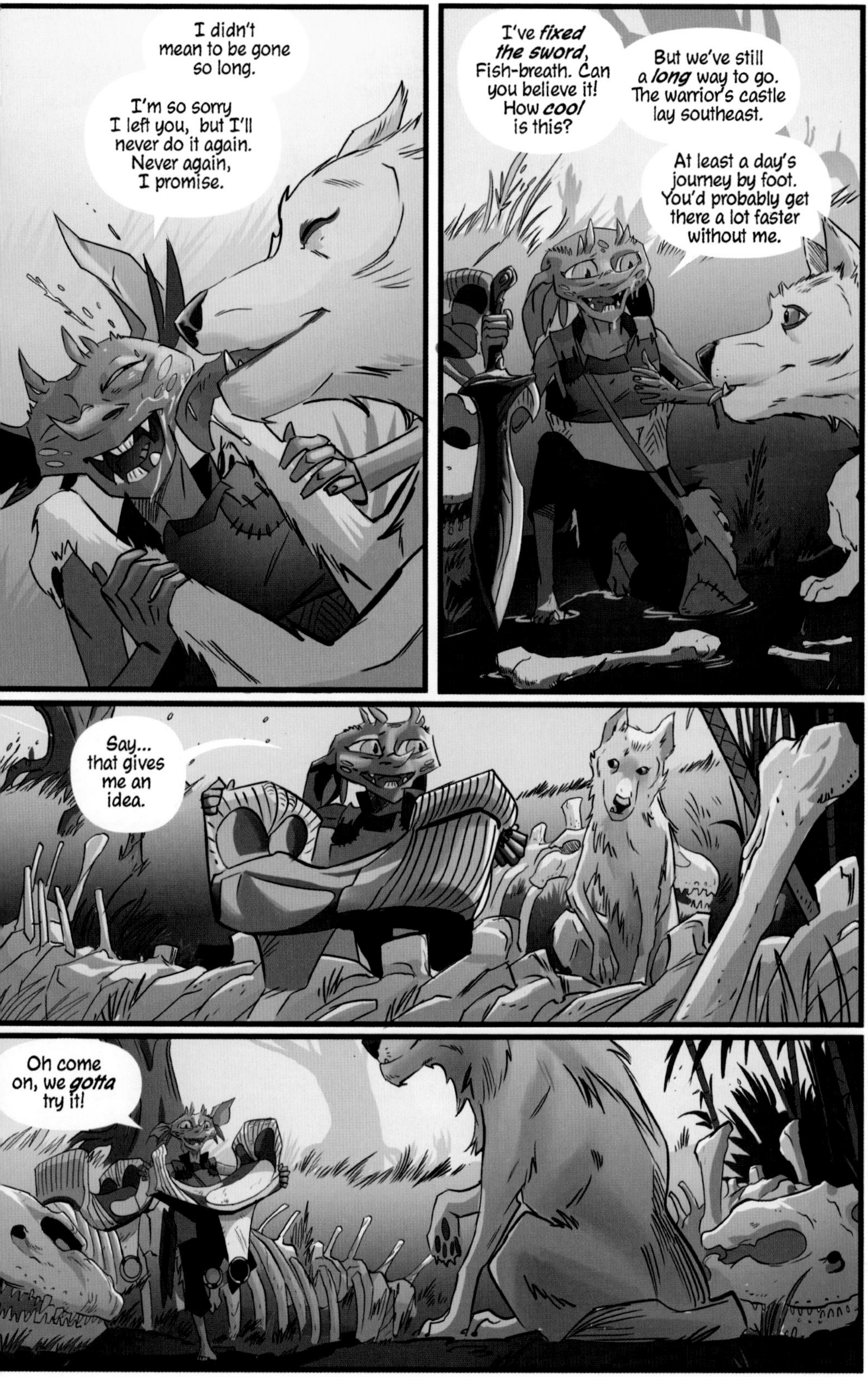
I didn't mean to be gone so long.
I'm so sorry I left you, but I'll never do it again. Never again, I promise.
I've *fixed the sword*, Fish-breath. Can you believe it! How *cool* is this?
But we've still a *long* way to go. The warrior's castle lay southeast.
At least a day's journey by foot. You'd probably get there a lot faster without me.
Say... that gives me an idea.
Oh come on, we *gotta* try it!

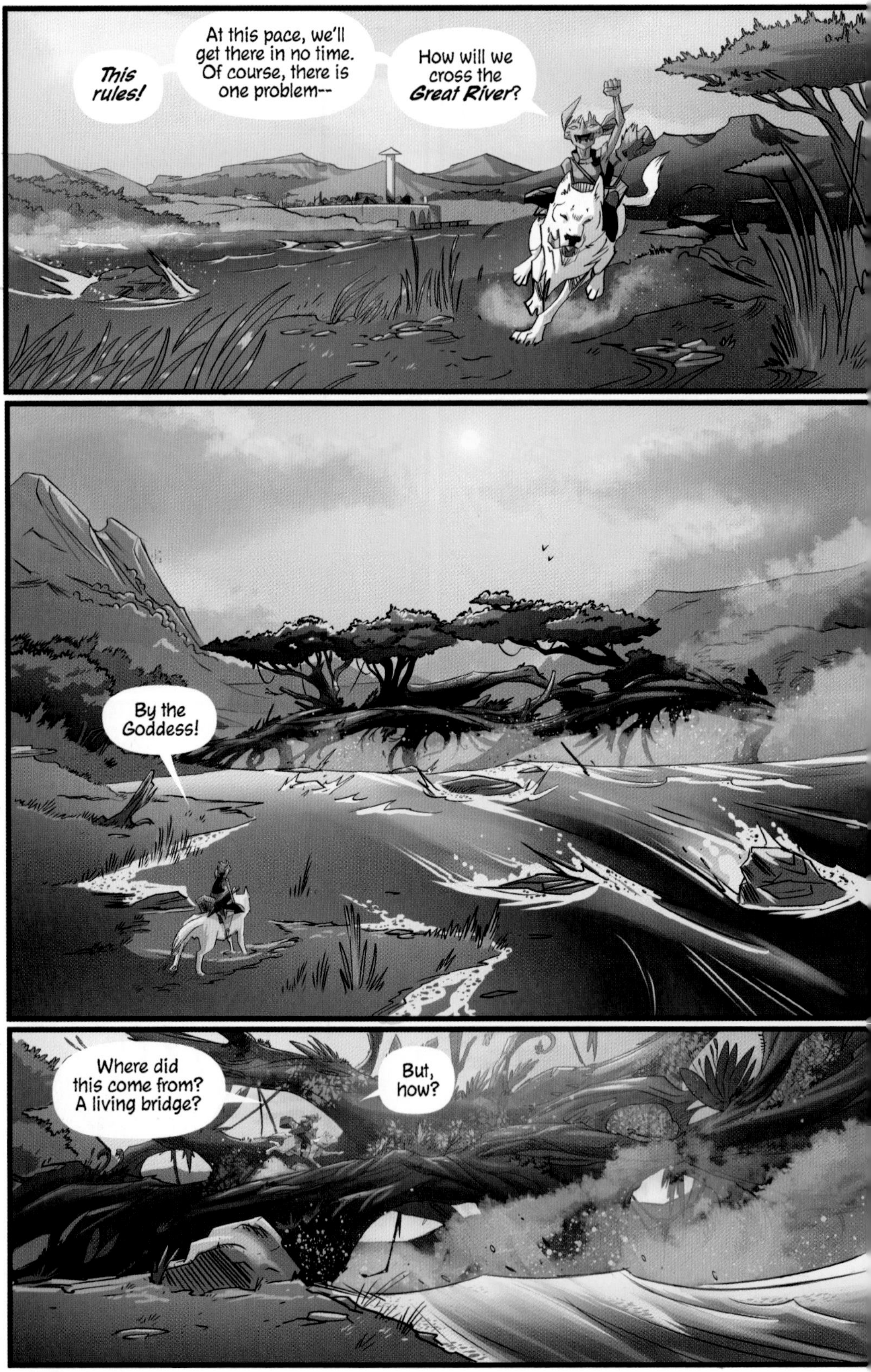
This rules!
At this pace, we'll get there in no time. Of course, there is one problem--
How will we cross the Great River?
By the Goddess!
Where did this come from? A living bridge?
But, how?

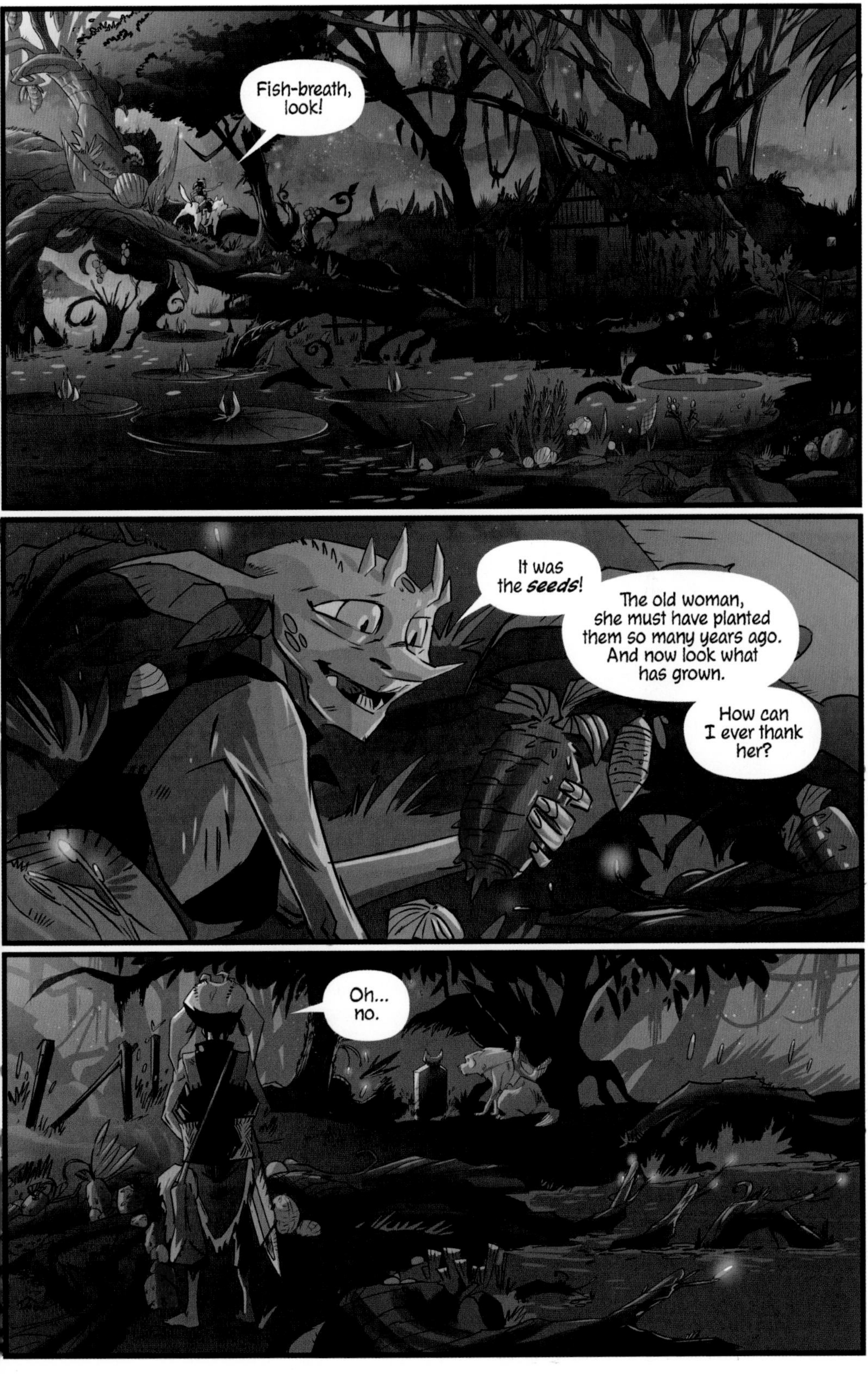
Fish-breath, look!
It was the ***seeds***!
The old woman, she must have planted them so many years ago. And now look what has grown.
How can I ever thank her?
Oh... no.

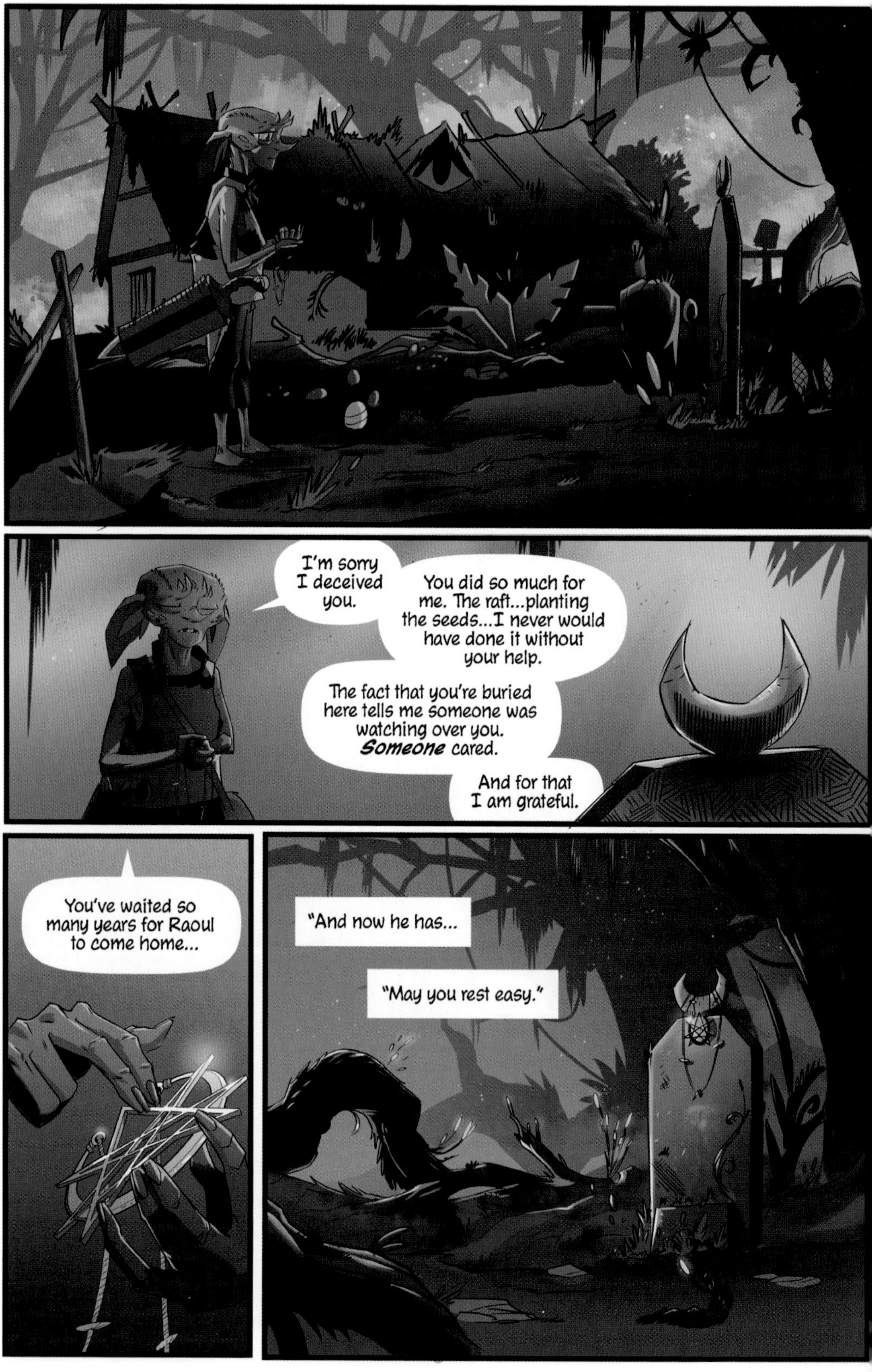
I'm sorry I deceived you.
You did so much for me. The raft...planting the seeds...I never would have done it without your help.
The fact that you're buried here tells me someone was watching over you. *Someone* cared.
And for that I am grateful.
You've waited so many years for Raoul to come home...
"And now he has...
"May you rest easy."

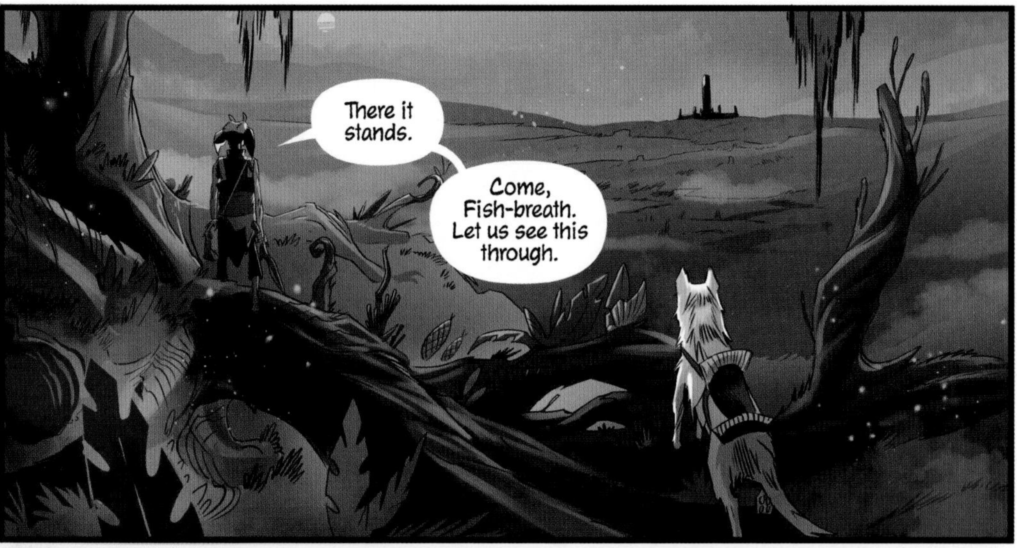
There it stands.
Come, Fish-breath. Let us see this through.

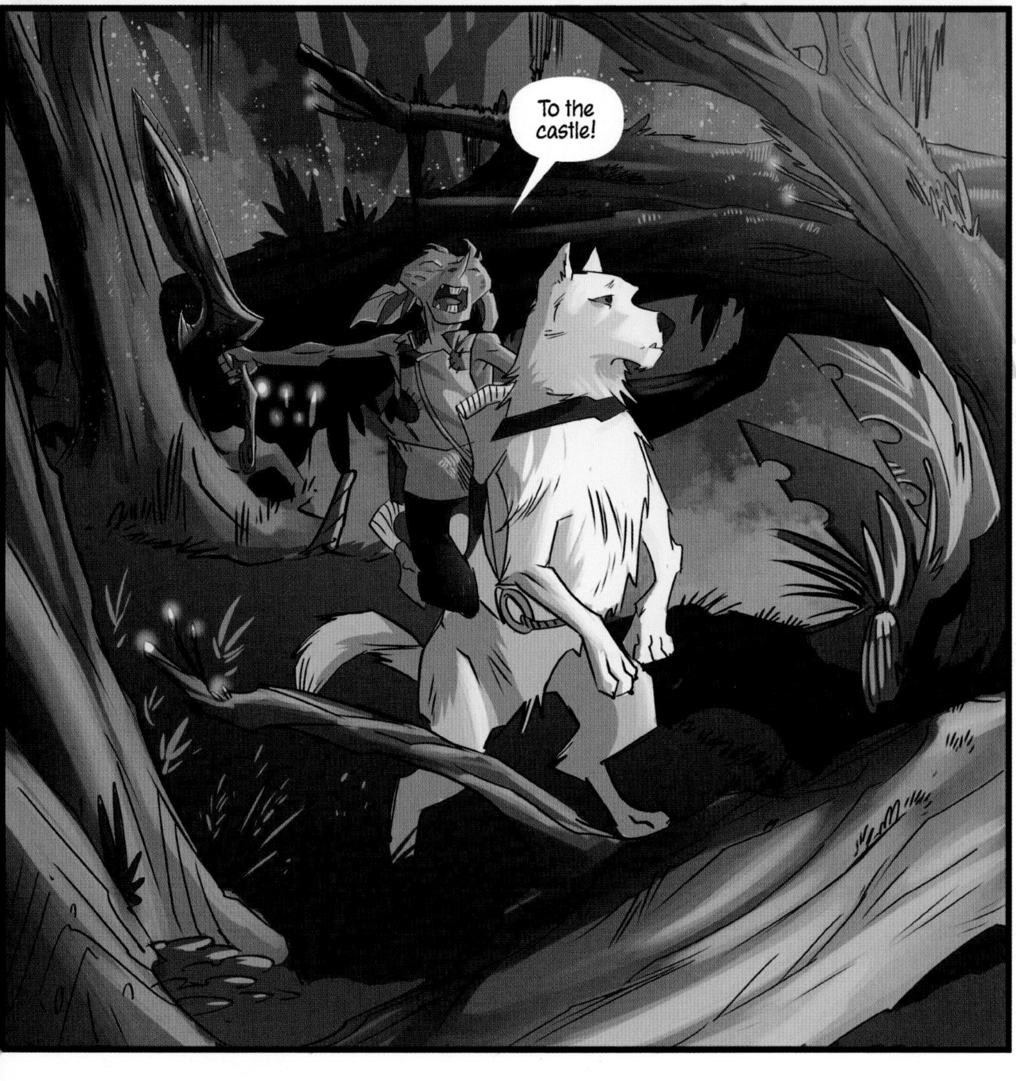
To the castle!

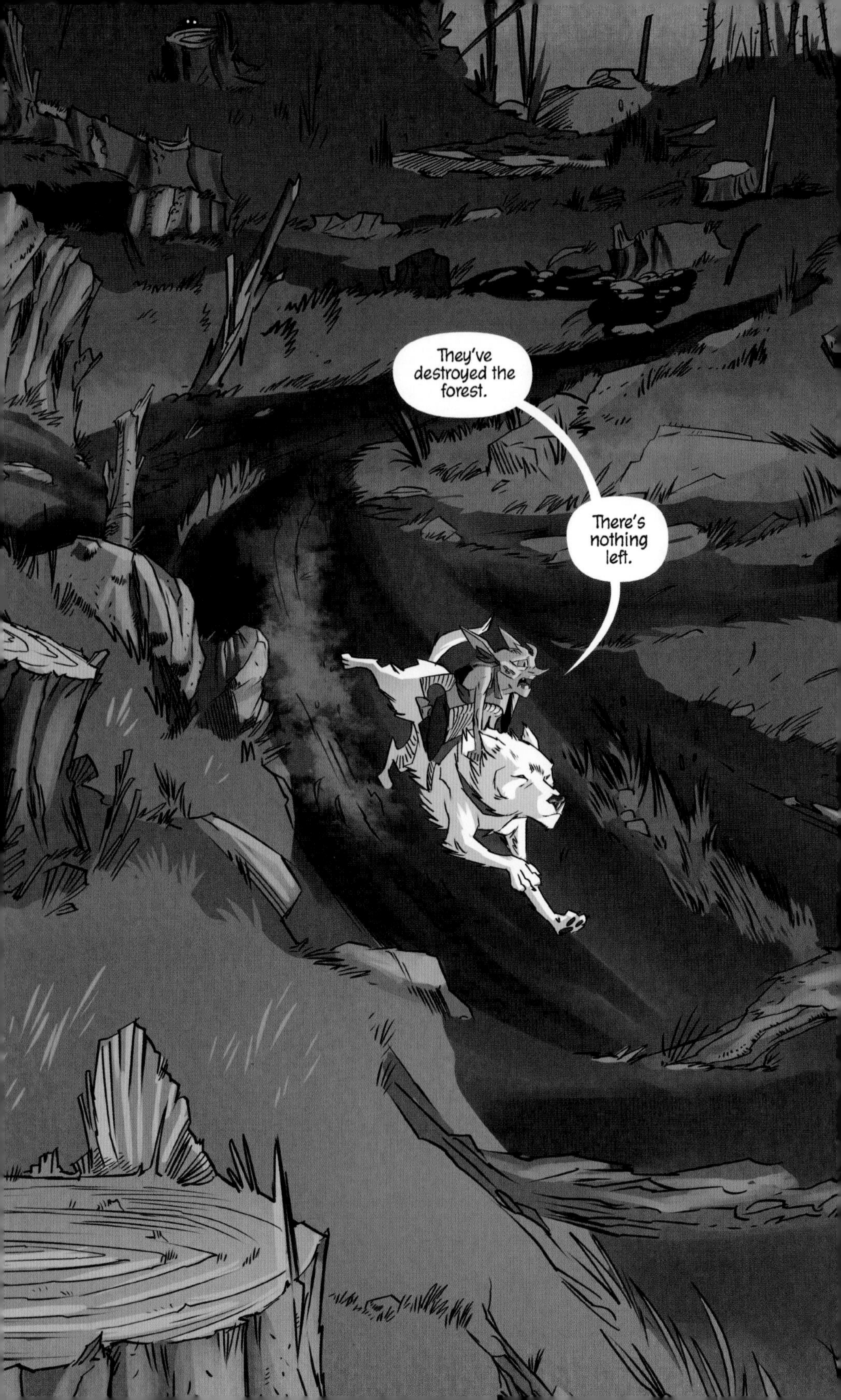
They've destroyed the forest.
There's nothing left.

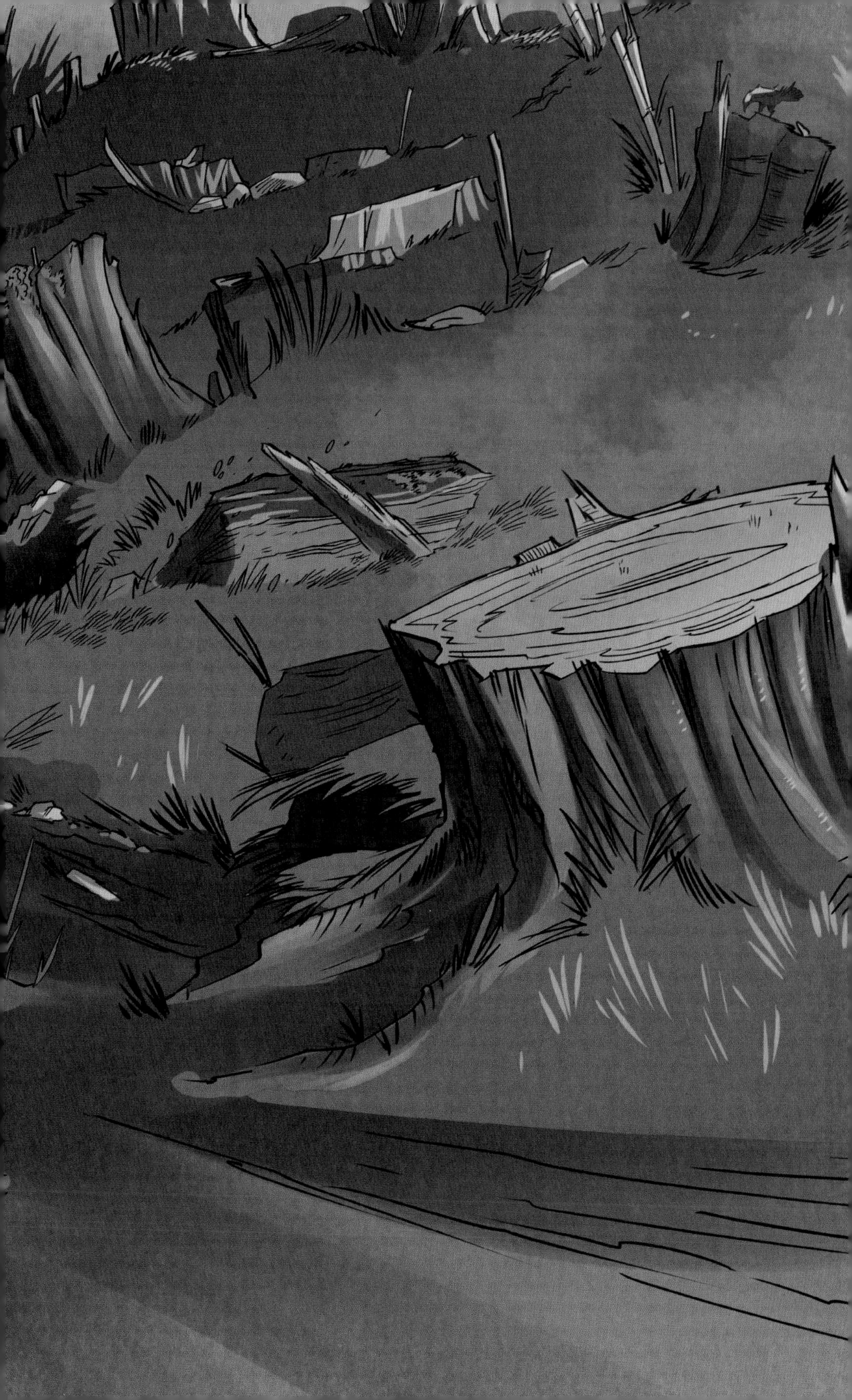

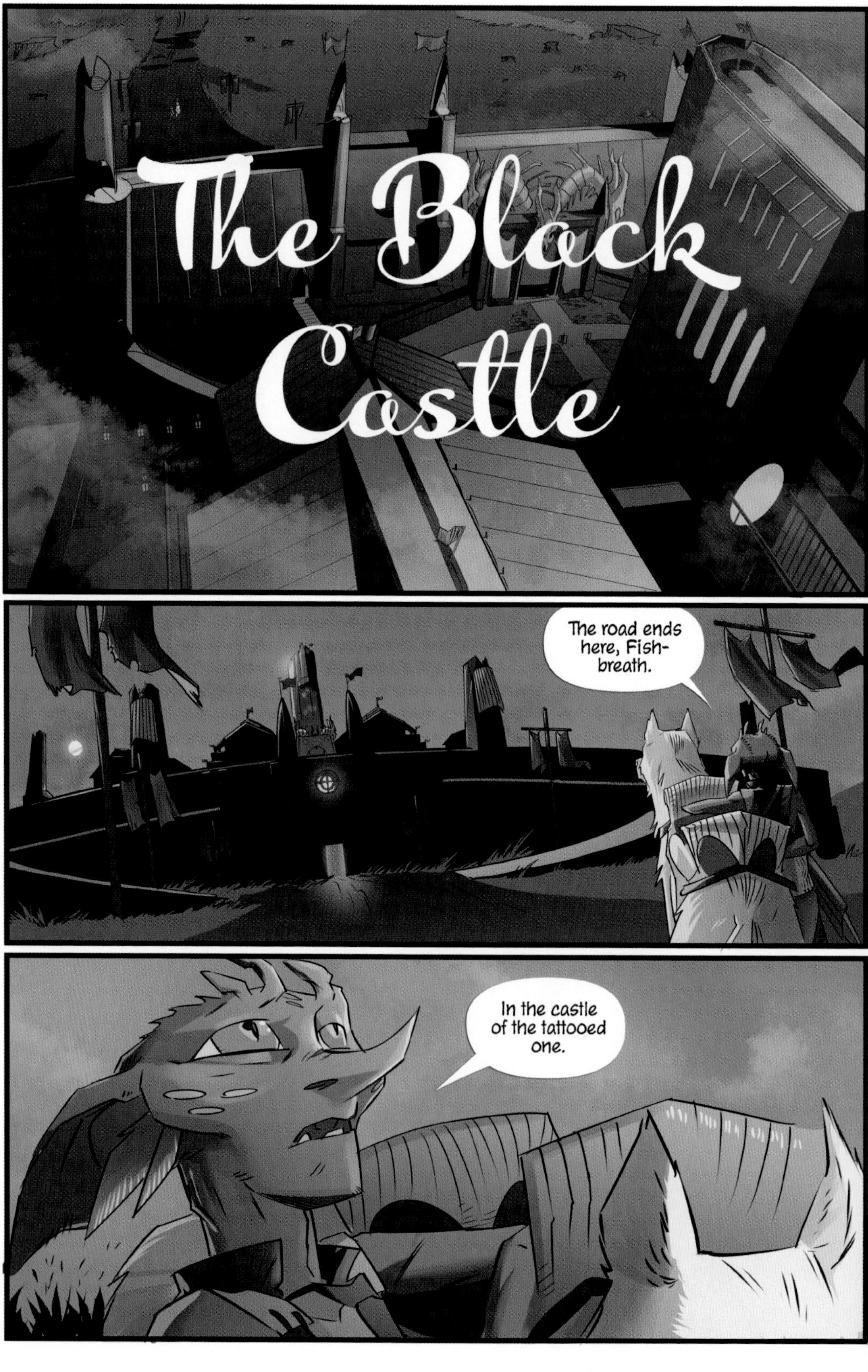
The Black Castle
The road ends here, Fish-breath.
In the castle of the tattooed one.

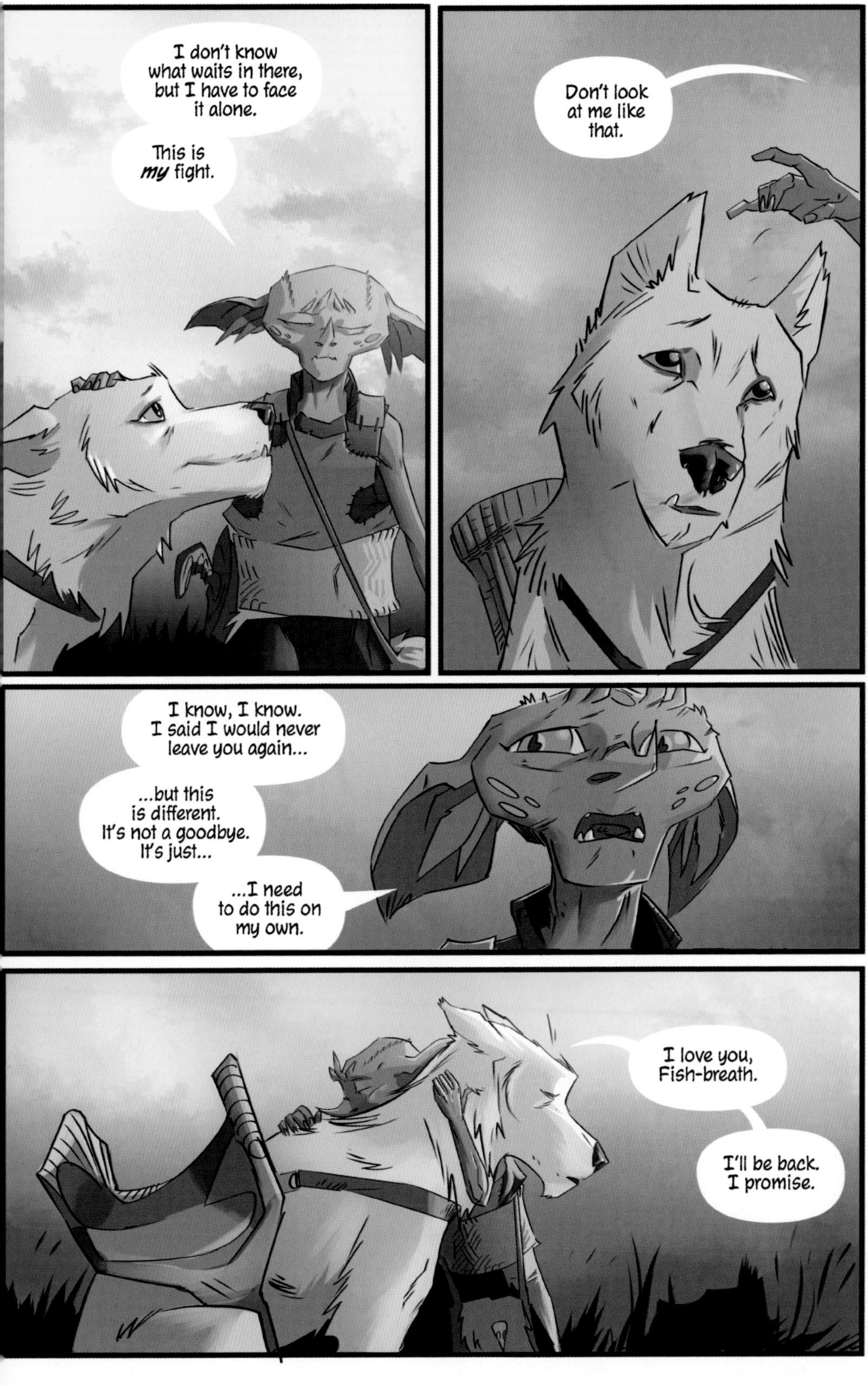
I don't know what waits in there, but I have to face it alone.
This is *my* fight.
Don't look at me like that.
I know, I know. I said I would never leave you again...
...but this is different. It's not a goodbye. It's just...
...I need to do this on my own.
I love you, Fish-breath.
I'll be back. I promise.

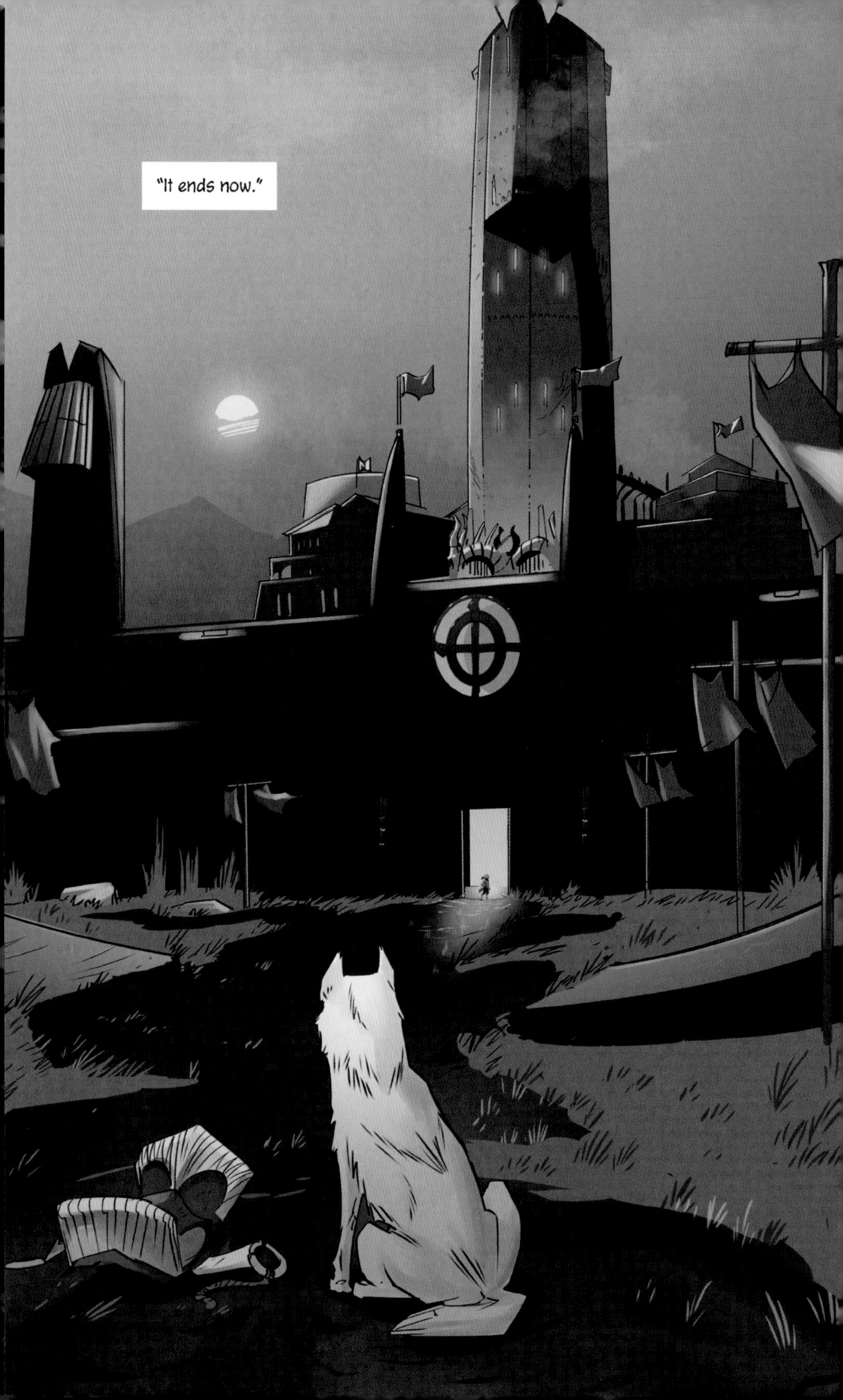
"It ends now."

CHAPTER ELEVEN
THE COST OF WAR

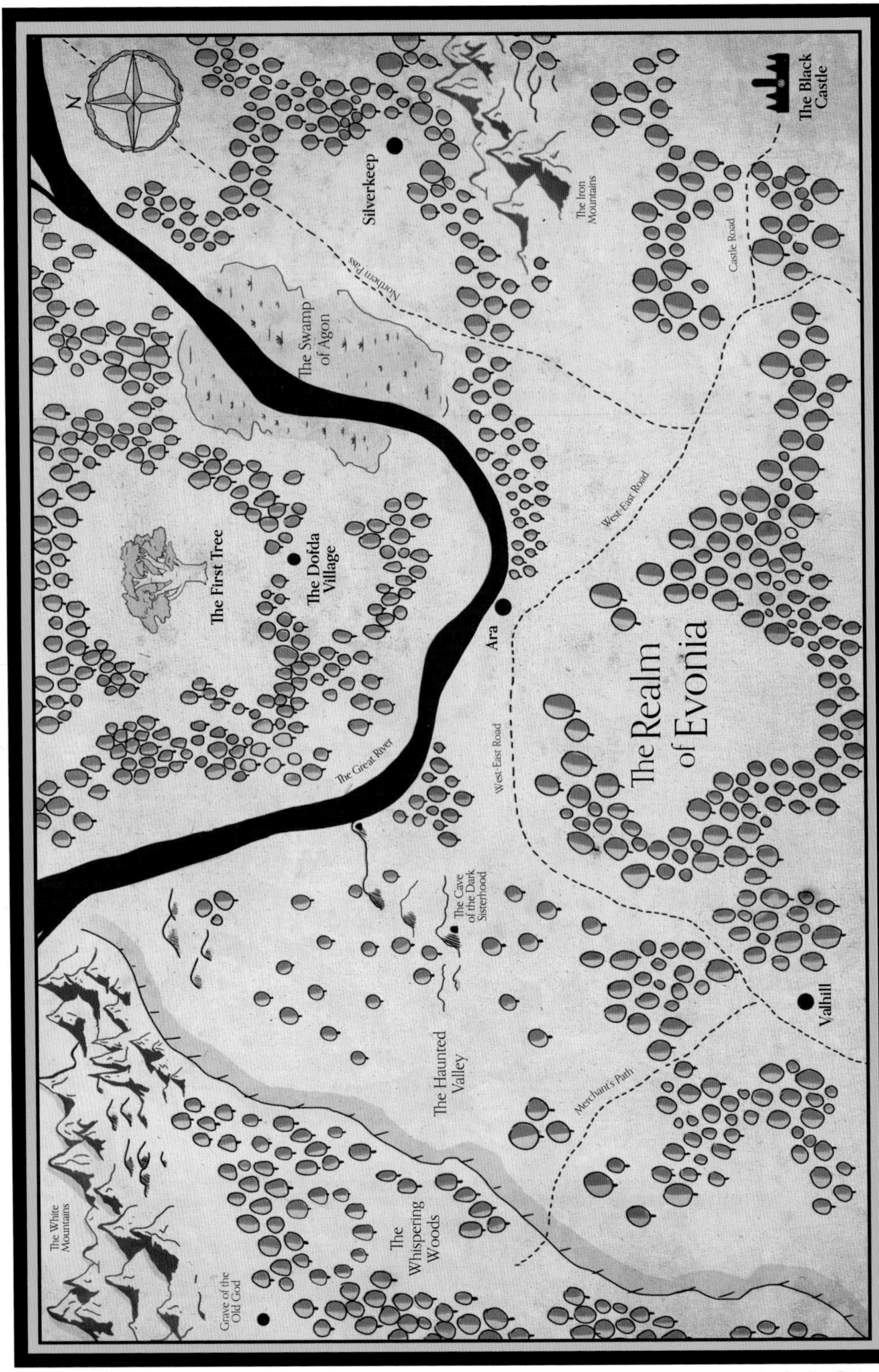
N
The White Mountains
Grave of the Old God
The Whispering Woods
The Haunted Valley
The Cave of the Dark Sisterhood
The Great River
The First Tree
The Dofda Village
The Swamp of Agon
Northern Pass
Silverkeep
The Iron Mountains
Ara
West-East Road
West-East Road
Merchant's Path
The Realm of Evonia
Valhill
Castle Road
The Black Castle

Map by Ava Grissom

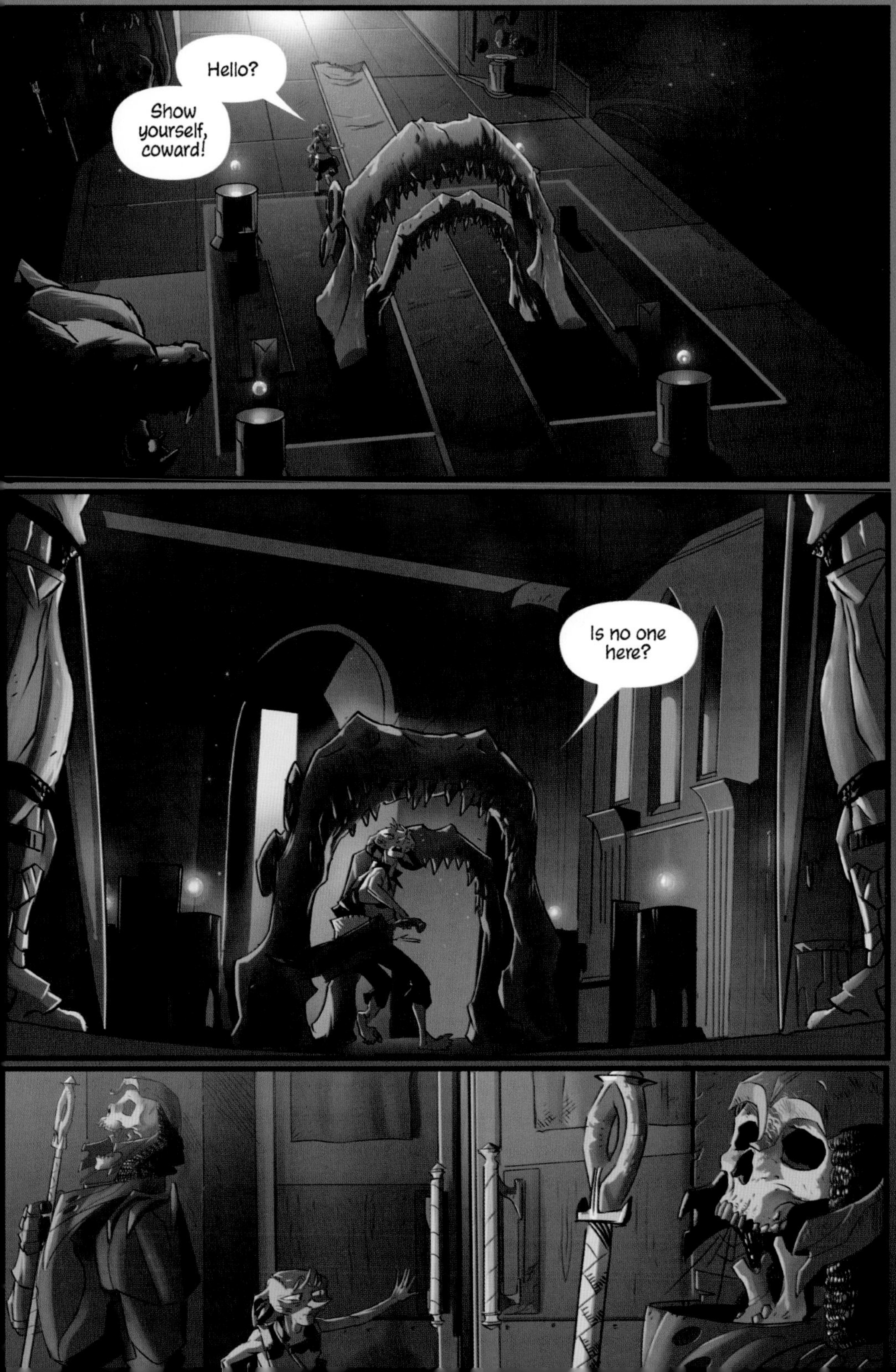
Hello?
Show yourself, coward!
Is no one here?

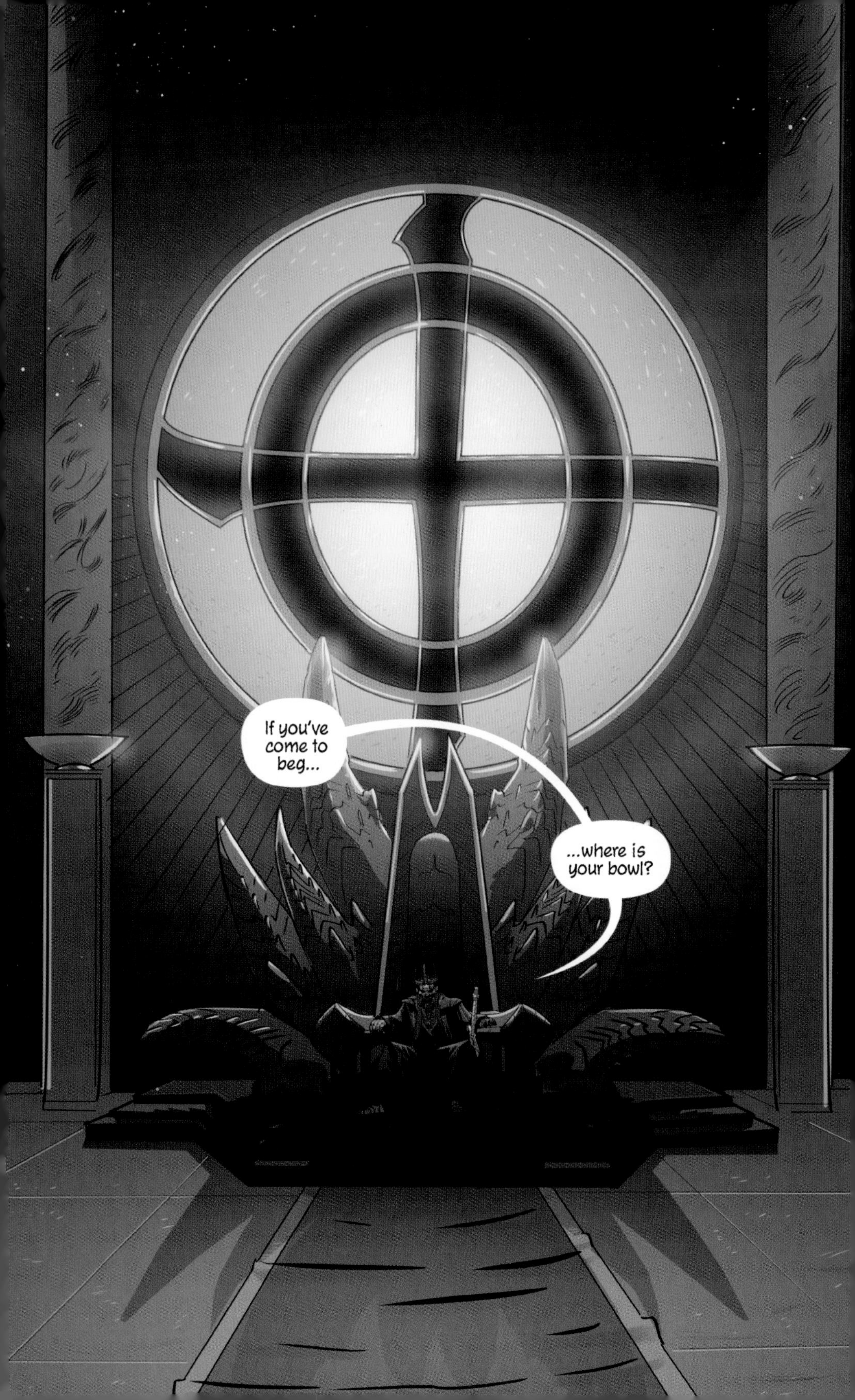
If you've come to beg...
...where is your bowl?

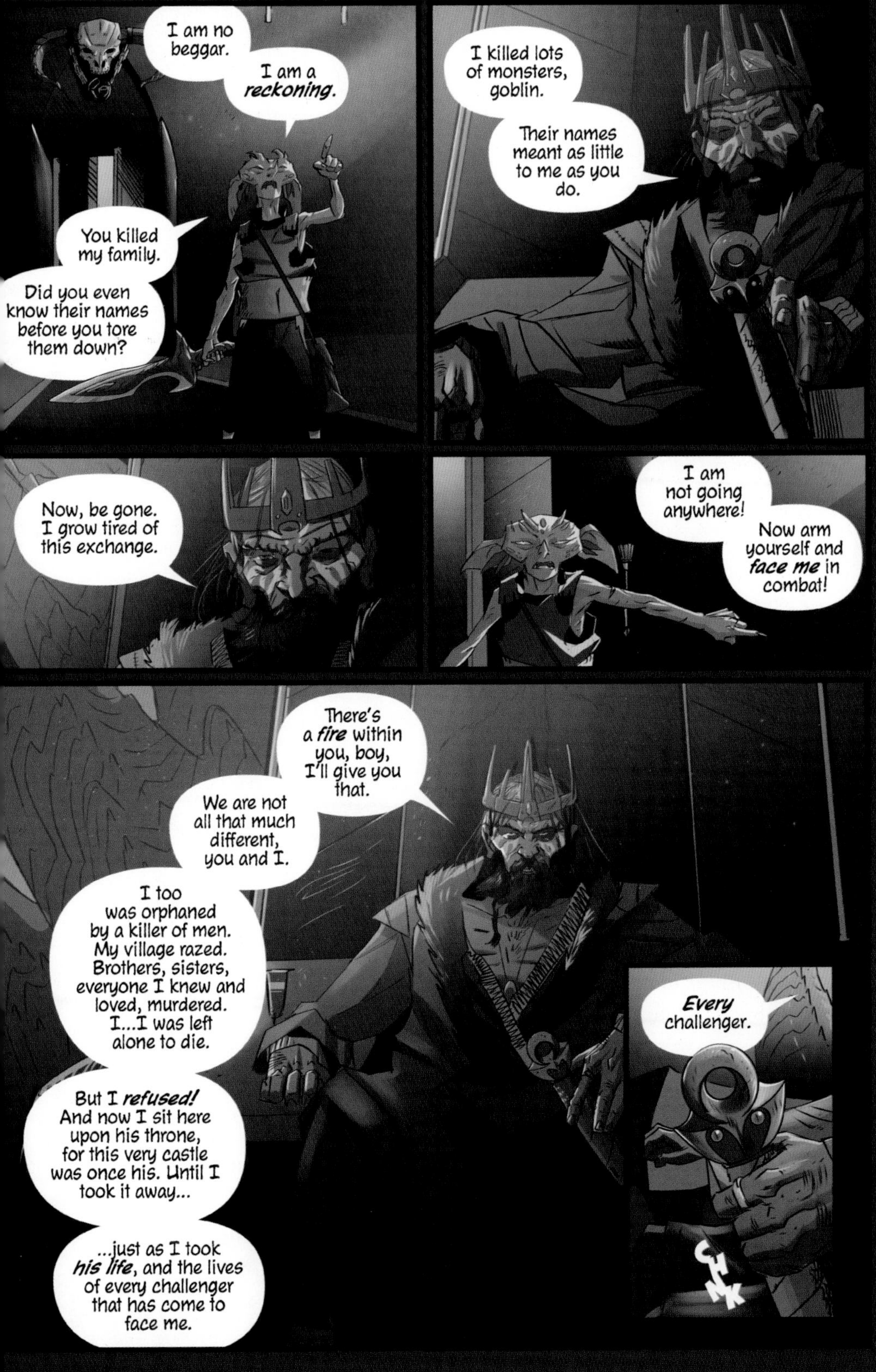
I am no beggar.
I am a *reckoning*.
You killed my family.
Did you even know their names before you tore them down?
I killed lots of monsters, goblin.
Their names meant as little to me as you do.
Now, be gone. I grow tired of this exchange.
I am not going anywhere!
Now arm yourself and *face me* in combat!
There's a *fire* within you, boy, I'll give you that.
We are not all that much different, you and I.
I too was orphaned by a killer of men. My village razed. Brothers, sisters, everyone I knew and loved, murdered. I...I was left alone to die.
But I *refused!* And now I sit here upon his throne, for this very castle was once his. Until I took it away...
...just as I took *his life*, and the lives of every challenger that has come to face me.
Every challenger.
CHNK

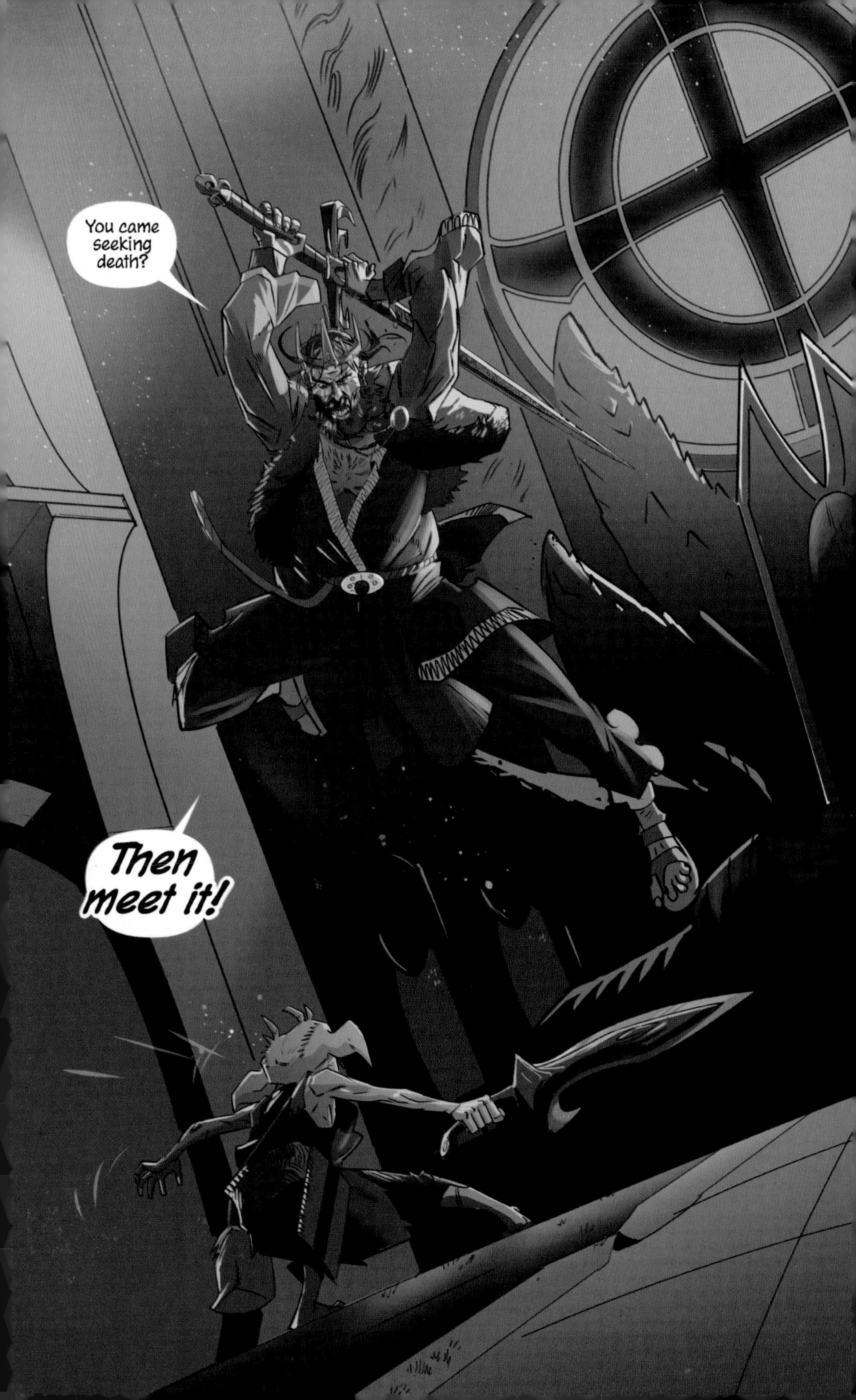
You came seeking death?
Then meet it!

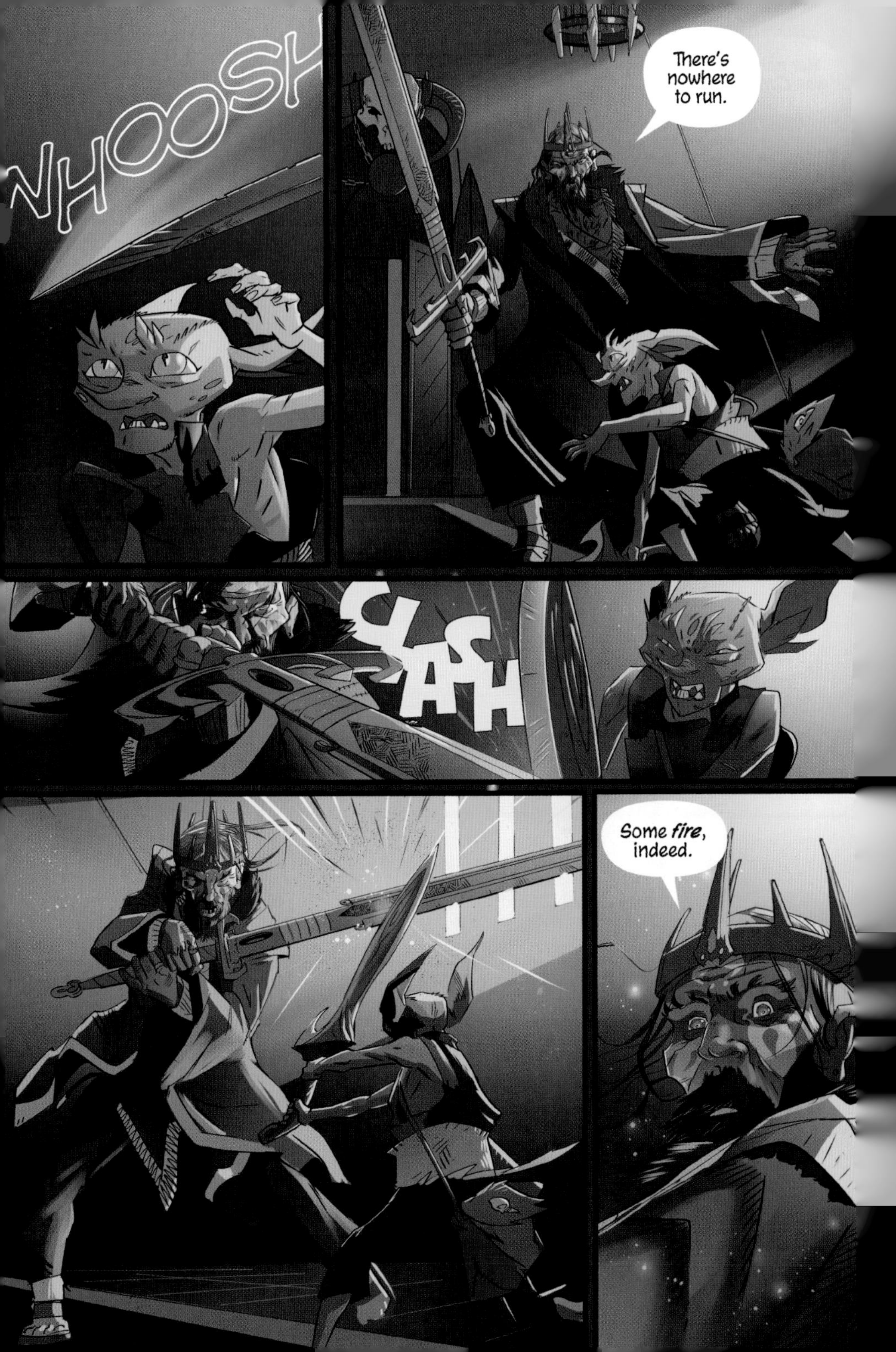
WHOOSH
There's nowhere to run.
CLASH
Some fire, indeed.

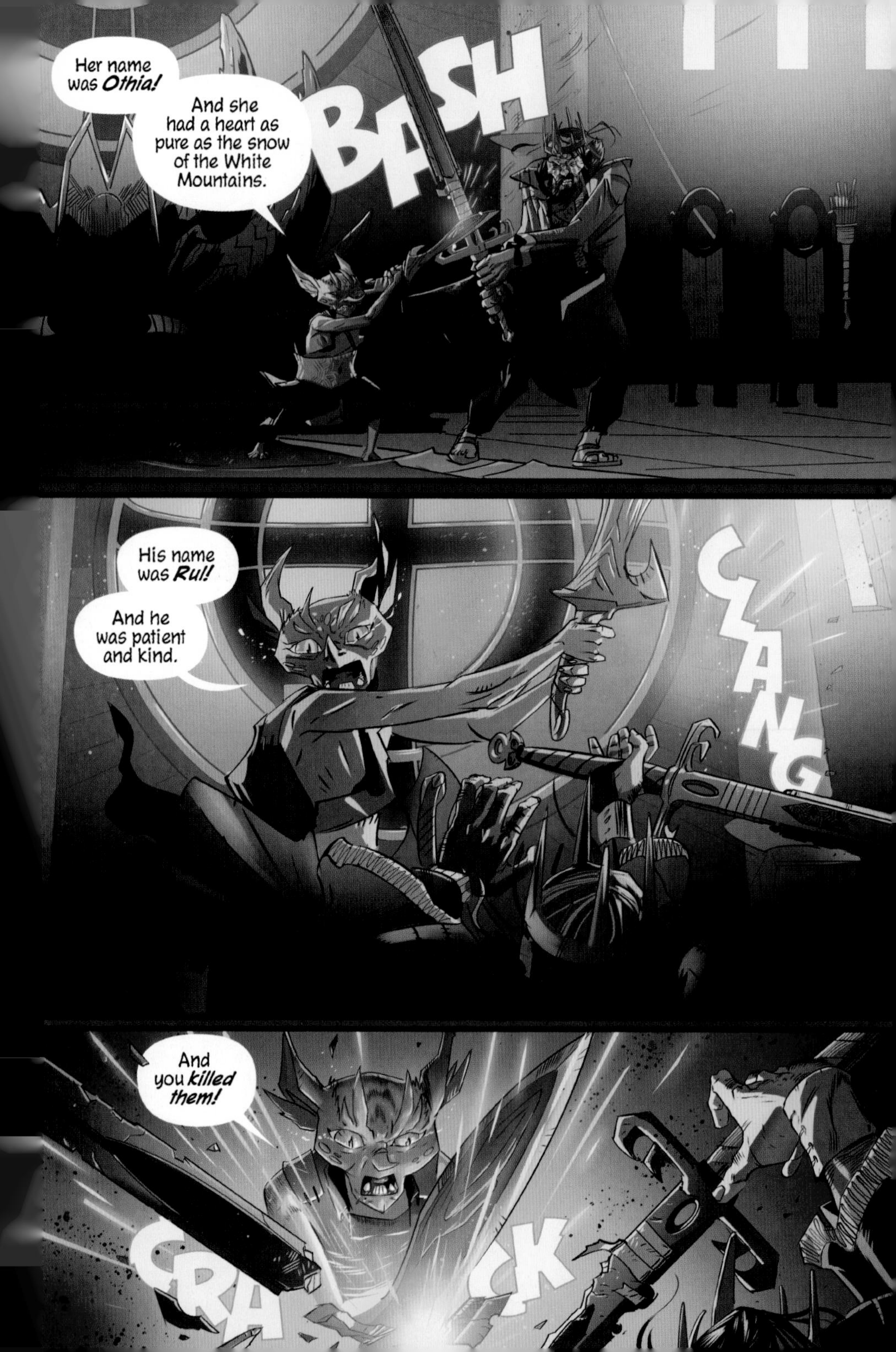

Her name was *Othia!*
And she had a heart as pure as the snow of the White Mountains.
BASH
His name was *Rul!*
And he was patient and kind.
CLANG
And you *killed them!*
CRACK

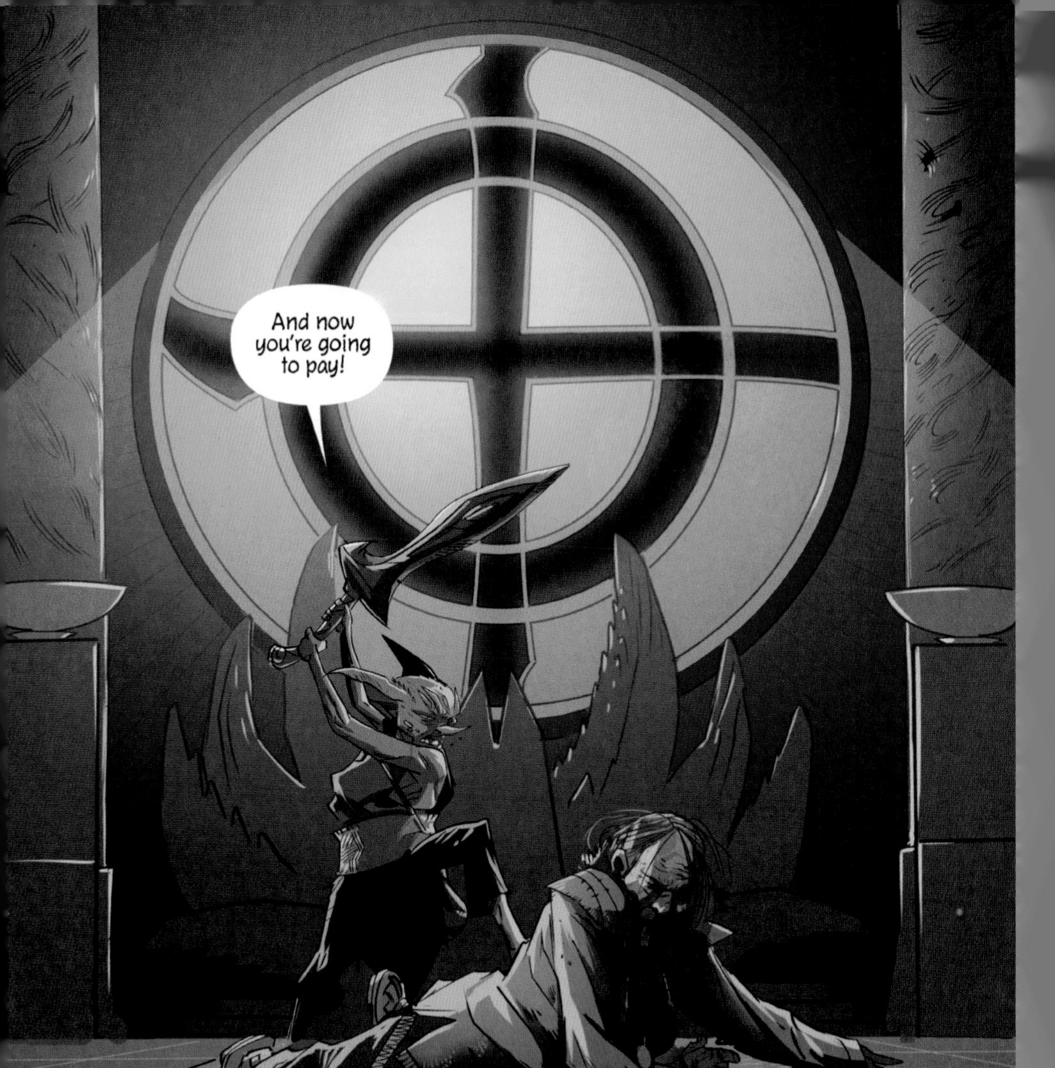
And now you're going to pay!

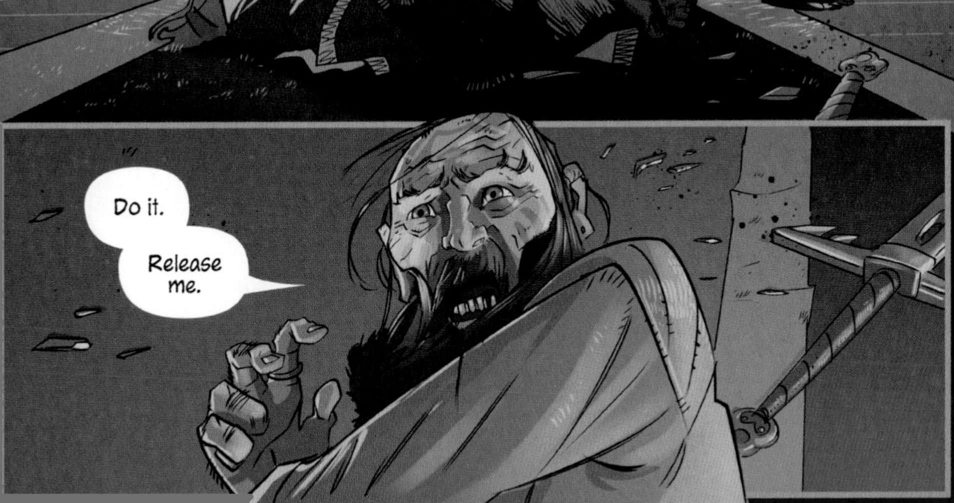
Do it.
Release me.

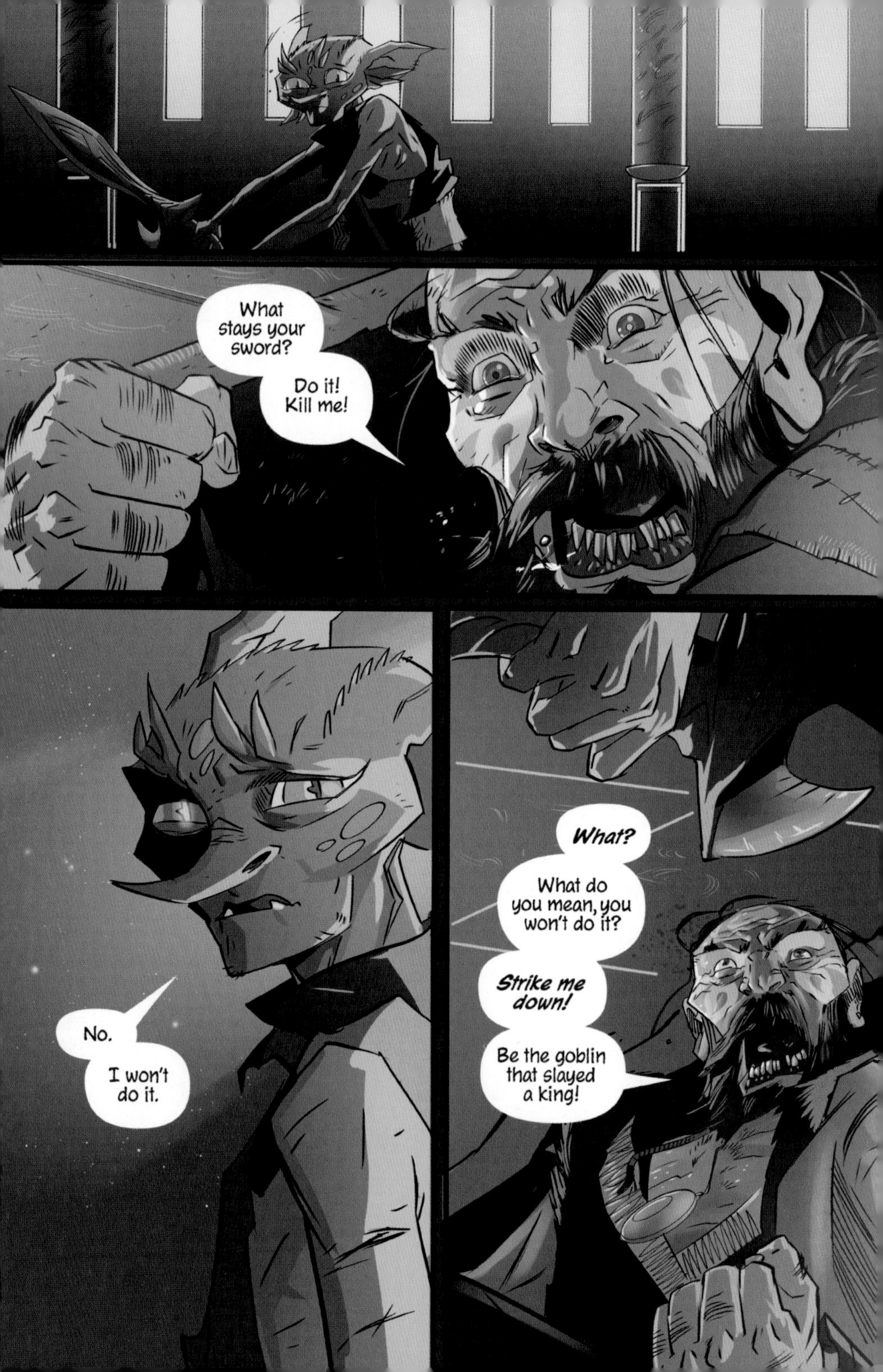
What stays your sword?
Do it! Kill me!
No.
I won't do it.
What?
What do you mean, you won't do it?
Strike me down!
Be the goblin that slayed a king!

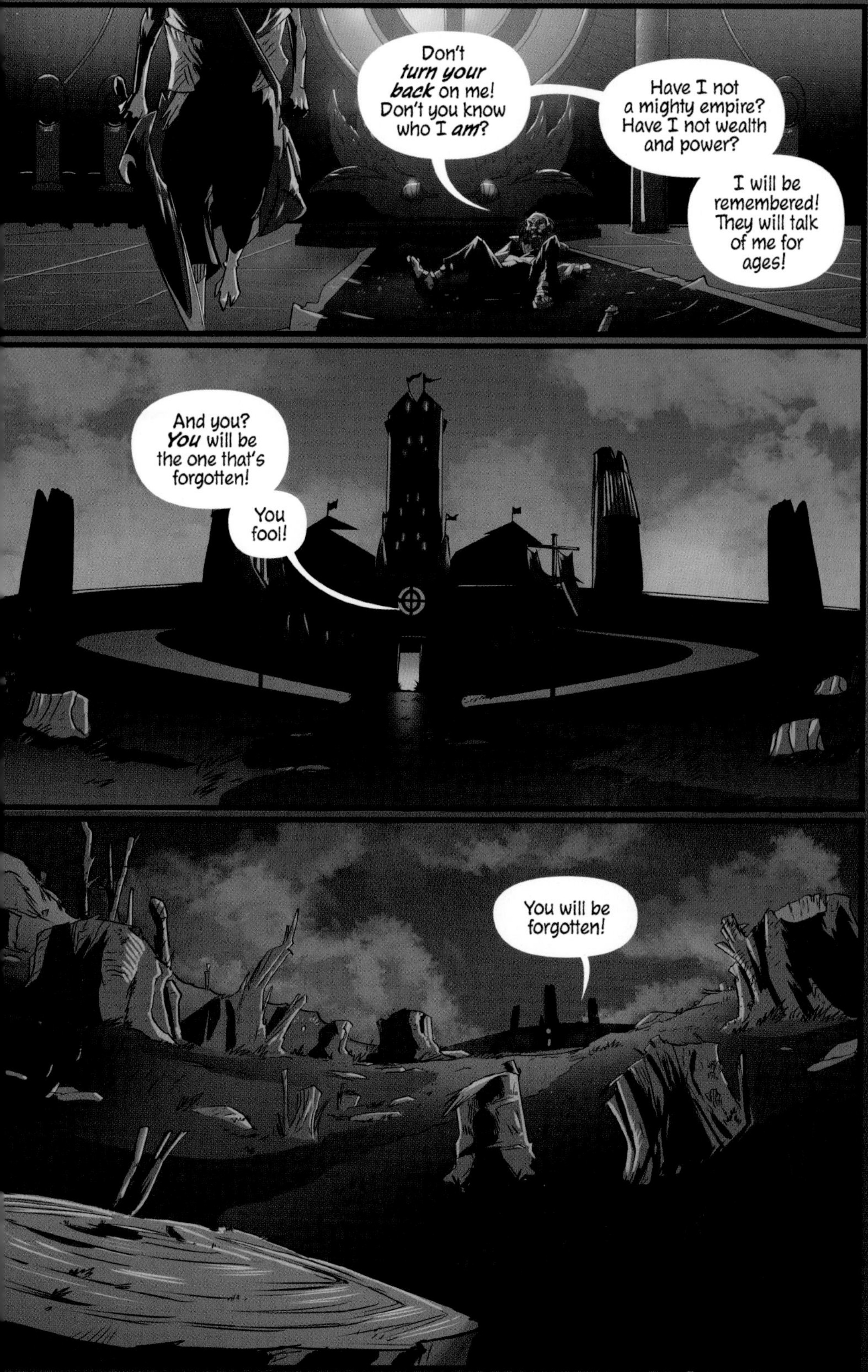
Don't *turn your back* on me! Don't you know who I *am*?
Have I not a mighty empire? Have I not wealth and power?
I will be remembered! They will talk of me for ages!
And you? *You* will be the one that's forgotten!
You fool!
You will be forgotten!

Epilogue

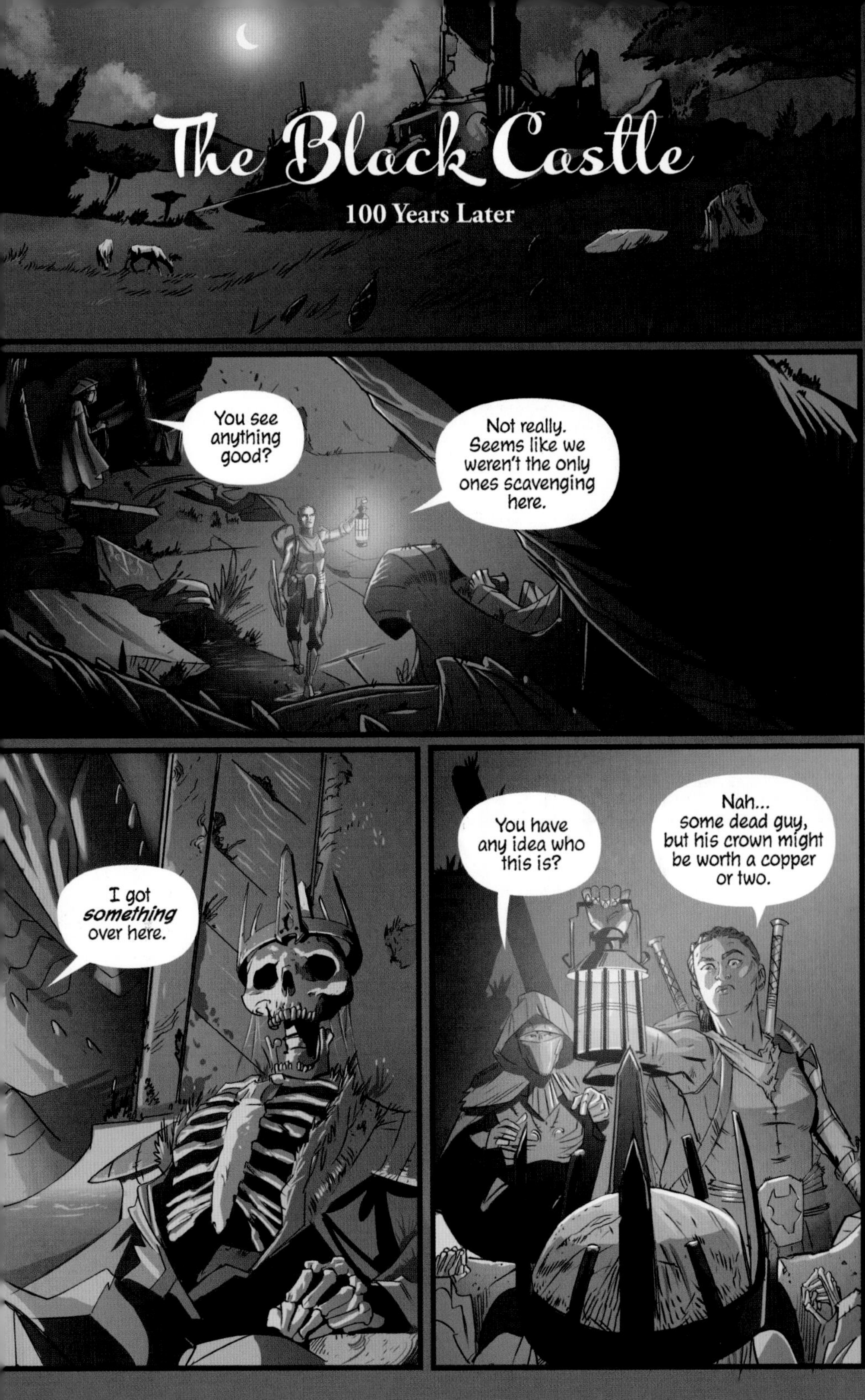
The Black Castle
100 Years Later
You see anything good?
Not really. Seems like we weren't the only ones scavenging here.
I got *something* over here.
You have any idea who this is?
Nah... some dead guy, but his crown might be worth a copper or two.

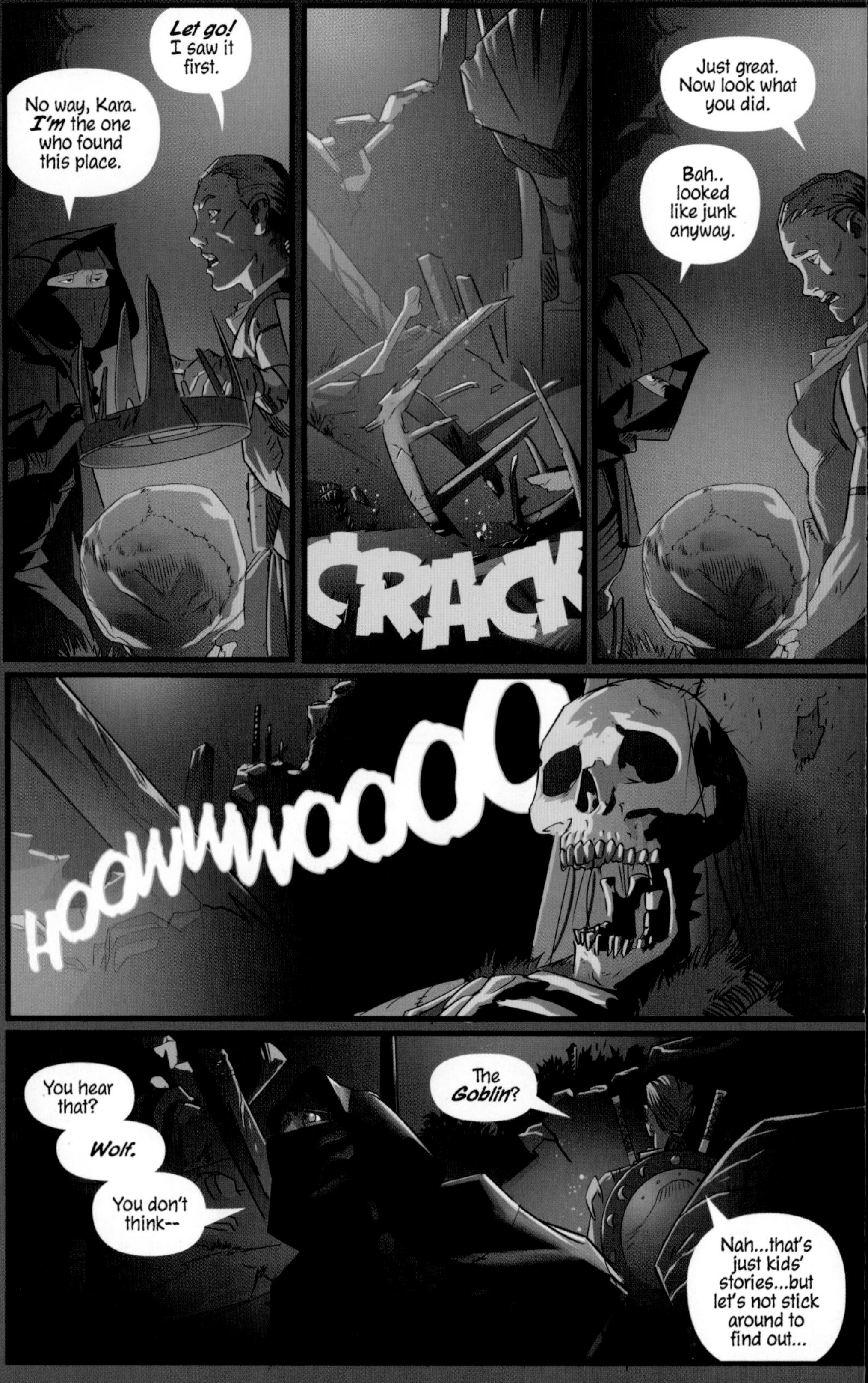
Let go! I saw it first.
No way, Kara. I'm the one who found this place.
CRACK
Just great. Now look what you did.
Bah.. looked like junk anyway.
HOOWWWOOOO
You hear that?
Wolf.
You don't think--
The Goblin?
Nah...that's just kids' stories...but let's not stick around to find out...

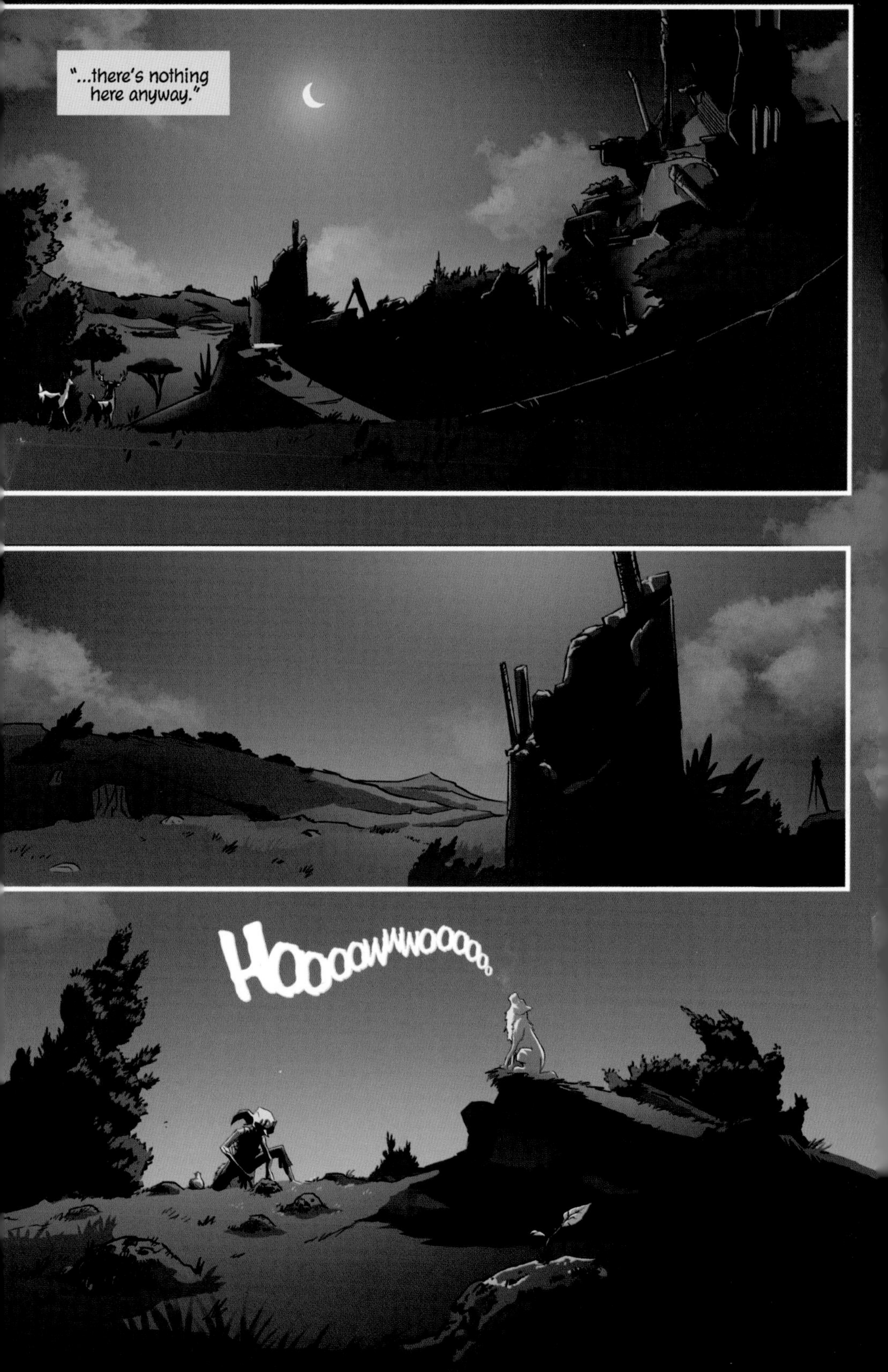
"...there's nothing here anyway."
HOOOAWWWOOOOOO

In memory of

SCOTT ROBERT PERKINS

1950–2020

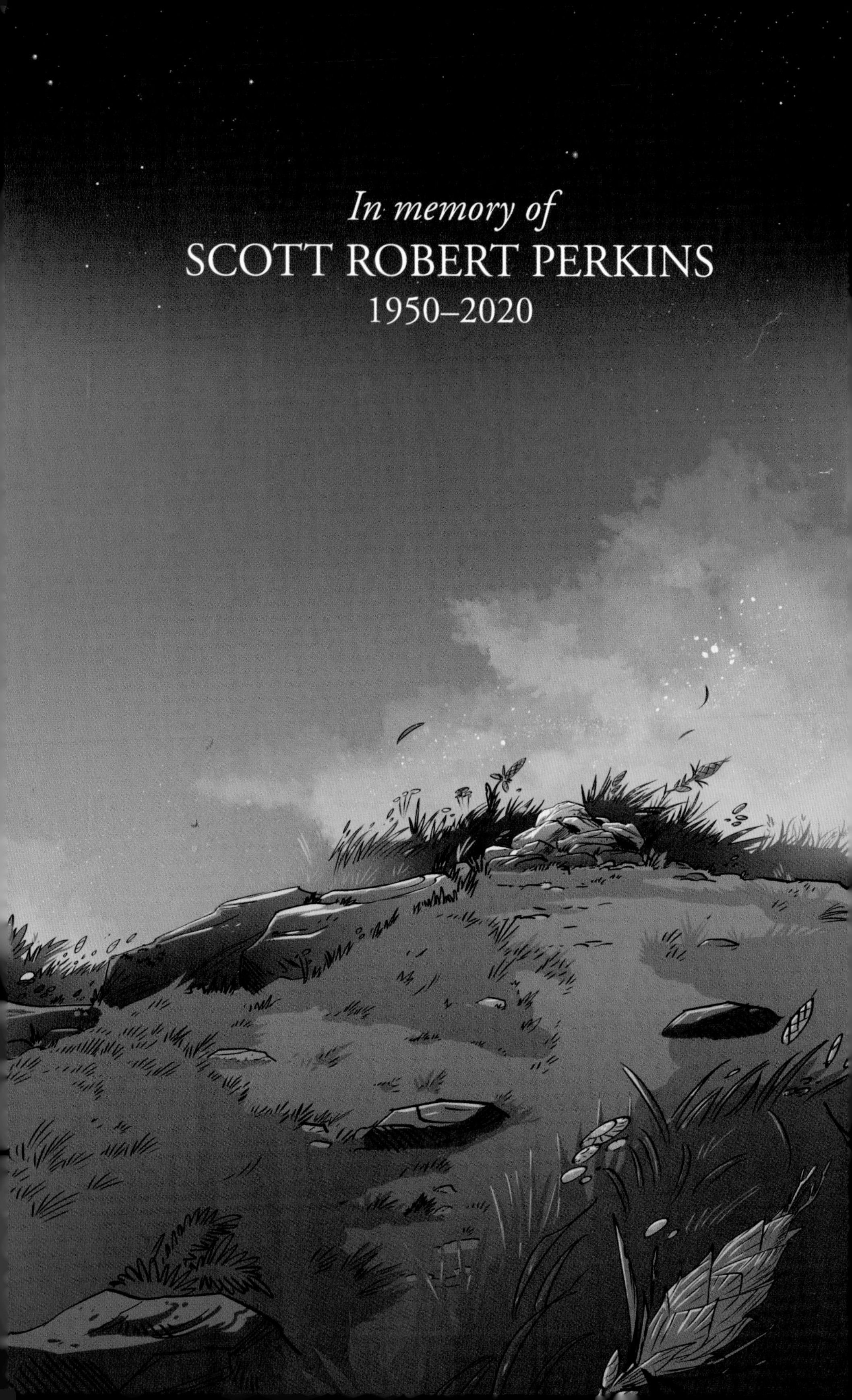